All for a Story

All for a Story

A NOVEL

ALLISON PITTMAN

Tyndale House Publishers, Inc.

CAROL STREAM, ILLINOIS

Visit Tyndale online at www.tyndale.com.

Visit Allison Pittman's website at www.allisonpittman.com.

TYNDALE and Tyndale's quill logo are registered trademarks of Tyndale House Publishers, Inc.

All for a Story

Designed by Ron Kaufmann

Edited by Kathryn S. Olson

Published in association with William K. Jensen Literary Agency, 119 Bampton Court, Eugene, Oregon 97404.

Scripture quotations are taken from the *Holy Bible*, King James Version.

All for a Story is a work of fiction. Where real people, events, establishments, organizations, or locales appear, they are used fictitiously. All other elements of the novel are drawn from the author's imagination.

Library of Congress Cataloging-in-Publication Data

Pittman, Allison.
    All for a story / Allison Pittman.
      page cm
    ISBN 978-1-4143-6681-4 (sc)
1. Women journalists—Washington (DC)—Fiction. 2. Women journalists—History—20th century—Fiction. 3. Newspapers—History—20th century—Fiction. I. Title.
    PS3616.I885A793 2013
    813'.6—dc23   2013019648

Printed in the United States of America

19   18   17   16   15   14   13
 7   6   5   4   3   2   1

Love knows nothing but moment to moment.
Be honest and true in each one.

ZELDA OVENOFF

ACKNOWLEDGMENTS

Many, many thanks go to . . .

Mikey and boys, for being such a wonderfully self-reliant family

My Monday night group, for your unfailing support and prayers and love

Bill, for having the best ideas

My Tyndale family, for making me feel so safe, always

The PITT crew, for answering ridiculous questions and keeping secrets

Beth and Matt, for lending me the essence of your polydactyl cat

Rachel, my Canadatwin, for your awesomeness in general

Above all, thank you, Jesus, my Savior and Friend, for bringing all of these wonderful people into my life. Because of you, I am never alone.

MONKEY BUSINESS

"Hop On Over, Friends"

A funny thing happened the other day when this little Monkey was making her way down a certain street. Seems the heel of my shoe was broken clean off. And I was proudly sporting my brand-new pair of vermilion patent-leather pumps. Cost me more than a month's rent, these shoes did, and here I was having to hobble. (What does the wounded turkey do? Hobble, hobble!)

Now, some monkeys might do fine in the trees, but I prefer the dance floor of a hot jazz jungle. So, lucky for me, I found the perfect little place to make everything better. Sure, I had to make it past a couple of gorillas, but what do you expect? When paradise is waiting in the treetops, it's worth a little bit of a pat-down in the lower regions.

But let me tell you this: be sure to bring your bananas. Bunches of them. You know the old saying about how the cobbler's children have no shoes? Well, yours might not either after a trip to this little shop. Whatever they're using to tan the leather is quality stuff, but you'll need the kind of scratch that doesn't jingle. Of course that means you'll be toe-to-toe with the king of the jungle, sharing a watering hole with a few elected big cats. Maybe even a few donkeys and elephants.

With water this cool and jazz this hot, it's a sure bet this little Monkey will be swinging through the jungle vines and landing in this tree house again.

❧ CHAPTER 1 ❧

I am really only myself when I'm somebody else whom I have
endowed with these wonderful qualities from my imagination.

ZELDA FITZGERALD

IT WAS JUST PAST DAWN when she hammered the final key on her portable typewriter, finishing up that week's installment of Monkey Business. Good thing, too, because the next sound to be heard above her percolating coffee was the familiar, timid knock followed by "Miss Bisbaine?" spoken in a voice not quite conquered by puberty.

Monica cinched the silk belt of her robe, not wanting to send the poor kid into some kind of preadolescent stroke, and opened the thin door of her small apartment to reveal Trevor Kelly shifting nervously from foot to foot.

"Perfect timing, as always," Monica said, stepping back to allow the boy ample space to walk in without touching her.

"Really?" Trevor looked around the room, obviously trying to avoid seeing both the unmade bed and the undressed tenant. "Because I thought I was running late."

"That's why you're perfect, love. I've just now finished. Coffee?"

"No, thank you."

The boy had just turned fifteen and no doubt had been given the tale that the stuff would stunt his growth. She wanted to tell him his fears were unfounded; after all, he loomed a full head above her, but his bony shoulders and scrawny neck testified to a weight that barely topped a hundred pounds.

"Milk, then?" The moment she offered, she realized the chances of finding a clean glass in which to serve it were slim at best.

"Like I said, I'm running late. . . ."

"All right, all right." He was a good kid, this one, but no sense of life. She shuffled over to her typewriter and lifted the foot to release the single sheet on the roller. "Let me give it one last read."

She pulled up the window shade just enough to illuminate the page and let her eyes—still stinging from a late night of smoke and booze—skim the column, making sure she'd given enough clues to attract interested parties but not enough to expose them outright. Satisfied, she gave the piece over to her first reader.

"My guess is upstairs from some shoe repair shop?" Trevor's wide eyes awaited her confirmation.

"Too easy?"

The kid scrunched his face, thinking. "Maybe instead of saying your shoe broke, something like, 'I had a bit of a problem with my walking paws.' Same number of letters."

"Do monkeys have paws?"

"Do you pay for hooch with bananas?"

"You have a point."

She grabbed a blue wax pencil from the cup on the table, drew a line through the sentence, and wrote Trevor's suggestion in the margin, initialing the page with a flourish before handing it back. "Good job. We wouldn't want anyone getting undue attention."

"No, ma'am." Trevor took the paper and placed it in a cardboard folder which he then tucked into the canvas messenger bag slung around his neck.

Meanwhile, Monica tried to look nonchalant as she riffled through her purse, then the little velvet drawstring bag on her bureau, and finally the preserves jar on her top kitchen shelf in a fruitless search for a nickel. Finding none, she offered a smile instead. "Sorry, kid. Double it next time?"

He shrugged. "That's okay."

"Just look extra puppy-dog pathetic when you hand it over to Mr. Moore."

Trevor snorted, and Monica understood. He'd have as much chance getting a nickel from Mr. Moore as finding a cherry blossom in November.

Once he left, she shuffled down the hall to the common bathroom that served the tenants in the four single-room apartments on her floor. One benefit of keeping irregular hours came in having the place to herself at these crucial times. Mr. Davenport, a high school math teacher, had probably left before Trevor took the first step in the stairwell. Mrs. Kinship worked overnight as a janitress and was already tucked in bed. Finally, a girl named Anna. *Girl* might not be the best word, since she had to be nearly thirty, but she was soft and pale and quiet, eking out a modest living from her job in the back room of the public library. She kept precise hours, leaving the house at seven thirty every morning and returning at six fifteen every evening, Monday through Saturday. When she spoke, she spoke in whispers, and she scowled at those who didn't follow suit.

Monica closed herself inside and sent a silent apology to Mrs. Kinship as the pipes groaned before the onslaught of water. She added a generous amount of sweet-scented bath salts before climbing into the tub, where she ducked her head under the spigot, hoping to wash away the pounding in her head.

When she got back to her room, she set a new pot of coffee to percolate on the electric hot plate and rummaged through her wardrobe and select piles of clothing on the floor to put together an outfit appropriate for the day, finding a relatively clean pair of thick cotton stockings, a long wool skirt, and an argyle sweater. With a pair of sturdy brown shoes she could pass as a college girl, maybe, albeit without the usual accompanying vivacity.

After dragging a large canvas bag from beneath her bed, she began to stuff it with as many garments as she could gather off the floor, draped over the chair, and piled on the foot of the bed. Mr. Varnos would scowl at her, but it was his policy to charge by the bag; she was just clever enough to take advantage.

Barely able to move under the weight of her laundry, Monica lugged herself and the bag down the three flights of back stairs in order to avoid her landlord's office parlor. A bitter wind whipped her face when she turned the corner from the alley to the street. Had it been this cold last night? She couldn't remember. The last bit of warmth from her single cup of coffee disappeared with the mist of her breath. Luckily, Varnos's Laundry was only half a block away, just in time to rescue her with its steamy, soap-scented warmth as she staggered through the door.

"My, it's like heaven in here," she said, trying not to grunt too loudly as she heaved the bag onto the counter.

Mr. Varnos, his thick, black brows joined together in his displeasure, did nothing to assist her. Instead, he stepped back, arms folded across his barreled chest, and stared Monica down.

"New policy," he said and cocked his head toward a neat-looking hand-lettered sign on the wall. "No more bag. By pound now."

"A nickel a pound? Mr. Varnos, that's robbery!"

"Is business."

"Well, not very good business if you ask me," Monica said, trying to regain some of her lost ground through charm. "Why, I'm only ninety-eight pounds myself. You could wash all of me and I'd owe you less than a fin."

Perhaps the line would have worked better were she not bundled head to toe in her favorite knit cap and sturdy gray wool coat, because Mr. Varnos—still frowning—grabbed her bag with effortless resolve and set it on a large scale. The red needle came to a bouncing halt just shy of twenty-two pounds.

A dollar and a dime.

Monica's smile froze. "That's not so much."

Wordlessly, Mr. Varnos scribbled on a little pad, tearing a ticket-size slip from the bottom and handing it over.

"Pick up Tuesday."

"Tuesday," she affirmed, wishing spring would get here a little sooner. Her clothes would be lighter. And if the grumbling in her stomach was any indication, so would she.

A dozen more steps against the biting wind, and she ducked into Sobek's Deli and Bakery, asking the plump, dimpled Mrs. Sobek for two *kolache*—on account.

Mrs. Sobek responded with her hand on her ample hip in a pose of mock disapproval.

"On account of what?"

"On account of my boss hasn't even paid me a compliment for the past couple of weeks."

It was a routine they'd mastered, a fair exchange of food for cleverness, exhibited with Mrs. Sobek's dropping the warm pastries in a white, wax-lined bag.

"I know you're too skinny, even under that coat. Come back later today for some nice soup." She winked. "On account."

"I will." It was an oft-repeated invitation, and even when Monica had a pocketful of nickels to pay, Mrs. Sobek would wave her off, claiming it was the scrapings from the bottom of the pot, about to be thrown out anyway.

The warmth of the meat and pastry filled her as she made her way to the most important destination of the morning. She was finishing the last bite and stuffing the empty bag into her coat pocket when she came up to the enormous glass window of Capitol Bank and Loan. She studied herself in the reflection, the *o* in *Loan* sitting like a halo above her head. She yanked off her hat and ran her fingers through her hair, licking them to tame the static. Inside, the place smelled like wax and wood and money, and she instantly regretted not wearing the little fox-fur collar on top of her coat. At least it had a friendly face.

"How may we help you?" The man at the reception desk, Harmon Peel, was thin and old, the latter explaining why—after more than a dozen visits to the institution—he seemed to have never seen her before.

"I'm here to see Mr. Bentworth," she said, signing the ledger.

Peel took a slip of paper, asked Monica's name—twice—wrote it on the slip, and sent a well-dressed page with the missive. Minutes later she followed that same page through the lobby and into the office of J. Everett Bentworth, the man she had grown up calling "Uncle Ev."

"Monkey . . ." He was up and out from behind the desk, drawing out the final syllable of the nickname for as long as it took to draw her into his arms. "What a nice surprise."

"Hello, Everett." The *Uncle* had been dropped when she'd turned sixteen, in deference to her sense of maturity. "You're looking well."

In fact, he looked exactly as he always had, though his hair was being overtaken by the gray that had always been present in a salt-and-pepper way. His upper lip receded to reveal a row of perfect teeth, and if she ever saw him wearing anything other than a navy-blue pin-striped suit, she probably wouldn't recognize him at all.

"As are you," he said, though when he held her at arm's length, his scrutiny said otherwise. "What brings you here? I wasn't expecting you for another couple of weeks."

"I'm a bit surprised myself." She swallowed hard. No choice but to go forward. "I was wondering, Everett, if there was any possibility I could get an advance on my next allowance." The statement made her feel like a child, and it didn't help that the chair he'd offered her was so deep that, if she sat far enough back, her feet did not touch the floor. So she remained on its edge, her toes tipped in the thick burgundy carpet while Everett settled himself in his own rich leather seat.

"Hmmm . . ." He opened a file drawer beneath his desk and brought out a folder. He needn't share the contents; Monica knew exactly what was in there. Her father's will, leaving everything to her mother, and her mother's will, leaving everything to no one. Well, that wasn't exactly true. She left quite a bit to the hospital that had given Dad such excellent care in his final days, and to her own army of nurses and maids, and to the League of Women Voters in honor of her own days as an ardent suffragette. But to her one daughter and only child? Nothing, save a modest trust fund and the monies from her liquidated assets.

"The terms of your mother's will are quite clear," Everett said, studying the papers. "One hundred dollars on the second Wednesday of every month. There's no other account for me to draw on for an exception."

"Really?" Monica steeled her toes and gestured wide about

her. "There's nowhere in this great institution that could make for an exception?"

"Is there something in particular that you need, my dear?"

His voice was low and cultured, making her ever more aware of the thickness of her own Baltimore accent. Who would have guessed that she'd ever been exposed to wealth?

"Well, in case you hadn't noticed, it's a bit cold out there, and I read a fascinating article about how food and a roof go a long way in preventing death by hypothermia. I thought I'd test the theory."

Everett's thin moustache—completely given over to gray—twitched. "I'm sure you exaggerate."

"Try me. If I don't show up, send a search party with brandy to my apartment over on Fourteenth Street. I'll be the little blue girl in the corner."

"One hundred dollars a month is quite generous, you know. Many people—even entire families—live on much less."

"They don't have as many shoes to support as I do." He looked unconvinced, so she pressed on. "It's part of my job—you know, dressing up and looking good."

One eyebrow, three shades darker than the moustache, arched high. "And what exactly is this *job* of yours again?"

If she didn't think she'd fall out of the chair, she would have kicked herself. Her anonymity was important. Not every speakeasy in town enjoyed the spotlight of the Monkey Business column, and if word ever got out that she was the Monkey herself, she'd never get another lead. But it was easy to see where Everett's mind was going with her last comment, and at this moment it seemed far more important to rescue her reputation—such as it was.

"I write a column for the *Capitol Chatter*. You might not know it—more of a tabloid than a newspaper. Anyway, I go places, clubs and parties and restaurants and such. Some of them public. Others—" she lowered her voice—"more on the private side, if you know what I mean. And then I write about it. What I did, who I saw. People kind of go around with me, vicarious-like."

As she spoke, a slow smile stretched under Everett's moustache, and the indulgent twinkle she remembered from childhood crept into his eyes.

"You're the Monkey behind Monkey Business?"

She twisted in her chair, seeing that no one was passing by the open door. Satisfied, she turned back.

"You read the *Capitol Chatter*?"

His face dropped back into aloofness. "My wife is a regular subscriber."

"Really? We don't have too many of those."

"Don't they pay you?"

She smiled wryly. "By the word. And my boss is pretty stingy with those, too."

"If your mother knew—"

"She'd die." She didn't feel the slightest pain at the joke. What affection she'd ever felt for her mother had long since callused into nothing more than an acknowledgment of lineage. They'd only spoken with each other a dozen times between the end of the Great War and the end of her life last spring.

"She loved you very much, you know," Everett said with a banker's measure of affection.

"So she disinherited me?"

"Legally, no. She left you a generous sum. And you'll receive the proceeds of the Baltimore house, should a buyer ever be found."

"Doled out in drips and drabs until I'm thirty."

"And then you'll have it all."

"Not the Georgetown house." She unhooked her toes from the floor and let her feet swing listlessly above the roses in the carpet.

"She only had your best interest at heart. I know she worried you might attract the wrong sort of man—one who would love you only for your money."

"And that won't happen when I'm thirty?"

"I suppose by then it might be the only thing that would get you a man at all."

He smiled, inviting her to join him, both of them knowing that must have been exactly what Mom had been thinking when she drafted the document. Monica's boyfriend, Charlie, had no idea about the money or her father's wartime profits that had generated it. Sometimes, though, she wondered if he might not feel differently about her if he knew. Differently enough to leave his wife. Perhaps she'd tell him on her thirtieth birthday. That was just over nine years away. Not quite a decade. She might have to send him a telegram.

"Let me do this," Everett said, pulling a wallet from the breast pocket of his jacket. "A personal loan. From me to you. Would ten dollars help?"

Ten dollars would indeed help. It would be half the rent— enough to sate her landlord for the next few days—or enough to buy the adorable brown velvet hat she'd seen in the window at Marcel's, or to buy a nice steak dinner at a place where she might get a lead on a new club. How to choose? Still, she should put up a bit of a fight.

"Oh, I couldn't." Her feet swung free, alternating. "I wouldn't want to be beholden." Besides, Charlie was good for a steak dinner every now and then.

"Not at all. I would consider it fair trade for just a bit of your expertise."

He said *expertise* in such a way as to still her feet. "Look, I don't know what you think—"

"Mona and I have an important anniversary coming up. Twenty years of wedded bliss, and I'd like to take her someplace . . . festive."

He said *festive* with the same conspiratorial air as *expertise*, and Monica responded with a wink. "I have just the place." She fished around in her purse until she found the yellow card. Approaching Everett's desk, she asked for a pen, turned the card over, and drew a comic-looking little monkey—with exaggerated eyelashes and a long string of beads—on the back. The same sketch appeared at the top of her weekly column. She held it by the corner and blew the ink dry before giving it to Everett.

"Shoe repair shop on East Sixteenth. Upstairs. Drinks are expensive, but strong. And the music was perfect for dancing."

"And this'll get us in?" He seemed somewhere between skeptical and amused.

"Worked for me. But take my advice. Dress like you're headed for an evening at the Carlyle. This place is classy. And not so much chatter at the door. If they ask where you got the card, tell 'em you got it from Miss Monkey Business herself, but zippo on my name."

"Mona will be thrilled," he said, placing two bills in her hand and folding it within his own.

"And don't tell her, either. Please, Everett. If word gets out and they know me at the doors, I'll never get back in. And if I never get back in, I won't have a job."

"It is a secret safe with me." He walked around to the front of his desk to offer a familial escort out of the office. "And you know, you can always come to me in your time of need. I'd hate to find you starving in the street like some rag straight out of Dickens."

"I'd hate that too." Despite the air of business behind their transaction, she gave him a brief hug—right in the doorway—and ignored the curious looks of all as she made her way back through the lobby.

The wind was just as sharp and cold as it had been before her visit to the bank, but it seemed to have lost its bite. She hummed "Ain't We Got Fun?" not so quietly, turning every third step or so into a jazzy backward kick. Safe again from the wolves that hounded her. She might just chip in fifty cents to the coal fund of her boardinghouse and spend the rest of the day in the big parlor downstairs, snug in a warm room under one of Mrs. Grayson's famous quilts. There was a new story niggling at the corner of her brain. Something about a banker and his wife celebrating their anniversary at a speakeasy. She would call it something like "A Night on the Town" or "The Ten-Dollar Ticket," and it would begin with the wife finding a mysterious yellow card in her husband's wallet, and she's immediately suspicious, thinking he's stepping out with another woman. . . .

Her thoughts carried her all the way through Mrs. Grayson's cozy parlor and up the steps to her own apartment, where she came to a sharp, startled stop at the sight of a familiar form crumpled in the doorway.

"Trevor?"

At her voice, the boy lifted his head from where it had been buried in his arms. His eyes were red, ruining any chance of hiding the fact that he'd been crying the tears he seemed now determined to fight.

"Oh, Miss Bisbaine. Have you heard?"

"Obviously not." She held out a hand to help him up, trying not to lose her own balance in the process. "Did the offices burn down or something?"

"Worse than that. It's Mr. Moore."

Mr. Moore. Her boss. Editor in chief and owner of *Capitol Chatter*. A small man with a bald pate fringed with hair the same length, volume, and consistency as his eyebrows. Constantly trudging, troll-like, through the tiny third-floor offices, leaving a trail of ashes from his perpetual cigar as he chomped and moaned about the lack of decent violence and vice in this hick town. He was fond of saying—daily, loudly—that all the real corruption was up there on Capitol Hill, and he was stuck with a bunch of hacks too stupid to know it and a load of readers too stupid to care.

"Did he drop dead yet?"

Trevor's eyes grew to saucers. "Who told you?"

❦ CHAPTER 2 ❧

*Take the adventure, heed the call, now ere the irrevocable moment
passes! 'Tis but a banging of the door behind you, a blithesome
step forward, and you are out of your old life and into the new!*

KENNETH GRAHAME

LOS ANGELES, CALIFORNIA

MAXIMILIAN MOORE'S SECRETARY, Ida, had taken the telegram over the phone, and he read the message now written in her precise, efficient hand.

*Edward Moore deceased. Request you come at earliest
convenience to settle affairs.*

Precisely who had sent the telegram was unknown. He hadn't any other family. No cousins or siblings anywhere. Uncle Edward had been his father's only brother, and Max an only child—his parents now deceased.

He walked over to the window and leaned his head against the cool glass, feeling very alone despite the manic activity on the street three stories below.

17

Three soft knocks and a muffled "Mr. Moore?" from the other side of his door sharpened his attention.

"Come in."

Ida's comforting, homely face poked through.

"My condolences, Mr. Moore, on your loss."

"Thank you, Ida."

"But he's in the arms of Jesus now."

Max folded the slip of paper smaller and smaller. He'd never heard his uncle Edward say the name of Jesus with any reverence, and his church affiliation seemed to be confined to the National Cathedral. Not attending, just a correspondence of letters and clippings during its construction. Still, it was not his place to judge the fate of any man's soul, and he quietly affirmed Ida's prophecy.

He took off his glasses, sending the whole office into a blur, and gave them an unnecessary cleaning with his handkerchief.

"Is everybody assembled in the conference room?"

"Almost everybody."

He didn't need to see Ida's face to visualize the look of thinly veiled contempt.

"Now, Ida, careful, careful. She does sign the paychecks, you know."

"With a solid-gold pen, if she could."

He chuckled and put his glasses back on, bringing the small, tidy office back into focus. "Call for me when she gets here."

"But you know she hates not to be the last to arrive. Likes to make an entrance, that one."

"Indulge me. I'm in mourning."

"Of course, Mr. Moore. I'm so sorry. My condolences, again."

In this short span of time, sweet Ida had offered Uncle Edward more kindness than the man himself had ever extended. And just what his "affairs" consisted of Max could only guess. The last he knew there was some sort of a small trade paper, *Capitol* . . . something—the name was on the stationery on which he'd written his annual brief Christmas note, as had been his habit since the death of Max's parents. For a man in publishing, Uncle Edward had very few words of comfort; in fact, at the moment, Max couldn't recall a single one.

He rolled down his shirtsleeves, fastened the cuffs, and was sliding his arms into the sleeves of his suit jacket when he heard her voice, strident and commanding, from the other end of the hallway.

"Ten fifteen is *not* ten o'clock, and we will *not* begin the meeting without Mr. Moore."

He was giving his lapel a final brush when the door burst open, and the woman herself—Aimee Semple McPherson—filled his office in a wash of silk and fur. The rest of the world knew her as Sister Aimee, world-renowned evangelist, the woman who had literally driven from shore to shore preaching revivals, winning souls to Jesus out of the spiritual fear of his imminent return.

"Good morning, Aimee," he said, as if her presence on the third floor were an ordinary occasion.

"Everybody's assembled in the conference room. Everybody." She was a small woman—smaller than anyone would imagine, having first seen her on a stage. Her dress and fur both her signature white, her face glowed with a healthy tan, and the tips of her fingernails deep red as she ticked off the list of those waiting downstairs. "Mr. Todd with the new cover, Mr. Crowley from sales and subscriptions, a few gentlemen from the radio, Mr. Lundi— everybody. We seem, however, to be missing our editor, which, in light of the fact that we are attempting to publish a *magazine*, seems to be a great, gaping maw. Wouldn't you agree?"

Sister Aimee hadn't built an empire by having people disagree with her, so Max slouched a bit, hoping to appear humble, and held forth his message.

"I've had a bit of bad news this morning. My uncle back east—he's passed away."

An immediate change came over Sister Aimee as she breached the space between them and grasped his hand in hers—icy cold despite the fur. She lifted her other hand high as she bowed her head in prayer.

"Father in heaven, I come before you on behalf of this man, asking for strength and comfort in this hour of need. May you carry him through this season of mourning. . . ."

Max stood, open-eyed and fascinated. His heart joined the prayer, but his mind drank in this vision. She was America's Angel, a woman who'd stood in front of millions of people, and here he was, a private, unworthy recipient of her intercessory power. People lined up around the block outside of her church, the Angelus Temple, with scant hope of such an opportunity.

Upon Sister Aimee's amen, he closed and opened his eyes and said, "Thank you, Aimee," with the appropriate warmth.

"Of course," she said, releasing him. "Now, we've business to attend."

He followed her out of his office and down the hall, staying two steps behind her clattering little shoes not out of defer-ence but out of habit. The hall opened up to a wide, winding staircase, which she descended like royalty—one hand gliding along the polished-to-silk banister, the other poised to wave at the people below. To think, she'd walked all the way up just to fetch him.

Given the expanse of the lobby, one would never guess that the offices above it were so small and cramped. The vast whiteness of the walls was interrupted with large, impressive paintings of biblical scenes. The ceiling stretched to the second story, where a skylight assured warmth and perpetual sunshine.

Max nodded at the two young women seated behind the enormous mahogany desk, pleased with the sweet, giggly way they returned his greeting. Tanya, one was named—the one with the soft brown curls pinned just behind her ears. And the other? Serena, perhaps—something exotic. She was newer and hadn't yet learned all of the details that came with being in the employ of Aimee Semple McPherson, because she held her smile a little too long and let the giggle out a little too late to capture it completely behind her hand.

Without warning, Sister Aimee stopped in front of him, almost causing him to run straight into her fur, and placed her hands on the desk.

"Serena," she said in that eerie, maternal tone she affected when addressing an underling of any kind, "do you honestly think that is the best way to comport yourself at a place of business, especially when you are representing the business of God Almighty?"

Poor Serena—yes, he'd remembered—looked toward the other girl and, stricken with confusion, said, "I'm sorry?"

"Give her a break, Aimee."

She whirled on him, and for a moment he enjoyed a hero's status as the pretty Serena sent a grateful smile from behind Sister Aimee's elbow.

"Are you encouraging this young woman's flirtatiousness, Mr. Moore?"

"Perhaps I am," he said, growing bolder.

"At least have the decency not to indulge in such right under my nose," she said, but a tug of a genuine smile was already forming. "And not on my time clock."

He sent Serena a wink—something he'd done fewer than a dozen times in his remembrance—and followed Sister Aimee through the lobby to the conference room, where yet another impressive piece of furniture, this time a massive oak table, dominated the room. Twelve chairs were spaced evenly around it, ten of them filled with men of all ages and shapes. Two were empty. One conspicuously so, as its back rose high above the others at the head. The other, his, fifth down on the left. It could have been filled by anybody or, Max was certain, left empty, and no one would be the wiser.

"My apologies, gentlemen, for starting late," Sister Aimee said, heading for her seat with the assurance that somebody would be waiting to go through the gentlemanly ritual of holding it out for her. "Mr. Moore has had some disturbing news from home—home, was it?—and we have been in a time of prayer."

Max made his way to his own seat, saying, as both apology and explanation, "My uncle passed away."

As a single unit, they nodded, expressing as much sympathy as each was capable. These were, after all, businessmen—lawyers, radio-air salesmen, publishers, public relations managers. Even the artists in their midst were of a commercial ilk, creating on command and within a specific frame.

Here he had brought all his journalistic dreams, heeding a call from one of Sister Aimee's varied pulpits where she spoke of bringing the Word of God to those who might never hold a Bible. A magazine of Truth for Today, its audience the very Bride of Christ. The title—the *Bridal Call*. When he had worried that he, a bachelor and a young one at that, might be unworthy of editing such a publication, she'd laid her hands on his head and anointed him, declaring him equally worthy and chosen and hired.

And then he'd taken his spot at the table, much as he did right now.

Sister Aimee led them in an opening prayer, as she did every meeting—every gathering, in fact—and this time he dutifully bowed his head and closed his eyes, lest somebody else equally bold catch him in his disrespect. He even joined his mind and heart to her words as she acknowledged God and his power and sovereignty in their lives and homes and streets and government.

"Reaching to the height and breadth and depth of our humble temple, in the waves that carry your message through the air, in every word and page of our magazine, we dedicate the hours of our days . . ."

She never spoke that she didn't sound like a million lost souls would find their way to salvation through her voice.

Max didn't need salvation, not in the same way Uncle Edward did. He tried to imagine Uncle Edward sitting in this chair, his fingers stained with ink, the iron-colored rim of hair tufted in all directions from being pulled asunder with each new idea. He would have lasted about thirty seconds into Aimee's prayer before pushing himself away from the table and declaring it was time to stop yammerin' already and start talking about how they were going to fill twenty-eight pages when the presses rolled next Tuesday. The publishing world had been his life—no formal education, no family of his own. Just one failed enterprise after another. Rags and tabloids, most of them. Now he was dead, and a slip of paper in Max's pocket summoned him to handle the last of the man's follies.

He shifted in his seat, the resulting creak and squeak the only sound, as Aimee's prayer had called them all to a silent search of hidden sin.

She ended with a plea to God that he would grant them

wisdom and fervor as they waged battle in his name, just as she always did, yet when Max finally opened his eyes, nothing seemed familiar. Or, if familiar, not comfortable. He was not a small man, but never before had the wooden armrests on the chair felt so confining. A sharp pain formed between his shoulder blades as he tried to fold himself to fit, and soon the only solution to his discomfort was to back away from the table itself and rest his elbows on the empty blotter in front of him. Such posture would have earned him a stern look from his mother, and so it did from Sister Aimee, who glowered from five seats up.

"Shall we begin?" Her question cut straight to him; he listlessly folded and unfolded Ida's message while all around him papers were shuffled and pens uncapped. Sitting directly at Aimee's right was Roland Lundi. Small and slick, his exact position in Sister Aimee's army remained somewhat a mystery—something between a servant and a squire. A well-dressed toady. He handed her a page of neatly typed notes before settling back in his seat, his responsibility complete.

"I've got everything prepared for the summer edition," Sister Aimee continued, sliding a thick folder down the table. It stopped right in front of Max and there remained, unopened.

"In the summer months, as you all are well aware, our collective minds turn to thoughts of patriotism and independence, so I've drafted an editorial in staunch condemnation of that so-called Miss America display that seems determined to take place year after year."

This was the point where he was supposed to speak up in agreement, perhaps offer some ideas for photographs or illustrations, but instead, he said nothing, until the silence all around the table became as uncomfortable as a wet wool suit.

"Well, Mr. Moore?" Sister Aimee said at last.

"Well, what?"

"Have you no opinion of my suggestion?"

"Why, yes," he said, speaking even as the idea began to unfurl itself. "I was thinking of writing a profile piece on Margaret Gorman. For those of you who don't know, gentlemen, she is the winner of the aforementioned contest in Atlantic City. And from what I've learned, she's a fine example of modern womanhood, high school educated and enrolled in college. My memory fails as to which university in particular—it's in my notes."

A fleeting smile twitched across Lundi's face, gone before Sister Aimee could capture it in her sweeping gaze.

"Mr. Moore, surely you are saying such a thing to vex me. Now, if we can get on with our business, have you any serious ideas to contribute?"

"Why in the world would you be interested in what I have to say?"

"Because, after all, you are the editor of the *Bridal Call*."

"Aimee, you and I both know I'm not the editor of anything."

"That's simply not true."

"Your name is on the cover. You choose, write, and approve every article. I'm lucky to get my name on the masthead."

There was an audible gasp from the men around the table, who had been moving their heads back and forth in unison, as if a slow-moving tennis match were taking place right atop the gleaming table. With barely a stretch from where he sat, Max reached across to grab a large brown folder from Mr. Todd, the cover artist—a thick, balding man who looked more like a dock-worker than an artist. He flipped it open, pulled out an oversize sketch of a woman looking bravely into the horizon, and pushed it across the table to where it came to a perfect stop right in front of Sister Aimee.

"I had absolutely no say in this."

"You should not let matters of pride cloud your judgment, Mr. Moore. Our readers know me. They trust me. This magazine represents my message to them—to all who cannot come to hear God's Word from my mouth. I thought you understood that."

She had a way of speaking—always—that captured equal measures of authority and grace, and immediately he felt the heat rising up the back of his neck. Not shame, exactly. At least not shame in this moment. But he could almost feel the clatter of the blinders falling from his eyes, and questions he'd never quite dared to ask himself began to demand answers.

"I suppose," he said, musing aloud, "I'm just wondering exactly what my place is here."

"You keep everything straight," Sister Aimee said as Mr. Lundi decorously returned the sketch to Mr. Todd. "You keep the articles balanced."

The rumbling sound he heard captured the agreement of the men around the table, none of whom he'd wager had ever looked beyond the cover of any issue of the *Bridal Call*.

"I count the words."

"If that's how you want to define it, yes."

"But I don't write the words. I don't approve or direct them."

"If you've ever a serious idea . . ."

There was that word again. *Serious.* It was the last of her diatribe that he heard before feeling the smile that his mother used to say opened up wide as a melon slice stretching across his face as the joke he'd been telling himself since his parents' death finally came clear. Uncle Edward, apparently, had been the punch line.

"I do have an idea, Aimee." He'd interrupted her mid-Corinthian metaphor about a body needing many parts, no single one more important than the others. She hated more than anything to be interrupted, and her mouth refused to accept the fact that she had been as she continued on, eyes to the ceiling as Scripture poured out of her in perfect citation.

"All right then." He spoke aloud, yet to himself, and backed his chair away from the table, standing to a towering height.

"Mr. Moore!" Sister Aimee leapt to her feet, causing a wave of like motion, but Max was already at the door.

"Gentlemen," he said, holding up a hand as if to stop the attack that would only come at Sister Aimee's bidding, "I received some sad news about a relative of mine. He passed away, you see, and I've been summoned to settle his affairs. I wish you well."

And he left, closing the door firmly behind him and waiting for a full count of ten exhalations to see if anyone would care to follow. Or simply track him down to drag him back.

Nobody did. Apparently, he was free.

He walked up the short hallway and found himself again at the reception desk where, to his surprise, Ida was waiting with a small cardboard box. Given the advantage of his height, he could easily see the contents: a football trophy, two diplomas, a thick black scrapbook, a Bible, and a ceramic cup of pencils in every hue.

"How did you know?"

Ida sniffed. "I had a hunch." The old girl had never been one for emotion, but even this short sentence bore evidence of fighting back tears. "Be sure you get yourself a good coat. They have real winter back there."

"I will." He took the box from her, set it on the reception desk, and took the older woman in his arms.

"You're leaving, Mr. Moore?" This from the lovely Serena, who made no pretense of hiding her disappointment. A little quiver had come to her adorable chin, and she stood, offering a delicate hand across the desk. "I guess this is good-bye, then?"

"It is," Max said, taking her hand. Then, in reaction to an impulse not even he could have predicted, he grabbed Serena by the shoulders, pulled her halfway to meet him, and planted a long, satisfying kiss right on her lips.

"I've wanted to do that forever," he said when he was finally able to release her. Her dazed expression and slightly smeared lipstick proved to be the most satisfying image he'd seen of late. That, and the beam of Ida's approval.

Serena touched the back of her hand to her lips. "What'd ya wait for?"

"I don't know." He gathered his box under his arm. "But I won't wait so long next time."

CHAPTER 3

Don't accept rides from flirting motorists—they
don't invite you in to save you a walk.
ANTI-FLIRT CLUB RULE #2

THE FUNERAL FOR EDWARD MOORE took place on a blindingly cold day in a small cemetery adjacent to a tiny Episcopal church. Though it was common knowledge that the deceased had loathed any adherence to religion, the task of the final arrangements had fallen to his accountant, Thomas Harper Jr., who stood near the gaping grave. The casket had already been lowered, and the small gathering of mourners—Monica among them—stood at a respectful distance.

"We coulda done this at the office," she said, speaking over her shoulder to Tony Manarola, the man who spent his days and nights hoofing from one police station to the next in search of the more salacious crime stories. "There's nobody here that isn't from the paper."

"Careful what you says," Tony replied, making a familiar

29

Italian gesture meant to ward off bad luck. "Chances are we'll be givin' the whole operation its final rest in the near future."

"Is somebody going to speak or something?" Monica shifted from foot to foot in an attempt to get warm. It wasn't windy, but the air was thick with merciless cold. She brought her mittened hands to her face and cupped them around her mouth, breathing deep.

"In the old country," Zelda Ovenoff, their office janitress, said, "if you die in this weather, we take you to the barn and set you on ice until the ground grows soft for digging. Only in America can one have a grave in the dead of winter."

Monica sent a sidelong glance at the lanky, rawboned woman who seemed oblivious to the cold despite the fact that her coat was worn thin at the elbows. Still, the look on her face was one of true sadness, unmatched by any of the others gathered there.

"Is there going to be a meal?" Trevor asked. He stood to Monica's right, wearing a black overcoat obviously borrowed from an older, larger relative. "Mom said funerals are usually the best eating. She wanted to come with me, but I said it didn't seem right, seeing as she didn't know him like the rest of us."

"There isn't going to be a meal." Monica's muffled words echoed back from within her gloves. And besides that, nobody here *really* knew Edward Moore—not outside the offices, anyway, where he was known to pace and growl as if the dingy string of space were his own personal lair. "Where would we go? Does anybody even know where he lives—er, lived?"

At this point, Thomas Harper Jr. deemed their conversation disrespectful and shot forth a cautionary glower. "We are waiting for the next of kin to arrive. And, ah, this must be him."

A lone figure was making his way across the cemetery, remarkable not only for his stature—even from a distance she could tell he was easily more than six feet tall—but for his gait, which appeared at once loping and purposeful. His face, however, remained a mystery, swathed as it was with a thick red wool scarf up to his nose and a black felt hat pulled low over his brow. What remained was a partially fogged set of round tortoiseshell spectacles. These trappings, combined with a fur-collared jacket, made him look equally suited to an expedition for Klondike gold as a midmorning funeral in a frostbitten cemetery.

Harper was the first to break rank and approach him, offering in one efficient gesture a greeting, introduction, and expression of sympathy for the loss.

"Thank you," the interloper said, though really, given the muffling, he might have said just about anything. He made his way down the modest line of mourners, introducing himself to each one, in a sort of reversed reception line. Each seemed to receive his undivided attention and gratitude for their attendance at his uncle's grave.

Monica watched from her spot on the end, fingers twitching within her mittens. This was a social occasion that called for precise, solemn decorum, and she worked to discipline her mind to speak along those lines.

So sorry for your loss.

I'm sorry we had to meet under such sad circumstances.

Edward was a good man. He'll be missed.

Next to her, Trevor stood rooted in silence, his pimpled neck stretched to meet the stranger's gaze.

"So sorry for your loss, Mr. Moore," his voice cracked the very pleasantry Monica wanted to claim for herself.

The next thing she knew, her hand was encased in something of a bearlike claw.

"Max Moore," said the voice behind the scarf by way of introduction.

"Are you sure?" she found herself saying, unable to stifle her cleverness. "Because I was half expecting you to introduce yourself as Griffin."

The eyes—crisp and blue like the sky surrounding his towering frame—opened wide behind the lenses, and his brows danced in confusion. "Excuse me?"

"Griffin. As in *The Invisible Man*. It's a novel, and this man— he's invisible, and he wraps himself up . . ."

In the midst of her babble he'd used his free hand to tug his scarf down, revealing a smile wide and crescent-warm. "I've read the book."

"Well, then, you know. And, my, what a nice face you have."

"I'm from California. Not used to the cold, I guess."

"Well, I hope you stick around long enough to get used to it."

Her eyelashes had taken on a life of their own, batting in punctuation, and he cocked his head to one side, looking both quizzical and amused. Before he could give any sort of reply, however, Harper cleared his throat with trumpetlike force and asked if they shouldn't get on with the ceremony. Max agreed, and as he moved to take his place at the head of the open grave, Harper openly glowered at Monica, hissing, "Have you no shame?"

She answered definitively with a wrinkled nose and stuck-out tongue—apparently she didn't. It was a harmless joke, a tiny flirtation, and if she'd offended the only Moore in mourning, he certainly hid it well. That was the problem with frosty old fogeys like Thomas Harper Jr. No sense of fun.

"Thank you all, once again, for coming," Max said with the air of a man clearly uncomfortable with public speaking of any kind. He had, however, unfurled his scarf until it merely hung down from his shoulders, and when he removed his hat in anticipation of prayer, he revealed a mop of wavy brown hair.

Tony Manarola and Zelda Ovenoff made dutiful signs of the cross and bowed their heads, as did the others, leaving Monica the briefest moment to openly study the new Mr. Moore before shutting out the daylight.

"Gracious Father," he began, without a shred of prayerful authority, "we gather together to honor the life of Edward Moore, a man who lived . . . a . . . life."

She risked opening one eye to find him shifting his hat from hand to hand, rocking on his heels, looking for all the world like a little boy faced with his first school recitation. His eyes were not closed, either, and he'd lifted his face to the sky, as if God himself would drop the words down to him. Initially amused, she felt a smirk tugging at the corner of her mouth. After all, in the year she'd known Edward Moore, there'd been very little about the man to be extolled in prayer. But then, after a deep sigh, Max moved his hat to cover his heart and looked down, catching her eye in the process. The sadness on his face reached out to her—silently imploring for rescue. Since one eye remained closed, she went ahead and twitched it in a wink before closing the other and offered a line.

"Amen."

Her voice rang out clear, inviting the others to echo, and when she looked at him again, the sadness had turned to relief.

"Uncle Edward," he began, sounding instantly at ease, "was . . . born July 2, 1863, not too far away from here." His brows hovered expectantly. "For those who aren't familiar, that was the Battle of Gettysburg, and our family has always joked that he was born under cannon fire, which accounts for his explosive personality."

They rewarded him with a round of warm chuckles, as Moore's temper was indeed legendary.

"But I think that also made him fearless. You worked with him; you know. He never backed down from a fight, not in all his days as a reporter or an editor. Publishing was his world, and you—well, you all were his family. And me, of course . . ."

The nervous discomfort had returned, but he avoided Monica's gaze, opting instead to glance to some invisible attendant to her left, then down at his feet until a deep breath revived him.

"I admired him—for his courage, if not his character. And I might have even loved the man, had he ever given me the chance."

It had never crossed Monica's mind that she would be moved to tears at Edward Moore's funeral; they'd been sparse enough at her own mother's, and those that appeared were born more of guilt than grief. But when Max's eyes took on a glinting sheen, she herself welled up, and the chorus of sniffles around her brought her to an unforeseen, heartbreaking camaraderie.

He smiled then, broadly enough to engulf them all, and if they hadn't assembled at the graveside as family, they certainly felt so now. At least Monica did. Through Max's words, Edward Moore had been transformed from intolerable tyrant to heroic old crank, and the scars from his predictable tirades took on certain nobility. Even Trevor, who'd always turned a shade of sickly green whenever Moore spoke to him directly, stood with a distant smile under his sparse growth of moustache while Zelda Ovenoff, who had arguably treated him with the most kindness, openly and loudly wept.

"Obviously we can't go back to Uncle Edward's for a meal," Max said, holding his gloved hands out in apology, "but there's a deli not far from here that Mr. Harper tells me was one of his favorites, and they've assured me that we are all due a complimentary lunch in his honor. Will you join me?"

Of course they would, and Monica's mouth began to water at

the thought of the warm pastrami and tart potato salad waiting at the District Deli—a haunt familiar to them all.

Max took three purposeful steps (in the wrong direction, before being corrected by Harper) and the mischief of mourners followed. Monica held back, keeping a pinch of Tony Manarola's coat sleeve between her fingers until the others were several steps ahead. Then, linking her arm conspiratorially through his, followed. Tony was one of the few men near her own height, and her whispered words drifted just under the brim of his hat.

"What do you know about him?"

Tony had hoped to be a Pinkerton when he came to America, only to find that his stature would keep him from joining the elite detectives. His investigative prowess, however, had served him well as a journalist. In fact, it was Tony who'd broken the news to her that Charlie had a wife in a modest three-bedroom home and that his small string of automobile repair shops generated enough income to keep her quite content there.

"Ed was his father's uncle. Family in Philadelphia at least two generations before him, so good American stock."

"He *does* look a little like a farm boy."

"And you was wrong to flirt like that, circumstances being what they are."

"I flirt with everybody."

"The man's in mourning for his last living relative, God rest his soul."

Monica wasn't in the mood for a lecture, so she conceded the point with a sigh. "What else?"

"Well, you're wrong about the farm boy, anyway. Grandfather a professor, father a lawyer. Both parents died in a house fire— God rest their souls—seven years ago. No brothers, no sisters."

"So he really is all alone," she mused. So rare to find another who shared her fate. "What do you think he's going to do with all of us?"

She felt Tony shrug against her. "I'm your man for diggin' around in the past. Leave the soothsayin' to someone else, you know what I mean?"

"Yeah. I know what you mean."

By now they'd left the little churchyard far behind and were walking along a busy street thick with afternoon traffic. Sleek, expensive automobiles jockeyed for position alongside older models, making it impossible to imagine that little more than a decade had passed since the same streets teemed with horses and buggies and wagons. On the sidewalk pedestrians fought a similar battle, not having the benefit of a designated direction. Luckily, when it came time to cross the street, a police officer stationed in the middle of the intersection blew a shrill whistle, bringing the traffic to a stop for safe passage.

Max and Harper led the way, followed by Trevor, who—quite the gentleman—took Mrs. Ovenoff's arm. Monica and Tony followed and were nearly to the opposite side when the *ah-oogah* sound of a honking horn startled her so, she dropped his arm, stopping dead in her tracks. The hearty sound of a man's laughter came from the car nearest the curb.

"I thought that would get you to drop the geezer's arm!"

Monica stared down the shining blue hood of the car to where a rakishly handsome face smiled at her through the windshield. The top was down despite the cold, and the driver leaned out to get a better look at her.

"Give a girl a heart attack, why don't you?" But she smiled wide so he'd know there weren't any hard feelings, really.

"Baby, I'd give your heart anything it needs. Ditch your daddy and come play with me for a while."

"Hey, come on, fella," Tony said, bristling beside her. "Leave her alone."

"And if I don't?" the man shot back.

Before Tony could say another word, the impressive figure of Max Moore appeared. He stood in front of her, blocking the entire view of the automobile, and said, "The lady is not welcoming your attentions, sir." Then, without another word, he turned and draped a shepherding arm across her shoulders.

"You heard the man," Tony said. "G'on."

If the driver had any reply, it was lost in the rev of his engine. Monica hurried for the last few steps until she was safely on the sidewalk.

"You've got a lot of nerve," she said, ducking herself out from under his arm.

"I'm sorry?"

"Beefing on that fellow like that."

"Oh." Max looked over to the intersection, as if expecting to see the fellow still waiting. "I thought he might be bothering you."

"Just some harmless flirting. Right, Tony?"

"You kids. Nothin' but sex, sex, sex. It's broad daylight, for pete's sake."

Monica felt her cheeks flush despite the cold and found a rush of words to defend her honor.

"Why are you making such a federal case out of it? A little honk, a little wink. No harm done."

"I think perhaps you might want to be more cautious in your response to a man who is so publicly brazen in his behavior," Max said. They'd arrived at the deli, where he opened the door and held it for her.

"Oh, I don't know," Monica said, her voice thick with sarcasm.

"I mean, here you are so *brazenly* holding that door for me. What kind of a girl would I be if I just walked right inside? I mean, we've barely been introduced. Right, Tony?"

"Six-dash-six-four-seven," Tony said, glancing at his ever-present little notebook. "That's the license number of the fella's car if you want I should track him down for you. In case it's a matter of true love or something."

He took the responsibility of holding the door, and Monica scooted past, returning a scowl for his smirk. Once inside, the din of conversation made further discussion impossible, at least for as long as it would take to shoulder through the crowd of regulars to the assembly of small tables at the back of the room. Three open seats remained—one in the center by the window, and two crammed into the corner at the head. Tony's determined step from behind knocked her flat into Max's back, and before she could ask what all the rush was about, he'd claimed the center seat, leaving her to be squished in the corner at Max's right hand.

Clearly their arrival had been greatly anticipated, for they'd barely settled in before Harper lifted his hand in a signal, and a trio of red-moustachioed deli men, each wearing a meat-stained apron, descended on their table. They were led by Peter MacDougal, as famous for his unpredictable Irish temperament as he was for the generous portions of delicious food. With them came a steaming platter of corned beef along with a pyramid of sliced rolls, a bowl of warm cooked cabbage, another of potato salad, and finally a double-decker cake iced white and festooned with garlands and blue roses.

"To honor Edward Moore," MacDougal said. "Three, four, maybe five times a week did he come here. Always the same thing, corned beef on a white roll, cake, and coffee. Sat on that stool right there, he did." He pointed to a raised seat along the counter that sat empty, draped in black wool. "When I told him that my mother, God rest her soul, was longin' to come here from the old country, he asked me flat out, 'Peter?' he said. 'Is it your mother that taught you to make such a fine corned beef?'

"I told him, yes, sir, 'twas indeed, and the good man came back the next day with a check. Bought her a first-class passage on the next ship out of Dublin."

MacDougal wiped an unchecked tear with the back of his wrist. "I tell you, there's nothing I'd like better than to raise a glass to the man. Cursed law it is that a friend can't have a drink to honor the life of another. But I trust you'll eat hearty, the way he'd want you to, God bless him."

"We will," Max said, standing to offer his hand.

"You're the family?"

"I am. His nephew—" But the final syllable came out as little more than a puff of air as Max was crushed in the embrace of a man who spent his days working a meat slicer.

"I always told your uncle," MacDougal said once he'd released Max to an arm's-length grip, "he was more of a man than anybody knew. Get it? *Moore* of a man?"

Everyone around the table laughed at the cue, including Monica, though she was more amused by the dazed look on Max's face than by MacDougal's pun.

"I look for you to be the same, young man. The very same." By now tears flowed freely down MacDougal's red face, disappearing into his generous moustache. He wished them all a good lunch as a start to a long life of good health, then took his men back behind the counter to meet the needs of the growing line of customers.

"Everybody, please," Max said, holding his hands out toward the tableful of food. "Enjoy."

They immediately tucked in to obey, passing platters and bowls and filling their plates. In the midst of the activity, Max leaned in close, the timbre of his voice low enough to be heard under the chatter around them. "Did you know that? About the check and the old country?"

"Nope," Monica said, buttering her roll. "I was half expecting the man to come up with a bill for a lifelong tab. I always figured Edward to be the guy to take a sack of pennies to the five-and-dime."

She immediately wished she'd had a bit more tact than to insult the memory of this newly discovered generosity, but Max's smile eased her conscience.

"It was good to hear. And by the way, I think we can all rest assured that Mr. MacDougal has had plenty of opportunity to raise a glass to his friend."

"Really?" As if such a thing were unheard of.

She piled her roll high with corned beef and added the warm, peppery cabbage before pressing the top of the roll down on the overflowing sandwich. In retrospect, she should have given more thought to her lipstick than her appetite, as there was no way to continue without making a complete mess of her makeup. Still, she opened her mouth wide to take a bite and felt completely vindicated by the deliciousness of the combination.

"And about all that business with that fellow in the car." Max was talking to her again. "I do apologize if I insulted you, Miss . . . Miss—"

"Bisbaine," she said, or something like that.

"Bisbaine," he said, as if tasting the sound of it along with the warm potato salad. "Bisbaine. You know, I looked through several issues of *Capitol Chatter* this morning, but I don't recall your name in a byline. Are you an editor? Copy editor?"

"No," she said, swallowing.

"Secretary?"

"Ha!" A crumb of something flew past her lips, but she caught it in time with the back of her hand. "Fine day it'll be when I'm a secretary. No, Mr. Moore, I'm a writer. I simply choose to publish anonymously."

Tony made a monkey sound from down the table. Max's eyebrows rose at its shrieking apex.

"That's you? Monkey girl?"

"Monkey *Business*. And yes, that's me." She leaned forward, elbow planted on the table, her sandwich dangling over his plate. "Are you scandalized?"

He shook his head. "Nope. Should I be?"

"It's a very popular column, you know. People write letters, wanting to know where I'm going next and where I buy my clothes. Even though they can't see them. I write about what I'm wearing, and they want to know where they can buy the same thing. They love me."

"Imagine that." Max sliced his corned beef and stabbed it along with a forkful of cabbage. "People who don't even know you love you. All those readers who don't know your name. That fellow in the car."

Monica sat back, angling her body and tilting her chin in the way that hours of study in the mirror confirmed to be the most enticing. "What are you implying? That I might only be lovable to those who don't know me?"

"Not at all. Just making an observation."

She waited for something to crack—a smile, a humorous glint from behind his spectacles—anything that would belie the inscrutable seriousness of his expression, but there was nothing.

"Well, I should hope not," Zelda said from the opposite side of the table. "You are a lovely girl. Mr. Moore was quite fond of you."

"Really?" The news—and indeed, it was news—warmed her

as much as the food. "With him you could never tell." She tore off a piece of her roll and wedged it in the corner of her mouth like Edward's ever-present stump of cigar and twisted her face to match his scowl. "'Monkey!'" she said, matching his gravelly voice to near perfection. "'You call this writing? I can knock a kid down in the street and steal his copybook and get better stuff than this. Ever hear of a verb?'"

The table burst out in laughter, Max among them, though his chuckle seemed to stem more from curiosity than amusement.

"Oh," Zelda said, wiping her eyes with the corner of her napkin, "you have captured him completely."

Monica received the compliment with a small bow as she chewed and swallowed the bit of bread. Max stood beside her and lifted his water glass.

"To Edward Moore," he said, "who apparently will live on in the hearts of us all."

"To Edward," they echoed, touching their glasses to one another's. Monica's eyes met Max's over the clink, and there she saw the humor that had been hiding before.

Do you see? Someone we both knew loved me.

She kept the victorious truth to herself as she sipped her water and confidently imagined Max conceding the point as he did the same. It was a first, if silent, truce.

After that, the floodgates of conversation opened, and until the last crumb of cake was gone, stories of Edward Moore's secret generosity and blatant orneriness flowed from one end of the table to the other. Max mostly listened, taking in his uncle's most recent history while contributing very little about the man Edward had been before.

"What?" Monica said during a lull. "No childhood traumas to share?"

"We weren't close," Max said with a finality she dared not breach.

She shrugged. "That's family."

"It doesn't have to be." He scooted his chair back as far as the confines of the corner would allow and stood. "Thank you, everybody, once again for taking the time to share your memories with me. I can see that my uncle has left me quite a void to fill, and I'll be taking a few days to look over his affairs before I decide what the future of the paper will be."

"Wait a minute," Tony said. "There's a chance you might shut us down?"

Max held up a reassuring hand. "I haven't made up my mind. I'll be meeting with Mr. Harper to see how viable the business is. There are a lot of factors to consider. This was my uncle's vision, not mine. But we will continue on the publication schedule for the next issue, at least."

It was as if a pitcher of cold water had been dashed across the table, dousing every bit of the crackling camaraderie. In the midst of the wash, Max thanked them once again for their time and their memories before taking his leave.

They watched him, some turning in their chairs to do so, as he once again wrapped himself against the cold and walked past the windows that ran the length of the store.

"So what if he does shut us down?" Tony said at last. "Not like any of us's gettin' rich from writin' for this rag."

"You're right," Monica said, voicing the others' downcast agreement. If she were indeed dependent on the pittance she earned from her column, she'd be begging for scraps in the street.

"Still," Zelda said, "we are rather like a family, are we not?"

"Yeah," Monica said, "and you see how much family means to him. His own uncle, and he's got nothing to say."

"Do not be so harsh." Zelda turned to Harper. "You, Mr. Harper, you know better than any of us. What do the books say?"

Thomas Harper Jr. straightened his tie and cleared his throat. "That, I'm afraid, is information I'm not at liberty to share at will. Suffice it to say that to take the helm of this publication would be a matter of affection, not business acuity."

"You're saying Edward kept on with the paper because he loved us?" Monica asked.

Harper bristled at the thought. "Because he loved the industry, I would say."

"Well, Mr. Maximilian Moore is inheriting both," Monica said. "He seems like kind of a big, cold cod, but let's hope he warms up to one of the two."

❧ CHAPTER 4 ❧

*The stranger came early in February, one wintry day, through
a biting wind and a driving snow, the last snowfall of the year,
over the down, walking from Bramblehurst railway station, and
carrying a little black portmanteau in his thickly gloved hand.
He was wrapped up from head to foot, and the brim of his soft
felt hat hid every inch of his face but the shiny tip of his nose.*

H. G. WELLS, *THE INVISIBLE MAN*

HE'D GONE STRAIGHT TO THE FUNERAL from the train station,
and then, with his belly full of corned beef and cake, not to mention a head full of visions, met with a junior associate of Bolling,
Bolling, and Smith—the law firm handling Uncle Edward's estate.
Nelson Bolling, at least a generation removed from the men who'd
earned the name on the door, thumbed nervously through a thin
portfolio of papers, clicking his tongue in time with the office clock.

"It's a fairly . . . simple . . . affair. . . ." He spoke slowly, no doubt
an attempt to stretch the billable hour. "Your uncle, Mr. Moore?
Which would you prefer, that I refer to him as your uncle? Or Mr.
Moore? The latter could be confusing, as you are also Mr. Moore. I
suppose I could go with Mr. Moore Sr., although that isn't entirely
accurate, given that he was not your father—"

45

"Why don't we go with Edward?" Max sat forward in his chair, elbows resting on his knees. The train ride had been long, the lunch delicious, and the office now overly warm, and he fought back a yawn while the young lawyer made a fastidious note on his blotter.

"Ed-ward. Got it. Now, there is a will—" he removed a single sheet of paper—"in which you are named as sole beneficiary of Mr. Moore's—Mr. *Edward* Moore's—estate. I will read this to you now."

Thirty ticks later, Bolling had located a leather case from which he withdrew a pair of thin spectacles, and when they were perfectly balanced on his equally thin nose and the case replaced in the top drawer, he cleared his throat, adjusted the paper to the correct distance, and read, "'My nephew, Maximilian Edward Moore, gets everything currently held in my name.'"

Bolling looked at Max over the rim of his glasses. "Would you like me to repeat the reading?"

"He was a newspaperman. Brevity and precision."

Bolling blinked as he processed the idea, repeated the ceremony of the spectacles in reverse, and reached into the portfolio.

"Here is the deed to the home, and it is assumed that all of the contents therein are also now in your possession. And you are now owner of . . ." His voice trailed off as he retrieved his spectacles and scanned the current papers in his hand. "Ah, *Capitol Chatter*." He looked up again. "It's a weekly tabloid. I read it often. Quite salacious."

"I am familiar with it," Max said, though before today he'd seen very few copies. At its inception, a sense of family loyalty made him a subscriber, receiving issues via post until Sister Aimee, in an impassioned sermon during which she'd littered her stage with a thousand such publications, declared their sensation and scandal unworthy of the very soil that nurtured the trees slaughtered to print them. *Capitol Chatter* was no doubt among the papers, and he'd spent that morning reading a lurid tale about a woman captured and bound in lascivious torture before a heroic rescue by her brother-in-law. The details of the story had been hidden from the public but ferreted out by a journalist of Tony Manarola's ilk, if not Tony himself. Max had left the rest of the paper unread that day, and for the balance of the year lined his efficient apartment trash barrel with each new issue.

"Both his personal and business accounts are at the Capitol Bank and Loan." A further search yielded the address of the institution, seemingly close by as the logistics of the city began to take form in Max's head. "You will need to take a copy of the certificate of death and the will to gain access to the accounts. But you are free to take over the operations of the paper immediately, or as soon as you see fit. There is a Mr. . . ."

"Harper," Max offered in an effort to expedite the conversation.

"That's right. Harper. He should be able to enlighten you on the business details. And if you find yourself facing another libel suit, may I say on behalf of our firm that we have successfully defended you—your uncle, Mr. Moore, Mr. *Edward* Moore—and *Capitol Chatter* in the past."

This last bit of conversation was delivered with a handshake, the words spoken at twice the velocity of all those previous. The portfolio that had seemed so thin at the beginning of the conversation now felt thick and burdensome as Max took it from across the desk.

"Libel?"

"I, of course, wasn't given the case," Bolling said, suddenly looking too small for his suit, "but I do remember the lovely basket of fruit your uncle, Edward, sent over after the verdict. Very little bloodshed—as they say—as I recall."

"Very little," Max repeated, feeling a slight twist of the corned beef. "Good to know."

He gathered his hat and coat and scarf and gloves from the receptionist, cocooned himself in their warmth, and stepped out into the street to hail a taxi. Perhaps if he had the privilege of Miss Bisbaine standing beside him he'd have more instantaneous results, as she'd shown herself quite capable of attracting vehicular attention. Instead, he had his brand-new coat with the fur collar that he hoped gave him an air of affluence, and the fact that he stood outside a law office holding an impressively thick portfolio certainly added to the ruse. In the end, it took only a few minutes before a cab pulled to the curb in front of him, and he rambled off the memorized address lest the driver take him for a tourist and double the fare.

He divided his attention between the city unfolding on the other side of the window and the contents of the portfolio. Included with the paperwork was a small yellowed envelope that contained a key affixed to a card on which the address of Uncle Edward's home was written. Its copy had been in the small box of things Thomas Harper had discreetly presented him with at the deli, and it now hung on a ring in Max's pocket. There'd also been a worn leather wallet, a silver pocket watch, and a small pebble worried smooth. These items were nestled in the depth of his overcoat.

By the time the cab came to a stop and the driver announced his outrageous fare, everything had been neatly reassembled. He handed the driver a folded bill, instructed him to keep the change, and wrested himself from the car. It wasn't surprising that his uncle wouldn't have a car, and he'd have to either resign himself to walking or find access to a steady supply of cash.

As the car sputtered away, he found himself standing in front of a neat, modest redbrick home with three shallow steps leading up to a white front door. Beside the steps, partially hidden by a hardy piece of shrubbery, he saw the corner of his suitcase, having been delivered from the train station. He took in a deep, stinging breath and mounted the stairs, stooping to pick up his bag on the way. In it was almost everything he owned, minus his few household items he'd left for his landlord in exchange for grace in the breaking of his lease. Two good suits, a dozen shirts, photographs. Ida had been charged with packing and shipping the books both at home and in his office, as he was not willing to disrupt his library until he was certain of its new home. Abandoning an assembled mass of pots and dishes was one thing, a lifetime of selectively collected tomes quite another.

He secured the portfolio beneath his arm, freeing his hand to slip the key into the door, and soon stepped across the threshold into the darkened room. Dark only because the curtains were drawn against the light, and his first order of business after dropping his bag was to grasp the surprisingly heavy material and pull them open, wincing at the sound of the metal rings against the rod.

The room flooded with light, and something in him wondered if this wasn't a rare occasion, as the surroundings immediately looked unaccustomed to the exposure. There was a small woodburning stove and next to it a comfortable-looking leather chair with an afghan strewn across its back. A rolltop desk—its contents covered by the louvered top—a footstool, and a freestanding lamp comprised all the rest of the furniture, unless one wanted to throw a cushion on the steamer trunk under the window. One wall of the room was dominated by a massive bookcase that stretched floor to ceiling, each shelf packed with volumes of every size and shape crammed from end to end.

"Wow," he said to the empty room, thinking of his modest collection, though he'd never thought of it as such until this moment.

He stepped around a corner into a small kitchen—sink, icebox, two-burner stove, and a square table sporting an oilcloth cover. Here he placed the portfolio, his hat, gloves, and scarf, draping his coat over one of the two high-back chairs. That's when he realized the house was stone cold.

Before exploring the rest of the house, he went to the stove and was pleased to find a neat stack of wood ready to be lit and a full bucket of logs beside it. Possibly the work of a well-meaning neighbor, or a cleaning woman, or even Uncle Edward's own habit. He took a long match from the box attached to the wall, lit it, and touched the flame to the kindling. Already the house felt a little more like home.

A short hallway introduced a tiny bathroom and two bedrooms. At first glance it was impossible to know which had been Uncle Edward's, as each held a narrow quilt-covered bed, four-drawer bureau, nightstand, and lamp. Further inspection, however, gave clear preference to the room where a lone sock peeked from underneath the spot where the quilt grazed the floor and a shoe-blacking kit waited expectantly next to the dresser. After only the slightest hesitation, Max opened the top drawer to find a neat assembly of socks and underwear and garters, shirts in the drawer below that. Two suits hung in the closet above a pair of well-worn galoshes. The walls were largely bare, save for a few amateurish paintings of what he recognized to be DC's famous cherry trees in full bloom.

Even though Uncle Edward hadn't died in this house, it was still comforting to Max to know that he wouldn't have to sleep in the dead man's bed, and he deposited his suitcase on the bed in the second room. Within just a few minutes he'd completed the task of unpacking, filling the empty drawers and closet, and placing his shaving kit on the dresser for now, along with the two framed photographs—his parents at their wedding, and the three of them shortly after Max's Army induction, weeks before their death. This he studied closely, never quite recognizing himself in uniform. Not that he had any glorious—or inglorious—memories to coincide. As an only son of deceased parents, he'd served his country from behind a desk in an Army communications office, typing up reports of battle and heroism to be filed away as if such occurrences were little more than bureaucratic details.

The house was small and silent enough that he could hear the faint crackling of the fire in the stove in the other room, but at this moment, the lure of the bed was stronger than any warmth. A rummage through all the dresser drawers yielded a second quilt, and after stripping down to his long johns, he climbed in beneath both of them and squeezed his eyes shut.

"He didn't die here," Max said under the quilt he'd pulled up to his nose, and he repeated it a few more times, urging his mind to reconcile with his body and give in to the rest he so desperately needed. But it wandered, thinking briefly about the last man who slept in this house, and how he now, too, lay flat on his back, eyes closed, cold and alone.

Buried.

Invisible.

"Griffin."

And then he saw nothing but the tiny woman with the enormous brown eyes who wrote for a rag and read H. G. Wells. Suddenly his mind and body were in accord, completely rejuvenated, driving him from the bed. He donned a pair of pajamas and his dressing robe over them, grateful for the extra layer of warmth, and headed to the front room to search the bookcase, even though the odds of finding the book were not in his favor.

By now it was late afternoon, and the front room dangled on the edge of darkness save for the sliver of light from the fire behind the grate. He pulled the little chain on the floor lamp and, thankful that the cord reached across the room, held it to the uppermost corner of the bookshelf and began to scan.

There was no rhyme or reason to the organization of the books. Biographies next to travel journals, poetry, history, but enough novels to be optimistic that he would eventually find the title he sought. And then, there it was, a smallish red book; on its cover, an eerie etching of a masculine form in repose, wearing a long smoking jacket—much like his own dressing gown—and slippers. He'd read it long ago. In fact, this might well have been the same copy he'd devoured over the course of a series of stormy winter's nights much like this one, thrilling at the idea of passing through the world unseen.

Little had he known just how possible it was to do so.

The novel beckoned him as it had in childhood, but so did his stomach. When he'd left the deli that afternoon, he had no idea he would ever be hungry again, and his thoughts turned fondly back to the meal and to those with whom he'd shared it. One in particular, with sleek black hair and wide doe eyes. Clearly she'd been flirting with him throughout the afternoon, but he wouldn't be duped by such flattery. Just as clearly she flirted with everyone. Including total strangers who honked from automobiles.

No, she was a woman to be admired. The only woman he'd ever met who had a working knowledge of both science-fiction novels and underground illegal drinking establishments. Neither of those attributes warranted the thoughts that followed, thoughts about the laughter that picked him up and carried him away with the joke, or about the bit of cabbage dangling from the corner of her vermilion lips, and how he could have reached out and—

Hungry. He was hungry, so he took himself to the kitchen with little hope that his deceased bachelor uncle would have left any kind of viable meal in his cupboards. When he was a kid, a funeral meant a houseful of food, and he and his friends would dodge the gathered mourners and fill plate after plate with loved ones' best offerings. But Uncle Edward had lived an invisible life, as far as he could tell. Still, he opened the first cupboard to find a sparse collection of dishes along with a single pot and a single pan. In the next, however, he was greeted with an array of boxes and cans and a note written on the back of a photograph:

He is a loss to us all.
Welcome to the "Family."

It was a photograph of the *Capitol Chatter* staff, all of them gathered on the steps of what Max knew to be their office building. Uncle Edward sat in the midst of them, scowling, as was young Trevor, given that the old man's cigar smoke must have been wafting directly into his face. Amusing as that was, his eyes went straight to Miss Bisbaine, who stood on the far right, her body contorted in a flapper's pose worthy of the cover of the *Saturday Evening Post*.

Smiling, he tucked the photograph into the front cover of the book and set about heating up a can of Campbell's tomato soup. Once it was poured, steaming, into a sturdy white mug, he took it and the book into the front room, where he found Uncle Edward's leather chair to be the most comfortable piece of furniture a man could imagine. He spread the crocheted afghan over his lap, took a cautious sip, and opened to the first page of the novel.

It occurred to him briefly that he might not want to spend his first evening in a dead man's home reading about another man who had the ability to pass through life undetected, but any fear he might have had disappeared when he envisioned her face, Miss Bisbaine's face, a sparkle in her eyes as fresh as snow, saying, *"I would have called you Griffin."*

And so he embarked on the story of Griffin, but he got no further than the first few sentences before his sputtered soup was sprayed upon the page.

"How could she . . . ?" His question lingered in the silence of the house as amusement and wariness came over him. To be sure it wasn't a matter of a half-willing trick of the mind, he read the words out loud. "'The stranger came early in February, one wintry day, through a biting wind and a driving snow . . .'"

Max thought back to the picture he had made coming across the snow-covered cemetery that afternoon, and Uncle Edward's house filled with the rich sound of his own laughter.

"'A fire, in the name of human charity!'" he said, quoting the text with dramatic good nature. "'A room and a fire!'"

It was all Griffin required at the outset of his tale, and here Max found himself with not only a room and a fire, but a blanket and a book and warm, satisfying soup. If he could have one other thing, it would be to tell her—as if she didn't know—how perfectly she'd greeted him. But it would be days before he'd see her again, not until the scheduled meeting for the staff, and by then the joke would have grown as cold as the night outside. So he savored all that the Invisible Man sought, reading until, having marked his page with the photograph and tucked his spectacles into the breast pocket of his dressing robe, his head dropped in sated sleep.

MONKEY BUSINESS

"A Monkey in Mourning"

Here's a Monkey Riddle for you. Why is Monkey wearing a black dress in the middle of the day? Why are tears puddled up in her big brown Monkey eyes? Why is she at a church on Thursday and sitting home, feeling sad, on a Saturday night? The answer to all three is the same. This little Monkey is in mourning.

Last week, *Capitol Chatter* lost its most important critter: our Big Gorilla, Edward Moore. If it weren't for this Gorilla, there'd be no little Monkey running around in this great big jungle. Sure, he could hoot and holler and howl when Monkey was late to work, but it never took more than a song to soothe him. A song—and a cruller from Sobek's Bakery. Sometimes two. Most gorillas love a good pastry.

So if the jungle seems a little quieter, it's also lost one of its greatest characters. He loved this city, with all its dirt and grime and secrets. All of us at *Capitol Chatter* swing through the vines bringing our stories back to the nest he built for us. This little Monkey might be in mourning, but she'll keep swinging. And she doesn't mind wearing black, given she spent half of her allowance on a new Coco Chanel number last month. She can't wait to wear it on a new adventure. That's what the Gorilla would have wanted.

CHAPTER 5

*By the pricking of my thumbs, something wicked this
way comes. Open, locks, whoever knocks!*
SHAKESPEARE, *MACBETH*

MONICA RIPPED THE DRAFT of her column from the roller of
her little typewriter and gave it a final read.

"Edward Moore, Gorilla." She smirked to herself. He would
have loved that. "Shoulda thought of that earlier."

Today there'd be no Trevor to deliver her work to the office. In
fact, he'd been here last night with a notice that she—along with all
the other staff—were to be in the office at nine sharp for a meeting with the new boss. She couldn't remember the last time she'd
been anywhere on a Monday morning, let alone at nine o'clock.

Sharp.

It was already past eight thirty, so sharpness would be impossible, especially since she wasn't even dressed yet. With all of
her best stuff still in hock at the laundry, she could either wear
the same black number she'd worn to the funeral ("bought" on
account at Nellie's) or the green tartan and sweater that made her
look like she lost her bagpipes in a tumble across the moors. The
stockings she'd washed the night before weren't completely dry,
and she cringed against the cold as she stretched them up her legs.

Peering into the mirror above her sink, she used her tiny silver scissors to give a fresh, crisp trim to her bangs before tugging a heather-colored tam to a perfect angle.

"Sharp."

She carefully rolled the article and tucked it into the pocket in the lining of her heavy wool peacoat, ignoring the crunch as she belted it. With a little fast hoofing, she might actually make it to the office on time, but the minute she'd typed the word *Sobek's*, she wanted a warm cherry Danish and coffee, and her peacoat had been hiding a dime.

In the end, she wasn't more than twenty minutes late—forgivable by any standards with the exception, apparently, of Maximilian Moore's.

During the days between Edward's funeral and this morning, the common area in the middle of the run-down third-floor office space had acquired an enormous wooden table, like something from a Victorian rummage sale, around which were squeezed an assortment of mismatched chairs. Max stood at the head of the table, tapping a pencil against his palm. He said nothing as the door clicked behind her but shot a meaningful glance at the large round clock on the wall.

Her colleagues—including a couple of reporters she only knew from their bylines—sat in awkward silence as she shrugged off her coat and hung it on the rack by the door. The tam, of course, would stay.

"Sorry," she said, remembering to pluck her article out of the inner pocket. "Couldn't catch a cab."

"Top o' the mornin', lassie," Max said, running his eyes across her outfit and speaking in a deadpan brogue.

Her mind raced through Shakespeare's Scottish play in search of the perfect smart retort. "'Thy letters have transported me beyond this ignorant present, and I feel now the future in the instant.'"

"*Romeo and Juliet?*"

"*Macbeth*. I played Lady Macbeth in my junior year." She tapped her temple. "Still have it all right here."

"Well, why don't you bring *it* and the rest of you over here and have a seat so we can continue?"

Max pointed to a chair that would have been inaccessible for most people, but her dainty stature made passage possible, if awkward. She felt his eyes on her, and she tried to show her figure off to its best, sprinkling apologies and greetings as she made her way. When she finally arrived at her designated spot, Max was there, having pulled the chair from the table in a most gentlemanly fashion. The moment she sat down, however, she understood why this place hadn't been claimed by anybody else, as the seat was embarrassingly low. While no one could deny Monica's short stature, this made her downright childlike, with her chin mere inches above the chipped, dry surface of the table. Moreover, she sat a full head shorter than the snickering Tony on her left.

"Can it, Manarola," she hissed, not quite under her breath. "You're probably sittin' on a dictionary."

"Kids," Max implored, having reclaimed his place at the head of the table, "the better we focus, the quicker the *Chatter* gets up and running again."

"I was only twenty minutes late, for crying out loud. When did we stop running?"

"He's taking us in a new direction," Tony said, and from the sound of his voice, the direction wasn't good.

"I just thought we might want to sweeten some of our content with the milk of human kindness," Max said over the disgruntled rumblings that erupted after Tony's comment. To illustrate, he held up an issue from the previous fall. "For example. Here we have a story about a woman whose husband tied her to the stove after he suspected her of adultery. We have an interview with the husband and the wife. Very dramatic, true. But why not the story of the heroic milkman who discovered and rescued her?"

"Because the milkman wasn't talking on account of his own wife," Tony said.

"Point taken," Max said. "This story, however, highlights the violence without ever calling for reform. It could have been used as a platform to call for stiffer prosecution of crimes committed against women."

"The guy spent the night in jail," Tony said, "went home; two weeks later, wifey whacked him upside the head with a potato masher and ran off with the milkman. Excuse me—the *hero*."

"Maybe that wasn't the best example," Max conceded, "but my position remains the same. As editor in chief, publisher, and *owner*, I'd like to see us do something with less vice and more virtue."

At this, Monica snickered out loud. "Where does that leave me? Monkey Business goes to the ice cream parlor?"

"Why not? This is a city full of history and museums and art. Why should we devote column space to what is essentially illegal activity?"

"Because it's fun."

"Lots of things are fun."

He tossed the paper he'd been holding onto the table and plunged his hands into his pockets. This, she recognized, was his victory stance. She was about to retort with a doe-eyed question about just what, exactly, he saw as *fun*, when the door to the offices of *Capitol Chatter* burst open, and two men brandishing pistols entered and stood—guns at the ready—on either side.

The loudest scream was that of Zelda Ovenoff, who, within a hair of a second, dove underneath the table. The rest of them followed suit, with Monica feeling exceptionally grateful that her seat was already so close to the floor that she need only slouch a bit and slide off to safety. From there, she looked around at all of the terrified faces in the shadow of the secondhand table.

Tony, ever the professional, already had his notepad and pencil at the ready, furiously scribbling. Trevor seemed to be working very hard at appearing brave, probably berating himself for playing hooky from high school to attend Maximilian Moore's Morality Seminar. Zelda seemed to be reconciled with her fear, her eyes now narrowed as she summoned the courage of the Cossacks. Everybody else stuffed the semidarkness with imperfectly silenced whimpers.

Monica scanned the faces, her own heart pounding. There was one notable absence. In the place where Max's broad, affable—yet understandably terrified—face should be, there was only a pair of dark trousers, and with the unassuming tone of a store clerk, she heard him ask, "May I help you, gentlemen?"

"We're looking for a certain monkey."

The voice was cultured, almost courteous—like the kind of gentleman her mother would have loved. Perhaps this was her way of reaching beyond the grave to find Monica the perfect husband. Under any other circumstances, Monica might have giggled at the thought, but there were, after all, guns involved.

"There must be a mistake," Max said. "This isn't the zoo."

Polite laughter followed, during which time Tony moved Zelda aside to look out from under the table. Immediately he ducked back down, grabbed Monica's sweater, and pulled her to him.

"That's Jim King," he whispered. "They call him Doc."

"Why?"

"On account of he used to be a doctor before he started runnin' hooch."

"I want an explanation for this," the well-mannered voice said as two shiny brown shoes approached the table.

"Cute," Max said. "But as far as I know, we don't have a regular cartoonist on staff. But then, I'm new here. You might have heard my uncle recently passed away. Natural causes."

More polite laughter. "We just want to talk to her."

"You are," Max said. "We call it a pseudonym in the business."

"You're the one running around in silky dresses and high heels?"

"Like I said, I'm new here."

"I appreciate an honorable man, as am I, in most circumstances. This being one of them. I just want to talk."

"Then I'll need to ask your friends to leave," Max said, rising on his toes as he said so.

"Gentlemen," King said, before a shuffle of footsteps were silenced by the closing of the door. "Now, where's my monkey?"

Knowing it was quite possible that King had his own gun and that even the most refined man could be provoked to violence, Monica determined that Max would not be her hero anymore that day and slowly backed out from underneath the table to face her foe.

He was, in a word, handsome. Edwardian, with a well-trimmed beard and short-cropped hair, both a perfected shade of brown. His face was broad—almost square—and his nose narrow. He stood like he had been planted to the floor, his hands posed in front of him, all ten fingertips touching, and he used this entire configuration to point toward the familiar yellow card sitting in the center of the table, from which her hastily sketched monkey smiled.

Her scalp tingled icily beneath her tam, and she prayed for Zelda Ovenoff to grab and yank her back under the table.

"Do you know where I got that?"

Monica swallowed and nodded.

His face completely placid, King reached into his jacket, at which time Monica scrambled along the back of the chairs and threw herself against Max, burying her face in his shirt, grateful for the strong arm which more than made up for the strength that had fled from her legs.

"Are you a subscriber?" Max said, which prompted her to peek through her fingers and see King holding a folded copy of the latest edition of *Capitol Chatter*.

"Subscriber? No. I'm afraid my days allow very little time for leisure reading. But it was brought to my attention that my personal establishment held a prominent position in your latest edition."

King spoke like he belonged in a parlor, with a tiny pocket of air softening each syllable.

"I wouldn't call it prominent," Monica mumbled, having always resented her tiny corner on page eight.

"It is more prominent than I would like," King said. "There are reasons we don't advertise; wouldn't you agree?"

She nodded, feeling Max's shirt against her skin as he drew her closer.

"After all, you are careful to keep your identity separate from your shenanigans, aren't you?" He paused, his mouth open slightly, indicating the answer to his question was understood. "And yet . . ." He positioned his copy of *Capitol Chatter*, scanned for a bit, and read, "'You'll be toe-to-toe with the king of the jungle.'" He looked up. "King?"

She nearly dropped, but Max held her up. "I didn't mean you. I don't know you. I didn't even know your name until Tony told me a few minutes ago."

"Is that so?"

At that, Tony slowly stood, pad and pencil in hand.

"Good morning, Mr. Manarola," King said, greeting him as a peer.

"'Morning, Doc."

"You know I'll insist that this visit be off the record."

"And you know I don't make no promises until it's all played out."

"Fair enough." King turned his attention back to Monica, who by this time had taken a few deep breaths but had not released her grip on Max. "Reads like a puzzle, doesn't it, with all the hidden clues and gobbledygook slang. So-called writers like you will be the death of the English language."

"Now just a minute—" This was too much, and she might have made a physical leap for him had Max not grabbed a handful of sweater to hold her back.

King held up his hand. "I apologize, Miss, ah, Monkey. Sometimes it's hard watching the world grow young around you. But let me understand—" he balanced a pair of thin-rimmed glasses on his nose and looked back at the paper—"'big cats, donkeys, elephants . . .' I assume you're referring to our guests."

"You bet I am," Monica said. "All those elected officials, breaking their own laws." She twisted in Max's grip to look up at him. "There's the real story—what we should be writing about."

"You mean something like *real* journalism?"

"Exactly."

"Well, maybe if we get out of this alive, we'll talk. In the meantime, let's listen to what the gentleman has to say."

Monica followed Max's lead and turned her gaze back to Doc, who seemed pleased to once again be the center of attention.

"I am sorry," he said, "if I gave you all a fright. Please know that my intention was only to meet with you face-to-face to discuss these important matters. I am nothing if not a reasonable man. An honorable man. And I trust—" here he directed his attention straight at Tony—"this bit of ugliness will go no further than this room."

"What ugliness?" Max said with an air of confidence not even Monica believed.

"Good boy." A smile had unfurled beneath Doc's narrow nose. "Now, if you'd like to bring your people out from their hiding."

"They're not hiding."

Monica felt her chest swell with pride at the words. Never before had she felt herself standing beside a leader, and with those words, Max had become exactly that. A young patriarch, an untested general. She willed her fellow employees to emerge from their places beneath the table, not in obedience to Doc King but as a show of loyalty to the man willing to protect them. The response was slow at first—nothing more than the slight scooch of a chair, and another as Zelda, then Trevor, then Thomas Harper Jr. and those two other guys unfolded from the darkness like so many soldiers crawling from the foxholes in the cautious light of day.

Slowly and—Monica thought—unnecessarily, Max dropped his hold on her, abandoning her to an equal standing with her fellow *Chatter*ers.

"That's better," Doc said in a voice as smooth as a cigar before sending out a piercing whistle that brought his armed companions crashing back through the door. Above their clatter, he calmly assured his host that, provided nobody moved, nobody would get hurt. And though she wanted nothing more than to be once again safely tucked up beside her new hero, Monica didn't move.

"I just wanted my men to have a good look at all of you." Doc stood perfectly still himself, eyes panning from left to right. Behind him, his men expanded his study, using the barrels of their guns so that everyone—Monica included—had an opportunity to stare down those dark metal holes. "I want them to memorize your faces, as I am memorizing your faces, so that should I see you—any of you—near the door of any of my places, both they and you will remember this as the day I showed you mercy, though you gravely insulted both my patrons and my establishment."

"I said the music was wonderful, and the drinks—"

Immediately both guns were aimed squarely at her, and the imagined *rat-a-tat* of their firing proved only to be the hammering of her own heart. Eerily enough, Doc's expression hadn't changed a mite.

"Second warning," he said calmly. "You—and all of you—stay away from what is mine, and I shall stay away from what is yours."

"Fair enough," Max said, with the same ability to match the coolness of Doc's tone.

Doc acknowledged the agreement with the slightest nod. Presumably on the off chance that the staff of *Capitol Chatter* might make a dive for their own weapons, the three men took the first of several steps backward, never taking their eyes nor their guns off the assembled group. To be sure, nobody moved until the door was once again closed and their shadowy figures disappeared from the other side of the frosted glass.

The only sound was that of Tony's pencil furiously filling page after page of his little notebook. He glanced up. "What do you say, Bisbaine? Can I get a statement?"

"No comment," she said. "But a question—how am I supposed to know which joints are Doc's and which aren't? He doesn't exactly have his name on the doors, you know."

"Easy," Max said with the same authority he'd held when the gangster was in the room. "You don't go into any of them. At least not officially, not for the paper." He clapped his hands together as if to preemptively squash any protest. "Now, with the exception of Miss Bisbaine's next column—and may I assume it's one less likely to bring gangsters to our office?"

"It is," Monica said, hoping he would regret his condescension once he read her tribute to his uncle.

"Then we have the next issue ready to go to press—am I right?"

Hums and nods of agreement overruled Monica's sulky glare.

"Terrific." He rubbed his palms together, looking like a man ready to work, and then surprised them all. "We're shutting down for a while. No writing, no digging, no stories. We'll meet here again, two weeks from now. Nine o'clock—" he gave Monica a soft punch on the shoulder—"sharp. I need some time to assess."

Monica assumed she spoke for each of her comrades when she asked, "Assess what, exactly?"

"What you've done here," he said. "And given the events of the last few minutes, whether or not we're going to continue."

❦ CHAPTER 6 ❧

O Hope! Dazzling, radiant Hope!—What a change thou bringest to the hopeless; brightening the darkened paths, and cheering the lonely way.
AIMEE SEMPLE MCPHERSON

HE KEPT A FIRE constantly burning in the woodstove throughout the days. He might have spent his childhood in the equally bitter Philadelphia winters, but years spent in temperate California had thinned his blood.

The first order of the day was breakfast, and as the bacon sizzled in the pan, he thanked God for the generosity of Uncle Edward's neighbors. One by one they'd trickled by, always carrying some grocery gift—pies, sausages, loaves of bread, jars of pickled beets.

"We didn't know your uncle well," they'd said, bearing the burden for his misanthropic ways, "but we hope you'll feel welcome just the same."

Always Max smiled, took the gift, and thanked them for their hospitality, though clearly the true motives changed depending on the giver. Matrons came with jars of hearty soups for the poor

69

young transplant. Little boys, banded together in groups of three or four, had combined their pennies to bring him bottles of ketchup or Coca-Cola, and they contorted themselves to get a glimpse of the house behind him, no doubt allaying their fears that its previous owner was some kind of child-eating monster.

And then there were the young women. Dolled up in coats and hats befitting an occasion of much more importance than a social call to a new neighbor, they came in pairs, arm in arm, offering tins of sardines and boxes of crackers. They giggled behind their soft, leather gloves phrases about not being able to cook—not in the kitchen, anyway—and knowing of some fun places where a fellow could go to make some new friends. These were, he assumed, the daughters of his neighbors, older girls living at home, maybe working in some of the local shops or even attending a local college, but some were clearly no more than sixteen years old. Between the bulkiness of their coats and the layers of makeup, it was sometimes hard to tell the difference. Both he and any one of the girls might have faced a world of trouble if not for the constant presence of Sister Aimee in his head.

"Today's young woman thinks nothing of the treasured gift she's been given, and if we cannot train them up to prevent the mass suicide of their virtue, we will rely on godly men to protect it in daily battle."

Fortunately, it was a battle easily won. This morning it had been two sisters, easily in their teenage years, bearing a loaf of cinnamon bread and an invitation to accompany their family to church the following Sunday.

"If that's something you enjoy," the older of the two added, leaving him no doubt that she held such convention in disdain. "But afterwards there's lots of us who go to the pictures. Some even as old as you, and they don't mind going around with a bunch of kids."

Max had accepted the bread, promised to consider the invitation to church, and politely declined the invitation to the movie. Now, with the neighborhood streets quiet, having emptied all of their occupants to school or work, he enjoyed the scent of the bread wafting from Uncle Edward's electric toaster and dropped an egg in to fry beside the bacon.

A week had gone by since shutting down production of *Capitol Chatter*, during which time he'd met twice with Thomas Harper and felt less hopeful after each encounter. Truthfully, he'd imagined the financial situation to be much worse, given the small number of subscriptions and the newsstand competition with at least ten other publications of its kind, but Uncle Edward ran his business with the same spartan approach as he did every other aspect of his life. A shoestring writing staff, no freelancers. Advertising cheap and plentiful, and little time or energy spent on the pursuit of redeeming society. Story after story of vice and crime—all things plentiful enough in the city, and endless enough to keep the bottom line bobbing in the black.

"But don't you think we could do more?"

"Your uncle was never a man driven by profit," the complacent Harper had replied.

"I mean more for our readers. More for this city. Stories about heroes, maybe. Good people doing good things. Certainly that is all just as plentiful."

"It is a little harder to dig up."

Max thought of this conversation now as he dug into his breakfast, wishing he had somebody with whom to share his thoughts—somebody not so invested in the paper. Not that *he* had any investment in it, because the cleanest option would be to simply shut it down and walk away. It might mean a small refund to the subscribers, but there were few enough of them to buy off with the paltry amount in petty cash. Chances were slim that riots would break out at newsstands when the tabloid failed to make its weekly appearance, and the staff was small enough to be absorbed by the glut of other papers just like it.

And Max? Well, he could make his way back to Sister Aimee, blame his outburst on the grief over losing his only living relative, and rely on her grace to take him back into the fold. Working on the *Bridal Call* might not have been the most satisfying position he could ask for, but at least their staff meetings had never been interrupted by a group of new converts crashing through the door with guns. Surely Manarola would find another home for his particular set of skills, and Mrs. Ovenoff could continue on as janitress for whatever tenant took over the office space. As for Monica . . .

Here he paused, took a sip of his coffee, and stared at the empty chair on the other side of the table. He could still remember the feel of her tiny body tucked under his arm, the way she practically vibrated with what he thought was fear, but upon further reflection saw to be something more like indignation.

"Monkey Business," he said out loud, just to hear the sound of it.

He finished his breakfast, rinsed his dishes in the sink, poured himself a second cup of coffee, and went into the front room to sit in the comfortable chair by the fire. His few halfhearted attempts to bring order to Uncle Edward's book collection had only resulted in a more confusing jumble as he'd become engrossed in more than one volume as he perused it to determine just where it should be shelved. Now a stack knee-high sat between the arm of the chair and the wall, topped with *The Invisible Man*, of which about half remained to be read. Beneath that, *The Tragedies of William Shakespeare*, with a ribbon marking act 1, scene 1 of *Macbeth*. For now, though, the less-than-wobbly pile created a perfect place to rest his coffee cup as he settled back into the chair. Already the leather seemed to know him, conforming to his body in that perfected melding of man and furniture.

His Bible lay beside the pile of books, and the leather scrunched as he reached down for it, along with the stenographer's notebook in which he kept a journal of his thoughts and prayers. As testament to his state of mind of late, the last few pages were full of notations and numbers, offering to God the details of the choices put before him. He did not record his questions, for all of them could be summed up in a single petition.

Show me, O Father, what to do. There's no one else whose counsel I trust.

He stared at the numbers, hoping God would supernaturally arrange them on the page, spelling out a clear message, much like he did for King Belshazzar. Even if it spelled a message of doom, pointing out Max's clear unworthiness to create even the modest success that Uncle Edward had, at least he would know what to do. He didn't need a promise of success, only a nudge of direction.

It was his habit to begin each daily devotional time by reading a chapter from Proverbs, especially during those times when he was in need of wisdom. Quoting from this book had been a staple of his father's conversation, but Max lacked the ability of precise recall. Too often, he hated to admit even to himself, his eyes skimmed over the all-too-familiar words, but sometimes, like today, everything came to a halt at a single verse. Proverbs 15:22: "Without counsel purposes are disappointed: but in the multitude of counsellors they are established."

Max looked out the window to the iron-gray morning and laughed out loud.

"And this multitude of counselors, Lord? Who would they be?"

73

Harper had staunchly refused to offer any advice, remaining mathematically objective on the paper's viability. "Maybe Trevor? He's young, but he's sane."

For the duration of the cup of coffee, his Bible remained open and unread as his gaze focused and blurred and focused again on Uncle Edward's bookcase.

No, *his* bookcase. His books, his house, his chair. His publication. All given to him not because he'd proven himself as a reliable steward but simply because of who he was in life. This wasn't exactly a legacy; it was a weekly twelve-page tabloid. It would bear his name only because he bore his uncle's, but no mistake—it was *his*.

He set his cup back down on the stack of books and thumbed through the pages of his Bible until he found the well-worn folded slip of paper. One of his first assignments as part of the staff of the *Bridal Call* was to create a page listing the parables of Jesus, chapter and verse in corresponding Gospels. *"The words of Jesus Christ,"* Sister Aimee had said, *"our Rabbi, our Teacher. In them lie the answers to our questions of how we are to live as his disciples."*

And she'd insisted that they were all disciples, Christ's followers and students, daily at his feet, attuned to his voice through the Scriptures. It had been Max's job to create a cheat sheet.

His eyes skimmed down the column, though he knew exactly what he was looking for. The parable of the talents. Though he nearly knew the passage by heart, there was something comforting about the soft turn of the pages. The Bible was a gift from his parents upon his graduation from high school, and one of the few things he had from his childhood home.

He adjusted his glasses, focusing on the red text, and took in the familiar story of three men, each entrusted with a portion of their master's fortune. Two double their portions' value; the third—much to the master's ire—simply buries his.

Which would he be? Already an answer was beginning to form.

Just when he began a second reading of the parable, a familiar form passed by his front window, and a purposeful knock soon followed. Curious, he left his Bible open in his seat and moved to the door, trying to hide his surprise at the sight of the woman standing on his front step.

"Mrs. Ovenoff?"

"Is Tuesday," she said as a way of greeting and brushed past him. "I did not come last week out of respect for your privacy to mourning. But I am here today."

She was wasting no time, tugging off her gloves and taking off her hat. Once she'd shrugged off her coat, she opened the small closet and hung it on a hook inside—clearly a task of habit.

Max backed out of her way. "Can I get you something? Put on some coffee?"

Zelda looked at him indulgently and clucked her tongue. "Sweet boy. No, I am here to clean. Every Tuesday, nine o'clock. Until ten thirty. Then we have tea."

"Tea?"

"Your uncle and I had tea."

Her voice caught on the final word, and a shadow crossed her narrow face. The woman who, to this point, had exhibited the strength of a Russian bear seemed to be on the verge of girlish tears, and he brought a hand out to touch her thin shoulder.

"That's nice, knowing that the two of you were friends outside of the office."

"Yes," she said, obviously fighting for composure, "that's what we were. Friends. Good friends. Edward was a good man." Her eyes darted around the room. "Messy, though. I see you are like him that way."

Max estimated that woman was old enough to be his mother, and he fought the emptiness that threatened to push him into her arms. Whatever made him think she would welcome such an embrace had already passed, as she was rolling up her sleeves and trudging toward the kitchen with a purposeful step.

"I sometimes bring food," she said, speaking as if he were following her, so he did. "But I did not know what to bring for you." She stopped short in the kitchen and sniffed. "You cook?"

"Just bacon and eggs," he said, feeling sheepish in the shadow of her subtle approval. "And as for food, the neighbors have all been so generous. I think I'm set for a month."

"That is how long you are staying?"

He tried not to recoil at the directness of the question. "I haven't decided, yet, exactly what I'm going to do."

"Hmph."

Zelda disappeared into the tiny mudroom long enough to retrieve a bucket, which she set on the floor with a clatter before opening the tap on the kitchen sink, filling it with steaming water.

"I can take care of those," Max said, feeling self-conscious at the idea of watching this relative stranger wash his dishes. But she ignored him, and with that same strange familiarity, found the box of soap flakes in the curtained-off space below the sink and sprinkled in a generous amount.

"If you will gather your clothes, I will take them to wash. I will have them back on Thursday."

"Mrs. Ovenoff, please." He'd hit the necessary note to make her stop, turn, and face him. Outside of the few neighbors who had barely made it past the threshold of the front door, this was the first guest he'd entertained in this home. She might present herself as a mere cleaning lady, but she was a cleaning lady of prior acquaintance, and one who clearly held a place in her heart for the former occupant. More than all of that, she may well be one of the many counselors promised in the proverb he'd read just minutes before her arrival on the porch.

He gestured toward the table. "Please. Sit with me. Have a cup of coffee."

She looked suspicious. "We usually have tea after."

"We can have both."

She stiffened. "I don't care for coffee."

"Then just sit with me. Ten minutes while the dishes soak."

This—in light of the congealing bacon grease—won his argument, and though she didn't look particularly pleased, she brushed past him and stood while he pulled out a chair for her. By the time he'd excused himself to fetch his cup from the other room and poured himself a cup rich with the final dregs from the pot, she'd used the back of her hands to gather every errant crumb and dropped them into a scrap of rag that must have been hiding in her apron pocket.

"I didn't know my uncle well at all," Max said once he'd settled in across from her. "Do you think you can tell me a little more about him?"

She folded the rag into a small, tight square and worried it between her fingers. "I came to this country twenty years ago with my sister and her family. Her husband had a good job working in the steel, in Pittsburgh. Good for an immigrant, because he spoke English already, and we all lived in a little apartment. I helped with her children, and they gave me a home. That was not in this town."

Max nodded but remained silent, curious to see how this would eventually come to answer his question.

"They had more children, and the apartment got smaller, so

small that I slept on a couch in the kitchen. I know they wanted me to get my own family, to find a husband of my own. But I liked being useful. I never was a beautiful woman, so I did not have many men interested in me. My brother-in-law was trying to save enough money to buy a little house, and I knew they did not want to take me with them. I worked as a janitress for our building, and I asked if the landlord would keep me, to let me have a single small room. He told me the owner had several properties in different cities, so I came here."

Journalistic instinct told him there was much of the story missing, and she had yet to even mention Edward. He leaned forward. "I mean no offense, Mrs. Ovenoff, but I've never heard of a landlord transferring a janitress. Why didn't you stay in Pittsburgh?"

She studied the cleaning rag in her hand. "I had to get away. It was not good, those last days. So crowded, and my sister pregnant again, hardly enough room for her husband in the bed."

Now he understood, or he thought he did, because unmistakable shame had invaded their conversation. Why Zelda would have chosen to reveal such a story he had no idea, but he felt the urge to rescue her from the memory.

"And that's how you met Uncle Edward?"

She brightened. "It was a little more than five years ago. He had just taken the offices for his newspaper, and they were a mess. I worked in that building, mopping and such, but not for that tenant. I saw him that first day, pacing in the hallway, so angry and scratching his head." Zelda fell into an accurate impersonation, her face adopting his scowl. "And he is saying, 'Oh, what will I do?' I was walking by and he grabbed my arm—" she demonstrated—"and begins to yell at me, saying I must not do my job because this place looked so terrible, like pigs and goats had been doing their business in there."

"What a charmer," Max said.

"So I clean his office. One hour later, he was looking and looking for something to complain about, but I left him nothing." She smiled, reliving the satisfaction. "He would always say, 'Zelda, you could make porcelain out of pig—' Well, I won't say the word he used. But you understand. He appreciated me, and he paid me above what the owner paid. And we would talk almost every day. I would see him being nice to me, talking so sweet right after yelling and cursing at someone else."

"You were friends."

She nodded—short, severe nods that carried through clear up to the loose bun of hair on the top of her head.

"One day, he asks if I can come to his home and wrote the address on the envelope with my pay, and I worried that it would seem improper. But it was for me to clean, only."

In his mind's eye he saw her, carefully grooming for that first visit, brushing and pinning her hair, pressing her blouse. "And tea after?"

"Yes. To clean, and tea."

She couldn't look at him, and a sweet tinge of pink enhanced her regular rosy complexion. The silence that followed told him clearly that there had been more. Lovers, perhaps. But at the very least, companions.

He reached his hand across the table to still her fidgeting ones. "I'm glad to know he had someone who cared about him."

"Everybody think he was such a grouchy bear, and he was. But he had a tender side, too."

"Did he ever talk about me?"

Now it was Zelda's turn to look upon him with something between affection and pity. "He did."

Max was prepared to press no further, but Zelda patted his hand with motherly affection.

"He wondered, often, how he could bring you into his life, I think because he did not want you to be all alone like him. I say to him, 'Call the boy. Or write a letter.' But men are stubborn. One month goes by, and then a year."

"I didn't try any harder than he did."

"You are young. You don't have a road of loneliness to look back on." She took her hand from his and stood, smoothing her apron. "That has been ten minutes, I think. And if you will please gather your laundry? Just your clothes—I get the sheets from the bed."

Max stood too. "Certainly. And I don't know if you can do anything about the bookcase—"

Zelda cut him off with a guffaw. "I don't touch the books, except to dust."

"Fair enough." He remained standing there, hands loose in his pockets, not sure what to do with himself, when the telephone jangled in the front room. Relieved, he answered it, identifying himself to the familiar voice on the other end—Nelson Bolling, Uncle Edward's attorney.

"Are you free tomorrow morning, Mr. Moore?"

Max looked at the precarious pile of books and the open, waiting Bible. "I am."

"Very good. If you will meet me at Capitol Bank and Loan, let's say nine. They are prepared to sign over the contents of your uncle's safety-deposit box."

"I'll be there."

He hung up the phone and sat back down, feeling welcomed by the chair. The Bible remained open in his lap, but the text did not call to him. Instead, he leaned his head back against the crocheted afghan and listened to the sound of the crackling fire accompanied by the soft humming of the woman in the kitchen. In that moment, he knew for certain that, whatever the extent of their physical relationship, Uncle Edward had loved this woman, because he found himself on the brink of caring about her too.

"Mr. Moore?" she called out, interrupting her tune. "May I have the remains of your coffee?"

A curious question, given she'd declared earlier not to like coffee. "I'm sorry, Mrs. Ovenoff. I drank the last of it."

"No, I mean this." She stood in the kitchen doorway with a pile of coffee grounds on a piece of newspaper.

"I suppose so, but I'm afraid you won't get a very good drink out of them." He didn't want to hurt her feelings or sound suspicious, but what in the world would a woman do with a pile of coffee grounds?

Zelda laughed. "Oh, it is not for drinking. I mix with an egg white, makes a nice scrub for the face."

"Really?" Come to think of it, she did have remarkably few wrinkles for a woman of her age. "Do women know about this?"

"Some do, I suppose. Poor women, maybe, who cannot afford to buy such fancy things."

She was back to her humming, leaving Max alone with his parable, the wisdom of Solomon, and a fresh, blank page in his journal. At the top of it he copied the verse from Proverbs that had seemed so bitterly amusing less than an hour ago. Underneath the verse, he wrote the word *Counsellors*, with a bold underscore. And beneath that, he wrote a single name: *Zelda Ovenoff*.

Now he would wait for God to bring him the multitude.

⤷ CHAPTER 7 ⤶

"Perhaps," she said, leaning forward a little, "you will tell me
your name. If we are to be friends—" she smiled her grave
smile—"as I hope we are, we had better begin at the beginning."
ELIZABETH VON ARNIM, *THE ENCHANTED APRIL*

MONICA WAS STILL UNDER HER COVERS, not quite asleep but
not ready to face the cold, when she heard the faint knocking on
her door.

"Miss? Miss? A package for you."

The voice belonged to Mrs. Kinship, Monica's neighbor who
worked overnight as a janitress for some of the government buildings downtown. For a quarter a week she'd clean the individual
apartments in this building, too, but Monica was well suited to
live with two bits' worth of dirt and clutter. The other service Mrs.
Kinship offered to her fellow tenants was the delivery of the mail,
as it often arrived at the door to the common parlor shortly after
her return from work. Before retiring for the day, Mrs. Kinship
would slip the various envelopes under the appropriate doors.

Occasionally, usually after reclaiming a letter that Mrs. Kinship had "forgotten" to deliver, the occupants of the apartments would put a dime in an envelope and slip it under *her* door—just to thank her for her troubles.

At first, Monica had refused to participate in this minor postal extortion, figuring she didn't have a soul alive who would be writing her a letter anytime soon, and what could be the harm if her creditors' notices piled up under Mrs. Kinship's greed? But that was before Charlie and the almost-daily missives Monica received from him. Little notes describing his ardent desires, addresses and directions for places they could meet for discreet drinks and dancing. And occasionally, a trinket.

She threw her quilts off and ran across the stinging-cold floor, plastering on a broad smile as she opened the door to her neighbor, who hadn't bothered to do the same.

Mrs. Kinship was one of those gray women—her hair, complexion, dress, and demeanor completely without life. Right now the only spot of color was the bright-red box tied with a silver ribbon that she held in her open claw.

"This from your gentleman?" she asked, as if she had the right to know.

"Well, I don't know. I haven't opened the card yet. There is a card, isn't there?"

Mrs. Kinship sniffed. "Not my duty to inspect the packages. Just to deliver them."

Monica wanted to correct her, saying, no, in fact, it wasn't her duty to do even that, but unless she wanted to take it upon herself to sit at the front door in the mornings and grab the early post, it would be best to keep her smile.

"Thank you for that," Monica said. She took the package from the older woman, who left her hand palm up and open, waiting.

"I thought I'd get some soup from Sobek's later this afternoon. Shall I bring you some?"

Mrs. Kinship seemed to be weighing the chances that Monica would follow through. Satisfied, she worked up a bit of a smile, saying she hoped the package was something nice, obviously hinting that she'd like to stay and see just what it was.

"If you're asleep," Monica said, inching the door closed, "I'll leave the soup at your door. Have a good rest."

Once alone, she lit a fire in her stove and huddled next to it. As it turned out, there was a card, but she set it aside, eager to see the gift beneath the passionate red paper. Slowly, to savor the experience, she untied the ribbon, thinking it might be nice to embellish a hat or something later. With the ribbon gone, the paper fell away, revealing the more exotic, fiery-red—nearly orange—box, featuring the familiar image of a phoenix in flight.

Perfume. Mavis perfume. Not expensive or extravagant, but still . . .

He remembered. Valentine's Day. She hadn't even reminded him. In fact, she hardly remembered herself, unless spending the previous afternoon doodling cupids and arrows counted as remembering.

She grabbed the jewel-shaped cap, twisted it, and brought the bottle up to her nose, inhaling. *Irresistible.* That's what the ads always said, with their pale, elongated women surrounded by exotic pillars and peacocks. Charlie was irresistible. No matter how many times she tried to put him aside, to move on to some other guy—it just took a note, a visit, a nuzzle to her neck, and she was back. Or *he* was. Charlie was warmth when she was cold, a joke when she was blue, a drink when she was lonesome. Most days that was enough.

The fragrance drew her back, the way Charlie always did, and then again, and she knew why. She'd smelled this before. On his collar. On his skin.

It was the fragrance of his wife.

That should have been enough to hurl the bottle across the room and curse his name as it shattered. Bad enough that she lived with secondhand affection—now a secondhand scent? But whose fault was that, really? Even she knew he was in love with his wife.

Then again, if he *did* love her, why did he bother with Monica at all?

She studied the bottle. At least she knew she wasn't getting the cheap end of the deal here. Not like wifey bathed in something Parisian while she made do with Mavis. She was an equal in that way, at least, to the woman with whom Charlie chose to share his name and his life.

The fire in the stove was well blazing now, or at least enough to offer legitimate heat. In its glow, Monica dropped her nightgown to the floor. She tipped the bottle, bathing the stopper, and touched it to her skin. Behind her ears, in the hollow of her collarbone, along the pale vein running the length of her inner arm, the curve of her waist, behind each knee. Then she slipped on her silk kimono—black and emerald green with twisting, gold-stitched dragons—and ran a brush over her hair, its sheen rivaling the silk of the robe.

"I think of you when I'm with her."

Because Charlie's wife probably clomped around the house in something ratty and calico, quilted so she looked like a piece of furniture making flapjacks in the morning. And all the time nagging at him. *"Where've you been? Why were you out so late? What time are you going to be home?"*

Questions Monica was not allowed to ask.

"I think of you when I'm with her."

That was the closest thing to a promise Charlie had ever given. But if she was honest with herself, she had to wonder if it wasn't the other way around. He was all the time fretting about lipstick and face powder on his shirt, worried that his wife might figure it out. Now he wouldn't have to worry about the scent of his skin.

She pushed the thought away and focused on the pretty box. The cut-glass bottle, the ribbon, and finally the small, square envelope. With a steady finger, she opened the flap and pulled out a card. On it, two lovers dressed in disheveled Victorian garb reclined in each other's arms beneath a budding tree with a caption underneath.

Would I could die in a field of your kisses.

The words were the sentiments of the artist, not Charlie. His message, far less romantic, was scrawled on the back.

Friday night. 7 p.m.

Her place, probably. That was where their dates usually began and ended.

Well, no use getting drippy about it all now. Today was Bank Day, though she wasn't looking forward to facing Uncle Everett after the run-in with Doc King. He—Everett—had sent her a note soon afterward, explaining that he'd been forced to surrender the card and hoped there wouldn't be any repercussions. She'd wanted to send one back saying they all got a whole lot more than ten dollars' worth of excitement out of it but decided it was best to say nothing. He might not be so easy with the money next time if he thought it would get her into trouble.

She'd spent her last eighty-two cents the day before getting her latest batch of laundry out of hock, with a promise to Mr. Varnos to return with the balance later in the afternoon. All of her clothes had been wrapped in neat, brown paper packages and tied with string, but she'd spent the evening playing one record after another on the gramophone she purloined from Mr. Davenport until all had been pressed into the small closet or tucked away inside one of her three dresser drawers. She had her pick of her wardrobe and chose a heather-gray dress of light wool jersey with a band of rose-colored ruffles descending like a sash from the collar to her waist. The same ruffle graced the cuffs of her long sleeves and the tiny flowers stitched into her gray stockings. She slipped her feet into black patent-leather high-heeled shoes and, as she buckled them, hoped that the day would prove to be more cold than wet.

With a tiny dab of pomade sleeking her hair to perfection, she applied her lipstick and lightly kohled her eyes, opening them wide in her best in-sincere-need expression, but the only coat that would do was the tailored knee-length gray wool with the wide mink collar. After all, like her mother always said, nobody wants to give money to someone who looks like they need it.

The question of whether or not to wear a hat was settled the minute she got a glimpse of her face framed in shining black— the mink collar pulled up to her ears, just meeting the matching sheen of her hair.

"Perfect," she said to her reflection, pleased with her dramatic red pout.

It was half past nine by the time she reached the bank. Early, but not desperately so, and every head in there snapped to her attention when she walked through the door, even the addled Mr. Peel at the reception desk.

"Miss Monica Bisbaine here to see Mr. Bentworth." She tried to appear aloof as she tugged each finger of her camel-colored kidskin gloves before taking up the pen to sign the register. "A matter of personal business."

For the first time, Mr. Peel seemed to recognize her and was announcing Everett's otherwise engagement when Monica stopped short, seeing the name written in the ledger just a few lines above her own. Maximilian Moore.

She glanced up and around, as if the man would materialize from the lobby's rich paneling.

"Miss?" Mr. Peel was standing now, a long white envelope in his shaky hand. "Mr. Bentworth left this for you."

Monica kept her own hands cool and controlled as she stepped away from the desk to peer inside the envelope. In it, a short note on a slip of Capitol Bank and Loan stationery.

Monkey—
Sorry for the ugly business in your office last week. If it helps at all, Mrs. B and I had an enchanted evening.

Uncle E

Besides the note, there was a draft for her one-hundred-dollar monthly allowance and a crisp portrait of Grover Cleveland on a twenty-dollar bill. She quickly closed the envelope and struggled to regain a look of composure. It was just a hundred and twenty bucks, for pete's sake, not a bucket from King Solomon's mines.

"Thank you, Mr. Peel."

She glided across the lobby floor to the row of tellers at the back and endorsed the draft with the pen resting in the gilded pedestal at the window. When she slid it across to the anonymous, bespectacled man on the other side, saying, "I'd like to deposit this into my personal account," she made sure to look up and away the moment the teller came into contact with her current balance.

"And if you could exchange this for its value in smaller denominations?"

"Certainly, ma'am," the teller said with the professional disguise of his thin-lipped smirk.

With her cash safely tucked in her purse, Monica turned away, allotting herself a cleansing sigh of relief. What to do next? Pay off her laundry? A nice warm lunch? Perhaps she'd go shopping for a Valentine's gift for Charlie. A tie clip or something. Better yet, something for her—for him. A new silk peignoir to wear with her perfume when he came to visit Friday night. Then to the butcher's for a couple of steaks the landlady maybe would let her fry on the stove in the kitchen downstairs. And then to the bakery for a little cake—strawberry with a buttercream icing. Or chocolate . . .

"Miss Bisbaine?"

The voice cut through her reverie, and she turned midstep to see Max Moore emerging from Everett's office.

"Monkey!" Everett said, leaving Max's side to come offer her a peck on the cheek. "Did you get—everything?"

"I did." She gave him a playful tap on his sleeve with the envelope and shot a glance up at Max. "How did you hear about our trouble at the paper?"

"We must never forget just how small this town is, darling. But it seems all is well?"

Monica couldn't help noticing the look exchanged between the two men, but she chose to maintain her ignorance.

"You were more than generous, *Uncle* Ev."

"Stay warm," he said with an affectionate tone that surprised her, considering this stranger to them stood so nearby, "and if you need anything, you know where to find me."

"Of course." She stood to her toes, reaching up to plant her own kiss on his smooth-shaven cheek.

He turned to Max and offered his hand. "Anything else I can do for you, Mr. Moore?"

Max, who had watched the entire exchange with a bemused expression on his face, told Everett that no, thank you, he'd be fine from here, at which point Everett disappeared back into his office, leaving the two of them in a state of awkward togetherness. At least it was awkward for Monica, because she'd barely had a chance to breathe between her thoughts of a new peignoir for Charlie and a confrontation with the man who may or may not be her boss in the next couple of days.

She cocked her head toward Everett's closed office door. "Business?"

"Personal, actually."

"Oh."

She waited for him to inquire as to her reason for being at the bank that morning, but he simply stood, calm as water, as if he could stay right there all day.

"He's not really my uncle," she blurted out, not nearly as comfortable in the silence as he. "Everett's an old family friend. Closest I have to family these days, I guess."

"My uncle did his business here," Max said. "He had a safety-deposit box. I just got the key."

"What do you think is in it?" Her mind swam with possibilities.

"I have no idea."

And what was more maddening, he didn't seem in any hurry to find out.

"By all means, Mr. Moore, don't let me keep you."

She backed one step away, surprised at just how reluctantly she did so, and even more surprised at the little leap of joy when he said, "Why don't you come in with me? We'll have a look together," even though his invitation carried with it the same enthusiasm as if he'd offered her half a sandwich.

"Is that allowed?"

"It's my box. I get to say who's allowed."

She didn't know if she should legitimize his invitation by taking his arm, but then he didn't offer it, so she simply walked beside him as they approached the vault. When they arrived at the outer room, however, the portly keeper looked at Max over the thin spectacles perched on his nose.

"Quite sorry, sir. But all of the rooms are occupied now. Perhaps you could return in, say, half an hour? Ten o'clock?"

"Of course."

It was the same response she'd had for Everett, but lacking in conviction. If Max's disappointment was anywhere near Monica's, it was some kind of fight to hide it, and the slight hitch in his breath was the only betrayal that he felt any frustration at all.

He turned to Monica. "I'm sure you have other things to do."

"What would I have to do?"

"I don't know. Buy some diamonds? Fund an orphanage?"

"What?" His comments were funny, but not in a way that made her want to laugh. Instead, she studied his face, trying to discern if he seriously believed what he said. "Why would you think such a thing?"

He reached out and ran the back of his fingers along the mink collar on her coat. "This. It makes you look like some millionaire maven. I guess Uncle Edward was paying you more than I thought."

"I have bad habits and expensive taste. It can be a deadly combination."

He gave her collar a tug. "It was certainly deadly for this little guy."

This time she did laugh and swatted his hand away. "Leave him alone; he's precious. Ten more payments and he's mine."

"Congratulations."

The word carried just enough irony not to be insulting, and the lilting humor in his voice made her feel that she'd been scooped up and taken away to some amusing new dimension.

"So," she said, knowing her thin, arched brow was quirked most becomingly, "if I'm still invited to tag along into the vault, I know a charming little place where we can have a cup of coffee while we wait. Not far from here."

It was a bold thing to do, even for her, but her skin was crawling with the scent of another woman's perfume, something that could only be soothed by the company of another man. This man, though, was taking a lifetime to decide, making her work very hard not to push the offer.

He leaned in, close, giving her a whiff of his shaving soap. "Will I have to know a password?"

"Yeah. 'Cream and sugar.'"

"Well, then." He opened the door to the street. "Lead on."

❧ CHAPTER 8 ❧

Beauty made you love, and love made you beautiful.
ELIZABETH VON ARNIM, *THE ENCHANTED APRIL*

MAX FELT like he was chasing a raven. Monica kept a good few steps ahead of him as they maneuvered through the streets and sidewalks after leaving the bank, walking with a kind of nervous energy that propelled her at a sprinter's pace through clumps of businessmen who never failed to tip their hats and follow through with an admiring glance. Whether or not she'd done anything to warrant such attention he didn't know, as her face was hidden from his view, surrounded on all sides by the black fur collar she'd pulled up around her ears.

"This is it."

She turned to him with a dazzling smile of breathless triumph more fitting of having led him safely to a mountain summit than to a modest bakery. She reached for the door handle, forcing him to make a heroic leap to open the door for her.

"Why, thank you, sir," she said before swooping inside.

They were instantly engulfed in warmth both from the ovens

filling the air with heat and yeast and sugar, and from the effusive welcome from the soft, stocky woman behind the counter.

"Monica!" Even the word was warm, the vowel sounds rounder and an extra syllable tacked on, making the greeting more like *Moni-ka*-la. The woman reached her hands over the counter, simulating an embrace that Monica returned by blowing a kiss—both women seeming to understand that flour-dusted hands on a mink-collared coat would be a disaster.

"Mrs. Sobek, this is my new boss, Max Moore."

Mrs. Sobek made a clucking sound deep in her throat and gave him a sidelong glance. "Much more handsome than the old one, isn't he, *ptáček*?"

Monica looked at him with a gaze parallel to Mrs. Sobek's. "Oh, I dunno. I'm sure he thinks so, but I haven't decided yet."

"Well, until you've decided," he said, "I guess the coffee's on you."

Her expression changed immediately into one of mock indignation as she twirled back to the counter.

"Two coffees and two *kolache*. And not on account." She opened her purse and took out a crisp one-dollar bill. "I actually have money today."

Mrs. Sobek looked doubtful. Not at the money, but at Max.

"You're going to give this big guy one *kolache*? That won't fill up his little toe."

"All right," Monica conceded. "One more, and a fruit Danish for me. And before you say anything, it's February. I have two more months to wrap up in a coat before I have to worry about my figure."

Mrs. Sobek gave an admonishing waggle of a finger before turning to an enormous tank and dispensing coffee into two large mugs. In the meantime, Monica took off her coat, revealing a column of soft gray material dissected by a pink ruffle, hugging her frame in such a way that left Max to worry about her figure—or at least about his reaction to it.

He busied himself pouring cream and spooning sugar into the rich, dark coffee, then walking with it carefully back to a small two-top table where Monica was already sitting and sipping.

"You don't take anything?" he asked, pulling out his chair.

"Delays the time between the pouring and the drinking," she said, preparing once again to wrap her lips around the cup's rim.

Mrs. Sobek arrived with a coffeepot and a white plate covered in waxed paper. She set the plate on the table and replenished the inch of missing coffee in Monica's cup. Then, after softly touching Monica's cheek with the back of her knuckle, she slipped away.

"She seems like a lovely woman," Max said, reaching for the warm pastry.

"She's wonderful," Monica said. "Like what I think a mother should be. As in, nothing like mine."

He remained silent, mesmerized by the interplay of her emotional display. She delivered the word *mine* with her hand to her heart and a smirk on her face, but she held both the gesture and the expression a bit too long to pass off its exaggerated humor.

He opted to be deliberately obtuse in order to preserve her dignity. "I take it your mother wasn't much of a baker?"

"Ha-ha." She wrapped her hand around the mug. "My mother cared about two things: herself, and what others thought about her. And by *others*, I don't mean me."

Cared. Past tense, and she spoke with the bitterness of one dealing with not only a loss, but a loss tinged with disharmony and regret.

"I'm sorry," he said, softening his tone from that of banter. "When did you lose your mother?"

She scrunched her nose, thinking. "Almost a year ago? It's hard to remember, sometimes, because I barely ever saw her for the two years before she died. We did not get along."

Not for a minute did he believe her cavalier routine, even less as she transformed into some other creature right before his eyes. Darker, colder—something no amount of Mrs. Sobek's hot, strong coffee would resuscitate, much less his own weak words, so he simply repeated, "I'm sorry," and sipped his own sweetened, weakened drink.

It must have been the right thing to say, because she softened behind the ribbon of steam rising from her coffee, and a genuine, warm smile mirrored its curve.

"We used to be rat-poor, and she hated it. Always harped that she'd 'married down' when she married my dad. Also dead. He owned a little sewing shop back home—Baltimore—and never aspired for anything bigger. Until the war came." She picked up one of the *kolache*, took a bite, and chewed thoughtfully before proceeding. "He won a government contract to make uniforms for the Navy. Made him a lot of money, and he worked himself to death filling it. Ended up dying on Armistice Day. All that cheering in the streets."

"That must have been difficult for you." He wanted to reach over to her in some way, to warm her hand with his own, or even something as gentle as Mrs. Sobek's featherish touch, but she seemed too brittle.

"Not as difficult as seeing the relief on my mother's face. Dad never let us spend any of the government money, always talking about feast and famine and such. When he died, Mom packed us up and moved us here, found a house in Georgetown nobody wanted on account of it was fresh from a murder-suicide. We couldn't even get a neighbor to say hello to us for a year."

He said, "I can't imagine anyone ignoring you for that long," and was rewarded with a bit of the girl he knew.

"She enrolled me at the Visitation; never mind that we hadn't been to Mass since before the war. I almost forgot we were Catholic. The girls hated me. I didn't have a single friend. But the university boys?" She winked. "There's a different story."

A different story, indeed. He could imagine the acceptance Monica found with the university boys. He knew too well the wild nature of a young man granted independence and access. It was bad enough in his day, before the entire country seemed to lose its mind with peace.

"You see," she said, "boys don't care how old your money is as long as you don't want to marry them. Mom couldn't decide if she should be scandalized by my behavior or proud of my ambition. She settled on scandalized when I couldn't get us invited to a family dinner. I tried to tell her that she should send me to college, but she wouldn't. Too much hassle, she said. And when I cut off my hair and said I was going anyway, she threw me out."

She signaled for Mrs. Sobek to bring more coffee and tore off a corner of the fruit Danish, pushing the plate across the table, encouraging him to try a bite.

"We okay here, *ptáček*?"

Monica nodded, seemingly restored by the woman's touch, and Max found himself sending God a silent thanks for this nurturing woman and for the love he carried with him from his own mother. Fond as his memories were, he found himself drawn to Mrs. Sobek's enfolding warmth; he could only imagine the strange, unfamiliar lifeline it must have been for Monica.

"My mother was sick for ages," she continued after Mrs. Sobek walked away. She leaned forward on her elbows, holding the steaming coffee just in front of her chin. "When she died, she left a will that mandated the sale of the house and everything in it. All that money—and really, it isn't so much—sits in the bank. I get an allowance. One hundred dollars on the second Wednesday of every month."

The timing seemed odd, and he said so.

"You don't know the old nursery rhyme? 'Wednesday's child is full of woe.' I'm her little Wednesday child, until the money runs out."

There she was, floundering in a sadness deep enough that he could taste it, beyond the rescue of a substitutionary maternal touch. Instinct kicked in. "So," he said, reaching out and wrapping her up with nonchalance, "I'm having breakfast with an heiress? That's a first for me. Now I feel much less guilty for letting you pay for it."

She indulged him with a small laugh, and to prolong the moment of lightness, he grabbed the second *kolache* and finished half of it in one bite.

"People will think we're lovers," she said at a whisper. "Why else would we be together at this hour?"

Thankfully, he'd swallowed his bite, or the brazenness of her comment might have induced a choke.

"Do you always say exactly what's on your mind?"

Her thin, arched brows answered first. "Always."

"You don't worry that you might get yourself into trouble?"

"Always."

Her grin was catlike, deceptive and dangerous, and he felt himself on the edge of being snapped up in it.

"We should go," he said before gulping the rest of his coffee.

"Sure." Her tone was unmistakably patronizing, and she settled back in her chair with no visible sign of budging. "I just want to finish this."

"As you wish." He backed his chair away, ignoring her protests as he crossed to gather his overcoat and hat from the rack by the door.

"All right, all right." There was nothing even faintly feminine about her now as she folded the remaining Danish in half and dunked it into the coffee, shoving the soggy mass into her mouth and wiping her chin with the back of her hand. Mrs. Sobek sighed at the sight.

She was still swallowing when Max helped her into her coat.

"Very nice to have met you," he said to Mrs. Sobek with a tip of his hat.

"Come back again," the woman said. "Talk of happier things."

At the moment, there was nothing he'd rather do, but he couldn't very well devote his days to sharing breakfast with Monica Bisbaine. It wasn't professional or, really, prudent in any way. Moreover, Monica herself hardly chimed in agreement.

They spoke very little as they retraced their steps to the bank; for this leg of the trip, she walked beside him, no matter how unhurried his pace.

"You don't have to accompany me if you don't want," he said finally, wondering if her silence wasn't the product of sullenness.

"Nothing much better to do. After all, I don't even know if I have a job or not."

"You'll know by this time Monday."

She looked up, squinting into the sunlight. "No chance of a hint right now?"

"No chance."

"Come on. You can make it my Valentine's Day present."

He looked at her closely, wondering whether the request that left him completely nonplussed was meant seriously or in jest. "Sorry. Then I'd have to do the same for everybody, and I'm not about to give Tony a Valentine's gift. Besides, I'll bet you have a dozen boyfriends leaving cards at your door. Am I right?"

She tucked her arm in his. "You don't care if I have a dozen sweethearts. You only want to know if I have *one*."

He wouldn't have thought so until she said it, but once she had, he wanted an answer. Not any answer, but the truth. What he would do with such confirmation he had no idea, and she certainly didn't *act* like her affections had been claimed by any man, but he felt unable to leap to the next thought without knowing.

"Do you?"

"Maybe I'll tell you Monday. Who knows? If I don't have a job, I might need a new boyfriend."

Check and mate. She conversed like a game of chess, three moves ahead, anticipating his strategy. Now they'd reset the board for a new match, but neither seemed in a hurry to begin. At some point their pace slowed to a stroll, and as they came to the final block, Max was beginning to question the wisdom of his invitation.

"I don't have to go inside with you if you don't want me to," she said, answering a move he hadn't made.

"I have no idea what to expect."

"But aren't you curious?"

"Of course I am. He was my uncle. The last of my family. I guess part of me is hoping I'll find something . . ."

"Monumental? Valuable? Scandalous?"

"Interesting," he said simply. "Something that tells me more about him."

They were at the door of the bank, and she dropped her arm, ostensibly so he could open it for them, but the resulting separation left him immediately and illogically lonely. Without thinking, he placed his hand at the small of her back as she crossed the threshold, leaving no doubt in either one's mind that he wanted her by his side.

The details were dispatched with quickly enough. With all the paperwork signed, it was merely a matter of recording their names in the ledger book—both of them—and being led into a small, windowless, paneled room. The bank officer backed out, closing the door behind him, leaving Max and Monica alone with the metal box perched on the tall, felt-covered table. It was larger than he'd expected—taller, anyway—with a hinged lid on top.

"Here goes," Max said, slipping the key into the lock and twisting it. Immediately, Monica's hand was on his.

"Would you rather I didn't look? I mean, do you want me to go stand in the corner or something, so you can have the first few minutes alone? Just in case it's—"

"Scandalous? Valuable?"

"You know. Private."

"You'll never be a journalist if you give up on your curiosity so easily."

"Then I guess here goes."

"What's the worst that could be in there?"

"My cousin Pandora said the exact same thing."

It was the perfect thing to say to slice the tension of the moment, and after a ceremonial count to three, they lifted the lid to gaze inside.

His first reaction was one of confusion, but not Monica's. Hard to believe this was the same woman who, just minutes ago, had offered to step away from the contents to let him discover them in private. Before he could say a word, she'd reached inside the box with an enthusiastic "ooooh" spilling from her pretty lips and pulled out one of three glass bottles, bringing with it a few stray sticks of straw.

"This is the real stuff," she said, her voice filled with awe as if she held a brick of pure gold rather than a glass bottle filled with pale liquid. "I mean, I think it is. Why bother going to these extremes to hide a bunch of hooch?"

"It's whiskey?"

"Better." She was already working the cork. "Scotch."

"Are you nuts?" He took the bottle from her hand and set it on the table beside the box.

She pouted for about half a second, then peered inside. "You're right. There's already an open bottle." She pulled it out, revealing no more than three inches of liquid remaining.

"Isn't this illegal?"

"This stuff was beginning its life in bonny Scotland when Volstead was in short pants. Look at this. *1898.* We could take this to Doc King and get a thousand bucks. Or . . ." She dug back into the box and emerged holding a shot glass. "We can drink a toast to the man who knew enough to ferret this away for better times."

There was no stopping her. The glass was on the table, the cork out of the bottle, and two fingers of the drink poured out.

"To Edward Moore," she said, offering the drink in salute. "May he rest in peace as his legacy lives."

Then the same lips that had earlier thoughtfully sipped hot coffee, that had sent him smiles and puckered in a way that made him think of kisses, touched themselves to the rim of the glass and, with barely a tilt of her head, took a slow, satisfying swallow, leaving an imprint of her lipstick. The look she had on her face afterward was nothing short of rapturous, and he was seized with a sudden, illogical desire to find and do anything that would give her that look again. Something that didn't involve his dead uncle's liquor stash.

"Now you," she said, poised to repeat the ritual of pouring.

"No, thank you." His head was foggy enough.

She arched her brow in a way that was more enticing than anything in any bottle ever could be. "'Lips that touch liquor will never touch mine'?"

"No," he said, feeling hollowed out like a schoolboy. "It's just—there's more in here. Look, actual papers."

With a rush of relief for the distraction, he lifted them from the box, brushing off the straw. The first item to draw his attention was a bundle of four—no, five—sheets of paper, carelessly folded. The first few pages were typed, but midway through the third page, the information was recorded in a harshly precise hand. Max's eyes scanned the material quickly, recognizing right away its content.

Monica had moved around to peer at it alongside him. "What is it? Some kind of list?"

"These are his books. The titles of all the books in his house."

"Oh my." Her enthusiasm didn't quite reach the level it had when she found the Scotch, but she seemed nonetheless appreciative.

He flipped to the last page and read aloud. "*Babbitt* and *The Enchanted April*. Probably the last books he bought. Or at least the last he recorded."

She snatched the paper from his hand. "*The Enchanted April*? I've been dying to read that."

"If I can find it, I'll lend it to you." He'd said it before thinking of the consequences. Loaning a book meant waiting around for its return. Otherwise, it was a gift, and he wasn't ready to give Monica Bisbaine a gift. But she smiled, sealing the deal, and he knew right then he would spend his evening searching the disorganized shelves for the title.

"What else is there?" she prompted.

There was a brown envelope made of thin cardboard, bound with a winding string. Suddenly his fingers felt too clumsy to open it, and he wondered if maybe he should have had a shot of whiskey to calm his nerves. After a few bumbling attempts, he gratefully handed the whole thing over to Monica and watched her nimble hands make short work of it. Once the envelope was opened, she handed over the first photograph, never taking her eyes off of his, allowing him to be the first to see the image.

It was Uncle Edward and Max's father when they were both young men. Probably younger than Max was now. They wore dark slacks and shirtsleeves, and they stood without any hint of motion or expression on the familiar front porch.

"1885." She was reading from the back of the photograph. "Doesn't that seem like forever ago?"

"It was." He showed her the photograph.

She peered at it closely. "Your father?" Then looked up at him. "I can see you in this."

Strengthened, he took the envelope away and reached in for the next picture, studied it briefly, and handed it to her. "My parents, their wedding." And then a fat-cheeked baby surrounded by tapestry. "Me, I guess." The familiar handwriting of his mother confirmed.

"Well, lookee lookee." Her eyes lit up and danced between the photograph of the baby and the man in the room. "What a fat little snack you were."

Again, that hollow feeling. There were more: himself at growing ages, culminating in the portrait taken for his high school graduation; various groupings of the brothers, his parents, him and his uncle, his solid three-person family; and Edward—alone, distinguished, aging.

"Why would he keep them here, locked away?" Monica

whispered, the atmosphere growing more reverent with each photograph.

"Because his family home—the house I grew up in—burned down. Destroyed everything. These are the only pictures of my family that exist."

He spoke from a power outside of himself, because his gut and throat and head were too full of newly resurfaced grief to be of coherent thought, let alone conversation. Somewhere in between those photographs came the time when some rift had occurred, fueled by both selfishness and apathy, that caused his uncle to cut loose and drift away. The same four faces appeared over and over—his father, his mother, Uncle Edward, Max. They were all each other had, and now, after years of estrangement, only Max remained, sifting through the prized possessions of a man who died alone.

And then, a new image.

"What do you know?" He'd piqued Monica's attention and savored the final moments of a secret.

"What is it?"

It was Zelda Ovenoff, an image from some years ago, but not many. Her hair was neatly arranged in a prewar coif, and she looked directly at the camera with a smile that rivaled that of Mona Lisa.

Speechless, he handed the image over. He had a feeling there wasn't much in this world that would surprise Monica Bisbaine, but this sure seemed to do the trick. What a delight to watch understanding dawn.

"But why . . . ?"

"I think they loved each other. At least, he loved her—that's clear."

"I never knew. I don't think anybody did."

She handed the photographs back with a certain reverence, and he packaged them again in the envelope.

"He came here often," Monica said with certainty.

"How do you know?"

"This." She ran her finger along the spine of the envelope's flap. "It's worn, almost broken. I think he must have come here, looked at them, and drank a toast."

As she spoke, the scene unfolded in front of him, so clear that he could almost smell Uncle Edward's cigar. Perhaps she could be a top-notch reporter after all.

"I think we should do the same," she said, pouring another drink.

"You already did."

"It's no fun to toast alone."

"There's only one glass," he said, though his initial idea of protest had weakened.

"There's a glass," she said, handing it to him, "and a bottle. To Edward."

She held up the bottle, and he touched the shot glass to it, the resulting clink sounding muffled in the small room. And then, just as Monica touched the bottle neck to her lips and tilted her head, he drank. He'd braced himself for burning, or bitter, but found neither. The taste was, instead, smooth, and even that small amount seemed to break up and wash away the final vestiges of anxiety.

"What's next?" she asked, looking up at him as if ready to go along with anything he said.

"For starters, this—" he took the recorked bottle from her and placed it back in the box—"will stay safely here. And these—" he tucked the photographs under his arm—"are going home with me."

"And the glass?"

"Why don't you take it?"

"Thanks. I'm honored." She took it from him and stashed it in her coat pocket. "One more thing before you walk out there." She brought her thumb to her mouth, licked it, and reached up. He stood, frozen, as she grazed it across his lip. "I left a little smudge on the glass; you picked it up. Don't want you walking around with a smear of Scarlet Passion on your mouth. People might wonder just what we were doing in here."

"They might indeed." In fact, *he* was beginning to wonder just what was happening between them, but knowing Monica, it was nothing more nor less than what it would be if she were locked in a small room with any other man and a bottle of liquor. He focused his attention on arranging the whiskey bottles back in the box, packing the straw around them—at her instruction—to keep them upright.

"Shall we do this again?" she said as they left. "Say, about a month from now? Celebrate my allowance?"

"It's a date," he said, fighting the urge to count the days.

CHAPTER 9

Don't ignore the man you are sure of while you flirt with another.
When you return to the first one, you may find him gone.
ANTI-FLIRT CLUB RULE #10

THE FRONT PARLOR smelled heavily of cabbage, meaning Mrs. Kinship had custody of the kitchen for the evening. Mr. and Mrs. Grayson, the elderly couple who owned the house and occupied two rooms on the first floor, were quite generous with their tenants, allowing them to spend evenings in the comfortable furniture downstairs and cook as they pleased, provided they prepare enough for the entire household on occasion. Mrs. Kinship must have spent some time cooking for troops, because she always prepared mounds of food, enough to feed the landlords, herself, Mr. Davenport, Monica, and even Anna when she was home from the library at mealtime.

The old-fashioned, sour smell perfectly complemented the wailing of the opera spiraling from the Victrola. If Mrs. Kinship commanded the kitchen, Mr. Davenport dominated the gramophone, having a collection of records at least six inches high. He sat in the high-back chair, his head lolled to one side. His fingers, tufted with long, white hair on the knuckles, accompanied the mournful aria, suspending themselves on the high, sustained notes.

Anna had draped herself across the back of the sofa, a forgotten mystery novel in her lap, and stared out the front window.

"Looks like it's snowing again," she said, her words dredged with malaise. "Nature's blanket to protect the most tender of shoots."

"Yeah?" Monica strode across the room to look for herself. "Well, it's going to ruin my most expensive of shoes."

"Hush," said Mr. Davenport, who sometimes forgot that he wasn't standing in his high school classroom.

Anna twisted to catch Monica's eye. Her long hair had streaks of gold, and her eyelashes were a dark, almost copper color. Two enviable marks of beauty, yet she seemed to take no pride or purpose in them.

"Going out with your gentleman friend again? What is it you girls say? Your *daddy*?"

Her question was met with two angry glares—one from Monica for the ridiculous use of slang, and one from Mr. Davenport for speaking at all.

"Where to this evening? Something exciting, no doubt. That's a very dramatic dress you're wearing."

"It's new," Monica said, holding her arms akimbo to show its full design. It was blood-red wool trimmed with black piping that gathered across her narrow hips.

"I could never get away with wearing such a thing," Anna said, and it was true. Not because of her face or figure but her lackluster demeanor. Much as she spoke of her longing to go to Paris, Monica couldn't imagine a less likely event.

"I decided to treat myself. A girl needs to do that every now and then. Lifts the spirit, you know?"

"Oh, I'm sure." Anna smoothed her thin, blonde hair. "Just the other day I walked past a shop that had the most attractive hats, and—"

"Ladies, if you please." Mr. Davenport's eyes were still closed, and he had to raise his voice considerably to be heard above the competition between the conversation and the chorus.

It was as good an excuse to quit talking with Anna as any, so Monica resumed her methodical pacing of the room.

"You should wait up in your apartment," Mrs. Kinship said, having come into the room wiping her hands on a comfortably stained apron, no doubt to announce that supper was ready for all who would partake. "So when he gets here, he has to wait. It's better that way."

"Not so *obvious*," Anna said, whispering the last word.

"This is hardly the first time the gentleman has come calling," Mr. Davenport intoned, one eye open. "No need to create a false sense of propriety now."

The music came to an end, filling the room with silence buffered by the sound of the Victrola's needle scratching into the endless vinyl of the record.

"Supper's ready, anyway," Mrs. Kinship said finally. "Stuffed cabbage, and plenty for everybody."

"Not for me, thanks." Monica sat on one of the more uncomfortable, rickety chairs and picked up a magazine. "I'm sure we'll be going out for supper. Maybe for a steak somewhere. And then dancing. So, no, I won't be having any stuffed cabbage."

It was rude, she knew, and she'd well offended at least Mrs. Kinship by the time she thought to smile and say, "Thank you." Anna maintained a bit of wistfulness on her pink face, and Mr. Davenport busied himself returning the record to its sleeve.

"Well, he's welcome too, just so's you know," Mrs. Kinship said.

Monica took another stab at sincerity, saying, "Thank you" once again, knowing full well she'd never invite Charlie to a family dinner, no matter how patched-together the family might be. Table talk would mean lots of questions, some she'd never even had the nerve to ask. Like where did he live, and where was he from, and did he ever think of settling down?

Soon enough she was alone in the parlor, and she slammed the magazine down on the side table. What if Charlie didn't get here before all of them were done stuffing themselves with Mrs. Kinship's stuffed cabbage? They'd come strolling back in, and here she'd be, still waiting for her young man. Her *daddy*.

She peeked out the window again. It was still snowing—the wet and sticky kind that would make the thin leather of her black shoes feel like tissue paper. All the more reason to stay off them, she'd offer, practicing a wicked, seductive grin on her pale reflection. Dinner at a hotel, maybe, and then a room. Maybe out in Silver Spring. She might even pack a little bag to make it seem more legitimate.

Just as she was about to run upstairs for her train case to make good on her plans, the telephone jangled the house's ring—two long, one short.

Her stomach dropped. She was practically the only one who ever got telephone calls, and those were mostly Charlie—either canceling plans, or postponing them, or whispering an address to meet him.

Reluctantly, she made her way to the telephone table and lifted the earpiece from its cradle, bringing the candlestick to her lips.

"Hello? Grayson residence."

There was a pause on the other end before a familiar voice came through.

"Hello. Yes, I'm looking for Miss Bisbaine. Miss Monica Bisbaine."

Max. Immediately, her mind filled with the memory of a small, warm room, good Scotch whiskey, and the feeling of being the only other person in the world.

"This is she, Mr. Moore. Whatever are you doing calling on a Friday night?"

She knew the question would take him off guard and bit her bottom lip, enjoying the audible sound of his squirming on the other end. Like a baby, this one was. She could knock him over with a bat of her eyes.

"I, um, I have your book."

"What book?"

"Well, not exactly *your* book. It's my uncle's. Mine now, of course. The one you wanted?"

"Mr. Moore, I have no idea—"

"*The Enchanted April.* It was on his list, and you said you wanted to read it. I found it."

"Oh," she said, all traces of amusement gone. "How nice of you. I hadn't given it another thought."

"Oh," he said, sounding just disappointed enough to make her feel guilty. "Well, I thought that maybe, if you're not busy tomorrow, we could meet somewhere and I could lend it to you?"

"Why not Monday?" Before he could answer, the front door shuddered against an impatient knock, and she said, "Hold on a second," before setting the phone down to answer it.

"There's my Miss Mousie!" It was Charlie, his leather cap damp with snow. He wasted no time waiting for an invitation but leapt over the threshold, taking Monica in his arms and burying his cold nose in the warmth of her neck.

"Charlie!" She screeched at the cold but gave in to his embrace. In no time at all his hands traveled just about every bit of her north of her knees as she made giggling, halfhearted attempts to swat him away, saying, "Unhand me, you beast."

He snarled one last time and then took a step away, devouring her with his eyes.

"Sweet grandma's pudding," he said, savoring the sight. "Look at you."

"It's new," she said, feeling less inclined to show it off the way she had for Anna. "With tonight being a special occasion and all."

"Special occasion?"

"Valentine's Day? I mean, officially it was a couple of days ago, but tonight it's ours."

"Oh, sure, sure." His eyes glanced over to the phone. "You talking to someone?"

She looked for the slightest hint of suspicion, but his question came off as one of pure curiosity.

"Yes. Just one minute, and I'll be ready to go." Once again she picked up the telephone, turning her back to Charlie as she did so and saying, "I'm sorry, I've just had a guest arrive."

"What a relief," Max said. "It sounded like you were under attack."

"Oh no," she said, choosing her next words carefully. "Just a date."

"Is he wearing a straitjacket?"

"Don't be silly—"

"Because those aren't exactly ideal for a night on the town—"

"Max—"

"Let alone dancing—"

"You were saying something about a book?" Spoken with the urgency of smashing a brake. She could picture his smirky grin through the line and felt her own being tugged along.

"*The Enchanted April.*"

She glanced over her shoulder, pleased to see the interest Charlie had taken in the conversation.

"Yes," she said, adopting a voice resplendent with breathless longing. "Of course, Max. I don't know if I'll be free tomorrow. I might be out of town."

"Eloping?"

"Hardly. Just a little fun."

"Then Monday it is."

"Perfect." She sent a wink over to Charlie. "I'll see you then."

He was behind her the second she placed the earpiece in its cradle, his arms wrapped around her, his lips against her ear.

"You have another fellow besides me?"

She twisted around and pulled him close for a kiss, letting him stew. When he pulled away, she said, "It's nobody. Just my boss."

"He's takin' over the paper?"

"I don't want to talk about work." She kissed him again to emphasize the point. She especially didn't want to talk about Max. And she wanted even less to think about why.

"Okay, okay," he said, drawing back and glancing at the staircase. "Want to try to sneak upstairs?"

"No." She slapped his arm in disgust, not quite mock. "Look at me. Do I look like I want to sneak upstairs?"

"So we're going out? You got a lead on a place?"

"Not tonight. Can't we just go on a date? Like two normal people?"

"Sure we can, sweetheart. Go get your coat. It's some nasty weather outside."

"All right. But I'll need to change my shoes, too. Wait here."

She ran upstairs, all wild ideas of taking a train to Silver Spring flown clear out of her head, replaced momentarily with the thought of a snowy-cold morning, occupying a table at Sobek's, reading *The Enchanted April.* That, too, was shaken to the side as she opened the door to her room and crossed to the armoire, where her shoes lived in tumbled piles on the bottom shelf. In no time she'd found her black T-straps—less dramatic, but infinitely more practical given their thicker heels. She was sitting on the edge of her bed, fastening the buckle, when her eye caught the jewel-shaped lid of the Mavis perfume. She'd applied it faithfully as she dressed and now lifted her wrist to take in the scent.

And for the first time since the first time, she didn't want to go back downstairs.

They sat in the back of a cab with an unaccustomed distance between them. Usually time alone was such a rare commodity, little of it was ever left to comfortable silence. Not that this silence was comfortable.

Monica stared out the window, lulled to listlessness by the hum of the engine. Occasionally the car would hit a bump or lurch for some other reason, and she'd steel against the impact, once even grabbing at the seat in front of her to keep balanced and upright.

"Shoulda stayed back at the house," Charlie said at last. "Things was a lot warmer back there, if you know what I mean."

She knew what he meant. When it came to *that*—or any topic, really—the man was about as subtle as a train at a racetrack. One deep breath was not enough to infuse her with the energy to agree, or disagree, or even care.

"Sheesh, if I wanted the silent treatment, I coulda stayed at home."

She wanted to say that there were lots more things he could get at home, too, but that would start a fight, or as much of a fight as they ever got into, meaning he would pout his way through dinner and then drop her off alone. In some ways, tonight that didn't seem like such a bad deal—maybe curling up in the parlor with a good book and a mug of that hot chocolate Anna made sometimes. There were worse ways to spend an evening.

Keeping stock-still, she shifted her eyes over to Charlie. He was staring straight ahead, giving her ample time to study his profile. Had his face always been so soft? So square? The night they'd met at a little underground club on K Street, he'd seemed different from the other guys. Rounded, affable, safe—and thus he'd remained all these months. He stayed with her for three solid days after her mother died; nights, too. Never so much as a whisper about his wife, or his home, or his family. He was a boon of her imagination, coming to life only when he drifted in line with her gaze. Existing nowhere but here, beside her. Disappearing into a dark void the minute he left her bed, moving with surprising silence for a man of his girth.

He called on that same stealth now, because the next thing she knew, his broad face filled the curve of her neck.

"I see you got your gift."

"I did." She stared at the back of the driver's head, giving Charlie nothing. "What an unexpected surprise."

"Well, I remembered what you said about me never giving you a bottle of perfume. So I thought I'd set that right."

"It's very nice. Usually the cheap stuff makes me break out in hives, so I'm keeping a watch. You'll let me know if my neck turns red, won't you?"

"Ah, Mousie, you know I do the best I can for you."

"What I know is that you gave me the same scent your wife wears."

An unmistakable snicker from the driver prompted Charlie to

nudge the back of the seat as he twisted his body in a protective shield around her. His face disappeared in and out of shadow, depending on the streetlight. Like a film projected in slow motion, she watched his face turn from confused to surprised to hurt at her accusation.

"Sweetheart, I don't buy my wife perfume. She buys her own. I don't pay any attention to that kind of stuff."

"Well, it's an amazing coincidence, don't you think?" For her part, she kept her face the same. Cold.

"I told the lady it was for a beautiful girl, hair black as midnight. I said you looked like some beautiful Egyptian princess, only, you know, with this perfect white skin. And then she shows me this ad, and I could picture you in that silk robe you wear sometimes, and it seemed perfect."

Her mind wandered through the fabric of his story, looking for tufts of truth. Maybe he really didn't know the name of his wife's perfume. He probably did have some conversation with a store clerk. He thought she was beautiful. Other men thought so too, given the way they flirted and carried on until Charlie became some big, fuzzy shield, staring them down and sending them away. He'd never let anybody hurt her. In fact, *he* would never hurt her. Not if he could help it. Unless she let him.

The lie he told tonight—and other, smaller ones she barely remembered—was meant to protect her. To keep her miles away from the tragedy of their truth, to make her feel like she was the only woman in his life. The only woman in the city worthy of Mavis perfume. It was just the kind of lie a girl needed every now and then.

"Oh, Charlie." She kissed him before the driver's doubts could worm their way into the backseat, and she didn't stop until the car did.

⋅⧸ CHAPTER 10 ⧹⋅

Don't flirt: those who flirt in haste oft repent in leisure.
ANTI-FLIRT CLUB RULE #1

WHILE CHARLIE COUNTED OUT a generous tip for the cabbie, Monica tilted her little mirror toward the streetlight, fixed her lipstick, and powdered her nose. The air outside the car felt refreshingly cool and clean, inviting her to forget her previous touch-up and turn her face toward the now-intermittent flakes drifting lazily down.

Charlie swooped in beside her, taking her under his arm as if to shield her from the snow. "You hungry?"

"Starved."

"Good."

He kept her close to his side, hurrying the few slick steps to the black-and-red canopy over the restaurant's door.

Romo's was a steak house on K Street. A fifty-cent cab fare from Monica's apartment, making it far enough away to seem like an adventure. In fact, it had been an adventure the first time they went, on a tip that ordering the *crêpe flambé* for dessert would get diners a pass into a back room where they could sip an after-dinner brandy while listening to a sonata played by a string quartet made up of the proprietor's daughters.

"I love this place," Charlie said as their cab eased its way through the traffic-clogged street. "Steaks as big as my face, right?"

"Yeah."

Monica, rather, chose to remember the dark-paneled room, lamps with red-tinted domes, and the haunting music that made the light and the brandy join in as a perfect blend for the senses. That's what she'd written, anyway, without giving any clues to the location or the name or even the code word to gain access to the hidden treasure. This was one place that deserved to be both celebrated and protected.

They were met at the door by a man just her size who took their coats and disappeared while another led them to the only free table, which just happened to be tucked away in a perfect dark corner.

"A secret place for secret love, am I right?"

The host's olive skin gave an aura of mystery and romance to his words, and Charlie answered with a slug to his arm. "What are you trying to say, pal?"

"Only that a woman this beautiful needs to be kept under lock and key, lest someone steal her away."

Charlie looked at her, his arms open in surrender. "What did I tell you, Mousie?"

"You told me you were hungry," she said before turning her attention to the simpering host. "I'll bet you'd have a whole other line if we had to take a table by the kitchen."

He smiled deferentially before bowing away, leaving her to look at Charlie across the table by the flickering light of a low-burning candle. Hushed conversations swirled around them, filling the absence of their own for a while, at least until they'd been served two glasses of water and ordered their supper.

"So tell me," Charlie said, tucking his napkin into his collar in anticipation of the meat to come, "what's new in your life since last we met?"

Monica smiled at his attempted lyricism. "You first."

"Same old, same old."

"How lucky for you. My boss died, our office was held at gun-point on account of the Monkey Business story about Hoofers, and I got two swigs of genuine thirty-year-old Scotch whiskey."

He sat back, impressed, though she wouldn't venture to guess which headline intrigued him most.

"Please tell me you got that bottle stashed in your purse."

"Did you hear me, Charlie? Guns. Doc King, not apprecia-tive of the way I rendered his joint in the press. I could have been killed."

"But you weren't, were you? And good thing for him, too, because I would have knocked his block off. Ought to do that just for scaring you."

She chose not to mention Max, how he'd held her close to his side throughout the ordeal. No doubt any bullet meant for her would have had to go through him, or at least she liked to think so.

"Now—" Charlie leaned across the table—"about that whis-key. Where'd you stumble across that? From that gangster?"

Monica smiled. "No. It was Mr. Moore's. We found it with some of the, um, things he left behind."

We. Would he wonder?

"Imagine. Checking out of this life and leaving something like that behind."

"Imagine," she confirmed, choosing instead to think of all

Edward Moore had *not* left behind—namely a hint of the heart he'd kept hidden. "But it makes a person think, doesn't it? What we're leaving behind, I mean. You know what I got from my mother? Nothing. She sold the house, gave everything away. I didn't have claim to anything I didn't take with me when I left."

"But you're doing okay." He wrapped his paw of a hand around her wrist, rubbing his thumb under the gold bangles encircling it.

"Sure, but then what happens to it when I go? Say Doc King made good on his threat?"

"Let's not talk like this." He gave her wrist a squeeze. "How many nights do we get to sit down to a nice dinner? Why are we going to spoil it with talk like this?"

Two sizzling steaks were set in front of them. Charlie immediately dug in with gusto, tearing in with his knife and fork, while Monica tried not to wince at the trickle of pale blood released by his attack.

"You might not even know," she said, speaking as much to the meat as to him. "I could be gone for days and days, and you wouldn't know until you showed up at the Graysons' only to find some other person renting my room after they box up my things and take them to the orphanage or something."

"No orphan pull off that dress," he said, pointing with his fork.

"I'm an orphan, Charlie. You don't know what it's like to be all alone in the world."

He at least had the courtesy to look chagrined.

"And what about you?" she continued. "What if something happened to you? I might never know. I'd be sitting around some Friday night, waiting, and no one would even know they were supposed to telephone, or send me a telegraph, or anything. And who would I ask?"

"What? You want I should check in with you every day, just so's you'll know I'm alive?"

"Isn't that what people do for each other?"

He was chewing. "Not people like us. We live. I've got a wife to watch me die."

She sliced a sliver of steak and held it aloft; Charlie devoured three more before she could bring herself to take the first bite.

"What's the matter?" he asked. "Not cooked right? You need me to send it back?"

"No," she said. "I mean, it's fine. It's perfect." She cut and ate another slice to verify.

"Good. I like to keep my girl happy."

The bite barely cleared the growing lump in her throat, and she set her knife and fork aside.

"You know I'm crazy about you, right, Charlie?"

"Same here, Mousie." He lifted his napkin to wipe his chin and lips, misreading her direction.

"But I think we have to stop. This has to stop."

"Ah, now . . ." He tore the napkin from his collar and sent it drifting to cover the decimated meat on his plate. "Why would you say something like that?"

"I don't want to die alone. I don't want to *be* alone."

"Well, that doesn't make any sense, does it? Won't you be more alone without me?"

"No," she said simply, feeling the brush of her earrings as she shook her head.

"It was the perfume, wasn't it? Look, I'll buy you another—"

"It wasn't the perfume. Not completely, anyway."

"Oh no. You can't fool me. If it's one thing I know, it's women."

He'd kept her for this long, so the statement might be just as true as it was delusional.

"I've just been doing some thinking lately; that's all."

"Lately? More like the last five minutes. The way you was kissing me in the car didn't feel like you were ready to run me over."

"What can I say? I'm impetuous. That's how this whole thing started in the first place."

"So impetuous your mind right back."

She shrugged. "It doesn't work like that. Sorry. And I don't think it would be a good idea for you to try to keep a mistress against her will. Might get messy."

He looked sad. No, stricken. "I hate that word."

"Messy?"

"Mistress."

"Not as much as I do. Don't you think I deserve better, Charlie?"

He picked up her hand, held it, then brought it to his lips for a last, lingering kiss. She decided to forgive the trace of grease he left behind.

"Baby, you deserve everything."

In that terrifying second, she wished she could take it all back. Laugh it off like a joke, but he might not laugh with her. For all she knew, he was going to whistle his way out of this place, go back home to his wife, or maybe even find another girl. Certainly she wasn't the first. She might not be the only. But none of that mattered now. Her stomach roared with relief and hunger, and she couldn't wait to get her hand back.

"Don't suppose we'll be going out dancing after this."

He'd loosened his grip just enough that she drew her hand away, bringing it to rest on the table. "I don't think so."

"Then I guess it's time to take you home."

He was fighting something—a struggle between sadness and pride—as he reached into his jacket pocket and withdrew his wallet, opening it to retrieve a few bills, which their waiter handily arrived to take from him.

"I don't want you to take me home, Charlie." The long car ride in the dark, the familiar walk up the porch steps, the welcome darkness of the abandoned parlor, the silent reminder on the stairs to skip the third, squeaky step.

"So, this is it?"

"It had to happen sometime, you know."

"I never would have said so in a million years."

"Yes, you would have."

He looked away, conceding the point, and by the time their eyes met again, it was over.

"How are you going to get home?" he asked, his voice full of business.

"Same way I got here. Cab." She stopped him as he began to reach into his wallet again. "Please. I can take care of it myself. But thank you for supper."

"You haven't hardly touched yours."

"I know, but I plan to. I think you should leave now."

He sat back and up, surprised. "You're kicking me out of Romo's? Can you do that?"

She smiled. "Yes, and yes." The threat of tears whittled her sentences shorter and shorter.

He surrendered. "As you wish." Moving slowly, as if through water, he pushed his chair away from the table, stood, and walked over to where she sat. She filled her gaze with the flickering candle, forcing herself not to turn when she felt his lips touch the top of her head.

And then he was gone.

Her steak had congealed on the plate, as unappetizing as anything she had ever encountered, but she dared not look away. That would mean facing the roomful of people who had just witnessed her abandonment. She had to wait at least long enough for Charlie to get his own cab or maybe even just walk around the corner. For all she knew, he lived on the next block. But she couldn't just sit here with her uneaten supper.

Catching the waiter's eye, she summoned him over and asked him to take it away, which he did with aplomb.

"Hey, wait a minute," she said before he could take a second step.

"*Sì, bella.*" There was just a hint of suggestion in his smile.

"I'd like an order of *crêpe flambé.*"

The smile disappeared. "*Mi dispiace, signorina.* I apologize. We do not serve that dish here. Perhaps a nice custard?"

"Yes, you do. I've had it before."

"Perhaps you were accompanied by the nice gentleman. We are not in the habit of serving such to *una donna non accompagnato.* You understand?"

"*Capisco,*" she said, understanding too well what he feared. Too many single girls in a speakeasy, and a whole new set of crime might get under way. Still, she wanted darkness, and music, and a drink. She reached into her purse, took out a few folded bills, and slipped them between his palm and the plate. "*Capisci?*"

He did, and the next thing she knew she was being led to the coat check and, after a reassuring glance, ushered through a door behind it. With no frame and no knob—just a metal slide bar near the floor—she might not have known it was there, except that she'd been through it before. Then, tracing her fingers along the wall in utter darkness, she took a dozen steps down a dark hallway before turning a corner to find yet another door. This one, however, had a series of thin slats creating narrow stripes of light. She knocked, and a small window slid open near the top. She went to her toes, getting as close as she could to the onyx eyes and moustache, and whispered the words the waiter had whispered to her. The window slid closed; the door opened.

If she ever had a home of her own, something other than a room in a boardinghouse, she wanted a salon that looked just like this. Dark paneled walls; thick, plush carpet; overstuffed, comfortable furniture gathered in cozy combinations. The tables were small and low, perfectly placed for a languid stretch to retrieve a drink. Soft music came from the corner—classical, provided by the owner's daughters, two on violin, one viola, one cello. Conversation hummed just above it, laughter tinkling like ice cubes in a glass. Nobody here had any intentions of calling attention to themselves. In the days before Prohibition, this was a scene that might have unfolded in these people's homes, friends gathered after dinner for brandy. But the cost and the risk was too great, sending them scuttling into speakeasies like this one. For that, Monica was glad. One had to be invited to drink in somebody's home. This place welcomed a girl like her, provided she knew the correct words to get in.

The room was perfectly warm, mostly due, she assumed, to the fireplace dominating one wall. That same fire was largely responsible for the light in the room, casting all of the men and women gathered in its shadowy, dancing glow. It was reflected in the amber-filled glasses.

"The Devil's Lair" is what she'd called it the first time she walked in on Charlie's arm, and he'd whispered something deliciously evil in her ear.

Now she walked in alone, draped shoulder-to-shin in red. The minute she walked through the door, someone handed her a cigarette, and she bent absently to the flame proffered on her behalf. Her lungs filled with smoke—a sensation she failed to find as enjoyable as others did—and she surveyed the room for an empty seat. There were plenty, but none completely alone. Unless she went to the bar at the other side of the room, varnished black and lined with stools upholstered in rich, red velvet, she'd have to join a group. Easy enough to do if she'd had a date, but alone?

She took slow, measured steps across the room, aware of every eye observing her. It was a favorite line from *Pride and Prejudice*, when Elizabeth Bennet and Miss Bingley take a turn around the room to better show off their figures. The music was low and dramatic, the perfect score if this were a scene in a movie. She, the exotic unknown, and one of these men poised to succumb to her charms.

"Care to join us?"

The invitation came from a handsome, well-groomed model of a man. A touch of gray at his temples, a strong jaw, a suit expensive but not custom-tailored. He wore one ring with a dark stone—a garnet, perhaps—and another of pure gold with a Shriners emblem clearly visible in the firelight. It was in this hand that he held his drink, while the other gestured across the room, ordering her a— "Brandy?"

She nodded, agreeing to both, and settled on the far end of the vacated sofa. Why not indulge in a bit of a game? She needed fodder for next week's column and proof that she could charm another man, should she ever need to do so. Deep in the corner of her mind, like a shadowy figure in fading film, she saw Max's moonlike smile, but she pushed it aside.

Two other men, each wearing rings similar to that of the first, greeted her with easy smiles, their faces loosened by drink.

"We saw you earlier," the first man said, returning with her drink and sitting down beside her. Not too close. "Don't tell us your date has abandoned you."

Monica took a dainty, alluring sip.

"We had a parting of opinions."

"I think I'd go along with anything you say." This from one of the other two, who leaned across from his own plush wingback chair to run his hand along the top of her leg. The gold of his ring glinted in the firelight.

"Then I guess I've been wasting my time." She took another sip and waited for the alcohol to take effect. Once things became fuzzy enough, she could look at these guys and decide if any would be most worth her time. There were more important things than buying a girl a drink. There were dinners, furs, perfume . . . In the meantime, his hand was on her leg, his touch burning her to the bone, and she shifted beneath it, dislodging his grip.

If she'd offended him, he gave no indication. Not overtly, anyway, but when he settled back into his chair, he looked over the rim of his glass, and there was no mistaking the threat that lurked there. She would not invite another touch.

His companions laughed, including the man who first bought her the drink.

"Looks like my friend is out of luck for tonight," he said, sending a silent toast. "The lady knows a lounge lizard when she sees one."

"She sees three," Monica said, glancing at each in turn. She coyly spun the drink within her glass and took a sip, waiting to see which would rise to the bait.

Two of them chuckled.

She let her gaze linger on the first man. "What's your name, daddy?"

"Bernardo."

She knew it wasn't true, but she repeated it anyway. "Bernardo. Italian?"

"Perceptive." His voice was rich and deep, his lips soft and full.

She took a drag on her cigarette, exhaled, and asked, "And your friends?"

"Prefer to remain anonymous, as I'm sure you can understand."

In fact, it took a minute for her to understand. She was heady from the smoke, and though she'd had only a few sips of alcohol, it was strong. Quality, the kind only a select few were granted. Had she ordered her own drink, no doubt it would have been watered down. But this was every bit as good as the stuff in Edward Moore's safety-deposit box. This was what people drank before the law, or what they drank in spite of the law.

She took another drink.

"Are you gangsters?" The boldness was kicking in. "I met a gangster once. Stared down the barrel of his gun. Well, not *his* gun. But a couple of his hired goons'." She looked at the other two men with new understanding. "Say, you two aren't the goons, are you?"

The cigarette and the drink fueled her bravado; if her instincts were correct, that facade would keep her safe. Here, there was no Max to hide behind.

"I've been wondering," Bernardo said, "why it is a woman—lovely as you are—would choose to come into an establishment such as this unaccompanied. I find it disturbing."

He spoke in a deep, measured tone matched perfectly to the cello in the background. Anybody just listening in might think he was being unfailingly polite. But then, they wouldn't be privy to the black steel glint in his eyes.

"I just came in for a drink," she said, working to keep the fear out of her voice. "And I like this place. It's classy."

He nodded in a way that took credit for the compliment. "You've been here before?"

"Once or twice." They were warming up to each other, and with her silent consent, he gestured for another drink.

"With your boyfriend?"

"He's not my boyfriend anymore." She leaned back, comfortable. "Turns out he's married."

"No." Bernardo leaned back too, relaxed enough to allow his suit jacket to fall to the side, revealing a hint of leather holster beneath it. "What is a man if he has no honor?"

His companions echoed in agreement.

"Or a woman, for that matter," he continued. "May I ask you, Miss—"

"Monica."

"Miss Monica, are you a woman of honor?"

She took a final drag on her cigarette before stubbing it out in the cut-glass dish on the small table to the side of the sofa. "So far as I know."

"Then you can understand how I wish only to preserve that honor. A beautiful woman like you, in here alone, men might get the wrong idea." He sent a withering glare to his cohort who had been guilty of such a misunderstanding.

"Are you saying I should leave?"

"I think that would be best, yes."

"Then why do you keep ordering drinks for me?"

He chuckled, a deep rumbling sound that somehow made her think of warm caramel. If she were to look for a new boyfriend, he might not be a bad choice. Handsome, protective, powerful. He obviously felt at home here, and for a moment, she did too. A man in a crisp white coat came with a tray of fresh drinks. These were not the same as she'd been drinking before, but tiny shot glasses filled with a dark liquor.

"*Salute,*" Bernardo said, holding his aloft.

"*Salute,*" they—his companions and Monica—answered. Following their example, she downed the drink in a single gulp, not fully realizing its licorice-like flavor until after she'd swallowed. It so happened that their drink coincided with the final notes of the song being played by the quartet, and they set their glasses down amid a smattering of applause.

"It's a nice way to end an evening," Bernardo said. "Am I right?"

"You've got it, daddy." Monica licked the lingering liquor from her lips. His careful politeness kept shame at bay, and for that she was grateful, but his meaning couldn't be more clear. "'Course it's not quite that easy, for me at least. Like I said earlier, my date dumped me. He was my ride home." She planted a hand on the cushion between them and leaned forward, knowing this angle worked the neckline of her dress to her advantage. After all, this guy might even have a limousine.

He appeared unfazed. "How were you planning to get home?"

"Oh, I don't know." She shrugged the neckline that much wider. "There's usually someone headed toward my side of town. A girl can usually find a ride."

"I could give her a ride, boss." This from the intrepid man who had touched her leg.

"You see?" Bernardo said. "This is exactly what I mean. Girls like you bring trouble to an establishment such as this. Bad enough we have to tiptoe around the Volstead; we shouldn't be peddling flesh."

Outrage churned within her, but she chose instead to feign a coy confusion.

"I don't know what you're getting at, Mr. Bernardo. I came in here for a drink. Nothing more. It's a compliment to your place that a nice girl like me would come in here."

"Who said it's my place?"

Monica sat up straight, squaring her shoulders. "I'm a nice girl, Mr. Bernardo. Not a stupid one. You'd be surprised what I know and don't know."

Bernardo didn't blink. Instead, he reached beneath his jacket, setting Monica's heart on fire as she saw the iron glint of his gun in the firelight. Mother always said her mouth would get her into trouble. But Bernardo didn't seem to have taken much offense to her words, as he produced not a gun but a sizable bundle of cash. He opened the golden clip and peeled two bills off the top.

"Cab fare." He nodded to the man who'd touched her. "Go make the call. Get it here in five minutes."

"I don't need your money." Not bad enough to confirm his suspicions. Her shoes were comfortable enough.

"Take it. We can forget this unpleasant conversation."

He held out an amount that would have covered a fare halfway to New Jersey. The lingering liqueur turned sour in her mouth, but a sense of practicality won out. She took one of the bills, saying, "I don't live far," but stopped short of saying thank you. Hooded glances of the clandestine patrons burned the back of her neck, and if people were going to assume the worst, who was she to disappoint? She took Bernardo's face in her hands, leaned forward, and placed a long, lingering kiss on his soft, powerful lips.

"I'm not what you think I am," she whispered into his ear.

"Perhaps," he whispered into hers, "I'm merely the first to notice. *Buona fortuna.*"

~§ CHAPTER 11 §~

Don't be afraid to make a mistake; your readers might like it.
WILLIAM RANDOLPH HEARST

IT WAS SEVEN O'CLOCK in the morning when Max arrived at the *Capitol Chatter* offices. The night's darkness lurked outside the grimy windows as he typed up a dozen pages of scribbled notes and ideas, creating one coherent vision to be mimeographed and distributed when the staff assembled at nine. In truth, his message was a simple one; the scattered thoughts represented an attempt to keep his mind occupied over the weekend. Anything to chase away the image of the guy who had swept Monica away so effortlessly. That booming voice wrapped around her giggle had haunted him, taking his thoughts where they had no business going. Besides a brief visit to a dull church on Sunday morning, he'd spent two entire days with copies of every newspaper available, reading articles, studying advertisements, ascertaining tone and intent. Politics, crime, freakish events—sometimes all represented in a single story. He looked for joy, encouragement, faith, and found little.

The drafting of a letter to Sister Aimee occupied much of Sunday evening, asking her for prayer and advice in his venture. And then a sleepless night culminating in the predawn boarding of a streetcar.

The only sound was the spinning of the drum of the mimeograph machine, and he felt a great deal of satisfaction with each printed page that rolled out from underneath it. Here was a plan—*his* plan, divinely inspired and, hopefully, faithfully implemented.

Thomas Harper Jr. was, characteristically, the first to arrive, bringing with him a poster-board chart with lots of numbers and a big red line. This he set on a wobbly easel that seemed to maintain its balance in deference to the severity of his gaze.

Zelda Ovenoff came next, bringing with her a large white paper bag blotched with the telltale grease stains of doughnuts.

"Good morning, Mr. Moore, Mr. Harper. I'll make coffee."

It was the first time Max had seen her since that morning in Uncle Edward's—his—home, and she bustled about with the same controlled efficiency. This time, though, he could clearly see the beloved woman in the photograph beneath the animated janitress.

"Thank you, Zelda," he said, perhaps more tenderly than he ought, as she shot him a confused, guarded look.

"You have good news for us, I hope, Mr. Moore?"

"I hope so too."

She granted him a quick nod before taking the office's electric percolator to be filled, nearly colliding with Tony Manarola as she left.

"Hey," Tony said to the exiting Zelda, "where's the fire?" Then, turning to see Max in the doorway, said, "Sorry, kid."

"You know about that?" He searched his mind, trying to

remember if he'd told anybody about the fire that claimed the lives of his parents, but as far as he knew, only Mr. Bolling would have access to those details, and it was doubtful Uncle Edward had ever shared such a matter of personal tragedy.

Tony tapped his nose. "You don't just let someone walk into your family without doin' a little checkin' up, if you know what I mean."

"I guess I should be honored."

Tony shrugged. "It's what I do."

The office door opened again, this time by a red-cheeked Trevor, who graciously held it for the returning Zelda.

"Such a good boy," she said, resting a free hand against his cheek as she passed.

"Shouldn't you be in school?" Max asked with a quick glance at the clock.

"It'll be there later. This is my science hour, anyway. Mr. Tottle won't even know I'm gone."

Max resisted the urge to tell him that he simply wasn't needed here today. There'd be no errands, no messages, no mail to deliver or telegraphs to send. But the boy had already hung his patched-at-the-elbow coat on the peg right beside Max's own, so he simply clapped Trevor on the back and solicited a promise to be back on school grounds before lunch.

By eight forty-five, all the staff had arrived—with one notable exception—and the office was warmed not only by the heat coming from the radiators but also by the smell of fresh coffee, served in mismatched cups. Zelda's doughnuts were well received, with Tony being the first to dive for the platter and devour half a pastry in a single bite.

It was a contented silence that fell onto the room, with just a few comments about the cold and baseball and Charlie Chaplin

as the next minutes ticked by. It wasn't until she opened the door
that Max realized he'd been waiting to see her. Not just this morning, for this meeting, but since that afternoon at the bank when
they'd walked out the door and she'd gone to the right when he
turned to the left. And not just waiting, but worrying that she
might not come. That she wouldn't want to see him after that
clumsy, pathetic phone call.

The Enchanted April. The book was in his satchel hanging
on the hook behind his coat. Hidden, as if anybody could guess.

But here she was, piercing their presence with a loud com-
plaint about falling out of bed at the crack of dawn, and if she
wanted to keep bankers' hours she would have been a banker,
and there had better be some coffee left or she was turning right
around and heading home. The entire diatribe came out in a
single breath during the time it took for her to hang up her coat
and throw herself into the chair directly next to him.

"You're early."

"You're kidding." She twisted her body to look at the clock
behind her. "I must have been running to try to keep warm."

Zelda made a maternal clucking noise as she set a cup of steaming coffee down in front of each of them.

"He takes cream and sugar," Monica said.

"Does he now?"

Before he could stop her, Zelda had taken his cup away.

"Well," Max said, trying to rally attention to himself. "Thank
you all for being here so promptly this morning. And for making
coffee." This as she returned his drink, now two shades lighter.
"If nobody objects, I'd like to open our meeting with a prayer."

"And if we do?" Monica said, looking at him over the rim of
her cup.

"Do you?"

"Not really." She set the cup down.

Max took a deep breath, separating himself from their tug-of-war conversation. Praying out loud was not something he ever willingly embraced, but if he was to be in prayer for this endeavor, he wanted them all to know it. To hear it. He would not, however, command that everybody bow their heads and close their eyes, though he did as an example.

"Heavenly Father, we gather this morning grateful for the opportunity to do your will in our work. We seek direction and guidance, especially me. Help me to see, always, the answers you have for my questions. And . . ."

Words disappeared. Why it was that a man who had devoted so many hours to the study and perpetuation of eloquence was unable to string together more than three well-crafted sentences, he'd never understand. But there, his heart pounding in anticipation of pursuing some new, great thing, knowing full well he'd never accomplish it without some divine intervention, all he could manage was a stammer in the darkness.

"Tell us what to do, too." It was Zelda's voice, reaching out to him in a way that any touch to his hand never could.

"Amen." That was Monica, always—as he'd noticed—eager to end a prayer.

He, too, said amen and waited for Tony and Zelda to finish making the sign of the cross before clearing his throat and opening his journal.

"I'd like to begin this meeting with a few verses of Scripture."

Monica sighed, her eyes rolling so far to the backs of the sockets he feared they'd stick there. Tony, meanwhile, took out his pad, licked the tip of his pencil, and appeared poised to listen.

"It's a passage from the book of Philippians, chapter 4, verse 8." He opened his Bible to the place he'd marked with one of the photographs taken from Uncle Edward's safety-deposit box. It was, in fact, Edward, though only Monica would recognize him. Another secret shared.

That's when he knew he couldn't start with Scripture. Using his finger to mark his place, he closed the Bible and held up the photograph.

"This man, you should know, is Edward Moore. The date is 1885. Just after he finished college. Most of you can't imagine him ever being that young. Neither can I. I always knew him as old, opinionated. But nobody's born that way. I know Uncle Edward had joy—at this point in his life, anyway." He held up the photograph, blocking his view of Zelda. "And I hope that joy continued into his later years, in secret pockets of his life."

He went silent for a moment, struck with the thought that he was only just now giving the kind of speech he should have given at the funeral. But then, today marked a different death.

"Now, to the Scripture I mentioned." He opened his Bible, adjusted his glasses, and read. "'Finally, brethren, whatsoever things are true, whatsoever things are honest, whatsoever things are just, whatsoever things are pure, whatsoever things are lovely, whatsoever things are of good report; if there be any virtue, and if there be any praise, think on these things.'"

He looked around the table. "I want us to be a paper that thinks on these things, one that will make our readers think on these things. I want us to tell uplifting stories about honest people doing positive things in this world."

No response.

"You can't be all that surprised. I think I made it known early on that I wanted to take this direction, and then after our visit from Mr. King, well, I just don't think I want our paper associated with that level of society."

"I think this is good," Zelda said, making Max wonder if she and Uncle Edward hadn't had similar conversations.

"I'm glad you agree," Max said. "Because I want you to be a contributor."

Zelda's face registered surprise; Monica's voice burst forth in disbelief.

"What? She's a cleaning lady!"

"With wonderful ideas," Max said. "She could write about homemaking tips and things that might make the lives of our women readers a little easier. Recipes for cleaning products, or beauty."

Monica scoffed. "Beauty?"

"Like what you told me the other day about the coffee grounds, Mrs. Ovenoff." He addressed the table at large. "She makes some kind of paste, and then—"

"With eggs." The newborn pride in Zelda's voice gave him a brief jolt of victory. "It does wonders for the skin. You should try it, Miss Monica."

"What in the world is wrong with my skin, I'd like to know?"

Max turned to her, and he would have to agree that her skin was something close to flawless, save for the blotch of red stretching from her neck to her collarbone, an unmistakable sign of fury or frustration. Whatever the source, like a flame it licked across the table and destroyed what little bit of confidence Zelda had mustered. Once again the older woman's eyes were downcast, her hands engaged in invisible knitting.

"I—I don't know, Mr. Moore," Zelda said. "I don't write in English so good as I speak it."

"I'll get you help. In fact, perhaps Miss Bisbaine could spend some time—"

"And also, you know, with so much that was ugly, I don't know how many women even read this paper."

"This is crazy." Monica pushed herself away from the table and stood, planting her hands on its top. "We have plenty of women readers. And do you know why? Because of me. They want to know what I'm wearing and what I'm doing. Tell me, Maximilian Moore, what happens to Monkey Business?"

He'd anticipated this question. "It stays, but it changes."

She folded her arms and glowered. "Into what?"

Instead of answering directly, he turned his attention to the table at large. "I want to talk to each one of you individually this morning in my office. That way I can discuss with you more specifically my expectations, and we can share ideas." His words sounded weak, like his decision wasn't final and firm, and he hoped to have more courage fighting one lion at a time.

"Whatever you say, boss." Tony was closing his notepad and tapping it back into his jacket pocket. "But I have to tell you that all this happiness and sunshine might have worked with that magazine where you was at before, but here—this ain't no town of roses."

"We're going to see about that." He nodded to Harper, who stood, cleared his throat, and turned the piece of cardboard balanced on the easel.

"As you can see," Harper said, as if he were wrapping up a lengthy lecture, "even if we see a dramatic drop in sales, our paid subscriptions and current cash balance will fund publication for the next six weeks." At this point, his long, tapered finger came to rest on the point where the jagged black line turned blood red. "At which point we will need to reassess whether this direction is prudent."

"'Cause we'll be broke," Monica said, arms still folded in defiance. "Tell me, do you have any salaries factored into that black line?"

"Of course we do," Max said, overconfidently according to

the brief shake of Harper's head. He took a deep breath and tried to summon that confident, warm, reassuring tone his father had whenever Max needed direction. "Look, this is going to be a new venture for all of us. It's my first time to be in charge of—well, anything. And there's a good chance that we'll fail. But as a great, power-crazed, homicidal woman once said, 'Screw your courage to the sticking-place, and we'll not fail.'"

He ended his Shakespearean quote, fist raised in the air and all, and looked to Monica in triumph. She returned his gaze with one unconvinced raised eyebrow.

"You do realize," she said, "that *Macbeth* ends with the guy's head on a stake."

"We'll write that story when we come to it."

The paper still smelled of the mimeograph ink. Monica drummed her fingers on the pale, purplish typing. Max's instructions had been simple: take this sheet, read it, study it, and wait for a meeting in Mr. Moore's old office. She'd done the first, letting her eyes scan the written passage of the Bible he'd read at the meeting.

Just. Pure. Lovely. Good report.

As far as studying, though—what good did it do to study someone else's fantasy? She wasn't exactly the pure and lovely type, at least not that anybody'd ever said. If these were the new requirements, she had nothing to offer.

So she waited. Tony Manarola had been behind the closed door for what seemed like ages. Or at least three cups of coffee. Zelda waited too, dutifully writing something on a pad of paper, getting up to go to the pencil sharpener every time Monica ventured to the coffeepot. The rest of the staff writers had been a little antsy, finally opting to step out for a smoke.

Monica studied her now, dying to snatch the pencil from the woman's hand and ask her about her dalliances with Edward Moore. There was a story—the humble immigrant janitress and the lonely, irascible businessman. What secrets were locked inside that graying-blonde head of hers? Monica herself knew a little something about carrying on an illicit affair, but those two had no barriers to thwart their affection.

Zelda raised her eyes to the ceiling and tapped her lip thoughtfully with the pencil.

"I know about you and Edward Moore," Monica said, without ever really planning to do so.

Zelda looked at her straight on. "What do you know?"

"That you loved each other."

Zelda visibly gathered herself, sitting taller and drawing the pad of paper closer. "We did not."

Monica got up and moved to the other side of the table, sidling right up to the woman, who flipped her notepad upside down as if protecting her very thoughts from attack.

"It's all right," Monica said, wanting to assure the woman about both the notes and the affair. "And I'm sorry about what I said earlier in the meeting, about you being just a cleaning woman. Obviously you were so much more—"

"Stop this!" Zelda's accent worked to make the command sound like hissing steam. "There are things that are proper and things that are not, and I will not speak of it."

"What's improper? You're a woman, he's—was—a man. A bachelor, even, as far as I know. Unless you—" she cupped her hand over her mouth, catching the secret. "Oh, Zelda. Don't tell me you have a husband stashed away somewhere. Talk about bringing the old country into the modern age. I never would've taken you for a—"

Before she could say another word, the left side of her face exploded in stinging pain as Zelda's palm crashed against it.

"A lady does not speak of these things. I do not speak of these things. Not like you modern girls, flaunting yourselves with your smoking and your sex."

"Hey," Monica said, holding her cool hand to her burning cheek, "I don't flaunt anything."

Zelda made a noise that only a speaker of her native tongue could make. "Of course you do. All those nights drinking and dancing, and enticing other girls to follow. It is a shame."

"Edward didn't think so."

Monica knew the comment would be more hurtful than any slap, and she waited for Zelda's face to turn as red as her own. Instead of looking wounded, however, the older woman took on an expression of compassion—close to pity.

"Edward always worried about you. Going to those places."

"He said that?"

"More than once. And if he was here the day that awful man came . . ."

Monica felt herself on the precipice of guilt for having been such a burden to the man, until a certain resentment took over.

"Why didn't he say anything?"

"Would you have listened?"

For that she had no answer, at least not one that would satisfy either of them, so she dug into her purse, found her mirror, and checked to see what damage Zelda had done to her face.

"I should not have done that to you."

"No kidding, Katie." The sting had disappeared, but the tinge of pink remained.

"If you like, someday I will tell you about Edward. Better you should know the truth, rather than to make up your own story. Is that not so?"

"I suppose." But she didn't care anymore about Mr. Moore and Zelda Ovenoff, if they had a torrid affair or true love or a simple, secret friendship. She positioned her mirror, seeing one brown eye, encased in black kohl, beneath a brow tweezed to a thin, perfect arch. A modern eye for a modern girl.

"You modern girls." What did she care of one old woman's disdain?

She snapped the compact closed just as the door to Mr. Moore's office opened to allow Tony Manarola, looking more shifty and stooped than usual, to exit. The man shuffled straight to the rack, where he retrieved his overcoat and hat before taking his silent leave. Max stood in the doorway, watching.

"What'd you do to him?" Monica asked. "Knock him upside the head with your Bible or something?"

"Just talk." He crooked his finger, beckoning. "You're next."

She walked as if the worn wooden floor were piled with snow, her feet growing numb with each step, and when she stepped across the threshold, the chill spread to her entire body.

"No wonder Ed was such a crank," she said, vigorously rubbing her arms in an attempt to generate warmth. "It's colder than anything a lady ought to say in here. Ever hear of a radiator?"

"On the fritz." He gestured for her to sit down before settling himself behind Mr. Moore's plain, empty desk.

"Well, then we better make this quick before I turn into a penguin."

"Clever," he said in a way that wouldn't allow her to believe him.

Perhaps it was a good thing the office was so frigidly cold. It would keep her from getting too comfortable, too compliant. The cold sharpened her mind, kept her on edge, though it did tend to draw her to the only spot of warmth in the room—that being Max himself. She sat a little taller and thrust out her chin in defense.

"I meant what I said out there, you know. About keeping the Monkey Business column. I believe we do have readers who follow you and whatever shenanigans you choose to engage in. I'm merely suggesting a new focus."

"Let me guess. Tea parties? Tent revivals? Maybe a quilting bee?"

"No," he said, riffling through a pile of newspaper clippings. "Nothing quite so extreme. I thought you might be interested in this."

Max half stood from his seat to reach across the desk and hand her a square of newsprint. She, too, had to stand to take it, and rather than return to her chair, chose instead to ease one hip on the desk. When she did, their faces were at the same level—equal for a second—until he sat back down.

What he'd handed her was a photograph of a woman. Not a movie star, not some grande dame of politics. Just a plain, ordinary woman—*plain* being the kindest word possible to describe her features. The photograph was close-up and unflattering. More like a candid shot than anything the woman posed for.

"Am I supposed to know who this is?"

"Read the caption."

Monica unfolded the small strip below the photograph and read the brief lines.

ANTI-FLIRT LEADER, Miss Alice Reighly, is president of a club whose members say they are tired of being whistled at.

She looked up at Max. "So?"

"So, that's your next assignment."

She slid off the desk and returned to her chair. "Assignment as in, what?"

"As in, find that club, join in, and write about it. Let us see what happens when Monkey gives up the business of flirting."

He looked so smug sitting there behind the desk, nothing like the sweet guy who had shared a drink with her in a bank vault. There was an accusation lurking behind his cool facade, and she could either squirm beneath the unspoken weight of it or force him to speak it outright.

"What are you getting at?"

"It's an opportunity for investigation, just like you said you wanted to do. Go, blend in, find out just what these women are trying to accomplish by taking a stand against flirting."

"Are you calling me a flirt, Mr. Moore?"

Her intent had been to make him squirm, but he appeared to have anticipated her question and dodged it easily.

"It's what makes you perfect for the story. You look surprised."

"Insulted is more like it."

"You flirted with me the first day we met."

"I wanted you to feel welcome."

"It was my uncle's funeral."

"I wanted to lighten the mood."

"I don't think you realize that you're doing it. Flirting, I mean. More than that, I don't think you understand how dangerous it can be. A fellow could get the wrong impression—think you're the type of girl that you aren't."

The memory of Bernardo and his men flitted through her mind, but she kicked it away with a cross of her legs and leaned forward. "And just what kind of a girl do you think I am, Max?"

"You see?" He popped out of his chair and paced the width of the desk, hands jammed down into the pockets of his slacks.

"There you go again. I don't think you ladies realize what it does to a guy—the thoughts it puts into his head when you bat your eyes and show your legs, or come running when we whistle."

"Who's whistling?"

"That guy in the car when we were walking to the deli. And even that gangster, King."

"Well, he didn't kill us, did he? These might just be the big brown eyes that saved your keister."

He was directly in front of her now, leaning against the desk. "I worry about you."

She went a little flippy inside and moved her foot in a slow, calculated circle, hoping to buy both Max's attention and a little time to calm the tiny waves of pleasure at the thought of his concern.

"Tell me," she said at last, "this worry of yours. Is it just for me? Or for all of the fairer sex?"

"I'm trusting you to do the right thing for both. Now go. Be a journalist; find the story."

At some point the room had ceased to be so cold, or maybe her own body, fueled by pride and protection, simply brought itself to a compromising comfort. Either way, she remained motionless until Max, in a move of obvious dismissal, returned to his place behind the desk and began shuffling through his clippings once more.

❧ CHAPTER 12 ❧

Don't smile at flirtatious strangers—save them for people you know.
ANTI-FLIRT CLUB RULE #6

THE FIRST HURDLE was finding the meeting. For a woman bent on changing the way of women, Alice Reighly was sure secretive about the meeting place. It took an entire afternoon with Anna manning the telephone directory, calling every *Reighly, A.* in the book, asking if she (or he) was the one affiliated with the club. They found her just in time, as there was a meeting that very night. It took an hour combing through city maps to find the address on Harvard Street, then two streetcars, and finally half a block's walking before coming across a hand-lettered scrap of canvas hanging from the banister of a row of small apartments.

ANTI-FLIRT CLUB
7:30
DOWNSTAIRS (BASEMENT)

Basement. At least she'd dressed warm—wool skirt, sweater, and galoshes. The perfect outfit to blend in with the other plain

153

Janes bent on wiping the wink off the face of the earth. Her crushed-velvet hat was pulled low over her ears, but she maintained that its silk lining served dual purposes: to warm her ears and serve as a reminder that no serious journalist should ever relinquish her grip on fashion.

A walkway stretched along the fronts of the apartments, bending around the corner of the last in the row. She walked cautiously, hunkered down, embracing more secrecy than she'd felt with any speakeasy. She should have called Max, let him know the address so when some lowbrow tabloid unapologetically reported the discovery of a pretty girl found chopped up after being lured by the promise of a more pious existence, he'd be able to identify the body.

The walkway ended with a set of narrow steps dimly lit by a single bulb and a strip of light peeking out from beneath a solid door at the bottom. She took a deep breath before taking the first step, then held it for all the rest, exhalation being the promised reward for not turning back. Once there, she pressed her ear against the door, hoping to hear some clue that she'd come to the right place. Nothing—although the muffled silence could be attributed to the cushion of silk and velvet between her ear and the door.

Then, the sound of conversation. Women, and giggles, and footsteps descending the stairs at a quick pace.

". . . and so I told him, 'Look, Mr. Morton. You might be my boss, but that doesn't give you access to my personal files, if you know what I mean. I'm a secretary, not a secret Mary.'"

"So'd you slap him?"

"Nah. I'm two weeks behind on my rent already. I just—oh, hello."

The women appeared to be close to Monica's age, and since

the narrowness of the stairwell wouldn't permit them to walk side by side, the first sped up for the final steps and came straight to Monica, hand outstretched.

"I'm Junie. Are you here for the club?"

"I am," Monica said, surprised by the girl's grip. Mr. Morton had better mind his mischief.

"I'm Stella," the second girl said, keeping her own hands firmly clasped within each other. "What's your name?"

"Maxine," Monica said without hesitation. It was a decision she'd come to on the second streetcar—a necessary step to protect her anonymity. Thankfully, neither girl had offered a last name, leaving her free to guard her own.

"Good to meet you." This from Junie, obviously the more talkative of the two. "Come on, we'll show you in." She grabbed the door and dragged it open—no easy feat, as it appeared to be made of solid steel. Stella entered first, and Monica followed, thankful to be sandwiched between two returning veterans of flirting forbearance.

They entered a plain hallway, lit only by the light coming from an open door halfway down.

"Why all the underground secret stuff?" Monica asked, instinctively dropping her voice to a whisper.

"Oh, it's not a secret," Junie said, further establishing herself as the more forthright of Monica's two new friends. "I think it's just part of Miss Reighly's philosophy of modesty."

"Interesting." Though she'd hoped it was more to do with a fear of attack by forward-thinking flappers.

While the journey thus far had been spartan and cold, crossing into the actual meeting space more than made up for the previous eerie atmosphere. The room itself was set up modestly with rows of chairs numbering no more than twenty and a battered wooden podium at the front. No flowers or ribbons or decorations of any kind. What the room lacked in ostentation, it more than made up for in charm. And warmth. Obviously the beneficiary of an active heating system, the room offered a warm embrace and encouragement for a girl to banish her overcoat to one of the rows of hooks along the back wall. Monica was wrestling with the buttons of her own when a different kind of warmth assaulted her—that in the form of a bleached blonde determined to help her with the process.

"Welcome! I'm Arlene. Let me get that for you."

"I'm fine," Monica said, knowing her notepad and pencil were tucked into the lining.

"Nonsense. Since we don't have any men around, somebody's got to help a girl out."

In a flash, Monica's coat was gone and Arlene was enveloped by a flock of chattering girls. She'd been prepared to face a roomful of crab apples; instead, she found herself in the midst of vibrant, vivacious voices streaming from women of all shapes and sizes—most of them her own age. Nobody looked like she'd fallen out of a fashion magazine, but neither did anybody lack a comfortable, modern style. These were shopgirls and secretaries with bobbed hair and light makeup. Quite a few were smoking cigarettes, and an impromptu foxtrot lesson was taking place in a corner at the front of the room.

One by one they stopped and grabbed her hand. Lucy, Francine, Dalia, Marie.

"Maxine," she said, over and over, until she believed it more than she didn't.

A girl named Emma Sue with soft, rounded features to complement a mass of equally rounded curls took Monica's arm and led her to a long table covered with a white cloth, where platters of doughnuts and pots of coffee waited.

"Thanks," Monica said, taking a steaming cup from a tall, skinny redhead. She grabbed a doughnut from the top of one of the pyramids and submerged it.

"You're a dunker!" Emma Sue exclaimed with the enthusiasm of finding a long-lost sister.

Monica matched her tone. "Is there any other way?"

She'd eaten the pastry to a C when the staccato sound of a gavel pierced through the conversations.

"We're starting," Emma Sue said, and though Monica was perfectly capable of finishing her snack and finding a seat on her own, she gulped down the last of it, putting the empty cup in a washtub with all the others so she could stay by the girl's side.

"Have you ever heard Miss Reighly speak?" Emma Sue asked as they headed up the aisle.

"No," Monica said. "I only just heard about her a few days ago."

"In the newspaper?"

"Yep." True enough.

"You're in for a treat. She's fab, but be sure to listen close. She talks real soft."

"I wanted to take notes," Monica said with a wistful glimpse toward the line of coats on the wall. How would she ever find her own again?

"Oh, it's not like that. Not like a lecture or anything. There's no test. Well, I guess in a way there is. The test comes later, when you're out there."

"Out where?"

Emma Sue gestured vaguely. "You know, out walking around."

They'd made their way to the third row and were about to slide into two empty seats when a mimeographed paper was shoved into her hand.

"What's this?" Monica asked.

"Oh," Emma Sue said. "Those are the rules."

"The rules?"

"Precepts, guidelines, whatever you want to call them." She waved the girl with the stack of papers away, saying she already had a copy, thank you.

"What am I supposed to do with them?"

"Read them, silly. It's why we're all here, isn't it?"

Emma Sue fell into conversation with another girl, leaving Monica to read the purple print on the page.

ANTI-FLIRT CLUB RULES

1. Don't flirt: those who flirt in haste oft repent in leisure.

"Oh, brother," Monica said, rolling her eyes to the ceiling. Any hope she had that she wasn't in for a lecture from the original Mrs. Grundy disappeared with that sentence. She'd never once felt the need to "repent" of a flirtation. If you didn't count Charlie, that is. And that wasn't so much repenting as it was coming to her senses—something for which she deserved a little credit.

As if to avoid further judgment, she folded the paper into a neat little square and wished for a pocket to slip it into. By now her head was quite warm under her hat, so she took it off, set it top-down on her lap, and dropped the list inside.

"No need to keep it under your hat," Emma Sue said, jabbing Monica with her elbow and snorting at her own joke.

Monica offered no more than a polite smile before turning her attention to the plain, diminutive woman behind the podium.

Alice Reighly was substantially more attractive in real, animated life than the photograph in the newspaper allowed. Small in stature, her head barely cleared the podium, behind which she stood perfectly still, hands folded and resting as she scanned the room, waiting for the soprano chatter to die down. Obviously the gavel was not her weapon of choice, and she appeared ready to wait until dawn, but eventually the girls started hushing each other, and the chairs chorused in scooches as they turned to face forward. Not until utter silence had been achieved did Alice Reighly unclasp her hands, grasp the edges of the podium, and say, "Good evening, ladies."

"Good evening," they chorused back.

"My, what a nice, big group we have here this evening. Word must be getting out. Did you see me in the newspaper?" She punctuated this question with a cute, quick little gesture of a film starlet, to the rousing approval of the audience. Their cheers drove her to hide her face briefly, then grip the podium again as if to signal that the fun and games were over and it was time to get down to business.

"I want to welcome all of you tonight to our little club, especially those who are here for the first time. I won't make you stand up, but I hope you've been made to feel welcome."

Monica's newest and dearest friend patted her hand. Why hadn't she insisted on the aisle seat? She could have gotten up, grabbed her coat, and headed for the door before the next sentence. Instead, she leaned over to touch her shoulder briefly to Emma Sue's and determined to hear and memorize every one of Alice Reighly's words.

"Ladies—and you know that is the only title I will ever bestow on you. 'Women' seems somehow clinical, and 'girl' does not reflect the level of sophistication for which I hope to see you all strive. You are not 'dames' or 'shebas' or any of the modern, derogatory terms the uncultured man on the street might hurl at you. And you are nobody's 'baby' but your own mother's."

This last bit provoked a healthy spate of laughter, another chorus from which Monica abstained, though her lips succumbed to a smile.

"You, my sisters, are ladies. Through and through. And though we may seem at times to be nothing more than victims of objectification, I believe—I stake my reputation and my heart on this truth—that if we will strive to comport ourselves as ladies, the world around us will embrace our efforts, and we will eventually turn back this tide of harassment and assault."

Applause and cheers. This time Monica joined in, lest her abstinence rouse suspicion. As it was, she hoped nobody noticed she held her fingers crossed as she clapped, keeping her eyes closed and repeating *nobody's "baby" but your mother's* three times. Whether or not she would ultimately agree with what the woman had to say, she was determined to work the clever phrase into the next column—with full attribution, of course.

"Just the other day," Alice Reighly continued, "I observed a young lady walking on the sidewalk in front of the drugstore. I say 'lady' out of a spirit of kindness, though her actions do little to justify the title. When she was not three steps away from the door, a man leaned out of his car window and howled like he was a licensed wolf. No doubt if she'd heard this same sound coming from the dark of the woods she would have run for shelter, but given the setting of the urban street, she abandoned her errand to turn and strike a pose for his pleasure."

Monica could well picture the scene. So well, in fact, she half expected Alice to describe the woman as a cute, petite brunette with Louise Brooks hair and a fox-fur collar.

"That woman rewarded his behavior, you see. The next time he howls at a woman he will expect the same reaction, and my fear is that he will soon be unsatisfied unless his wanton attention is acknowledged. I do not consider myself a prude, nor would I wish that slur to be associated with our club. I simply encourage you to refrain from open flirtations with strangers, for both your own reputations and the protection of the freedoms of our sex."

No amount of finger-crossing and repeating would enable Monica to remember all of these words. Miss Reighly was soft-spoken and eloquent, and Monica really did need to lean forward in her seat and focus all her attention in order to catch every phrase. This was not the fist-wielding passion of one of Mom's suffragette sisters, nor did her language drip with moral preaching. Still, there was something about the message that settled right at the base of Monica's spine, eventually clawing itself up vertebra by vertebra every time a memory proved to illustrate a dangerous scenario.

"And so," she said, in a blessed tone of conclusion, "I am happy to report that I was able to meet with the mayor last week, and he has agreed to allow us to declare the week of March 4 Anti-Flirting Week."

Applause, applause, punctuated by declarations of wonder and joy—all of it loud enough to disguise Monica's derisive snicker. As the noise died down, one woman near the front stood up and, to Monica's relief, asked exactly what such a week would entail.

"An excellent question," Alice Reighly said. "Those of us in this room have committed ourselves to resisting the urge to flirt with men on the street. Our week in March will extend those efforts, wherein I will challenge all of you to remain flirt-free in every area of your lives for the week. And I hope the publicity generated will allow others to join our cause."

"With all due respect," said another girl with peroxide-blonde hair and bright-red lips against her pale skin, "I don't know how many more girls we can fit down here. We might have to move to an auditorium or somethin'."

"Well, of course I don't expect them all to come *here*," Miss Reighly said after allowing her own laughter to dip briefly in with the others'. "I'm hoping young women throughout the city will be flirt-free out in our streets and in their homes or places of business. Everywhere."

Flirt-free. Fun-free. Monica crossed her arms. And her legs— for once not giving a hoot about how much leg was showing.

"How are we going to let everybody know about it?" This from Junie, the girl she'd met on the stairs.

"We're preparing a press release," Miss Reighly said. "And sending it to select papers. And it would be lovely if a few of you could be here Thursday midmorning for a photograph to run along with it."

This invitation garnered squeals from several girls, along with loud protests from those who wouldn't dream of being in a newspaper photograph.

"Once the public sees you—" Miss Reighly accompanied the pronoun with a wide, sweeping gesture—"and can see the Anti-Flirt Club is not merely a bunch of dried-up old prunes—what's that slang term those flappers use? Mrs. Grumpy?"

Mrs. Grundy. Another voice in the audience corrected her aloud.

"Ah yes. Mrs. Grundy, crab apples, wet blankets, what have you. When they see that we are comprised of healthy, vibrant, beautiful young women, they'll listen to what we have to say."

Monica scanned the room as inconspicuously as she could, outwardly applauding, inwardly verifying Alice Reighly's assessment. For the most part, she agreed. Besides the occasional dowdy dress and long hair, these were perfectly decent girls, but she couldn't imagine any one of them capturing a man's attention— much less drawing him in—without a concentrated, targeted flirtation. Why, she herself, as vibrant and attractive as she objectively knew herself to be, would lead a lonely, man-free existence if not for the practiced use of her eyelashes, her pout, her legs, her list of well-crafted suggestions. And even that was no guarantee. Take Max Moore for instance. She could flirt with him until her head fell off, and he wouldn't even notice. Maybe that should be the topic of the next meeting: men who find flirting to be a nuisance.

"Are there any more questions before we adjourn to partake of our lovely refreshments?"

Monica's head swam with questions, but she knew her anonymity hinged on a low profile, so she tucked them into the back of her mind and stood as the others around her did.

Alice Reighly then said, "Remember, girls. Don't flirt. Those who flirt in haste . . ."

"Repent in leisure!"

This was spoken in one resounding voice resplendent with feminine power. For a moment, Monica feared they might be called upon to recite all ten principles, but after this proclamation, the crowd broke into its previous smaller groups. Emma Sue excused herself to go take her turn serving coffee, but not before steering Monica straight into Alice Reighly's path and making an introduction.

"Hello, Maxine. So nice to see a new face."

Oddly enough, it was more difficult to hear her voice standing practically nose-to-nose than it had been when she was behind the podium.

"Thank you," Monica said, resisting the urge to shout. "I enjoyed your speech."

"And what made you want to join us this evening?"

"Oh, you know. Men . . . cars . . ."

Alice nodded, understanding. "They will treat us the way we allow them. Only we can demand and enforce respect."

"And how." It was all she could think to say, and it must have been enough because Alice gave her a warm pat on the arm before moving on to some other wide-eyed girl who was studying the list of rules as if bent on devouring them.

Monica made a break to the back of the room and walked along the wall of coats, finally finding her own. She shrugged into it, stuffing her own list of rules into one pocket while checking the other for her notebook. First stop she could—at a diner or coffee shop or even a little place nearby she visited with Charlie once last November—she would sit down and script out everything she could remember. Not for her own sake, of course, but for the sake of the story. Much of this was nothing but a load of applesauce. She'd had occasion to look over Tony's shoulder to see that sometimes the pages of his little notepad were dotted with blood. He'd been that close to the scene of the crime. Alice Reighly and her ilk were nothing less than a crime to modernity, no matter how many big words the woman wrapped around her weapons.

Several of the girls fluttered good-bye upon her exit, and she managed to leave without making any promise to return. She'd had enough. After retracing her steps in the dimly lit hallway, she flung the basement door wide open and let it fall shut behind her as she raced up the steps to the street level. It wasn't until she was at the top, when she knew for certain none of the sirens below would pull her back in, that she exhaled the last of the overly warm basement air and took in the full, fresh, stinging cold.

CHAPTER 13

In peace there's nothing so becomes a man
as modest stillness and humility.
SHAKESPEARE, *HENRY V*

MAX CONTINUED TO PACE the sidewalk in front of the apartments, giving himself one chance after another to leave before she found him. What kind of an editor follows a reporter to a story, anyway? Would he lurk over Tony's shoulder as they watched a body being loaded into the coroner's wagon? But then, he hadn't hurt Tony's feelings with a new assignment. Quite the contrary. Just the other day the man had called in with a lead on a story about a three-legged dog that led federal agents to the home of a man thought to have buried two of his three ex-wives in a garden plot beside his house.

"They think the fourth leg might actually be buried there too," Tony had said, his normally stoic tone losing ground to an enthusiasm obvious even over the phone. "People love a good dog story. What's more heartwarmin' than that?"

"Get the story," Max had said. It was a start.

Monica, however, had disappeared. He'd not seen a wisp of her since that meeting in his office, and while he knew her work ethic to be flighty at best, he had no way of knowing if she intended to follow through on his assignment. Phone calls to her boarding-house had been met with messages that she was unavailable, and even a visit from Trevor delivering a check written for a modest amount had the boy returning with a tale of leaving the envelope with a sleepy old lady.

Luckily, he'd been able to talk with a young woman named Anna, who not only knew the address but offered to accompany him, should he need her to do so. Declining, he found the meeting and now waited, as he had for the previous hour, for Monica to emerge.

At the first trickle of female voices, Max flattened himself against the back side of a massive tree, but the women who spilled out from the top of the staircase turned in the opposite direction, so absorbed in conversation that they would not have noticed him anyway.

Following them came a full minute of emptiness when he could have walked away, but then the staccato of a familiar step caught his attention, and there she was, hitting the final step at nearly a full-out run, then stopping at the top to catch her breath.

Slowly, with just a hint of trepidation, he approached her, coming up behind as she stopped, her hand on top of the iron banister.

"How'd it go?"

Though the question itself was innocuous, his appearance must have been anything but, because Monica's resulting scream was so shrill, it ricocheted off the surrounding buildings. Acting on some instinct to stifle the sound, Max grabbed her, pulling her close and covering her mouth with his gloved hand.

For such a small thing, she was surprisingly strong, as evidenced by her efforts to wrest herself from his grasp, and he was about to let her go when an onslaught of footsteps and female shouts rose from the stairwell, and his own fear caused him to cinch tighter.

"It's all right—" The pain of a set of sharp teeth clamping down through his glove kept him from saying anything more. Max released Monica, sending her spinning away from him until they faced each other, their breath panted puffs between them.

"Do you know this guy?" asked one of the two young women who came to stand flank-to-flank with Monica.

"It's me," he said, drawing his scarf lower and raising his hat. "Max."

"Aw," the other girl cooed. "He calls her Max. That's cute."

"I'm all right," Monica said, stepping away from the balustrade. "I know him."

Confused by the girl's comment about her name, Max attempted to further clarify the situation. "Yes. I'm her b—"

"My brother," Monica said. "He startled me is all. He's here to see me home. Ma don't like it if I'm out too late on my own."

The crowd of girls, now grown to a dozen, hit a unanimous note of understanding and began whispering among themselves. Their hands might have been cupped around their mouths, but they made little effort to hide the fact that their eyes cut straight to him.

"And, ladies," Monica continued with a sharp swing of her purse, "he's single, loves Jesus, and I guarantee has never whistled at a girl from his car." She walked over and lightly socked his arm. "Isn't that right, big brother?"

"Absolutely," he said, beginning to enjoy the idea of an enraptured audience. "But then again, I don't have a car."

The street rang with the peal of women's laughter, and Max stood a little taller, allowing himself to smile along with them as if he hadn't been the originator of the joke.

"Oh, brother," Monica said in a tone that had no familial connotation whatsoever. She tucked her arm in his and turned him toward the street, calling, "'Night, ladies," over her shoulder as they walked.

"Yes, good night," he called too, keeping his head turned until a yank on his arm got his attention.

"What are you doing here?" she hissed into his sleeve.

"Why do they think your name is Max?"

"I told them my name was Maxine. You know, to protect my anonymity."

"Clever."

They were still whispering, though they'd long left the range of being heard by anybody who would care about their conversation.

"You haven't answered my question. What are you doing here?"

"I haven't heard a word from you since we spoke in my office. I didn't know if you were intending to do the story or not."

"So you're checking up on me?"

"In a manner of speaking, yes."

"So you worry about my safety whether I'm going to speak-easies or drinking coffee with spinsters?"

"You could see it that way, I suppose. Or maybe I'd just like to know if you intend to do your job or not."

"I'll have a column ready for next week's paper."

That should have been enough to satisfy him, but she was looking up with such mischief in her eyes, he had to pry a little deeper.

"First impression?"

"Sweet girls."

He laughed. "You speak as if you have such an advantage of age. I'll wager at least half of those women are older than you by three years or more."

"Maybe I'm lumping myself in with them."

She was doing it again—flirting, though by now he wondered if she had any consciousness of doing so. Almost like a nervous tic. And as such, he must learn to ignore it, lest it lead him down a path that neither of them intended.

"Well," he said, "since everybody thinks I'm escorting you home, I suppose I ought to do so."

"How gallant."

He ignored her sarcasm. "Are we heading the right way?"

"It's early yet. No need to go straight home, is there? How about I show you a little bit of our fair city first?"

"It's dark."

"It's beautiful, especially by moonlight. Or streetlight at least. Hides the dirt. And all those big white buildings—"

"Are closed and locked up."

"Oh, who cares about what goes on inside. Bunch of old men in suits trying to hide their lies."

"This seems to be a strange place to live for someone so averse to politics."

"I don't hate politics; I simply find them endlessly amusing. If you like, I can take you to a few places where you'll see the leopards in their true spots."

Tempting. That was the word. Not the idea of unveiling elected officials but simply spending time with her. A light snow was falling—so light it was barely noticeable until a particular flake fell on an eyelash or cheek. Nonetheless, she tucked herself against him as if they were walking headlong into a blizzard. It was a quiet neighborhood, save for the occasional puttering automobile. She would have been perfectly safe without him, maybe more so if he were given the occasion to follow through on some of his less gentlemanly thoughts. The experience of the past few minutes had taught him that the best weapon against those thoughts was to keep talking.

"Tell me more about this evening."

"Nope." She made a slicing motion with her free hand. "It'll ruin my writing. I need to let everything soak for a while, write down my thoughts and the bits and pieces I want to get perfect."

Now there was a relief. "All the more reason to get you straight home."

"You would think so."

Her response sounded more like a trap than a concession, so he chose to ignore it and instead regale her with all the details he knew of Tony's current story.

"Poor dog," she said, surprising him with her sympathy. "I have a six-toed cat who comes around my place sometimes."

"Six toes?"

"Maybe more. Hard to tell. And he's not really mine. I don't know if he belongs to anybody. He must have a particular home in the winter. I'd like to think so, anyway. Someplace with a blanket bed, maybe bowls of warm milk at night. He quits showing around so much when it turns cold. I guess it's one of the reasons I'm looking forward to spring."

"If he's that footloose, you might want to be on the lookout for some six-toed kitten you could have as your very own."

She laughed. "Oh no. I'm not ready for that kind of responsibility. I can't even keep a boyfriend, let alone—"

She stopped abruptly, as if surprised herself at the turn in topic, and he chose not to press.

The snow continued to be lazy—fat and wet, each flake dissolving the minute it touched the surface of the sidewalk or a sleeve. Though they were far from alone, something about the intermittent snow made their surroundings feel like silence, and they continued walking at a slow, even pace, Max shortening his steps to match hers.

"I'll bet you don't have nights like this in California," she said after a time.

He answered, "Not even close," encompassing a lot of things. No snow, naturally, rarely cold enough to see one's breath, and never a night walking with a woman nestled beside him.

"Do you miss it yet?"

"No. Not really. I wasn't there long enough to think of it as home. In fact, I don't think anybody's been there long enough to think of it as home. Everything's too new. Too perfect."

"How can anything be too perfect?"

"Take this, for example." He pointed at the line of railcar track embedded in the street. "A hundred and fifty years ago, this very street was probably nothing more than a dirt road. Then maybe cobbled. Then paved. During all that time, men drove horse-drawn buggies up and down and up and down, until the electric streetcar came along."

"Thank goodness it did, or I'd never get anywhere."

"But the streetcar required electricity. And that meant poles and wires, cluttering up the sky." They'd come to a corner. He stopped and reached his free hand high and wide. "Just look at how beautiful this is."

"Like diamonds on velvet."

Her face was raised up, looking far beyond him. A single snowflake was melting among her thick black eyelashes. It was all he could do not to kiss her, and if she'd glanced his way, he would have lost that battle for sure. To be safe, he returned his attention to the sky.

"Imagine if that was marred by a bunch of wires. So now the power source is below us. Hidden, invisible, and ultimately more efficient."

"How do you know all this?" She sounded less impressed than he'd hoped.

"I found some papers in Uncle Edward's things. Apparently he was quite active in the movement to clean up the system."

"Really?" *Now* she sounded impressed. "I never would have thought he'd care about something like that."

"He chose to live in a neighborhood outside of the rail service. Maybe his own form of protest?"

"Maybe," she said. Then, "Speak of the devil."

The piercing beams of the railcar rounded the corner, and Monica grabbed his hand, running them to the opposite side of the street, where they'd board.

"Is this the right line to your place?" he asked as they waited for the car to reach its electric, screeching halt.

"I'll have to make a change at Fourteenth." She was on her way toward the steps, pulling her gloves off with her teeth before plunging her hand into her coat pocket. She was about to drop a nickel in the slot and ride away.

"Wait." Max clumsily eased himself between Monica and the car, fishing out two nickels of his own. "No sense my taking a cab from here. It'll cost a fortune."

"See? That's why you need a car."

Not even the bulk of her coat could completely hide her form as she ascended the steps. He couldn't possibly trust himself with a car.

They disembarked together ten minutes later in an area

decidedly different from where they'd boarded. Darker, rougher, where men and women moved like shadows.

"Changing lines?" he asked, trying to appear casual, though he inwardly cringed at the company.

"Eventually." She had no problem looking confident, and he suddenly knew what her neighborhood mice felt when confronted with her wayward six-toed cat. "I thought I'd show you a little bit of your new city that you might not see on your own. This is C Street."

He instantly understood. "No, thank you. I'd rather just see you home."

"I don't feel like going home yet." She was walking in front of him, only backward. Fearless of stumbling. "It's early. And I haven't been out in nearly a week. Just because I'm writing your silly assignment doesn't mean I have to give up all my fun, does it?"

He took a quick look around and lowered his voice. "I don't think it's a good idea for you to go into those places alone."

"So go with me."

"I think that's a worse idea."

"You're not even a little curious?"

"No."

"You're lying."

"You're right. But a little curiosity never hurt anyone."

"How do you know? It might have killed my cat."

He realized he'd been following her, matching step for step like some one-way impromptu tango. "I'll take my chances."

"Take a chance with me." She was actually beckoning with her fingers. "What's the worst that could happen?"

"Arrest." He poised his finger as if to tick off multiple examples.

"Don't be ridiculous."

"Beyond that—" he planted his feet—"it's just not something I do. Drink, that is. Not even if it were legal. Which it's not."

"Is it a Christian thing? 'Whatsoever things are pure' and all that?"

"That's part of it." They were standing in front of a crowded diner, not exactly the place he'd ever thought he'd be sharing his faith. "Why don't we go in there? Get a cup of coffee, maybe something to eat. I'm starved."

"I'm not." A glint had come to Monica's eye, something like what he'd seen in his office. A cold sheeting like she was freezing right in front of him. "But you go on ahead."

She had turned and gone five steps away before he caught up and grabbed her elbow.

"Monica, I said I don't want you to go in there alone."

She wheeled around. "Then prove it."

Her words and posture issued a challenge, and any choice to do otherwise fell away.

"You won't be sorry," she said without a hint of gloating at her obvious victory.

They continued past another diner, a Chinese restaurant, a pawnshop, and a cigar store—all of which appeared to be open for business despite the fact that the hour was approaching ten. Nobody on the streets seemed to have any inclination to go home, but even in these few moments they appeared much less threatening. Still, he would have felt better seeing even one police officer patrolling, especially when the street grew darker and narrower, when the warmth of yellow-lit storefronts bathed in streetlights became rows of three-story walk-ups with windows more dark than not.

He walked behind Monica, telling himself it was for her protection, as he would be able to see any potential attacker from a block away. He didn't tell her as much, though, for fear that she would either be offended or once again call his bluff by throwing herself into danger.

"This is it," she said without any preliminary hint that they were closing in. How she distinguished this particular house from the others was beyond him, as it was too dark to see any painted numbers and more than one had a dim light shining above the porch.

"How do you know?"

She looked at him like he was an idiot. "I've been here before."

Straight up the steps she went. Max would have preferred to lead the way just in case some armed gangster stood behind the door. But when he mentioned the possibility, she laughed.

"You've been reading too many dime novels, Mr. Moore."

"If you'll recall," he whispered, hoping she'd follow his example in doing so, "we had an armed gangster in our offices not long ago."

She rolled her eyes and tsked. "I am never going to live that down, am I? Trust me, the gangsters only come out if you don't know the code. Still want to go first?"

"No."

Taking on the posture of an orator, she said, "'Once more unto the breach, dear friends, once more; or close the wall up with our English dead.'"

Shakespeare again. He'd have to bone up if he wanted to keep up with her conversation. "It's the American dead that worry me."

She cupped her palm against his cheek. "'In peace there's nothing so becomes a man as modest stillness and humility: but when the blast of war blows in our ears, then imitate the action of the tiger.'"

"The war's over," he said, though her passion was coming close to kindling a mirrored one in him.

"The one over there, maybe. But there are a million battles right under our noses, and you don't even see it. Now, come on, tiger."

She rang the front bell, and a few seconds later, the door was opened by a woman with skin the color of freshly brewed coffee. She wore a red dress and a sequined headband wrapped around a mass of sleek, black curls. A ribbon of smoke curled from a cigarette in a long, thin ivory holder.

"Monica, baby," she said in a voice rich as cream.

"Celine." Monica stood tiptoe as the woman bent to exchange a kiss on each cheek. When the kisses were over, she said, "This is Max."

"Max, eh? Short for Maximilian?" Celine brought the ivory cigarette holder to her lips and took a long drag while studying him from head to toe and back.

"Yes, as a matter of fact." He wasn't sure if he should offer a kiss similar to Monica's greeting, and even though her right hand was occupied with smoking, he extended his anyway, waiting patiently for her to return the gesture.

"And how long have we known Max?"

"Awhile," Monica said. "He's practically family."

"Well," Celine said after another long look, proving she wasn't at all convinced, "I'd walk you in, but there's no one else right now to watch the front."

"Slow night?"

Celine shrugged. "It's early yet."

Monica grabbed his hand. "Come on. This is one of my favorite places."

They proceeded up the stairs, and as they passed the open doors of the bedrooms, he realized they were in somebody's actual home. He knew of restaurants with secret back rooms and underground clubs, but here there were framed photographs on the walls and quilt-covered beds. A new, dark idea struck.

"Wait a minute. This isn't a . . . ?" What term could he possibly use without causing offense? *Brothel? House of ill repute?*

"No," she said in that eerie way she had of diving into his thoughts. "My soul isn't that far fallen."

They came to a closed door, which she opened without hesitation. When it had closed behind them, they were in a narrow but not steep staircase lit with a single bulb. At the top was a second door, through which, as they climbed closer, he could hear faint sounds of music.

"We're actually going over to the flat next door," she explained over her shoulder. "It's a whole hidden third floor—no access from its own building."

"Smart," he said, feeling a twinge of guilt at his admiration.

"Now let's see," Monica was muttering as she studied a row of switches by the door. She hummed a bit of a familiar tune, then pressed the switches in a precise sequence. Faintly, over the music, he heard the replication of her tune in a series of chimes.

"Was that 'Take Me Out to the Ball Game'?"

"Yes," she said, pleased. "The proprietor played for the Senators for two years before they realized he was a Negro. I think this place is his way of getting revenge for that same kind of stupid law."

It hit him then that, upon crossing the threshold to this secret room, he would be knowingly breaking a law for the first time in his life. There was no separating the excitement from the fear churning in his stomach, and those elements—combined with a very real hunger—made him feel light-headed at the moment. So much, in fact, that it seemed his mind had left his body entirely, floating away with his better judgment, leaving the shell of himself to suffer the consequences of following a pretty girl on a snowy night. Wasn't that, in fact, the perfect beginning to a cautionary tale?

A small, square window near the top of the door slid open, and a dark face appeared, the whites of the eyes prominent as they searched out the waiting company.

"It's Monkey Business," Monica said, at which the little door was slammed shut, and the big door opened wide.

As soon as the door opened, the hint of music from the other side exploded into deep, layered jazz, leaving Max to wonder just how it—not to mention the sound of the crowd inside—had ever been contained.

"Monkey girl!" The man on the other side not only dwarfed Max by a good six inches, but he could not possibly be the owner of the establishment, as his nearly onyx-black skin would never allow him to pass as a white man for two minutes, let alone two years. The Monkey girl in question launched herself into his arms, and he swung her around as if she were no more than a child, then dropped her at Max's feet, saying, "An' who we got here?"

"This is Max. Max, this is Big Sam."

Big Sam took a step back. "Glad to see you got rid of that other fella. Never liked him."

"Oh, Sam," she said, "I don't think you'd like anybody."

Max extended his hand, tried not to wince at Big Sam's bigger grip, and said, "Good to meet you."

"Max is my new boss. At the paper."

Sam smiled, revealing two prominent gold teeth. "Well, how about that? This girl here, she somethin' else. Come in here, what was it, about five month ago? Late September. And ever since, people comin' in here all kinds of night askin' if this the place that Monkey girl writes about."

Monica turned to Max. "I come here all the time. I've probably written about this place more than any other."

"We do it up like family here," Sam said. "I ain't gonna pat you down, but I need to know if I have to worry about you shootin' up the joint."

"As in, with a gun?" Max asked, wondering if Big Sam knew just how ludicrous the question was. He didn't even own a gun, much less carry one around.

"He's straight," Monica said, patting Max's shoulder as if he were some sort of show horse. "You can't even imagine."

"Well, then," Sam said, backing away, "welcome to the Shangri-La."

The accompanying gesture had ten times more grandeur than the room could absorb. The entire space was one undivided room, with a bar set up along one side and a slightly raised platform on the other. There, a four-piece band consisting of piano, drum, saxophone, and clarinet played a sultry jazz number that may have been solely responsible for half of the heat in the room. A few tables were set up against the remaining walls, where small clusters of people sat amid pillars of cigarette smoke and empty glasses, but the heart of the room was its center—a space barely large enough for couples to maintain movement.

"Take off your coat," Monica said, shrugging out of her own and tossing it casually onto a pile under which must have been some sort of rack. "We can dance."

"I don't dance," Max said. Rather, shouted, given the volume of the music. He did, however, take off his coat as the near-sweltering heat of the space demanded. His inclination to simply drape it over his arm was thwarted when Monica grabbed it and threw it on top of hers.

"Then let's get a drink."

"I don't drink. You know that."

"Well, we have to do something, or Big Sam's gonna think you're a lawman. And you don't want to know what he does to sneaks."

She took his hand and led him to the bar, where she leaned over the rough-hewn wood so far that her feet dangled off the floor and ordered two of whatever was best. The man behind the bar was dressed in a starched white shirt and collar with a black bow tie, and he filled two squat glasses with a dark liquid without a single wayward splash.

"Pay the man," Monica said. "Four bits, am I right?"

"Yes, ma'am," the barkeep said.

"It looks trashy if a woman buys her own," she said, as if Max were hesitating due to frugality. Of course he would pay, both as a matter of etiquette and self-preservation, though he was already promising himself these would be the first and last drinks he would buy. When he made that same promise aloud to Monica, she raised her glass in a toast and said, "To the alpha and the omega of drinks," before downing half of it in one gulp. The other half, he assumed, would have to wait until she could untwist her face long enough to drink it.

"Not quite as smooth as Uncle Ed's whiskey?"

"Not by half." After a shuddering exhalation, she held the glass out to him. "Have a drink."

"No. But thanks just the same."

"If you don't, I'll have to drink it all. Can't let it go to waste."

"As you wish. But as soon as those glasses are empty, I'm taking you home."

Her face lit up with the thrill of a challenge, and he instantly regretted his words. Once again she brought the glass to her lips and tilted it, leaving a slick taste of the liquid on her lips.

"It's going to be a long night, Mr. Moore."

She left him little choice. He picked up his glass and took a burning swallow. Though he was inexperienced in the world of alcohol, he knew this was cheap but powerful liquor. By the time he set the empty glass on the bar, the stuff felt like it was burning a hole in his stomach. Monica, managing to keep the rim of the glass pressed against her bottom lip, laughed.

"My goodness, what you won't do to take a girl home." She opened the snap on her purse and pulled out a tuft of folded bills. The action caught the attention of the barkeep, who came immediately to her.

"Another round, ma'am?"

"Listen." She counted out the bills, four of them, and slid them across the bar. "I have a very important job for you. You see these glasses?" She clinked hers against his empty one. "No matter what, even if you have to drizzle in a few drops at a time, until I say so, don't let these go empty. Got it?"

He looked briefly at Max as if apologizing for his loyalty before saying, "Yes, ma'am." There was definitely more of a spring to his step when he scooped up the bills, left, and returned with a bottle. Max's glass was full again.

"Clever," he said, genuinely impressed. "But I'm not drinking that."

"It's drink or dance, Mr. Max."

Everything about her was inviting. The way her lips perched on the edge of the glass made him want to do the same. The way she swung her foot brought his own to life in the wake of the music. Reluctantly, he took his eyes away from her and surveyed the men and women coupled on the floor. The jazz sounded like a menagerie of moans, like heartache set to music, and the dancers clung to each other in the center of the room. It was a sight he'd never seen before. Not only because of the setting and circumstances, but the men and women—dark-skinned cheeks pressed against fair-skinned faces.

"Don't tell me you've never seen Negroes dancing before. Or just not with whites? Certainly they let the races mix in California."

"I'm not the authority," he said. "In fact, I've never given the subject much thought."

"What do you think about it now?"

His fingers closed around the glass, and he found the second drink to go down much smoother than the first. The moment he set it back down, empty, the bartender was on the spot to fill it again.

"That bad?"

"Not at all." How could he explain that this was one more layer to a strange new world he'd never had any intention of exploring? The music and the whiskey were twisting together, tying him in place, anchored by Monica's eyes. All night long he'd thought of nothing other than keeping her safe, and the way he felt right now, the greater the distance between them, the safer she'd be. "Finish your drink."

Her eyes checked his glass. "Finish yours."

"On three."

By agreement, they counted together, glasses less than an inch away from their respective lips, and when they declared, *"Three!"* he waited to see her follow through before doing the same. By the time the last drop had disappeared, he was wobbly both in his legs and in his head, but he somehow summoned the stealth to snatch her empty glass away and slam it upside down on the bar, his own beside it. When the bartender arrived yet again with his trusty bottle, Max put his hand over the upturned bottoms and said, "That's okay, buddy. We're done."

Monica pouted but hopped down from the stool. "Do you plan to devote your life to destroying other people's fun?"

Keeping his eye on her for all but the briefest of seconds, he crossed the room to get their coats. Not trusting her to leave under her own power, upon his return he took her arm, though with her drink to his three, she hardly needed the support, and ignored her question. The door to exit was on the opposite side of the entrance, to facilitate an evacuation in case of the threat of a raid, according to Monica, and there was no path to it other than traversing the dance floor. Suddenly, the result of inevitable friction with the other couples, Monica was pushed fully against him. Then, without his intent or permission, they were dancing. Rather pressed together, moving in a rhythm semirelated to the music around them. His mouth was full of the taste of liquor, his head with the smell of smoke, and his arms with this tiny, soft woman. None of it right. He might appear to be a man determined to destroy the pleasure of others, but for a few minutes at least, he would do nothing to spoil his own.

He bent low, felt her hair soft and sleek against his cheek, and asked, "What did you write about this place?"

"Just the things that are good. And pure." He felt her words through his skin. "Like you said to before you said to."

Nothing about this moment felt good or pure, and it wouldn't get any better by staying. He put his hands firmly on her shoulders, stepped back, and said, "There. You've had your drink and your dance. You won. Happy?"

"Blissful." By the look on her face, he almost believed it.

"Then we need to go."

This time he would not make the mistake of touching her at all. He waited for her to take the first step in the right direction and followed, stopping every few steps as she kissed cheeks and exchanged jokes about the boss man cutting short all her fun.

He was expecting another series of labyrinth-like tunnels to take them away from this place and was surprised to find that the door led straight to a third-story fire escape with a narrow iron staircase leading down to the alley behind the building. It wasn't until he began his descent that he felt the full effect of his drink, and he gripped the handrail despite its burning cold. After all, Monica was still walking ahead of him. One slip and they'd both tumble, with his body landing flat on top of hers. Nothing good or pure could come of that, either.

"You still going to take me home?" she asked when they safely reached land.

"Going to put you in a cab," he said, taking a quick mental count of the money in his wallet. There was still the question of getting himself home too.

"Not in this neighborhood you won't. Streetcars don't even stop here after ten."

"You might have told me that."

"You might have asked. But don't worry. A few blocks and you'll be in more familiar territory. The fresh air will clear your head."

Now there was a point they could agree on. She walked beside him; he not only matched her stride but trusted her to lead him, even though she'd given him no reason to trust her at all.

"You should read it sometime," she said after a substantial silence.

"What?"

"My column. About this place. Last October, I think, in case you have any of the old issues."

"Uncle Edward has them all in his office." And depending on just where they'd be able to hail a cab, he was closer to the office than home. "I'll look for it."

"I think you'll be surprised. Maybe I'm not such an empty-headed flapper after all."

"I never thought that for a minute. The whole reason I suggested the anti-flirting assignment is because I think there's more to you than what Monkey Business itself allows."

"Just read it," she said before breaking away and throwing her entire body into the hailing of a cab.

Unsurprisingly, a sleek auto with the word *Taxi* painted on its side headed straight for them. When it stopped, he opened the door and she climbed in immediately, scooting to the far side and patting the seat beside her in invitation. Max poked his head in, assessing the small, dark space, her smile, the fuzzed edges of his judgment.

"Tell the driver your address," he said, and upon the cabbie's estimated fare, handed a folded bill across the seat.

"What about you?" she asked, pouting again.

He touched his glove to his temple. "Head's not quite clear enough. Think I'd be better off walking. And one more thing?"

"Yes?" He must be imagining her hopefulness.

"I'll need your column tomorrow morning. First thing."

"Ten o'clock? Sharp?"

"Nine."

"Call Trevor. Tell him I'll have it at eight."

She leaned over, took the door's handle, and slammed it shut, leaving him to watch her disappear into the night.

MONKEY BUSINESS

"All the Dirt on Anti-Flirt"

This little Monkey doesn't like to brag, but she's been known to turn a few heads. What can you expect when a girl walks around in a perfect little package? Stylish clothes, careful makeup, and a hairstyle that will never see a braid or bun. She's a modern girl with modern dreams, and she likes all the perks that come from living free from pantaloons and petticoats. And so, what's a girl to do once the heads turn? To flirt or not to flirt? That is the question. If a man winketh, shall we not wink back? If he honketh his horn, shall we not smile and wave? Monkey's new club has the answer, and that answer is "No."

You might have noticed a little item in the papers, way in the back where nobody cares. Miss Alice Reighly and her group: the Anti-Flirt Club. If you're a woman ready to crawl back into the last century and wait for your cotillion escort to favor you with a dance, this might be the place for you. If you believe women should be silent, invisible, disappearing meekies, then you are a candidate. (Ladies only, please. They might find the presence of a man to be too frightening.)

There's a motto at the Anti-Flirt Club: "Those who flirt in haste repent in leisure." Ha! Ha! Any girl who's batted her eyes at the wrong sheik knows if she flirts in haste, she gets him first, before some other sheba takes him away.

Miss Reighly also says we aren't anybody's baby but our mothers'. True enough, I guess, but this Monkey remembers her mother marching in the streets for the vote. For equality. And what better way to show you're equal to a man than to give to him as good as he gives to you? Don't be fooled, my little monkey girls. Your power isn't in your vote. It's in your eyes. It's in any part of you that you can use to bend his will. Bat your eyes and blow a kiss. No reason you can't close the bank later.

✒ CHAPTER 14 ✒

I never gave away anything without wishing I had kept
it; nor kept it without wishing I had given it away.

LOUISE BROOKS

THE NEW EDITION of *Capitol Chatter* looked out from its familiar
perch in the magazine rack on the pharmacy wall. On the front
cover, modest yet above the fold, a small, serious picture of Max
Moore presided over the headline "The New Voice of *Capitol
Chatter*," directing readers to the editorial on page two where
Max-the-editor promised a new direction in content and tone.
He'd kept the actual text secret from the staff, and Monica knew
she'd have to shell out her own nickel if she wanted to read it.
That, or wait for the first disgruntled, disappointed, blood-lusting
customer to toss their copy in the gutter.

Then again, she could always just browse.

She ordered an egg cream at the counter before sauntering
over to the newspaper rack, where she ran her finger along the
titles, pretending great interest in each one. There were few other
customers in the place, and the gentleman in the white apron was

occupied with her egg cream, so with a nonchalant look around and behind, she slid the paper from the rack and opened to the second page.

"A Time to be Kind." That was the title of the piece, and with the first sentence Monica could hear his voice.

Edward Moore, the late editor of this publication, died alone. It's something I fear could happen to us all.

She read on about how Max wanted his publication to be a place where readers gathered to celebrate and rejoice, not to gawk at pain and vice. Yet somehow he wrote in such a way that condemned neither the writers nor the readers of the previous source of those exact elements. Her heart melted with his words, and she knew anybody else who read this would feel the same. He offered promises fueled by hope. Then, the final paragraph.

Even our lovable little Monkey seems ready to swing into new territory.

"Hey, lady! This ain't the liberry. You wanna read that, hand over a nickel."

Despite the innocent appearance of his starched white apron and cap, the guy behind the counter looked ready to do battle, even if his only missile was a tall glass of frothy egg cream.

Monica smiled, though he'd only see it in her eyes, as she held the newspaper to her face and fluttered it like a coquettish fan.

"Sorry, mister. I was just intrigued by the front page, about the paper turning all nice and everything."

"That rag," he said, setting the egg cream none too gently on the counter. "Not worth the pain of fishin' a nickel from your pocket."

"Gee," Monica said, lowering the paper to give him the benefit of her whole smile, "thanks, mister. That's awfully generous of you. And so unexpected."

He looked confused, then snarled. "I didn't say you didn't have to pay for it. I'm just sayin' it's a waste of money. Fork over or put it back." To illustrate his insistence, he held the egg cream like a hostage the whole time Monica dug in her purse for the money.

She read the rest of the paper leisurely, twisting on the soda-counter stool while she sipped the admittedly delicious treat. There was Tony's story about the dog, and another about a woman who found ten dollars in the street and gave it straight to the Salvation Army, saying, "It's the gifts from God that you have to give back." Monica couldn't remember the last time the word *God* appeared in a *Capitol Chatter* story, at least not in any positive context.

Another pleasant surprise was Zelda's debut column. The first paragraph or so told her story—an immigrant to this great country and a heartfelt desire to make it her home.

And for those of you who have always known your
home to be here, I want to help you keep it as beautiful
as it appeared in my dreams.

Her writing made no apology for her language skills, and Max had allowed it to go to press with certain subtle gaffes in syntax that complemented her natural charm. She promised the expertise of a maid and the warmth of a mother.

As Monica prepared to turn the next page, toward the back, where Monkey Business heralded the personal ads, a little knot of dread fizzed along with the sip of egg cream. She pictured her words—her rough-draft column—seeing it clearly as it emerged from the roller of her little typewriter at home. All those clever turns of phrase, her trademark snideness. It would be like some clanging cymbal in the midst of a charming interlude. But curiosity tinged with vanity prevailed. Her tongue was cold from the drink when she licked it against her thumb.

There it was, the familiar cartoon of the cheeky monkey wearing a strand of long flapper beads, its tail forming the second *s* in *Business*. And her own headline: "All the Dirt on Anti-Flirt." She smiled for the briefest second at her inimitable cleverness, but the self-satisfaction was fleeting at best as she noticed the text below:

> Editor's Note: The following is the first installment of a series. The sentiments expressed therein do not reflect those of the editorial staff of *Capitol Chatter*.

Monica sucked in her breath and grasped the now-empty glass, fully prepared to throw it should Max Moore happen to pop his head into the pharmacy. She settled for closing the paper and slamming the glass onto his picture.

In one swift move, she swirled off the stool, rolling and stuffing the paper into the pocket in the lining of her coat. She grabbed her purse, tugged on her gloves, and pulled her hat down low, preparing for battle as much as for cold. Once on the street, she walked with long, purposeful strides, careening through her fellow pedestrians. More than one gentleman brushed her shoulder, saying, "Hey, sister. What's your hurry?" But she didn't come close to breaking stride. Alice Reighly would be proud, and the thought of that made her walk even faster.

By the time she burst through the doors of the *Capitol Chatter* offices, she knew her nose must have been cherry red. Her intended diatribe, so carefully and silently rehearsed for the whole two blocks, would have to wait until she could take a generous breath. In the meantime, she stood and panted, perusing her colleagues, who seemed to be purposefully gathered around the shabby conference table. At least she thought these were her colleagues, given the dramatic changes each had undergone. Tony, for one, was wearing a new hat—black, unstained, and unrumpled. A small leather-bound journal sat open in front of him, and he was too absorbed in whatever he was writing in it to notice Monica's open stare. Next to him, Thomas Harper was making notations in his ledger. That in itself was a familiar sight, but this morning he was smiling.

But the biggest transformation of all was to be seen when the only woman at the table turned around at the shutting of the office door.

"Zelda?"

She'd cut her hair, and in doing so, lost the cloudy mass of gray, revealing instead a pale cap of curls the color of weak tea laced with cream. A pale touch of pink colored her cheeks, and even a bit on her lips, making them appear far less thin and pinched. Small, dark-rimmed spectacles sat atop her nose, and for the first time in memory, she did not immediately offer to take Monica's coat. Or make coffee. Instead, she simply said, "Good morning, Monica," while looking extremely pleased with herself.

"You—you look wonderful."

"As do you," Zelda returned without a hint of malice or, for that matter, humility.

The shock of it was almost enough to diffuse Monica's anger, and indeed it abated as she shrugged off her coat and hat and gloves. But then she heard his voice saying, "There's our little Monkey."

Max had walked out of his office, rubbing his hands together like some bachelor uncle heading for the Thanksgiving feast. His grin was more lopsided and goofy than usual, prompting Monica to reach for the rolled-up paper in her coat pocket and take a swing at it.

"You've got some nerve, Maximilian Moore."

Max took a deft step back, lifting his arms in not-so-mock defense. "What's with you? The rest of us are celebrating. Look, there's cake."

"I don't want cake," she said, though she did take her eyes off of her target for just a second to verify that his statement wasn't a mere tactical distraction. "This is a newspaper office, you know. Not some grandmother's dining room. We got along just fine without this monstrous table, and we never needed cake before."

"Monica—"

But she barreled on like a Keystone Cop. "And I don't want to be told exactly how many stories I'll write about what, and when I do write, I don't need some big, bold disclaimer at the top telling everyone how I'm not really a part of this, this little good and pure and lovely *family*."

And to her own horror, she felt her throat close up against any more words and tears pool in her carefully kohled eyes. He was looking down at her, his grin not diminished one whit. No compassion, no pity, just patient, befuddled amusement.

"Shall we go and talk in my office?"

"No." The only force keeping her tears at bay was pride. She couldn't bear to cry in front of Tony Manarola, Esquire, and Mademoiselle Zelda. She could feel their eyes on the back of her neck. The only sound was the scratch of Harper's pen.

"I think we should."

He laid a shepherding arm across her shoulders and shielded her from the prying eyes of the others as he led her in. Once inside, he shut the door and stood, leaning back against his desk, staring her down like the new owner of a lost dog.

"Now," he said, "first of all, this is a business. Not a family. Second of all, what makes you think you're not a part of it?"

"You didn't invite me to the party."

"It's not a party. It's called work. Some people, believe it or not, go to work every day."

"But there's cake."

"Because Zelda took it upon herself to bring it. If it would make you feel better, feel free to bring a sack of those delicious *kolache* next time you come in."

"And you called out my story. You told everybody that it didn't fit in with the rest of the paper."

"I'm an editor, Monica. I'm *your* editor. Right now I'm willing to give you some latitude, but I do have a vision for this paper. A very certain and specific tone I want to maintain. At some point you're going to have to comply with that."

"And if I don't?"

"Then stay true to yourself and write for someone else." He said so without a hint of threat. Just a fact, an option, as if doing so would be as easy as picking out a new hat.

"Maybe I'll go and do that right now," she said, hoping his statement was as much of a bluff as hers. "How would that make you look, telling everybody I was writing a series and then leaving them out to dry?"

"I'd manage. I'd tell them the truth, something you can surely appreciate."

"You'd expose me?"

"No. I'd just say that our Monkey found her Tarzan and swung away."

"You could do that?" And in that question, she wasn't

talking about her column anymore, and by the subtle shift in his posture—his shoulders sloped, his head bowed toward her—she knew he wasn't either.

"I wouldn't want to. But you have to understand. This paper, everything I'm trying to accomplish here—it's an extension of myself. *My* values. *My* vision. For the first time in my life, I have the opportunity to do what God has called me to do. I can't compromise on any level. It's hard enough facing what happens whenever you and I are . . . alone, together."

She stepped closer, her tears long gone, and lifted her gaze straight up into his. She dropped her voice to its lowest timbre. "What happens when we're together, Max?"

"You know. You were there."

"Tell me anyway."

"That first time, at the bank. Uncle Edward's whiskey. And then the other night. A speakeasy?"

She shrank away, deflated, and forced a joke into her voice. "Are you saying I drive you to drink?"

"I'm saying that it's becoming increasingly clear that spending time with you can be a dangerous thing."

"Dangerous for who?" She left her lips puckered around the word.

"For *whom*. And 'whom' is me."

"Well," she said, stepping back, "far be it from me to corrupt a choirboy. Anyway, you'll be happy to know that I am more firmly ensconced in the bosom of Miss Reighly's little club. There's another meeting tomorrow night. I was actually dropping by to see if you wanted me to keep up this little ruse, but that was before I saw your note."

"So you're going?"

"Of course. I'm writing a series, remember?"

"As a reporter?"

"As Maxine, secret Monkey spy."

"You shouldn't lie to them, Monica. They're nice girls, doing a nice thing."

"I have to write what I see, Max. You're the editor—publish what you want, or don't. Now, since this little group of saintly sisters seems to have captured your heart, tell me, how do I look?" She took yet another step back, struck a pose, and did a slow turn. "Will I pass?"

He was studying her, one eyebrow raised. "For what?"

"For one of *them*. They're taking a picture later this afternoon, and I fully intend to be a part of it. My haircut's a little too provocative, but I figure I'll wear a hat—"

"Wait a minute. A photograph?"

"For all those other newspapers."

He slowly shook his head, wearing an expression of reluctant admiration. "Do you have any shame?"

"Not so much. Not for this, anyway." She glanced at the clock. "I'm supposed to be there in less than an hour. Hopefully none of them have had a chance to read the column yet. Might make for some awfully sour pusses in the picture."

"Just keep talking. Distract them."

Slowly, an idea dawned. "Or maybe *you* could."

"Me?"

"Want to come with me?"

"Why would I?"

"As Maxine's older brother, of course. Protective and all that. And for something else."

"To keep you from saying something stupid?"

She made a face. "No. To flirt."

"But you're supposed to be my sister."

"Not with me, silly. With the other girls. You saw how they looked at you the other night. Like a big stick of candy in a kindergarten. One smile from you, and those girls will forget all of Miss Reighly's rules, right under her pinched little nose."

"Trust me, Miss Bisbaine, the world is full of women immune to my charm."

"I'm not asking you to seduce them. Just smile, be friendly, and see if they aren't *friendly* back."

"Remember just a few minutes ago, when I said that time spent with you could be a dangerous thing? Case in point."

"Please? And after, we can do whatever you want. You can even take me to church."

"It's Thursday."

"So take me to the front steps. I don't know if there's one that would let me in anyway."

He glanced at the clock. "Think there's time for cake first? I'd hate to disappoint Zelda."

"There's always time for cake." Monica moved aside to allow him to open the door. "You don't think she's too modernized to make coffee, too, do you?"

The question answered itself when they walked out of Max's office to see the big table set with slices of cake on small plates and steaming mugs of coffee at each place. At some point the rest of the staff had arrived, and someone—undoubtedly Zelda—had thought to give Trevor a double portion, which he eyed with the insatiable hunger of youth.

Monica moved to what she regarded as "her" place, across from Zelda, who had procured a glass of milk from somewhere for Trevor.

"You really do look beautiful," Monica said, hoping the change in her tone would suffice as an apology for her earlier abruptness.

"Thank you," Zelda said. "I am a writer now. I should look like one. I wish I could stand to smoke cigarettes."

Monica laughed. "I can't stand to smoke cigarettes, and I'm a writer. So you're in good company there. Then again, I can't make cake, so you are now in a class all your own."

Zelda laughed. "It's good not to forget the old ways, even when new ones come along. Too much modern, and everybody would starve."

Then Tony came to the table, and Trevor, and Harper even closed his ledger and slid it to the side. Monica picked up her slice of cake and was lifting it to her mouth when Max stood at his place and said, "Let's take a minute, if you don't mind, to say a prayer."

His eyes searched the table for a volunteer as Monica slowly lowered her cake back down. Tony removed his hat and made the sign of the cross.

"I will pray," Zelda said; then she, too, stood. "Our mighty Father God, for this life, we thank you. And these friends. And all that we have. For our strength, we want to give you glory. May we honor you always. In the name of the Father, and the Son, and the Holy Ghost. Amen."

Each word was so carefully measured. Perfect and even, and the last of them chorused with Tony. He and Zelda both crossed themselves again, with Tony punctuating the ritual with a quick kiss to his fingers. It seemed quite a show for a slice of cake.

✥ CHAPTER 15 ✥

Don't use your eyes for ogling—they were made for worthier purposes.
ANTI-FLIRT CLUB RULE #3

"ARE YOU SURE it doesn't look doubly suspicious? The two of us showing up together?"

"Nah. I told them last time you were my brother and Ma doesn't like me going around without a chaperone. Might seem suspicious if you *weren't* here. Besides, I need somebody to hold my coat. If I'm going to have my picture in the paper, I want everybody to be able to see my figure."

They'd just rounded the corner of Harvard Street, where already a modest crowd of women had gathered on Alice Reighly's porch.

"You know, if they read that column, you might not be welcomed with open arms."

"It's early. Nobody starts their day with the *Chatter*."

"I still think you could finish the assignment without appearing in the photograph."

"Of course I could, but it wouldn't be half the fun, now would

201

it? Besides, what better way to keep them in the dark? Who would be stupid enough to try to keep a secret with a photograph?"

"I don't like lying." It had been a familiar refrain for most of the twenty-minute walk.

"Yet you're here, aren't you?"

"Only because I relish the opportunity to prove you wrong. People do stand by their principles, no matter how far-fetched those principles might be."

Monica took two brisk steps ahead of Max, turned, stopped, and held out her hand. "Care to make a bet?"

"And add gambling to the growing list of vices you've suckered me into? No, thanks."

"Not money or anything. And maybe not even a wager. More like a promise between friends."

"I'm listening."

"If you're right, and those girls over there resist your charms, with not so much as a giggle or a wink, then I promise my next column will be full of nothing but praise for their effort."

"Fair enough."

"But you have to promise me something too. You have to lay on the charm, toss out the compliments, tease a little, you know."

After what appeared to be serious consideration, Max took her hand in a grip that gave no deference to her delicate gender and said, "Deal."

"Good." She didn't let go.

"Now," he said, showing his own reluctance to break free, "what if the unthinkable happens?"

"Which would be?"

"What if some poor, unsuspecting girl falls madly in love with me? It hardly seems fair to toy with an unsuspecting heart."

"It's a risk you'll have to take. The girl should know better, anyway. You shouldn't fall in love with somebody who flirts with you. It's a given."

"Like a rule? I thought you didn't like those kinds of rules."

"Not a rule, exactly." Unless her imagination was playing a trick, he was reeling her in, closer and closer, with almost imperceptible tugs. She gave in and modified the grip they had on each other, encasing his hand in both of hers and bringing it up to nearly touch her cheek. "More like—" She looked up, amused to see his amusement, inviting her to play with the moment. "Those teasing looks, and touches, and even kisses, sometimes, when they get passed between strangers, it simply isn't *real*. Not like love."

"What do you know about love, Miss Bisbaine?"

Just like that, the game changed, losing any hint of humor. The only answer she had was Charlie, how she thought she'd loved him. And how he must have loved her, considering the risk he was willing to take to see her time and time again.

"Love comes back," she said finally.

He wanted to say something; she could sense it. His lips parted, he took a breath, and if he were anyone else, she might have thought he was about to kiss her. But he was buttoned-up Max, and if this wasn't the place to wax philosophical about the ways of romance, it was even less an opportunity to practice it. Not that there'd be time for either, anyway, because at that moment, Emma Sue—her companion from the first meeting—was waving frantically from Alice Reighly's porch, calling, "Maxine!"

"Your first victim," Monica said, taking Max's arm in a much more familial way. "She's a nice girl. Try not to devastate her."

Emma came down off the porch and, with a quick, almost trotting gait that made her seem more youthful than Monica would have imagined, linked her own arm through Monica's free one.

"We have to hurry up," she said. "The photographer says

he can only stay for about fifteen minutes. It's one or two shots and he's off. And only a few girls showed up. Alice is terribly disappointed, but most of us are working girls, you know? Can't just step off the shop floor to pose for a picture, now can you?"

"You made it."

"I don't have a job. Unless you count babysitting for my neighbor's kid. Which I don't."

By then Emma Sue'd completely stolen Monica away from Max, leaving him a good two paces behind them. She twisted in the girl's grip in an attempt to make an introduction.

"Did you meet my brother the other evening? Max, this is—"

"I think he should stay back," Emma Sue said, quickening her step. "He might be distracting to the other girls, and already it's hard to keep everybody focused. You understand, of course."

"I—" But they hurried so, there was no opportunity to press the issue. One glance over her shoulder proved that Max had clearly slowed his pace to widen the gap between them. Now he stopped and plunged his hands into his pockets, rocking back on his heels and grinning at the demise of her carefully crafted plan. The rotten irony of it all was that he looked so cute, if Emma Sue would so much as turn around she'd be a goner for sure.

"I'll be waiting right here, Sis," he called with a touch to his hat. "Holler if you need me."

"That's sweet," Emma Sue said with a sisterly squeeze. "If every girl had a big brother like that, we wouldn't have anything to worry about. He seems a bit overprotective, if you know what I mean."

"Yeah, funny how *brother* rhymes with *smother*, isn't it?"

Emma Sue giggled. "You're clever."

They'd arrived at the white railing of Alice Reighly's apartment, where a small swarm of girls gathered, primping each other's hair and checking their lipstick in tiny mirrors. Off to the side was Alice, wearing the same conservative suit she'd worn at the meeting. Only now she wore a small brown hat, utterly void of fashion, with fine strands of her hair dripping down from beneath it. Despite it all, however, she looked radiantly happy. Perhaps it was the brilliant wash of the winter's sun or the pennant she wielded with the conviction of a soldier going into battle.

Then again, it might have something to do with the photographer. He was tall—easily over six feet—and the cut of his wool coat revealed a physique worthy of immortality in marble. Broad shoulders, narrow waist, and from what she could see that wasn't obscured by his camera, a handsome, clean-shaven face.

"That's it, doll," he said from behind the lens. "Beautiful, just beautiful. Let me see that smile."

Doll. The Alice Reighly who had spoken so passionately the other night would never have stood for such a nickname. Or *sweetheart*, either, yet he punctuated his directions with that one, too, asking her to turn a bit so she didn't look so squinty.

"Oh my," Monica said to Emma Sue, speaking softly. "Isn't he a handsome one?"

Emma Sue fluttered her hand near her heart. "He is, like something from the movies. Rather a test for our resolve, I think."

Monica tsked, as if anyone would plan such a thing, and followed Emma Sue up the porch where that bossy girl, Junie, was handing out sashes for all of them to wear, draped shoulder to hip, like those young women in that Miss America pageant in New Jersey. They were white silk with the words *Anti-Flirt Club* emblazoned in royal-blue paint. Monica followed the example of the other girls and shrugged off her coat, thankful that the temperature had risen to something close to fifty degrees, and lifted her arms to allow Junie to adjust the sash to perfection.

"You're so tiny," Junie mumbled without a hint of compliment. "People are going to have to look behind you to read the whole thing."

"Well, it's just for the photograph, isn't it? I mean, we're not going to be expected to parade all over town in this thing, are we?"

"I would." She stepped back to assess her work. "That would keep the wolves away."

"And everybody else, too." But Junie had already moved on to the next girl.

Monica shielded her eyes from the sun and looked down the street where Max stood, waiting. That rat. She could sense his amusement from here.

"All right, ladies." The photographer's voice invaded their chatter like a warm swallow of coffee, deep and smooth. "What do you say you chickens all perch up there on the railing? Between the columns. Looks like you'll just about fit."

"Are you sure?" Junie asked, sounding both skeptical and suspicious. "Couldn't we just stand along the stairs? That would show off the sashes better."

He allowed his camera to hang freely from the strap around his neck and stepped away from the group to both study and admire.

"You might have something there." His eyelids fell to half-mast, drawing attention to a fringe of dark lashes any flapper would give her teeth for. "It does something to your figures." He held up his hand, as if touching them from a distance, and to Monica's amusement, Emma Sue leaned forward, as if to create a bridge between them. "The way it dissects—"

"I think the railing would be fine," Alice Reighly said, her soft voice breaking the spell without resorting to chastising authority.

Monica stared at the railing in question. It came nearly to her waist, and she planted her hands on it, wondering how in the world she would ever hoist herself up when she felt the brush of a masculine shoulder behind her. Their photographer, apparently sensing her plight, had bounded up the stairs to the rescue, and the next thing she knew, her waist was almost completely encased in his hands.

"Let me give you a boost there, little sheba." He spoke close to her ear, and the thrill made her collapse to near deadweight in his grasp. The ground left her completely as he lifted her up, and then the narrow railing became a precarious seat beneath her.

"Steady . . . ," he intoned, keeping one hand around her waist as the other scooped beneath her knees and slowly turned her to face the street. "Does that feel all right?"

"Yes," Monica said. "Fine."

"Good." He clapped his hands. "Anybody else need help?"

Emma Sue was the first to raise her hand, though she was certainly tall enough to swing one long leg over the railing and sit just fine. She submitted to the ritual, though, and once she was settled next to Monica, she risked gravity to lean back and whisper, "I don't think your brother was too keen on all that."

Monica gripped the rail beneath her and stretched her neck to see where Max had, indeed, taken several strides closer, his posture and countenance far less gregarious.

"He takes a woman's honor very seriously."

Girl after girl was lifted, giggling, to her perch. One protested in vain that she must be far too heavy for him to lift, to which he replied, "Ah, chickie, you're nothing but a feather." Another cautioned that her shoes might get his lovely coat dirty, leading him to take the garment off to a collective squeal at the sight of strong arms in a skin-fitting white shirt. His smile at their reaction produced a pair of dimples that might have been a pair of bullets, seeing how they brought the girls to clutch at their hearts.

From the sidewalk, both Alice Reighly and Max, now side by side, watched the scene unfold. She with a look of consternation; he, more amused.

Monica, meanwhile, allowed her feet to swing freely. Too freely, in fact, because without warning one of her shoes flew from her foot, landing what seemed like miles away in the yard's patchy snow.

"I've got that," Max said, springing into action and scooping it up. As he approached, she held out her foot, bringing it precariously close to his nose.

"Be careful up there, Sis," he said. "It's a long way to fall."

"You're too good to me," she said. "I don't deserve such attention."

He wrapped his hand around her ankle, holding her steady as he slipped the shoe back on. The touch was strong and steady, and considering the jolt it sent through her body, was the only thing keeping her from launching backward into Alice Reighly's apartment. It crushed any memory of the handsome photographer even as it prompted a "Hey, buddy! Watch yourself!" from the man.

"It's okay," Max said, looking up at Monica with a twinkle in his eye. "I'm her brother."

Immediately afterward, Emma Sue kicked her shoe into the yard and heaved an audible sigh when it landed at the feet of Alice Reighly.

❧

Later, after the photographer declared his work was done, the girls scattered. Alice Reighly shook Max's hand, warmly thanking him for being a young man so concerned for his sister's safety.

"There should be more like you," she said, "dedicated to the virtue of young womanhood. I daresay men would think twice

208

about engaging in any lewd conduct if they thought they'd have you to contend with."

"I do what I can," Max said, looking sheepish in his lie.

"And she's grateful, I'm sure."

This last bit was spoken directly to Monica, who, for the first time, felt a niggling of guilt at her deception.

Max walked Alice to her door and wished her a good day before joining Monica back on the sidewalk.

"Coward," she accused immediately.

He shrugged. "I tried. The ladies would have nothing to do with me. Not with Mr. Handsome Photographer on the scene."

She made a little hop in triumph. "You see? They were absolutely brazen. My point proven. All on their high horse about the dangers of flirting, and they were practically throwing themselves off the balcony just to land in his arms. Oh, I can't wait to expose them."

"And how are you going to do that, exactly? Without exposing yourself, that is. It's one thing to be an anonymous face in a crowd, quite another to be one face out of a dozen in a photograph. How long do you think it would take for Miss Reighly to figure out who her mole is?"

"So what if she does?"

"And then the whole world will have a face to match up with their favorite Monkey."

"That's if she exposes me."

"Why wouldn't she?"

Monica grew silent and tried to hide her scowling ruminations.

"So you think it's best I don't write about the photograph at all?"

"As your editor, yes."

"Well, I guess that's all that matters."

"May I offer one bit of noneditor advice? More like brotherly?"

Something in his voice made her dread what might come next, but she said, "Sure," fully prepared to defend herself.

"They seem like nice girls."

"Oh, they are. The nicest, as a matter of fact." Her tone, however, swapped his sincerity for sarcasm.

"What I mean is maybe there's no story here. What if all you have is a nice bunch of girls who want to live a nice, normal life?"

"Unlike me?"

Now it was his turn to engage in a few silent steps. "I know you're dying to expose hypocrisy, but they seem sincere. Harmless, even."

She didn't dare stop beside him, lest the digging of her heels would root her in this place, clearly in view of Alice Reighly's home. "I happen to disagree with her and her 'rules.'"

"Which you made abundantly clear in your column. I don't see what more there is to say. Maybe it would be better for you not to go back at all."

"So now are you my editor? Or my brother?"

"A friend. Nothing more. And for the record, I think you're a nice girl too."

"Careful," she said. "Only one of us should be fooled at a time. Back to the office, then?"

"Nope," he said, making no attempt to hide his grin. "Remember? You said you'd owe me. That I could even take you to church."

"And you said it was Thursday. Which it still is, by the way."

"I want to go to the cathedral. The National Cathedral," he added when she seemed at first to be confused. "Uncle Edward wrote to me about its construction, rather fascinated with the process. He even went to the peace service they held there after the war."

"I can't imagine Ed Moore attending a church service."

"Some men are quiet about their faith, I guess. Anyway, I'd like to go. What do you say?"

"Are you paying the bus fare for both of us?"

He fetched a handful of coins from his pocket. "Will this get us there and back?"

Monica shrugged. "If not, what better place for a nice girl to stay?"

❧ CHAPTER 16 ❧

*At last he made a third appearance on the summit of the tower
of the great bell: from thence he seemed to show exultingly
to the whole city the fair creature he had saved.*

VICTOR HUGO, *THE HUNCHBACK OF NOTRE DAME*

IT WAS A TWENTY-MINUTE RIDE on an overly warm, crowded bus. Everybody on board seemed content to be silent, so Max and Monica joined them. It would never be like this in Los Angeles, where strangers openly—and loudly—bragged about their dreams and ambitions, mostly hoping that someone would overhear and make them come true. Here was a mixed bag of age and gender living stoic agendas.

Five minutes into the ride, Monica leaned her head back against the seat, closed her eyes, and let her mouth gape open slightly to allow the smallest of snores. He thought briefly about nudging her awake; after all, she might not appreciate being left in so vulnerable a state, but it was the first chance he'd had to look at her. A long, luxurious, open study of this woman who had drilled her way into his life. Here, he could see her youth as her face relaxed into something softer than she would ever allow. He tried to imagine her eyes without the dark shadow and black mascara that now dusted the top of her cheek. Her lips, so carefully painted, lost their drama in the soft parting of sleep.

In the midst of this reverie, a new concern overtook him. Why would she succumb to such sleep in the middle of the afternoon? On a bus, no less? His mind went to unpleasant places, picturing her in one predicament after another. A dark, smoky club. Drinking, dancing—and he'd danced with her before, so he knew how dangerous that could be.

She shifted and fell against his shoulder. Of all the times they'd touched—and he could clearly recall every single touch—this was the most satisfying. No guile, no defenses. He wanted to absorb the feel of her weight against him, and he prayed for a smooth ride.

His heart longed to pray for other things, too. Mostly that this would be a repeated scenario, her sleeping next to him. Neither of his parents would have approved, of course, and his years working with Sister Aimee did nothing to make him see this as a spiritually beneficial match.

"Your helpmeet is your partner in your journey with Christ," she'd said on more than one occasion. *"When our Savior makes his triumphant return to gather his church, do you want to be snatched away? To leave that man or woman with whom you've woven your years alone to suffer through the Tribulation to follow?"*

The smell of Monica's perfume wafted to his nose, and he smiled at the thought of it lingering on the shoulder of his coat. Her scent, woven in.

Lord forgive him, but he wanted her.

At the first screech of brakes, Monica startled awake, immediately bringing the back of her hand to her mouth to stifle a yawn. She took her time pulling away, revealing the imprint of his jacket on her cheek.

"Rested?"

"I'm so sorry," she said, now holding her fingers to cover the scar of sleep. "I was up half the night—"

"I don't need to know—"

"*Reading*, silly. The book you lent me. *The Enchanted April.*"

"That good?"

She put on an aristocratic pose and said, "Enchanting, dahling," in a British accent so terrible he had to laugh at it.

"Well, I'm glad you're enjoying it. Is this our stop?"

She strained to look out the window. "Yes. It'll be a block or so walk from here. But I could use the air. How about you?"

"Indeed."

When the bus came to its final, shuddering halt, they joined the others in the press to exit, and he filled his lungs with the cool, refreshing air once his feet hit the ground.

As usual, Monica took the lead, making him long for a time when they could be somewhere *she* could follow *him*. Maybe California, though she'd already made her feelings clear about that. Best to go someplace they'd never been, where they'd be on equal ground. New York City, perhaps. Or Chicago. Or now that the war was over, even Europe, like all the other great writers.

". . . Italy," she was saying. "And these women just pick up, pack up, and go. I could do that, you know. There's nothing holding me here. No family, no job—well, not one that I can't take with me, right? I could save my allowance, sell everything, and be in Paris by springtime. How long do you think I could last on four hundred bucks?"

"You? Forever. Some penniless baron would fall madly in love with you and whisk you off to his castle." He was only half joking.

The fact that he'd seen her in two different fur coats proved that girls like Monica didn't need a lot of their own money to live.

"Forget that," she said with a dismissive air. "*Penniless* isn't my cup of tea."

"Are you calling yourself a gold digger?"

"Not so much gold, but definitely green. Nothing makes a girl happy like a little extra lettuce, you know?"

She took his arm in the now-ubiquitous way she had, and he slowed his steps to match her shorter stride. If he'd hoped for a little firsthand history about the cathedral's construction or its impact on the city, he was in for a disappointment. Besides the occasional comment about a passing woman's hat, Monica remained oddly subdued. By the time they stood in front of the massive structure, she'd fallen completely silent and her shoes had turned to anvils.

"Are you sure we can go in?" Her grip on his arm was as tight as her voice. "I mean, is it open?"

"It's a church," he said, hoping he sounded more reassuring than condescending. "Churches are always open."

"I dunno." She let go of him, stepped back, and craned her neck to take in the sky-touching Gothic structure. "That's a lot of ceiling to come crashing down."

He reached for the door. "I'll take my chances."

She immediately contorted her body, dropping one shoulder and looking up at him with a twisted mouth and one droopy eye.

"Sanctuary . . ." She drew the word out in a low, husky voice, pawing at the door with a limp, clawlike hand. When he didn't respond, she stood upright and made a show of patting her face back into its original form. "Lon Chaney? *The Hunchback of Notre Dame?*"

"Ah. I've read the book; haven't seen the movie."

"Nobody has, yet. I just saw the pictures in *Movie Weekly*. Gave me the shivers."

She demonstrated with an actual shiver, and he pictured her beside him in a darkened theater, the screen filled with the image of a terrifying monster and his arm holding her close.

"Well, then," he said, chasing the image away, "maybe you should skip that one. See a Buster Keaton instead."

"Not a chance." She breezed past him, this time lifting her hands to tap an imaginary tambourine to accompany her gypsy twirl. "It's my favorite love story."

"That's impossible. It's tragic."

"Fine," she said with an air of concession. "It's my favorite tragedy. But think of it. La Esmeralda is so beautiful, but she's awful. I mean, really not a kind person at all. And yet, all these men—they love her."

"They *want* her," Max corrected, drawing from memory. "There's a difference."

"Not Quasi." She smiled, as if she held a personal fondness for the misshapen hero. "And he knows he could never have her, he knows he would never be able to enjoy her *beauty*, but in the end he shouts his love to the city." She resumed her caricature and pawed pitifully at his sleeve, saying, "'There is everything I have ever loved.'"

"But she was already dead."

She resumed her small, authoritative stature. "Then he shouldn't have waited."

Inside the vestibule, a conservatively dressed woman took their coats and Max's hat and, speaking in a half whisper, directed them toward the entrance to Bethlehem Chapel. They thanked her, with Monica adding a self-conscious move rather like a curtsy. Not sure whether or not she intended the gesture to be a joke, he stifled a good-natured laugh.

She's nervous, he thought, justifying his own spark of

queasiness. He tried to brace himself, but the first step on the marble tile took his breath, and he didn't catch it again until he felt Monica's small, cold hand in his.

"Golly," she said, and he found it to be the perfect word for the moment, full of a childlike awe at the pure majesty surrounding them.

The walls were made of massive stone—limestone, if he recalled correctly from Uncle Edward's letters—fitted together in smooth, almost seamless perfection. Stained-glass windows set within their own arched alcoves lined the walls, and the ceiling stretched high above a series of Gothic arches stretching to the grandeur of the altar at the front.

Monica stepped away and went to the first of the massive columns lining the center aisle.

"It feels ancient," she said, pressing her hand against the stone. "Like something medieval."

He closed the space between them. "You've really never been here before?"

She shook her head. "I've only ever been to church a couple of times since my confirmation. Christmas, mostly. Midnight Mass." She looked around. "Where do you suppose they keep the confessionals in this place?"

"They don't have those here. It's not a Catholic church."

"Good thing," she said with the little laugh he recognized as something she did when attempting bravado. "We'd be here awhile. Maybe 'til after dark, and you might not catch the right bus home."

She was leaning back against the column, her pale skin awash in the lavender light of the stained-glass windows.

He leaned forward, close enough to feel the cool emanating from the stone. "You shouldn't talk that way about yourself."

"What way?"

"I don't believe for a minute that you're half as scandalous as you say. I don't know why you're trying so hard to convince us all of your own mythology."

"Is that what you'd like to believe?"

There was a shift in the light coming from outside—a cloud drifting, most likely—and a new prism of color graced the top of her cheek.

"It's what I know. You see, every now and then, this charming little girl makes her way straight to the surface. She's who you are deep inside."

"You don't know anything at all." She brushed past him and stood in the aisle. "What's that up there?"

"That's the altar."

She batted his sleeve. "I'm not a total dummy. I mean—" she leaned forward, squinting—"I can't tell . . ."

"Come on." He touched his hand to her waist and they made a strolling ascent amid the sea of plain wooden chairs. An elderly woman pushing a dust mop appeared from a door at the front of the chapel and, upon seeing them, leaned on its handle to watch.

"We'd better be careful," Monica said, speaking out of the side of her mouth. "People might get the wrong idea."

"Technically, the groom doesn't walk the bride up the aisle."

"Who said anything about bride and groom? It looks like you're about ready to give me away."

"Two problems with that." By now they were nearly to the altar. With the emptiness of the room capable of carrying his words to the far corners, he dropped both his head and his voice. "One, I'm not old enough to give you to anybody. Two, you're too much of a brat for anyone to take you."

She looked up at him with a playful pout. "Oh, Daddy, how you tease."

He guided her into a row and they sat, assuming an identical posture, with their elbows propped on the seats in front of them. For a full minute, Max's eyes scanned the scene carved into the white stone behind the altar—Mary and the Christ child, a manger behind them, angels looking on.

"It was carved from a single piece of stone," he said as both an expression of awe and an attempt to inform.

"How do you know so much?"

"Uncle Edward. I was working with Sister Aimee and, in case you haven't heard, she's built an enormous . . . temple—" there was no other word for it—"in Los Angeles. We traded postcards and photographs." He chuckled at the memory. "It was almost like a competition. Who could build a bigger, better church."

"Who won?"

Her interest seemed genuine, and while he hadn't given the Angelus Temple much of a second thought since leaving California, his mind suddenly filled with memories of the place from the laying of its cornerstone to the final service he'd attended.

"Hard to say. It doesn't have the grandeur of this place. The windows and the carvings. It's huge—"

"This place is huge."

"Not in comparison. Sister Aimee's is like a theater. Five thousand seats. Modern in every way. I think you'd like it."

Monica narrowed her eyes in suspicion. "Why are you spending so much time trying to analyze me? Who I am 'deep inside' and what kind of church I would or wouldn't like? Because there's nothing wrong with me here." She tapped a dark-tipped finger to her hat.

"I'm sorry," he said, hoping the calming tone of his voice would halt her increasing volume.

"I don't need psychoanalysis—"

"I was just making conversation—"

"Or religion."

"I wasn't . . ." But her glare made it clear he would not be able to pass this off as merely an informal observation of architecture. Deep down, he wanted to know—needed to know—what Monica felt about faith and God and all those elements that would make her . . . what? Eligible? Worthy? And now it was clear that he'd hurt her. The facade she worked so hard to maintain was threatening to crumble before his very eyes, and her blustering did nothing to reinforce it. She perched on the very edge of her seat, looking close to panicked, and might have flown away if it weren't for the fact that she'd have to scramble over his legs in order to escape.

His first instinct was to soothe what feathers he'd ruffled, but something told him that doing so would only result in another snap. Instead, he leaned back in his seat, sending echoes of creaking wood bouncing throughout the sanctuary, and stared ahead, taking in every detail of the Nativity carving while effectively leaving Monica alone. After a minute or so, he heard her chair creak a little too.

"Those four guys?" he said after a time, pointing to the figures flanking the centerpiece behind the altar. "They're the writers of the four Gospels. Matthew, Mark, Luke, John." He pointed to each in turn.

"They all look alike," she said, but with no sense of malice.

"When I think about what we do—what I'm trying to do with this paper—I think about them. Their job, as it were, was to just write the story. To be accurate and truthful. They don't judge or editorialize or try to compel you to believe or not believe. They disappear behind the words and let Jesus speak for himself."

"So you want to create the Gospel of Max Moore?"

He chose not to see her comment as blasphemy. "I don't want

to tell anybody how to live or what to do, if that's what you mean. I just want our paper to tell good stories about good people. And then, maybe, our readers will want to be good people too."

"I don't want to disappear behind my words. Everything I say is truth, too, you know." He felt her clutch at his sleeve and turned. "You need to understand that, Max. What I write is who I am. I'm not some created character. I go to those places; I do those things. It's who I am, and I don't care."

"That isn't really true, is it?"

"Of course it is," she said, neither convinced nor convincing.

"So why isn't your name at the top of your column?"

She didn't recoil—not completely, anyway. Her hand remained on his sleeve, though her grip receded, and her face relaxed from its wide-eyed intensity.

"That was Edward's idea."

"Oh," Max said, holding back the wash of relief at his uncle's foresight.

"He told me it would be in my best interest, for now. In case, I suppose, in the future, I ever wanted to do something a little more substantial."

"He was a wise man."

"He was a good man, Max. Really, truly good. I don't know why he didn't show that side of him more."

"I don't either." He covered her hand with his, and the sound of a subtle clearing of a throat came from the cleaning woman who now pushed the dust mop up the center aisle. "I think it's time for us to go."

"That's it?" Monica didn't budge. "Aren't we supposed to pray or something? Light a candle? Or is that reserved for Catholics too?"

"Sure. We could pray, if you like." Suddenly, though, he felt uncomfortable. Should they hold hands? Go up to the altar? Kneel? The opulence of the sanctuary seemed to call for more than whatever simple, humble words he could say—if he should say any at all. Perhaps she wanted to pray alone, silently. Or for both of them? How was it that the mention of a prayer called up the same squeamish discomfort he'd felt locked in a bank vault with a bottle of whiskey?

To his relief, she'd taken the *Book of Common Prayer* from the back of the seat in front of them and was running her hand over the dark-blue cover embossed in gold.

"Do you use the prayers in here? I mean, if you can't think of any of your own?"

"You can," he said, treading carefully. "Or during the formal service everybody might read them together. But even alone, sometimes, it helps to read someone else's words and feel a little less . . . alone." He took the book from her and thumbed through its pages. "The psalms of David are in here. Imagine, the prayers he wrote thousands of years ago, and they can be my own."

"Choose one." She hunkered close to share the book. "I'll read it with you."

He continued flipping pages. "I don't know how to choose."

"The first one." Like always, she sounded decisive, sure. He quickly found the Psalter, and together they read:

"'Blessed is the man that walketh not in the counsel of the ungodly, nor standeth in the way of sinners, nor sitteth in the seat of the scornful. But his delight is in the law of the Lord; and in his law doth he meditate day and night.'"

By the time he finished the second sentence, Max realized he was reading alone. Monica had let go of her side of the book. Her hands sat listless in her lap, her face downcast with a gaze that threatened to burn a hole through the page. Still, he read on about the righteous man being like a tree planted near water while the ungodly blow away as chaff, clear to the final verse proclaiming that the way of the ungodly shall perish.

"It's us," Monica said once he'd stopped. "You're this big, righteous tree, and I'm just a bit of blossom that'll blow away."

"I don't see it that way," he said, though he desperately wished he'd gone with the traditional twenty-third. "You're no more a sinner than I am."

"Really." She took the book from him, closed it, and ran her fingers along the gold-embossed title. "There's not a person alive who would believe that."

"Monica—" He moved to take the book from her, to settle it back in its spot so he could take her away from this place, but she would not loosen her grip, so he chose to seal her hand to the book with his own.

"My mother, of course, thought I was a terrible person. Not so much when I was little, of course, but later. I'll bet there were times she wished I would run away with gypsies, you know?"

He hated her sadness, especially as it blossomed in this place designed for worship, but he knew he had nothing to add. Nothing of his power could heal the wounds that seemed to be opening just below the surface of her bravado.

"But then," she continued, "my mother was a horrible person too. Just a different kind. And I ended up surrounding myself with these boys and parties, and part of me wanted to think that I was better than them. Better than *that*. But I meet you now, and I wonder—"

"Stop." He slid the prayer book from her, replaced it, and touched her chin to bring her gaze fully to his. "I don't like to hear you talk about yourself that way."

"Why?"

The question was a challenge, one he was not quite ready to meet. Not here, anyway, where only one of them felt safe.

"Because it isn't true."

"Or lovely? Or of good report?"

He smiled, somehow finding the strength to restrain his joy at her remembrance, frightened he'd startle her right back into hiding. "Exactly."

⋆❀⋆

The late-afternoon light had nearly exhausted itself by the time Max arrived at his own familiar front door. He opened it to find the day's mail scattered on the floor, including an official-looking envelope containing his final paycheck from his job with the *Bridal Call* along with a short, personal note from Sister Aimee herself.

Max—

While your talent and insight here are greatly missed, I am amazed at God's provision in filling the void your absence created. I find myself rising to editorial challenges for which he alone can equip me, aided by those he has brought alongside to be my Aaron and Hur as I attempt to hold up the vision set forth in our publication.

I pray that the God we strive to serve will bless your endeavors as well. Seek always to bring him glory, and he will make your path smooth.

I shall be more than happy to provide a glowing letter of reference to any establishment with which you seek future employment.

*Your sister in Christ and
co-inheritor of his Kingdom,
Aimee*

And so went any thought he might have of returning. The amount written on the check would make a hefty down payment on a new automobile or purchase a used one outright. Given the orchestrations of streetcars, cabs, buses, and shoe leather, such a purchase was seeming more and more attractive.

He wandered into the tiny kitchen, opened a can of soup, dumped it in a copper-bottomed pot, and stacked a small plate with slices of bread and cheese. A ring of blue gas flames leapt to life at the touch of a match and would have the soup bubbly and warm by the time the sky grew completely dark. In the meantime, he bit into a slice of bread, chewing thoughtfully, realizing that Sister Aimee's letter had nothing to do with closing off a path back to California. That decision was made the minute he sat in a church next to Monica Bisbaine. Or maybe the minute he sat down to corned-beef sandwiches with her after his uncle's funeral. Either way, at this moment she was integral to any decision he might make. He wanted to stay in Washington because she lived in Washington. He wanted to keep *Capitol Chatter* alive so she would have a place of employment. A place for her voice. And if that meant a place next to him, all the better.

The clock on the wall read quarter to six, still office hours in Los Angeles. After lowering the flame underneath his soup, he went into the living room, stuffed the last of the bread slice into his mouth, and tried valiantly to speak around it when the long-distance operator came on the line.

"Los Angeles," he choked, then gave the number of his former office.

"Mr. Moore!" Ida's voice held all the warmth of the West Coast. He would miss her more than anybody. "How marvelous to hear from you."

"Good to hear you as well," he said, though he was already

anxious to sever the final tie. "Ida, I'm calling about that final piece of business you offered to handle for me."

"Oh no. I don't like the sound of that. Final business."

He glossed over her statement. "I settled up with my landlord before I left, but my books are still there. Are you still willing to pack them up and ship them to me?"

"Of course, Mr. Moore," Ida said, her voice now bustling with business.

"See if you can send them with a promise of cash on delivery."

"Nonsense. I'll charge the shipping to Mrs. McPherson. It's the least she can do."

That was Ida, always his greatest champion. Another responsibility he would have to assume. He gave her the address and asked her to repeat it back to him, and with a final expression of gratitude, wished her well.

He returned the phone's earpiece to its cradle and went back into the kitchen to find his soup nicely thickened and steaming. With a towel wrapped around the pot handle, he poured it into a bowl and moved to the table.

It was far from the first meal he'd eaten alone, but this evening the empty chair loomed cavernous across from him. He bowed his head in the habit of asking the Lord's blessing on his food, but the tomato-laced steam carried with it the image of Monica's face in the light of stained glass. The weight of her head on his shoulder.

"I think I might love her, Lord," he said aloud, but he dared not ask for wisdom. Or guidance. Or any direction that might take her away. Instead, he asked that God would bless her meal too. Whatever—and begrudgingly, with whomever—that might be.

CHAPTER 17

Don't fall for the slick, dandified cake eater—the unpolished gold
of a real man is worth more than the gloss of a lounge lizard.
ANTI-FLIRT CLUB RULE #8

SHE SPENT THE NEXT DAY—all day—in bed, cocooned in a flannel gown and quilted robe, snuggled under a thick, voluminous comforter. Only the call of the coffeepot and the subsequent call of the lavatory enticed her out into the chill of her room. Otherwise, she sipped the black beverage and nibbled from a bag of pastries and imagined herself as one of a group of gracious women sharing a house in sunny Italy. At times she let the book fall open against her and stared out the window at the mass of leafless branches grown close against it.

What if she'd stayed true to her mother's wishes? Maybe if she'd played the good girl, met all the right boys, and behaved in all the right ways, she'd be married—or at least engaged—to a man who could provide some nice, comfortable life for her to grow old in. But she'd left that path long ago, and despite Max

Moore's attempt to elevate her virtue, the previous day's visit made it clear she wouldn't be returning to it anytime soon.

Charlotte Wilkins and Rose Arbuthnot may be fictitious characters in a novel, but they clearly showed marriage to be a trap—a long, tedious road leading to nothing but shared emptiness. A life lived alone while chained to another. What possible benefit could there be in that?

Unless, of course, it meant having somebody lying right next to you. Somebody who'd read the same story, who might have a different opinion, but who would have a brain to talk about it.

She'd marked her place in the book with the folded copy of Alice Reighly's rules for the Anti-Flirt Club. All that talk of "the one." Like a wink and a smile in one direction would build up a wall against the other.

What a load of crackers. Life wasn't one long hallway with the right guy waiting at the end of it. More like a maze—something from those great English gardens—with a new guy surprising you around each corner. A few dead ends, maybe, but always another one waiting.

But the next one, she promised herself, wouldn't be married. Not that Charlie would have been that much of a prize anyway, but she'd still wasted a lot of time on a man only to hand him back to his wife. No guy was ever a guarantee, but a married one? That was just like walking in circles, chained to a tree. Best to let the Mrs. Charlies of the world wait at home with all the inanity and ennui that drives a woman to rent a villa for the spring. Monica would take her chances facing this spring alone.

Well, maybe not completely alone, as the view from her window took on new life with the arrival of a gray tabby cat who immediately began scratching at it with his enormous six-toed paws.

"Paolo!"

His return was an early sign of spring, and she leapt out of bed to open her window to his demands. He was thin, as he always was this time of year, and felt like nothing but bones as she lifted him over the sill. She cradled him in one arm while shutting the window with the other. The Graysons would never allow her to keep Paolo as a permanent pet, and she scarcely saw herself fit for that kind of responsibility. Like every other man in her life, this one showed up, loved her for a time, and went away. The difference being, of course, that Paolo always came back.

Monica nuzzled her face in his furry neck and delighted in the resulting purr. "You're early this year, buddy."

She set him on her bed and slipped downstairs to the kitchen, where she found enough milk in the bottom of the bottles waiting by the back door to make a nice little puddle in a saucer. Further rummaging through the icebox produced a hardened wedge of cheese and a fatty piece of ham—nothing that would be missed by the other tenants. She tore the treats into cat-bite-size pieces and mixed them with the milk, carrying the dish upstairs quietly, but quickly, to avoid any confrontation with her housemates. Back in her room, she set the meal on the floor and herself right next to it, urging Paolo to come down from where he'd curled up on the end of her bed.

"If I had an egg, you'd almost have an omelet." She scratched behind his ears as he tentatively picked through the morsels. When he'd finished, his eyes half-closed with contented drowsiness, he jumped back onto the bed—this time with considerably more effort—and began to knead the comforter.

"Poor thing." She took a paw in her fingers and studied the deformity of having what looked like two paws fused into one. At first she'd thought it to be an accident of birth exclusive to her

Paolo, but Mr. Davenport assured her that it was a documented, if rare, condition. Polydactyl, these cats were called. Hence the cat's name, Paulie, changed over to Paolo in the quest for something more exotic. Not that a twenty-four-toed cat wasn't exotic in his own right.

"That's how I felt yesterday, you know? In that church? Like there was just something *wrong* with me. Like I didn't fit. And now tonight? Going to this shindig again . . ."

She didn't belong in the Anti-Flirt Club, either. Not outside of the story. And Max's note above her column still rankled: she didn't represent the views of *Capitol Chatter*. Someplace else she didn't quite fit.

Monica went nose-to-nose with Paolo, filling her vision with nothing but his green sleepy eyes. "Maybe I should follow you. Go wherever you go when you're not here. You might have a whole big gang of cats just like you. A clowder, isn't it?"

She climbed up into the bed and curled herself around him. Not that she didn't have her own clowders. Dance clubs and juke joints and dark, smoky bars. Those were her people; there she fit right in. Blended perfectly. At least she used to.

Tempting as it may have been to doze the afternoon away, she picked up her book, tucked her feet under the accommodating cat, and escaped to spring.

The meeting was held in the same basement space, and even though it was her second time to attend, she approached with apprehension. A group of girls gathered at the top of the stairs leading to the basement. What they were saying in their huddled whispers wasn't clear, but the hushed outrage couldn't be ignored. Sure enough, one of the girls had a folded copy of *Capitol Chatter*, and Monica walked down the steps to the sound of her own words, surprised at how sinister they sounded.

The atmosphere downstairs, too, was subdued—a far cry from the previous meeting. She went directly to the row of coats along the back wall and stood, her forehead buried in her sleeve.

"So you've read it." She knew it was Emma Sue not so much because she recognized the voice but because it came from so far above her. "It's awful, isn't it?"

Monica looked up.

"It's just so mean-spirited. Makes Alice out to be an Elizabeth Cady Stanton trying to stamp out the modern girl."

"Oh, it's not that bad."

"It certainly is. Just hateful. And worse—" she looked around and lowered her voice—"it was written by one of *us*."

"You don't know that. The whole city knows about this group. I learned about it from the newspaper."

"This wasn't someone who knows *about* the group; it's someone who *knows* the group. And Alice is just sick about it."

Monica busied herself taking off her coat and smoothing it over the hook before asking Emma Sue if there were any doughnuts like last time.

"Yes," she said, "and coffee."

"Good," Monica said, "but I might have to skip the coffee. I've been drinking it all day. Explains why I'm so jumpy."

In fact, she skipped the doughnuts, too, though she offered no explanation for that. How could she explain that her throat was so swollen with truth and guilt, she'd never be able to choke down a single bite? Instead, she headed for the back row of chairs and took a seat on the aisle, in case she needed a quick getaway.

As Alice Reighly took her place, the women followed suit, and once all had taken their seats, it was obvious this crowd was considerably smaller than that of the previous meeting. A tiny flicker of pride rose up through the quagmire of guilt. Women had read her column; they had changed their allegiance because of her words. A smile tugged at the corner of her mouth, and she worked to keep her face straight. Wouldn't do to be the only grin in the crowd of so many grumpy Grundies.

"Good evening, ladies," Alice said to the hushed room. "I do not think it is an exaggeration to say we have been dealt a traitorous blow. I have never been a regular reader of—" she paused to make a show of reading a folded issue of *Capitol Chatter*—"this piece known as Monkey Business. And I can rest assured that I have hardly been missing an opportunity to better my mind through substantive journalistic effort."

Soft laughter rippled through the room, Monica's included, though her derisive snort was meant to defend her from the girls. Most of them wouldn't know substantive journalism from a lovelorn romance.

"To quote this 'little Monkey,'" Alice continued, "we are nothing more than a bunch of women ready to 'crawl back into the last century.' I look at you lovely young ladies and cannot see anything further from the truth. You are all beautiful and modern, every bit as stylish as this writer claims to be."

Monica squirmed. *Claims* to be?

Emma Sue nudged her and whispered, "Don't worry. I think you're very stylish."

"Thank you," Monica said, not thinking to return the compliment.

"Nobody wants to turn back the clock of womanhood less than I do. I relish our freedom, but I also see the responsibilities we have to each other. Our days as chattel are over, if only the rogue on the street would remember that fact."

Cheers erupted, with Monica's polite applause in their midst.

"Do not fall prey to the hatred of men—or monkeys—who wish you to remain powerless. Just as alcohol robs you of your judgment, so does flirting rob you of your self-respect. I strongly suspect that is something this authoress lacks."

Monica sat stock-still as Alice's words fell around her, striking her like embers flung from fire. She dared not close her eyes, lest she open them to find the basement meeting room transformed into a cathedral with the Virgin Mary in all her fresco glory lining the walls. So she fixed her gaze directly on the diminutive woman behind the podium and burned.

"As most of you know, Monkey is the nom de plume chosen to protect the identity of this writer. She could very well be sitting among us this evening, as she was most certainly in attendance at a previous meeting. But I urge you not to seek her out, as I shall not. Let her stay and learn and grow. Nothing extinguishes the behavior of a flirt like being ignored. And I shall speak of this no more."

She made a show of folding the paper and dropping it into a rubbish bin clearly set on the stage for that purpose and lifted her voice to declare that they would now discuss more fruitful things.

Next to the fuming Monica, Emma Sue sat with her long, thin arms folded across her chest, openly expressing the anger that seethed beneath Monica's skin.

"Some nerve," Emma Sue hissed. "I'll bet she's ugly."

"Sshh." Monica feigned interest in the speech while the guilt she'd felt as she walked in twisted into something more akin to shame. Alice regaled the audience with the account of the handsome photographer, calling him a grand test of their principles.

"Not to mention that brother of yours," Emma Sue whispered.

"I'd rather you didn't," Monica said. "Mention him, that is."

Or even think about him, for that matter. Otherwise, it was just a matter of time before all the secrets were out.

Whatever Alice Reighly said for the rest of her speech was drowned out by a rushing sound in Monica's ears. She smiled when the others laughed, nodded along with the woman in front of her, and even unclenched her fists to participate in a smattering of applause. All the while, a single phrase hid in the crevices of her mind, whispering a haunting refrain.

They hate me.

As far as she knew, she'd never been hated before.

On the first day they met, Max had commented that she was the girl everybody loved but nobody knew. Now she was living the opposite truth. And here she'd never cared much about being loved or hated. She wrote what she wanted to, regardless of the consequences. She lapped up the praise and let the criticisms roll off her back, always distanced from it all by the force of anonymity.

She studied Alice Reighly. Meek, homely, soft-spoken Alice Reighly, able to stand under her own power, speaking her mind, championing her vision. She spoke her words. She *lived* her words in a way Monica never could—free of fear. Noble. This was not a woman suffering from a lack of self-respect.

Of everything, that assessment took root in her very soul.

What would that feel like? To stand up in the middle of this sea of women and say, *"It was me! I wrote it! Lighten up, ladies, it's a joke!"* Or maybe she should confront Alice privately, apologize for the snide tone if not the thesis. Perhaps Emma Sue beside her could be an experimental confidante; she could practice her confession in the guise of friendship.

Max would be pleased. He'd distanced himself and all of *Capitol Chatter* from her words—no reason she couldn't distance herself, too.

"Monkey's not real," she'd say with a shrug. *"Just a figment of my imagination. Sometimes she talks too much. I'll keep her on a shorter leash next time."*

Next time.

She was expected to turn in another column after the weekend, a continuation of her experimental study, and here she sat, hearing nothing, feeling nothing but regret for most of what she'd written so far. Maybe not regret so much as chagrin, like seeing her words in a new light that banished her wit into shadow. Then it came clear. If Monica could not make amends at the risk of exposing Monkey, Monkey would just have to apologize for herself.

Eyes closed, she tried to recall what Alice had said at the beginning of her speech. That she wanted the authoress to stay and learn and grow. She crossed her fingers and repeated the phrase three times.

Stay and learn and grow.

No reason next week's column couldn't open with a mea culpa.

Once the meeting ended with great enthusiasm for the upcoming Anti-Flirting Week, Monica managed to squirm away, avoiding interaction with the other girls. She suppressed the paranoid assumption that *they* were avoiding *her* as she slipped into her coat and out the door before she could fall victim to any of their disgruntled barbs.

Outside, she had the street to herself, and there the first tear sprang cold upon her cheek. She bit her lip, hoping to distract herself and stem those that would follow, but soon they were flowing faster than she could wipe them away. She doubled her pace to distance herself from any of the girls who might have followed.

"Monica?"

No! No! She quickened her pace yet again and turned a blind corner, not to get away from him but to lead him away from *them*.

"Monica!"

She ducked into a doorway—a stationer's shop closed for the night—and next she knew he filled it, shielding her from the street and any of the prying eyes that might have followed.

"Oh, Max." She grabbed two handfuls of his coat and drew herself up against him. "It was terrible, the things they said about me. You should have heard . . ."

He placed his hands on her shoulders in an embrace meant to keep her distant and stooped to look into her eyes.

"So they know it's you? That you wrote the column?"

She shook her head. "Not exactly. Not that I could tell. But she read the column out loud, and it was awful."

"Oh, darling." He drew her close, and she felt his hand on top of her head. "I think what you're feeling here is what some would call an attack of conscience." And then, to her utter horror, she felt him chuckle.

She would have swatted him away, but his embrace was becoming a familiar place of refuge.

"They think I'm a monster," she said. "Or that *she* is."

"Shall I be on the lookout for pitchforks?"

She lifted her face, then twisted it. "Sanctuary . . ."

He laughed again and gave her a good-natured push away. "Oh no. I told you not to go back."

"Technically, you said you didn't know if it would be a good idea for me to go back."

"And was it?"

"No. Is that why you're here? To rescue me?"

"Only from hunger. I've been meaning to repay you for the

kolache. In fact, I was planning to take you to dinner yesterday, after our visit to the cathedral, but you didn't seem in the right humor."

"Unlike the fountain of joy you see before you now?"

"I'll try to work up a few jokes between here and there."

There turned out to be a twenty-top diner just two blocks away. Light glowed warm from within, softened by steam on the windows. Inside, they were led to a high-back booth where Monica immediately drew her signature monkey in the steam.

"Brazen," he said.

"I've always been the wild child."

They spent a few moments looking around at their fellow late diners—not that nine o'clock was an unreasonable hour for supper. Several of their companions were older couples who sat in a silence equal to their own, yet comfortable. Giggles bubbled over from a tableful of shopgirls, no doubt to attract the attention of one or more of the young men at the counter.

She ordered a hearty meal of shepherd's pie, he a chopped steak with potatoes, and they settled in with cups of steaming tea to wait for their food.

"I've never been to this place before," Monica said. Looking around, she wished she had. It felt cozy. There was, however, a sweet little club about ten doors down from that stationer's shop, and upstairs. No music, just drinks—more like a parlor with a Victrola. She wondered if Max knew about that, decided he didn't, and kept her own mouth shut about it.

"My house is just a few blocks that way. I'm fast becoming a regular here."

The fact was evident in the familiar way the waitress had taken their order and attended to their—at least, his—needs. Not exactly flirting, but definitely special.

She calculated what she knew of the city. "That's quite a hike for you, then, isn't it? Into the office?"

"I guess Edward liked to keep his distance."

"I'm guessing it's about time for you to break down and buy a car."

Their food arrived, giving the waitress a chance to bestow a lingering touch on Max's sleeve as she promised to be right back with ketchup.

"I can see why you're a regular," Monica said, teasing.

"Take a bite, and *then* you'll see."

She obeyed, and he was right. The food was warm and comforting. The hurtful words of Alice Reighly and the self-loathing those words created melted away in the bits of seasoned diced meat and potato crust.

"Delicious?" he asked.

"Amazing." She stilled her conversation for three more bites. "I guess living near this place is worth the walk."

"Indeed. And, yes, it's a bit far, but not far enough to justify a car. I'm thinking it will be a little more pleasant in the spring."

She cocked an eyebrow. "So you're planning to be here in the spring?"

"So far, yes. No sense investing my money in the paper if I don't intend to invest myself, too."

"Well, if it gives you any hope at all, I had a sign today that spring is on its way."

"Your cat?"

He remembered. "Right outside my window. I fixed him a snack and he fell asleep on the end of my bed. I didn't have the heart to kick him out into the cold before I left. If he wakes up and starts howling, I might be kicked right out on the street with him."

"Landlord doesn't approve?"

"Claims they're filthy beasts that steal babies' breath. Not that we have any babies in the house."

"That's too bad. I've always had a fondness for cats myself."

Monica only allowed the next thought as much time to form as it took for her to eat the next forkful of pie. "You should take my Paolo."

"Paolo?"

"He's exotic. And it's still too cold for him to be homeless."

"For all you know, he lives in a senator's house during the winter."

"All the more reason to rescue the poor thing, don't you think?"

Max lifted his hands in surrender. "Okay, okay, but only for the rest of winter. I'd hate to steal away your closest friend. When shall I pick him up?"

"Not tonight. It's too late for me to have a visitor." Never mind that she'd had plenty of guests who arrived at this hour and stayed on until morning. Why not take a shot at establishing a little propriety? "Maybe I can bring him to your place? I can return your book."

He looked uncomfortable. "It's a little late for me to have a visitor too."

"You live alone."

"But I have my own sense of—"

"Propriety?"

"Respect. For you. I wouldn't want anybody to get the wrong idea."

"How kind of you." But a bit of coolness had crept up from her supper and into her voice. "Some other time, then?"

"Tomorrow night," he said, surprising her with his insistence. "Seven o'clock. That will give me time to tidy up and get a few groceries."

A bit of warmth came back. "Dinner, too?"

"To be honest, I was thinking of the cat. But of course, dinner, too."

She had a split second to collect herself and decide whether to be embarrassed at her gaffe or to laugh it off with something clever like *"Good. We both like ham."* But she waited too long, and before she could say a thing, the door to the diner opened and in walked a very loud, very inebriated couple, one of whom was all too familiar.

Charlie.

He looked oddly more squat and square than she remembered, but maybe that was due to his flattened hat and a coat that looked ready to burst its buttons. His companion was a good three inches taller than he, with hair the distinctive shade of blonde that implicated a bottle in its creation. They were wrapped around each other as if joined in some invisible, slow-moving potato-sack stagger.

Luckily the booths were tall and she was short. Instinctively she slouched down in her seat and grabbed a menu to hide her face.

"Hey, relax," Max said. "For a bachelor, I'm not that bad of a cook."

"Sorry," she said, keeping her voice low. "Bad penny just turned up."

He swiveled in his seat, easily looking over the back of the booth. "Which one? Him or her?"

"Both. But I can only vouch for one."

"Would you like to wear my hat? Can I get you a fake moustache?"

"Just act natural."

He slumped. "I shall follow your example." He proceeded to cut into his steak with such exaggerated furtiveness that she couldn't stifle her giggle. One peek around the edge of the menu showed that Charlie heard the familiar sound, and she could only sit, a helpless target, as they veered unsteadily toward her.

"There's my little Mousie." Charlie's words were thick and slurred. He took the menu away from Monica and trapped it on the table under his wide, soft palm. "Fancy running into you here. Must be some kind of fate or somethin'. Right, baby?" This he directed at the blonde. "Some kind of fate."

"Yeah, some kind," the blonde repeated. She openly stared at Max with black-smeared eyes. "Maybe you should introduce us."

"Yes," Monica said, tight-lipped. "Please do. I take it this isn't your wife, either?"

"Wife?" The woman seemed offended enough to fall off her shoes.

"Ah, now, Mousie. Why you gotta be like that?"

"You're right, Charlie," Monica said. "If this were your wife, you never would have come over here, would you? So let's just pretend—you're good at that—and you can go away."

"You always had a whole lotta mean in that little body. You broke my heart."

"Obviously."

"I think it's best that you go," Max said. He slid out from the booth and stood, towering over them both. "Or if it's easier, we will." He glanced down at Monica. "Are you finished?"

If anything could make this meal too undesirable to finish, it was the presence of Charlie and this woman. She pushed her plate away and would have stood, too, if Charlie weren't lurking just at the edge of her seat.

"This the guy you threw me over for?"

She didn't answer. Or move.

"Hey, buddy," Max said, "I don't think that's the way you want to talk to the lady."

Charlie spun in an unsteady circle, saying, "Lady? *Lady?* Any of you guys see a lady in here?"

This sent the blonde into a fit of giggles, and Charlie might have kept spinning indefinitely if Max hadn't done him the kindness of grasping his arm and bringing him to a stumbling stop, saying, "That's enough."

"Well, look who found herself a champion."

By now they'd attracted the attention of everyone in the restaurant, including the gentlemen from the lunch counter, who cracked their knuckles, appearing ready and eager to come to Max's aid should he need it.

He didn't.

Easily twisting Charlie's arm into an unnatural angle with one hand, Max dropped enough money on the table to not only cover the bill but also to compensate their waitress for the trouble caused by their uninvited guests. Monica quickly slid out, careful not to brush up against either of them, and wished the blonde good luck.

"Don't act like I wasn't good to you." Charlie's lips took on a sinister twist, and he craned his neck to look around Max at the blonde. "Be a good enough girl, and you might get yourself a little fox coat just like that one."

Monica felt every bit of herself drain away, like her head had been split wide open, leaving everything exposed to Charlie's acidic revelations. She burned from the inside, her face red from the volcanic rush, too hot for tears. Whatever Max said next was lost, but his meaning came through unmistakable as he drew back his free hand and landed a punch squarely against Charlie's nose.

"Baby!" The blonde rushed to his side as he staggered into a chair that was far too fragile to absorb the impact.

"Max!"

She grabbed his arm before he could deliver another blow, should Charlie find the strength to stand.

"Sir!" The waitress was at his side, wrapping an ice cube in a cloth napkin. "For your hand, so it don't swell up."

"How about a steak for his face?" the blonde said, cradling Charlie's head in her lap.

"Give me eighty-five cents, and it's yours."

"Come on," Max said, tugging Monica out the door. Once outside, he kept hold of her hand, walking swiftly enough to force her to run until they reached the nearest streetcar stop.

"Are you all right?" he said, studying her face in the streetlight.

Her champion, Charlie had said, and she forced herself not to fling her arms around his neck and kiss him.

"You're the one who socked him. How are you?"

He held up his hand, and she could see the knuckles still red and already swollen. This, without a thought, she kissed. "No one's ever defended me like that before."

"'Twas an honor, milady."

"He's . . . Charlie . . . He was an old boyfriend."

"So I gathered."

"Not so old, I guess. I mean, it's only been a little while since—"

"You don't need to explain."

Of course she didn't. Any questions he might have had about her character were answered in the revelatory light of Charlie's lewd suggestion. She'd never be able to wear this coat again.

A car arrived and came to a stop, emitting a few passengers onto the street.

"Is this one yours?" he asked.

She nodded.

"Do you have a dime?"

She nodded again, not wanting to let go of his hand, despite his obvious dismissal. "I suppose you'll want to cancel our—" she hesitated to use the word *date*—"dinner tomorrow."

He grinned and recited a series of numbers on Ninth Street. "Seven o'clock. Bring the cat."

CHAPTER 18

And so, slowly, beginning at his hands and feet and creeping
along his limbs to the vital centres of his body, that strange
change continued. It was like the slow spreading of a poison.

H. G. WELLS, *THE INVISIBLE MAN*

WHY HAD HE SAID ANYTHING about dinner? For that matter, why did he say anything about anything?

And those were the more innocuous questions that pestered him as he lay on his narrow, cold bed.

How "old" of an old boyfriend was that Charlie guy? Before Max met her? After she started on this ill-fated anti-flirt espionage? And just how long did it take for her to figure out he was married?

Dear Lord, he prayed, *there have to be half a million girls in this city. Why did you have to cross my path with hers? And just what am I supposed to do with her now that she's mine?*

"Not that she's *mine*," he said into the darkness. Just because he thought about her, prayed for her, protected her, saw her face and heard her laugh when she was nowhere to be found. Didn't every pretty girl make a guy choke on his heart when he saw her standing with him in a church? Couldn't a fellow punch another fellow in the face without laying claim to the girl in the middle? After all, he had no desire to sock it to Miss Alice Reighly, and *she'd* hurt Monica as much as anybody. No, in that matter he wanted to smack himself for starting that whole ball rolling.

If any woman ever seemed like one who should send him running, it was Monica Bisbaine. She had none of the qualities his mother had urged him to look for. Her life was a living example of everything Sister Aimee warned the world against. Loose, if this jokester tonight were to be believed. A lush, given her ease with and desire for drink. Even lazy—wasting a quick wit and sharp writing on a crummy last-page column in a two-bit tabloid.

But she's mine.

This time the words didn't belong to him.

She's mine, Max.

He tried to imagine anyone else levying that same list of accusations against her. Charlie called her loose, and he socked him. Alice Reighly insulted her writing, and he'd burned a little in anger, wishing to rise to her defense. As for the drinking? Well, even he couldn't defend the government's interference there.

She's mine, Max. And I love her.

"I know you do, Lord. I wish she knew that too."

And despite all the reasons he shouldn't, Max knew he loved her too.

Knowing he'd pushed sleep further away than before, he sat up in bed and reached for the chain on the bedside lamp, turning his eyes away from the initial illumination. Books were stacked on the table, his Bible among them, and while he knew his first recourse should be to look for comfort and clarification in God's Word, he couldn't help but dread what he might hear.

Two wandering souls, they were, each orphaned and alone. The hunchback and the gypsy, though their roles seemed interchangeable. She fancied herself, he presumed, the twisted, unlovable soul, yet here he harbored an unspoken love.

His mind went back to that first day, those first moments before he knew what a quagmire lurked behind those big brown eyes, when she'd called him Griffin. The Invisible Man. Little did he know then that she lived just as invisibly as he did.

That novel, too, lay on the bedside table, marked with the ribbon where he'd left off at his last reading. He grabbed it now, put on his glasses, and smiled at the chapter title: "The Invisible Man Sleeps."

"Not likely." He swung his legs over the side of the bed and slipped his feet into his slippers. His thick robe hung from the bedpost. He put it on, took his book, and headed into the dark kitchen. A glass of warm milk was in order; he'd take it back into bed with him, feeling defiant in doing so despite the years he'd spent without accountability for his behavior.

As the milk warmed in the pan, he thought about all the responsibilities he would have for tomorrow's evening with Monica. A "date," as she might call it. As anyone might call it, actually. The house remained fairly clean between Zelda's visits, though he might straighten the bookshelf. And perhaps a new oil-cloth for the table. Something pretty—women liked those things. Flowers for the center. And food.

He thought no further than *food*.

Whatever had compelled him to agree to making dinner? *Bewitched* might be more accurate. He wasn't even sure what he should get for the cat.

This was the disadvantage of living invisible. A stranger in a strange land. He'd never invited a woman to his home before, having gone from his parents' house to Army barracks to a one-room apartment under the scrutiny of an evangelist with a strangely personal reach. Maybe he'd assumed Monica—a bachelor in her own right—would be satisfied with a can of soup and a ham sandwich.

Then he remembered the way she'd tucked into that shepherd's pie.

❧

First thing in the morning, after the hours of restless sleep that finally came, he called the *Capitol Chatter* offices, knowing Zelda Ovenoff would be there, straightening and dusting, no matter her new responsibilities as a contributing writer. Whether or not she'd answer the phone, however, was a different question altogether.

He was in luck.

"Hallo. Is Zelda."

"Zelda. It's Max."

"Mr. Moore?"

"Yes."

"Oh, the phone! It has been ringing and ringing all morning. At first I did not answer, but over and over."

If this were a regular Saturday occurrence, it was the first he'd heard of it. In fact, he could count at the most twenty phone calls to the office since he'd arrived. His mind flashed back to the image of Doc King's gun-wielding thugs, and he winced. "Who's been calling?"

"So many people. They want to buy advertisement, and I tell them I'm only the cleaning lady, to call back on Monday. So be prepared that day to be very busy."

"Well, what do you know?"

"Nothing, Mr. Moore. Not about any of that business."

He laughed. "That's all right, Zelda. You did just fine. I don't know why they would be calling this time of week anyway."

"*You* called, Mr. Moore."

250

"For completely different reasons, I assure you." Over the next minute, he explained his predicament to Zelda. That he'd invited a friend to dinner, and he had no idea what to prepare.

"It is a woman?"

There was no lying to Zelda, not even over the phone. He cleared his throat. "It is."

"It is our Miss Monica?"

Had he not already set a precedent of truth, he might have denied it, but already he'd hesitated long enough to confirm her guess.

"It is, actually." He felt no compulsion to tell her about the cat.

"Oh, Mr. Moore. I will be there in one hour to take care of everything."

Zelda didn't exaggerate. By late afternoon, Max was sitting in a spotless house with the smell of pork shoulder and turnips roasting in his oven. Foolproof, Zelda had said. "Just don't touch it until you eat it."

The kitchen table was covered with a crocheted cloth the color of champagne and set with china decorated with flowers painted in gold.

"I have four sets I took from my sister," she'd said with a hint of triumph. "I convinced her no-good husband to give them to me so I'd keep my mouth shut about his shenanigans."

A modest number of carnations stood in a clear cut-glass vase, but he'd drawn the line at candles.

"But, Mr. Moore," Zelda had implored, "they make for such romance."

That's when he told her about the cat, and they agreed the risk of fire would be too great.

Every book on Uncle Edward's bookshelf stood upright, spine out—a task Zelda had been wary of until Max convinced her he didn't share his uncle's overprotectiveness toward them. After she left, he'd spent the afternoon in the soft leather chair staring at it. A lifetime's collection. He settled in to read *The Invisible Man*, hoping to finish it before Monica arrived. Then, perhaps, he'd lend it to her, giving them another book to share. And when she finished, she could bring it back. Choose another. When he looked at the vast array of titles on the shelves, he saw nothing but endless opportunities for visits and conversation. He could be the Rudy Valentino of librarians.

His eyes raked through the pages, but few of the words registered. He glanced up at the clock. Two more hours and she'd be here. Then another glance fifteen minutes later. The excitement of the book's final chapters held no fascination for him. He'd read it before. He knew how it ended—the angry mob descending on the Invisible Man. The mob beating him to death, and his slow reappearance, vein by vein, to show him pitiful and weak.

The room had grown nearly dark around him, so much so that he'd moved the book clear up to the end of his nose, absorbed in the act of reading if not the story. The knock at the door was more surprising than startling, though he did momentarily lose his grip on the book.

She knocked again, and from his vantage point he could see her in full profile, one hand poised at his door, the other straining to hold a large covered basket.

The cat.

He closed the book, ran his fingers through his hair, straightened his glasses, smoothed his shirt, took a deep breath, and opened the door to find her now holding the basket with both hands, offering it across the threshold.

"I present to you," she said with exaggerated grandiosity, "Paolo the cat." Without any other hint of invitation, she walked across the threshold of his home and set the basket on the floor.

"Please," he said. "Come in."

She was already unbuttoning her coat, which she handed over along with her hat with the clear expectation that he had some sort of a plan for what to do with them.

"Isn't this cozy?" Her eyes were taking a slow spin around the room, but her whole body turned when her gaze fell upon the bookcase, and her face took on an expression of near awe. "Look at those!"

"It is an impressive collection," Max said, unable to keep himself from feeling an undeserved sense of pride. "He has everything—history, biography, atlases, travel guides . . ."

She'd stepped closer and was running her small, tapered fingers along the exposed spines of the books.

"They're not in any sense of order right now." He felt himself babbling but couldn't stop. "When I first got here, they were a mess. Just crammed every which way on the shelf. We've worked to just get them facing one direction. I guess organizing them into categories will have to wait."

Resting her hand on a book, she turned to look over her shoulder. *"We?"*

"Zelda and I. Mostly Zelda."

She made a sound indicating she needed no more information.

A muted howling sound called Monica's attention away from the books and Max's attention away from Monica.

"Is he vicious?" Max eyed the basket warily as it made a tiny scooting path.

"Not usually. But then again, as far as I know he's never been stuffed into a basket and hauled around on a bus before. Let's just hope he's forgiving."

"I'll let you do the honors," Max said, giving her a wide berth. "It might be best if the first face he sees is a familiar one."

"How—thoughtful of you. And not at all cowardly."

She knelt down, slipped the basket's leather thong out of its closure, and opened the lid. Two green eyes stared from its depths.

"Vieni," Monica urged, with a soft clicking sound. *"Vieni qui."*

"You speak Italian?"

"No. But Paolo does, I think." And again she cooed, *"Vieni."*

What emerged was a gray tabby cat, wholly unremarkable save for the fact that each of his feet looked to be encased in a fat, furry mitten.

"*Ciao*, Paolo," he said, playing along.

Monica softened her voice to something identifiably feline. *"Buona sera, signore."* She was petting the top of the cat's head, and he purred loudly in response. In fact, he walked his mittened feet right up Monica's leg and touched his whiskers to her face.

"He looks like he doesn't want to leave you."

"Don't be fooled." She touched her nose to Paolo's. "He leaves me all the time." She gathered him in her arms, kissed the top of his head, and set him back on the ground. "Help me up?"

She was stretching her hand up to him, and he took it, resisting the absurd urge to gather her into his arms in just the same manner. Once she was on her feet, he let go, and they stood, not quite side by side, not quite facing each other, but awkwardly angled. She took another deep breath and a quick look around; he stuffed his hands into his pockets and rocked on his heels. Paolo made his way to the stove, gave his back one good arch, then curled up on the braided rug in front of it.

"I think he'll be fine," Monica said. He couldn't see her face, but something in her voice caught his attention. He reached out, touched her chin, and turned her toward him. Tears pooled in her eyes. "It's silly, I know." She shook off both his touch and her tears. "I'll just miss him is all."

He wanted to tell her she could come visit anytime, but since she'd come into the room, coherence eluded him. How was it that within five minutes of arriving, both she and this cat seemed more at home in this place than he ever did? Already she'd returned to the bookcase, studying the gold-embossed titles.

"I finished *The Enchanted April*. I would have brought it back, but I was afraid Paolo might rip it to shreds."

"Another time. Or you can bring it to the office."

She gave no indication whether she'd heard him or not, as she remained engrossed by the wealth of Uncle Edward's collection. "We had a library in our house," she said, speaking as if her mind were as far away as any of these books would have taken her. "Not the house I grew up in, but the one . . . later. In Georgetown. At least, it was supposed to be a library, because it had all these shelves. Every wall, just lined with them. I remember telling my mother that I couldn't wait to fill it up. With books. I had this image of myself lying in the middle of that room. No furniture, even. Just the floor, surrounded by books, and just reading and reading and reading."

"Did you fill it up?" He regretted the question the moment he asked, even more when the droop in her shoulders and the stiffening of her body heralded her answer.

"Hardly. My mother wasn't going to waste any of our precious money on books. Not when we had to buy expensive furniture and knickknacks to impress all those people who never came to visit."

"Well, these are here for you. Whenever you like."

She turned and looked at him with eyes that made him want to give her everything he'd ever own. "Can I even sit on your floor? Right here, next to Paolo?"

"You'll have to," he said, grateful for her little joke to ease the mood. "I only have one chair."

"Is that where I'm going to have to sit to eat my supper?" She tilted her nose and sniffed. "It smells delicious, by the way."

"Of course not. This way." Not daring to touch her, he gestured around the corner into the tiny kitchen, which by now had fallen into gray shadow. Candlelight may have been in order after all.

"Well, isn't this lovely?" Monica said once he'd flipped the switch to illuminate the kitchen in safe, bright light. Her tone oddly matched the identical phrasing of when she'd called the living room "cozy." "Tablecloth? China?" She leaned over the table and inhaled the scent of the flowers.

"All the work of Mrs. Ovenoff, I assure you." He busied himself finding a tea towel to protect his hands as he took the roast out of his tiny oven. Suddenly he felt like Paolo, with extra fingers and thumbs making his movements more clumsy than usual. The kitchen, while always small, seemed to have shrunk to doll-sized proportions. He bumped into cupboards, bumped into Monica, nearly dropped the roaster's lid.

"Zelda trusted you with her dishes?"

"Hard to believe, I know."

Somehow, he managed to get the roast and vegetables into a serving dish and then to the table, where Monica took over the task of transferring the food to their plates.

"I'm so glad you invited me over tonight. It's Mr. Davenport's night to cook, and he only knows one thing: corned-beef hash."

"My father made corned-beef hash on nights when my mother had her ladies' auxiliary meetings."

"Is that so?"

There was something different about her this evening. She

seemed cool, restrained, almost distant. All the worries he'd had about being alone with her—here, in his home—quietly went away, only to be replaced by new ones. Had he so offended her in the church that she'd erected some barrier between them? Had the incident with that goon in the diner fed whatever embarrassment he'd initiated? Sitting across from him, poised to dig her fork into supper, she seemed politely disconnected from him. It took a few minutes for him to really understand what he felt at the moment, but then it came clear.

He missed her.

In fact, he'd been missing her all day. All night, even, since the diner. Before that, since the cathedral. Before that . . . And now, here she was. And wasn't. Monica was in his kitchen, but something was missing. *Someone* was missing.

She'd left the Monkey behind.

That was it. Not once, not for a moment, had she flirted with him. He cut into his roast, took a bite, and pondered everything she'd said, every expression, every nuance since her arrival. No batting of her eyelashes. No pouting, no touching. Even when he helped her to her feet, when she teetered in front of him, just a bit of balance away from falling against him. No innuendo, just pure, stilted, bland conversation. Not unlike the turnip on his plate.

"Well, isn't this delicious?" she said, interrupting his thoughts.

"It is," he agreed, adding that it was Zelda who deserved the credit.

From that point on, their conversation bounced between the texture of the roast, the flavor of the turnips, and Zelda's hair. Monica, it seemed, had come armed with the table manners of a finishing-school girl on scholarship, leaving Max somewhere between amused and befuddled at her performance. She clipped her words and touched her napkin to her lips and barely raised her eyes above the level of her water glass. Where was the girl who drank Scotch whiskey from a bottle? Or danced up close in Negro nightclubs? His mind was free to ponder such questions, as the conversation sat dull as butter on the table. No jabs, no jokes. She wore this persona like a duck in galoshes. Awkward, almost pathetic.

And yet a new frustration stirred within. His mind, now completely disengaged from the banality of her conversation, wandered, calling back memories of the steam that puffed from her lips on a cold winter morning, the feel of that tiny body tucked up against his, the featherlike softness of her hair. Desire so churned within him that he couldn't speak, couldn't swallow. His fork—newly useless—rested against his thumb. He watched her face, once again obscured by that stupid napkin, change as her eyes met his. They'd been dull all during dinner, but now they turned downcast. She dropped her napkin and stood.

"I think it's time for me to leave."

"No." He stood abruptly, sending his chair clattering behind him. The noise attracted Paolo's attention, and the cat came padding into the kitchen. Upon seeing him, Monica—without hesitation or permission—stooped to set her plate on the floor. There she remained, scratching the creature behind his ears as he lapped the juices and fed on the scraps from her plate.

"I do have food for him, you know," Max said. "Sardines. Five tins of them, in fact."

She didn't look up. "Who would want sardines when you can have something as tasty as this?"

"Well, he'd better not get used to it. Most nights I have a can of soup."

Monica bent to give Paolo a kiss on the top of his head, then rose and said, "Thank you for taking him in," before attempting to brush past him on her way to the front room.

He didn't touch her, but he stopped her with half a step to the side.

"You don't have to go."

"I do. I want to."

"Why?"

"Because I'm not having any fun. Neither of us are." She was daring him to contradict her, but her blunt honesty took him by surprise. "Look, I tried. Okay?"

Now, as he puzzled over what she'd said, she did slip by, leaving him to catch up in three long strides to where she was hurrying to put on her coat. He took it from her.

"Tried what?"

"To be *good*." She said the word as if he'd served her the sardines. "To be appropriate and proper, like that Alice Reighly says."

She made an attempt to snatch her coat back, and a folded piece of paper fell from the pocket. She retrieved it, unfolded it, and handed it over to him. "The rules."

His eyes skimmed the mimeographed type. A list of directives to distinguish the Stranger from the One. Which was he?

"You don't have to follow her rules, you know."

"But even you—back when we were in that church, you said—"

"I said that you should be true to the woman you are. Whoever that woman was at dinner? She wasn't *you*."

She tugged. "How do you know?"

He held firm. "Because you make me laugh. And you make me furious. And you make me want to do things like I've never wanted before."

Without meaning to, he'd pulled her closer, using the plain-spun wool of her coat like a lure, to the point where he could almost feel her body against his. Never before, he surmised, had

259

this garment ever been so charged to protect her from the elements of nature.

"Things like what?"

Nothing coquettish in her question. Her chin jutted forward, demanding an answer, and he knew what she wanted to hear. She didn't care that he'd never been in a brawl with a stranger, or tasted liquor, or faced down gin-joint gangsters. Her eyes begged him to tell of his desire; her lips were parted, waiting for a kiss. She unclenched her fingers from the coat, wanting him to drop it to the floor, removing the last physical barrier between them. He listened to her, engaging all of his senses to do so. Their breath was in perfect unison as were, he supposed, their hearts. At least in their rhythm. His own pounded, and if he dropped the coat and drew her to him, they would join in the next beat. And perhaps every beat thereafter.

She waited for an answer, and every part of him vied for the privilege of responding. His eyes wanted nothing more than to gaze upon her. His mouth begged to kiss her. His arms wanted to scoop her up; his legs, to carry the both of them to another room entirely. That's what she wanted to hear. That was the reaction and reassurance she sought.

But she deserved better.

"You, Monica," he said, stepping away, "make me want to do crazy things." Using her coat to protect his touch, he turned her around, facing her away from him so she could slip her arms into the sleeves.

She looked back over her shoulder. "Crazy, like what?"

"Like sending a beautiful woman out into a cold winter night." He reached for his coat. "After I walk you to the bus stop."

"Always the gentleman."

He could see that she was fighting a losing battle to keep the sadness from her smile, but there was a certain risk to offering reassurance—one that might topple his last stance of resistance.

"What is it you flapper girls say? 'Cash or check?'"

She pursed her lips. "I'm no flapper."

"Even so." His hand safely ensconced in a glove, he touched her face. "I'll take a check."

He opened the door for them both, welcoming the rush of the winter night's air. The walk to the bus stop was silent and quick, and a simple "Good night" ended the evening.

Back home, he took the opportunity to stand outside and study the little house with the lights glowing through the windows. The curtain rustled from within, and Paolo leapt up to the sill and sat, waiting. He couldn't remember the last time any living soul waited for him on the other side of a door.

MONKEY BUSINESS

"Monkey Culpa"

For those of you not up on your Latin, "Monkey culpa" is a ten-dollar way of saying that this little Monkey might have to take back some of her screech and chatter. Maybe because I've had a few days away from the zoo, but I've had a chance to step out of the monkey house and walk upright among the people. Mr. Darwin says that's what happened to all of us. We grew bigger brains and stood up straight. I happen to think that is a bunch of bananas, but there's more than one kind of evolution. For instance, this little Monkey might be ready to evolve into a new woman.

Want to know how your favorite Monkey has been keeping herself busy? She did some dancing cheek-to-cheek at a certain spot better known for its Nubian clientele. She had a late supper in a certain little diner and had quite a time watching a couple of gents duke it out for her honor. She even got a quiet dinner for two in the home of a regular Keeper.

Oh, there was one more escapade, when she grabbed a vine and swung back to visit her anti-flirting sisters. Yes, my monkey girls, I went back. (I'm waving at you RIGHT NOW from a very specific perch.) Furthermore, ladies— for that is what Miss Alice Reighly would call you—I'm taking the challenge. In my evolutionary endeavor, I think I'm going to stick it out. Going to try to stay and learn and grow.

From this column to the next, No Flirting. No winks, no grins, no swish, no sashay. No more pets and pats and whistles. No more dates with apes, and no more dancing near the wolf traps. I'll be the little dark cloud home all alone, leaving the sheiks to the rest of you shebas. Don't gobble them all up at once!

❧ CHAPTER 19 ❧

I have a gift for enraging people, but if I ever
bore you, it will be with a knife.

LOUISE BROOKS

THE SPECIAL DELIVERY ARRIVED at nine o'clock Tuesday morning, announced by Mrs. Kinship with a vigorous knocking on Monica's door. The strength of the knock was tempered by the hesitant, muffled question, "Are you in there?"

Little doubt why Mrs. Kinship would wonder. Monica had gone straight up to her room after the humiliating dismissal from Max's house on Saturday night, and with the exception of a foray to Sobek's for soup, coffee, and rolls, hadn't made her presence known. Her only communication with her housemates was a brief nod in the hallway while on her way to the washroom and a formally scripted note from Mr. Davenport stating that a Mr. Moore had telephoned and requested that she return the communication.

Sunday was, after all, the first official day of Alice Reighly's Anti-Flirting Week. What better way to comply than to lounge alone on her rumpled bed leafing through old editions of the

Saturday Evening Post? More than once she'd longed for the company of Paolo, even considered making the trek to reclaim him. But that would bring her face-to-face with Max, and her eyes were still a little too puffy for any such encounter.

Not that he'd been anything but a gentleman. Which was perfect, because she'd been trying so hard to be a lady.

The long stretch of Monday afternoon was given to the writing of her column, and she allowed a brief glimpse at the paper still rolled into the typewriter as she shuffled to her door, drawing her silk kimono around her shoulders.

"Mrs. Kinship?"

"There is a special delivery for you."

Monica slowed her pace at the announcement, unused to the trilling, songlike quality in Mrs. Kinship's voice. The woman sounded like she wanted a tip, and Monica wasn't in the mood to fork over a nickel.

"Can you slide it under the door? I'm not quite dressed."

"Oh no. Not these."

The woman sounded so pleased with herself that Monica's curiosity broke free of her muddled malaise. She slipped her arms through the robe's sleeves and was loosely tying the sash as she opened the door.

"For you," Mrs. Kinship said. "Delivered just now."

The box was long and flat with the florist's imprint stamped in gold. Monica ran her finger along the thick, burgundy-colored ribbon, thinking she could make something out of that—a headband or a sash.

"I think it's roses," Mrs. Kinship said, her nose close to the lid. "And expensive ones, too, from this place. Not from any street market."

"Thanks." Monica had to tug more than once to get the box

out of Mrs. Kinship's grip. Once she did, she thanked her again and used her shoulder to quietly, yet firmly, close the door between them.

She cleared the clutter of magazines and half-read novels to the floor and set the box on her tiny table. This wasn't the first time she'd received flowers—quite a few former suitors had plied her with such a gift. But as Mrs. Kinship had observed, those had been cheap, bedraggled bouquets often delivered in the sweaty clutch of the man himself. This? This was the gesture of a gentleman, a gentleman willing to spend at least five bucks on a lady.

"Aw, Max. You shouldn't have."

She carefully untied the ribbon, looking for a card before sliding it off the box. *Anonymous?* Leave it to Max's sweet, shy nature to have such a gift delivered with intrigue. Perhaps he wanted to follow in the footsteps of Edward and Mrs. Ovenoff, keeping a courtship shrouded in secrecy. Not that there was a courtship—not yet. She'd known enough men, however, to recognize a desire for something more in a man's eyes. Max might have turned her away and put her on a bus, but he'd done so reluctantly. Perhaps these flowers were an apology? Or a belated invitation?

Eager now to see the contents, she lifted the lid and let it drop to the floor. Large sheets of thin tissue paper rustled as they were folded away to reveal five blood-red roses nestled within. Monica exhaled, finding a tiny wedge of disappointment at the bottom of her breath, and counted again. *Five? That's not even half a dozen.* Though they were beautiful—deep in their color and full in bloom—it seemed an odd gesture.

"Don't send a lot of flowers, do you, Max?"

She lifted out a bloom to inhale its heady fragrance. This was a far cry from the modest bouquet that had adorned his dinner table, and wisely so, for no food could have successfully competed with this scent. Already the stale odor of old coffee and dirty stockings was bowing to its beauty. First thing, Monica would peek through the cabinets of the common kitchen downstairs and find a perfect narrow vase to house the long, thornless stems.

Returning the rose to the box, she found the tiny envelope. There *was* a note after all, addressed to her by the single initial *M*. Positively cloak-and-dagger, without the dagger. Hastily, she turned the envelope over and took out the card within. She didn't even have to read the message before her hand dropped away in disappointment brought on by the familiar ill-executed penmanship. And when, after summoning a deep breath of courage, she read the note, it did little to restore her joy.

I miss you, my little Mousie. One more chance? JJ's tonight.

She could feel every inch of the silk robe touching her skin, grating against it like sand. Charlie, as if she hadn't just seen him with another woman on his arm. As if he didn't have a wife somewhere. That explained the odd number of roses—probably all he could get with whatever cash he had on hand. Or maybe he'd bought the whole dozen: six to the wife, five to her, and the last one left on the pillow of that floozy in the diner. Suddenly the scent was cloyingly sweet, and Monica slammed the lid back on in an attempt to trap it.

She opened the door, unsurprised to find Mrs. Kinship lurking about, a faraway, romantic expression on her plain gray face. "A new admirer?"

"No." Monica squared her shoulders and gave her head a little toss, hoping to exude more swagger than she felt. "An old one, actually, giving me the brush-off."

"Really?"

There was no mistaking the thread of smug victory, but Monica chose to ignore it, knowing the older woman had been ignored far more than rejected.

"Why don't you take them downstairs, put them in a vase with some water. Brighten up the parlor."

"I'll do just that," Mrs. Kinship said, taking the box as though it were some kind of treasure. "And then I'm off to bed, if you wouldn't mind keeping the noise down."

She said this nearly every day; you'd think her fellow residents conducted parades up and down the hallways.

"I'll be out. All afternoon, once I get dressed."

"Well, don't you let this one worry your day," Mrs. Kinship said, hefting the florist's box as if it represented the man himself. "There's bigger and better fish out there."

"Yeah? Well, there's plenty of sharks, too."

Mrs. Kinship sniffed. "I can't imagine any of them would bother you too much."

"Only if you let them."

❧❧❧

An hour later, Monica walked as if facing a bitter headwind, even though the morning—well, midmorning—was clear and still. Head down, seeing only her favorite sturdy-heeled shoes poking out and back from under the hem of her sage-green wool coat. She kept her hands plunged deep within her pockets while relying on the confines of her pumpkin-colored cloche to hide her face.

Don't look up. Don't look up. Don't look up.

It seemed the best way to adhere to the tenets of the club, especially given Saturday night's disaster.

She'd tried. Honestly, really, and truly tried to be her best. Saturday night at Max's house, she'd used her eyes to ogle only his books. Not his jaw with its charm of soft stubble, or the breadth of his shoulders hunched over the stove, or even the way he touched his nose to Paolo's in sweet greeting. She didn't wink or giggle or pounce on that final unguarded moment when he was obviously ready to be a willing participant. There was a moment, right before the first bite of dinner, when she felt like she'd known him all her life. But maybe she just had her time all mixed up. Maybe she'd just been looking. Waiting.

What was rule number 7? "Don't annex all the men you can get—by flirting with many, you may lose out on the one."

Maybe he was the one, and that lunk Charlie almost messed it all up.

She kept her head low and plowed through her fellow pedestrians, stepping through this sea of strangers. At one point, while rounding a corner, her shoulder solidly collided with that of a stout older gentleman, who gave her an appreciative perusal as she staggered back.

"Might wanna watch your step, toots," he said with a tip of his hat. "An' if not, I'll watch it for ya."

"Sorry, mister," she said, and no great loss. Her first opportunity for sweet, constrained sincerity met an easy mark. Had he been young and handsome, she might have fallen into old habits—swished her hips and offered him something to follow. She might have even given this guy a jolt to the old heart, just for the giggle of it. Instead, she barely met his eye, didn't smile at all, and never thought twice about turning around to see if he was, indeed, watching.

Her strength stirred her confidence, and she kept her head a little higher, her eyes perfectly forward, paying no attention to whether or not any other man took notice. She heard more than one car horn honk from the street but resolutely refused to see if she was its target. By the time she arrived at the office, her shoulders had relaxed, the bounce had returned to her step, and when the handsome fellow from the property management office two floors below *Capitol Chatter* held the door open, she offered a measured "Thank you" and breezed right past him as if she hadn't spent a solid year wishing he'd ask her out on a date.

"You here to apply for the job?" he asked her midbreeze.

"What job?"

Still holding the door, he took the small cardboard sign that had been placed in one of its window squares and showed it to her.

Wanted for Hire:
Receptionist
Applicants proceed to the third-floor offices

Third floor? That was her floor—*Capitol Chatter* hiring a receptionist? When she'd be getting paid two cents a word for the heart and soul poured onto the page in her pocket?

"No," she said, handing back the sign. "I already have a job in the third-floor offices, in fact."

"That so?" He returned the sign to the window and smoothed the sticky gum back in place. "You're not the receptionist, are you? 'Cause if you are, looks like you're getting canned."

For the moment, irritation overtook any hurt feelings from the fact that he apparently had never seen her before. "I'm a writer. For *Capitol Chatter*? It's a newspaper."

By now he seemed impatient with the conversation and, without actually touching her, nudged her along. "Never heard of it."

"Well, you will. It's very up-and-coming."

Pleased that she sounded more haughty than coy, she continued past him without looking back. Two tests down for the week of not flirting. One old man and one young. She was ready for all the in-betweens.

As she rounded the final flight of stairs, the sound of hushed, excited female conversation wafted from above, growing louder with each step. Reaching the third floor, she turned the corner to find their usually low-lit, empty hallway lined with at least a dozen girls—nice girls with clean-scrubbed faces, hair coiled and pinned beneath plain brown hats. They spoke in hushed, sweet tones and fell into silence when the door to the *Capitol Chatter* offices opened, revealing the broad figure of Max framed within. A young woman scooted out from behind him. He thanked her, wished her well, consulted the paper on the clipboard he held, and said, "Mary Alice Murray?"

A fair-haired girl with freckled skin leapt to her feet, saying, "Here, sir," as she made her way up the corridor of applicants.

"Miss Murray," Max said, shaking her hand. Monica could feel the pressure on her own. "Do you have a letter of reference?"

"Three of them, sir."

Max cocked a brow. "Three?"

From her vantage at the corner by the stairs, Monica stifled a giggle. The girl couldn't have been more than nineteen and already had three jobs behind her. Max chose that very moment to look up and catch her eye from the other end of the hall. They shared a commiserating look before he ushered Mary Alice in for her interview.

Once the door closed, the gathering of girls erupted in a barely contained rush of giggling sighs.

"He could play Tarzan," effused the girl closest to Monica.

"Nah, too handsome," her companion said.

"The second one was handsome—what was his name? Something Polish."

"Gene Pollar," Monica said, butting in. "And I don't think a nearsighted Tarzan would have a lot of luck swinging through the jungle."

"Still," said the first girl, "what I wouldn't give to see that one in a loincloth."

The corridor erupted in giggles as Monica wished them good luck with that and strode straight for the door.

"Hey!" Tarzan girl called after her. "You can't just walk right in there. You gotta wait 'til he comes out again and gives your name for the list."

"Relax, sweetie. I already work here."

"You're a secretary?"

The question shouldn't have annoyed her as much as it did, but she spun on her heel to stare down the girl who'd posed it. She was a sweet-looking thing, frumpy and pale with the kind of gray, watery eyes that gave the impression that she was secretly ill or prematurely old.

"This is a newspaper, right? Well, I'm a writer, and chances are if any of you girls get the job, you'll be working for me just as much as for him, so don't waste your time thinking you can flirt your way to the position."

She felt like a crumb even as she spoke. After all, the girls were engaging in a little harmless bantering—something she herself was known to do. It was a far cry from jealousy, but she couldn't deny the territorial swell of protection she felt, no matter how rooted in hypocrisy it might be.

She grabbed the door handle with an air of privilege and was just about to slam it behind her when one final exchange of conversation caught her ear.

"You think she writes Monkey Business?"

"Nah. Monkey has a sense of humor."

To confront the error would expose her persona. Tempting as it may be to set the girl straight, she shrugged off her coat and took off her hat, hanging both on the brass tree. Harper's office door was closed, but Max's was open, and she could see the legs of Mary Alice Murray—modestly covered—as she sat for her interview.

Curious, Monica sidled over to see how they were progressing, but a chastising *"hssst!"* from Zelda Ovenoff at the conference table stopped her.

"Do not eavesdrop. Is rude."

"Who's eavesdropping?" Monica pulled a folded paper from her purse. "I have a column to turn in."

"Later. When she is done." Zelda summoned her closer and dropped her voice to a whisper. "And it will not be too long. That girl does not have a chance. Three jobs in less than a year. Always as waitress."

"That's a lot of dropped dishes."

The two women shared a soft giggle, and Monica was just about to point out that they'd managed this long without a receptionist when the telephone rang.

Zelda rolled her eyes and exhaled big enough to puff the soft clump of hair in front of her eye.

"Again, the phone. Always ringing." She walked over to the little desk at the front of the office that, as far as Monica could remember, had never been occupied, and took the earpiece from the stick. "*Capitol Chatter*. What may I help you?" A pause. "Stay, please, on the line."

She hung up the phone and walked to Harper's office, knocked twice on the door, and said, "Phone for you. Advertising," before sitting back at the table. "It is this all day."

"I still don't see why we need to hire anyone new. You're perfectly capable of answering a telephone, obviously."

"It is not good for a newspaper to have a telephone answered by a woman who does not speak English so good." Zelda's downcast eyes spoke more to modesty than shame; surely Max hadn't made such an observation.

"Even I could, I suppose, in a pinch."

Zelda looked up, a sly smile tugging at her lip. "I think maybe you do not want another young girl working here at the office. Most specially not all day, every day."

Monica steeled herself from squirming. "Don't be ridiculous."

"I don't think so ridiculous. I know you had dinner together a few nights ago."

"And it was delicious, by the way."

"Is this week's recipe. And I may just be a nosy old woman, but I hope the rest of the evening was just as good?" She waggled her eyebrows like some character from a comedy short.

"It was a nice evening." Monica shifted her eyes to Max's office, looking for any sign that Mary Alice was on her way out. She felt Zelda patting her hand.

"I am glad. He is a nice man, Miss Monica. You could use a few more nice men in your life."

A wave of defensiveness came and went as Monica let the comment pass.

She heard the scrape of Max's chair, and seconds later Mary Alice Murray, looking both hopeful and bemused, emerged from his office. Had Mary Alice been privy to the expression on Max's face behind her, she might have skimped on the hopeful.

"We'll let you know as soon as we have made a decision," he said, his voice on the kind side of a promise. "Look for a letter by the end of the week."

"Thank you, sir," Mary Alice said, turning to face him as she reached the door. "I'm a hard worker, just a little clumsy."

"We wish you all the best." Max held the door open for her, and the same rush of hushing came from the girls in the hall. He poked his head out the door saying, "Wait a few minutes, ladies," before closing it on Mary Alice's exiting form.

"Sweet girl," he said, turning around.

"She seemed so," Zelda said.

"Too thin," Monica said, capturing a skeptical response from both Max and Zelda. "I mean, she looks too much like a little girl. People will think she's Harper's daughter playing grown-up."

"I'll be sure to write as much on her rejection letter," Max said. "Better yet, I'll let *you* write the letter, since you're so gifted with a turn of phrase."

"I have other writing to do." Monica stood, holding out her column. "You might want to read it first and decide if it needs a fatherly disclaimer or not."

In response, Max gestured toward his open office door, following Monica inside and closing it behind her.

"I'm glad to see you made it home safely the other night." His voice took on a quality more suited to their privacy, though he came nowhere close to touching her as she sat down.

"I do know my way around this city," she said, scooting to the edge of the seat in order to keep her feet flat on the floor. "It's not the first time I've had to get myself home."

"I telephoned Sunday afternoon to check. I spoke with a Mr.—"

"Davenport? He delivered your message."

"Did he really? Because I asked you to telephone me."

"He's old. Forgetful."

"I was hoping to see you yesterday."

"My column wasn't due until today."

"I needed to see you."

She felt a twist, then a flutter at the thought of Max pining away these past days. Not enough to send her flowers, or even make a second phone call, but needing nonetheless.

"I'm here now," she said in a perfectly modulated way that would have made Alice Reighly proud.

Max leaned against his desk, and she watched, breathless, as he took off his suit jacket. In the outer office, the telephone was once again ringing, and Monica hoped against everything the call wouldn't be for Max. He extended his hand, and she inched farther up on her seat, stopping only when he hitched up his sleeve, revealing a series of long, raw scratches covering most of his forearm.

She exhaled. "Are you and Paolo not getting along?"

"Does it look like we're getting along? He hates me."

"That can't be. He's the sweetest cat in the world."

"Who doesn't like to be moved. Or touched. At all."

She dreaded his answer to the next question. "Do I need to take him back? Maybe he's better suited to roaming the streets than settling down in a nice home. Some cats are like that."

"No," Max said, and she tried to mask her relief. "I'm learning to let him stay wherever he plants himself, and if I do need him to move, I can lure him away with a toy rather than picking him up."

"A toy?"

He looked sheepish, embarrassed, like a little boy. "A wad of yarn tied to the end of a pencil. Endlessly entertaining. That's what Chaplin should use in his next movie."

"I'd love to see that." The minute she said it, Monica regretted having done so, especially given how the self-invitation fell between them like a brick.

Max rolled down his sleeve but left his jacket on the desk. "You have your column?"

"Yes." She handed it to him as he made his way around to his chair, then swung her feet nervously as he read it, brow furrowed.

"A change of heart?"

"Somewhat."

"You're taking on the challenge?"

"Full steam," she said with a plucky gesture.

"No flirting." He took off his glasses. "At all?"

She glued her feet to the floor once again. Resolved. Outside, the phone rang again, but this time she hoped it would bring Zelda to the door, knocking for Max's attention. The way he was looking at her fell short of being a leer but was clearly one of heightened interest, even if humorously so.

"Nope."

"Not even with some slick, dandified cake eater?"

She held a straight face. "I see you read the rules. And it's a good thing, too, because I think most of the girls waiting in the hallway haven't. You might have a hard time maintaining your sense of propriety with them. One of them thinks you look like Tarzan."

"Really?" He puffed up his chest. "What do you think?"

She bit the inside of her cheek, not willing to give him the satisfaction of knocking her off the flirting wagon.

"I'll tell you next week."

"Fair enough," he said, the spell broken. He stood in a clear gesture of dismissal, and she followed suit. "By the way, I think the column's good. Maybe we should move it? Might get lost in some of the new advertising."

"Page one?"

"Maybe four."

"I'll take it."

Max opened the door to reveal Zelda standing there, about to knock.

"The telephone. It was for Miss Monica. I take name, not wanting to interrupt." Her subtext was so clear, Monica dared not look up at Max.

"Who was it?" Monica asked, dreading that the next word out of Zelda's mouth would be *Charlie*.

"It was Mr.—" she brought the slip closer—"Everett Bentworth. At the bank."

Monica took the slip. "Uncle Everett? What would he want? I'm not due to visit him until next week."

"He says only that you need to visit him. Sooner rather than later."

Monica thanked Zelda, folded the slip of paper, and put it in her purse. She looked up at Max. "Any chance I could take the key to Edward's safety-deposit box? I might need a drink after this."

"Let me know, and we'll see," he said, giving her about as much hope as Mary Alice Murray had a right to claim.

He followed her to the front door, where he once again faced the gathering of potential receptionists, asking if there were any new names to add to his list.

"I am," a female voice said.

Monica ducked underneath Max's arm and would have passed by the girl entirely if she hadn't felt a hand on her shoulder and heard that same voice say, "Maxine?"

Oh no.

There was no sense hurrying away. She'd been seen,

recognized, called out. The best she could do was rely on Max's participation in one more lie.

"Well, hello, Emma Sue. What brings you here?"

"Same as you, I suppose. Applying for the job."

"Well, good luck to you."

"Nice of you to say, since you just came out of an interview."

"She's not here for an interview," said Tarzan girl, looking victorious at the opportunity to respond to Monica's previous attack. "She says she's a writer here. We happen to think she's Miss Monkey Business herself."

"Don't be silly." Monica ducked her head and tried to walk away, but Emma Sue's friendly touch turned into a viselike grip that stopped her midstep. She looked beyond her to Max. "Thank you for the opportunity, Mr. Moore."

The shake of Max's head might have been imperceptible to the other girls in the hall, but Monica couldn't miss it. In it was an apology—for suggesting this story, for allowing the ruse, for the fallout that was surely to come.

"Emma Sue, I can explain."

She watched the girl's face change. Her normally soft, heart-shaped lips stretched, as if barely containing the seething within. Her pinkish skin inflamed, making Monica want to duck away from the onslaught of some anticipated rush of anger.

"Explain what, exactly? How you played us all for fools? After everybody tried to be so nice to you. Then you write about us like we're a bunch of old sour apples?"

"I'm so sorry—"

"We should have known, you with your flapper hairstyle and all that makeup on your face. You're not a nice girl, Maxine. If that is your real name. Not a nice girl at all."

At this, Monica found herself slapped into uncharacteristic

silence. She wanted to run back into the safety of the office, if only to grab her article and prove her change of heart, even if that meant admitting to the ugliness of the ruse. Then again, what was there to admit? Emma Sue stood there as accuser, judge, and jury. *"Not a nice girl."* A sentence delivered by a peer.

"I can explain," she said once she'd found her voice.

"Don't bother. How would we ever know you weren't just spouting out another bunch of lies?"

"Now just a minute," Max said, stepping in, garnering Monica's appreciation and pity. He'd obviously had little experience dealing with an enraged woman. The term *fair* when applied to her sex was nothing if not misleading.

"You!" Emma Sue let go of Monica's arm and pointed an accusatory finger. "You're just as bad! This is not a nice paper at all! Never has been, and I don't care if you are turning over some new leaf; you're deceptive. Didn't even list the name of the company on the sign downstairs. And no wonder. Who would want to work for a rag like this?"

"Now just a minute," Monica said, her intervention exactly as effective as Max's had been.

"All of you girls—" Emma Sue turned to the row of shocked faces lining the hall, undaunted in her rant—"you'd do good to stay clear of this place. They're liars. And betrayers. And just, just—"

Depleted of words, Emma Sue burst into tears and ran the length of the hopefuls, her sobs and her footsteps echoing as she clattered down the stairs in retreat. A few of the girls silently gathered their things and followed, though Tarzan girl wasn't one of them.

"So you are the Monkey," she said, full of unrestrained admiration.

"Guilty," Monica said, not feeling a bit of irony in the word.

The girl glanced briefly at Max before pointing to herself, saying, "Me, Jane. And I love your column. I read it every week."

"Really?" It was Monica, then, who glanced back at Max. "Hire this one."

❧ CHAPTER 20 ❧

"And of this place," thought she, "I might have been mistress! With these rooms I might now have been familiarly acquainted! Instead of viewing them as a stranger, I might have rejoiced in them as my own."
JANE AUSTEN, *PRIDE AND PREJUDICE*

HE'D LEFT MRS. OVENOFF with instructions to take the names of the girls interested in the receptionist's job and caught up with Monica around the corner. It meant running at a good clip, clutching his hat to his head while his coat flapped behind him, but as he closed in on her small, unmistakable frame, he slowed himself to a long, loping walk, barely breathing hard as he pulled up beside her.

"What are you doing here?" she asked, more with surprise than suspicion.

"Needed a breath of fresh air."

She accepted that as explanation.

"So I guess I've been found out. Maybe it's time to give me a byline."

"It's a good piece of writing. You should be proud."

"I should send a note to Alice Reighly before Emma Sue gets to her."

Max thought about the fury in the girl's face. "Oh, I'm thinking it's probably too late for that already. But I think a note's a good idea."

"Maybe in the paper? Right under my column. An apology of sorts."

He considered it for just a few seconds before responding. "Not in the paper."

She looked up. "What about all that 'whatsoever things are true' stuff?"

"Journalistically," he said, choosing his words carefully, "you did nothing wrong. At all. You were investigating. If it makes you feel better, write the note to clear your conscience, but what you submitted to me already is mea culpa enough."

"Well, well . . ." She nudged him with her shoulder as they walked. "Look at you and me on common ground."

"Feels good, doesn't it?"

"I'm not getting too comfortable. I have a feeling it's a tiny island."

They walked in companionable silence for the rest of the way, and when they arrived at the bank, he opened the door for her in grand style, then stood back as she signed her name in the ledger.

"Here to see Everett Bentworth," she said to the ancient man behind the desk.

"Very good," he said, giving no indication he would quit his post to announce her.

Monica turned around. "Coming with?"

"Family business," Max said, backing into one of the benches in the waiting area. "I'll wait here."

She grabbed his hand in both of hers, tugging. "Please?"

Certainly she knew the effect she had on him—on men in general, he assumed. But there was no flirtatiousness to her plea. Rather, a genuine need—that tugging again—to have him by her side. And so, hat in hand, he followed her into Bentworth's office.

She gave only a courtesy knock before letting herself in, making Max want to apologize for her boldness, but she was welcomed with affection as Bentworth came out from behind his desk to take her in a fatherly embrace.

"There's my Monkey," he said, regaining some professional composure when he noticed Max in the room. Keeping Monica wrapped under one arm, he extended the other in greeting.

"Mr. Moore."

"Mr. Bentworth."

"I'm not due to get my allowance for another week, Uncle Everett," Monica said as he guided her to one of the leather seats facing his desk. Upon invitation, Max took the second. "And you'll be proud to know I still have nearly three dollars left. Do you want me to take you out to lunch?"

Bentworth's smile was hiding something—good or bad, Max couldn't tell. Eyes wide open, he sent up a prayer on Monica's behalf. The girl had suffered enough for one day.

"Well," Bentworth said, "the good news is you're about to become a modestly wealthier young woman."

It was the kind of news that should have elicited a joyful response, but when Max turned to offer his congratulations, he saw Monica profiled in shocked defeat and silence. He looked from one to the other for explanation.

"Her mother's house sold. She's due to inherit the proceeds."

"The Baltimore house? I didn't think it would ever sell. I

had no idea . . ." Her voice trailed away as she studied the deed Bentworth placed in her hands.

"It's a largely abandoned neighborhood, about to be destroyed. The developer bought all of the properties, including yours. Your mother didn't list it in her will—"

"She never looked back," Monica said, her eyes lost in the legal writing on the page.

"But as you are her sole heir, the money goes directly to you."

"When?" There was only one word to describe the expression on her face. Hunger.

"As soon as the sale is final."

"How much?"

He named a modest figure. "It's not a lot of money, but since it's not tied up in the trust, you can have it now. It may be enough for a small place here or at least a sizable down payment. I could help you secure a mortgage—"

"What do I have to do?" Monica broke in. "Do I have to sign something?"

"Not today."

"Then why am I here?"

Bentworth cleared his throat and proceeded with a compassionate caution. "They have hired a crew to clear the house for demolition, and there are a few items—perhaps of personal significance—that I thought you might want to see before they are taken away."

"What kinds of things?"

He consulted a list. "Papers, mostly; a few books. Some furnishings that you might want to have. It's all gathered neatly and may have even belonged to the interim renters, but I thought you'd like to know."

"Burn it," Monica said. Her tone could have lit the match.

"Wait," Max said. "It wouldn't hurt to take a look. There might be something there, some kind of memory. I know what it's like to have nothing left from childhood. Everything from my life *did* burn."

"I'm sorry," Monica said, chagrined. "That was a thoughtless thing for me to say."

Max waved her off. "That doesn't matter. What matters is, you have a chance, however slim it might be, to find something. Have something."

"The two of you could be on a train within the hour and back in time for dinner."

"You'll go with me?" Monica said.

Of course he would. And he said as much.

Monica turned to Bentworth. "Do I need anything? A key or something?"

"I'll make a phone call and tell the company you're on your way. I'll instruct them to leave the door unlocked rather than have someone meet you there, so you can have your privacy."

There was something about Bentworth's assumptions, lumping them together as one, each an equal part in the sharing of privacy, that loosened a stony resolve within Max. Never had he been so intimately connected with another person, let alone a woman. He found his hand reaching for hers in clear disobedience of his sleepless promises not to touch her again. But here, within the formality of a banker's office, surely he could bridge the distance between them. She closed her fingers over his, anchoring him in every way.

Bentworth opened his top desk drawer, producing a long, narrow box, which he unlocked with a little key.

"We'll call this official bank business," he said, producing a few crisp bills. "To cover your train fare."

"That won't be necessary," Max said, standing. "I'll cover it."

❦

"I love a train," Monica said as they were clearing the station. "The idea that you're going somewhere—anywhere. Think about it. For a few dollars, a train can take you to a whole new life."

"Indeed," Max said. "As one has for me numerous times."

She sighed. "I guess it's not as exciting for you, then. Not that this is exciting. Just Baltimore. A person can go to Baltimore any old day."

"You can go anywhere you want. You're young, healthy, fabulously wealthy. Pick someplace."

She played along. "Colorado."

They were sitting across from each other, and he leaned back as if to get a better look. "I don't know; you don't seem the cowgirl type."

"You're probably right. St. Louis?"

He laughed. "You can go anywhere in the country and you'd choose St. Louis? Obviously you've never been to St. Louis."

"All right, Mr. American Traveler, what do you recommend?"

He thought for a moment. "I like it here."

"Here, DC?"

"Yep. There's history, culture. It's interesting."

"I suppose." She sounded less convinced. "Sometimes you seem more like the small town, picket fence kind of guy. Run an eight-page shopper with headlines about pigs and corn prices."

It wasn't a flattering portrait. "Too hard to start over in a place like that. Those people have families going back generations. I've just got me. City's easier for blending in."

"Like, disappearing?"

"Not at all. Unless you want to, I suppose. More like finding other people, people who are just as alone as you are, and just fitting in."

"So, like a puzzle."

"Somewhat." He liked the metaphor, the completed picture. Less entangling than finding a family.

For a while there was nothing more than the rhythmic clack of the train until he asked if she remembered how to get to the house from the station.

Her brow furrowed. "It's been so long. Maybe we could take a cab?"

"Why not? We've shared a streetcar, a bus, a train. Cab makes sense."

"Looks like you'll have to buy a car."

"Or a tandem bicycle."

She smiled enticingly and clucked her tongue. "Henry, Henry—" Then broke into song: "'I won't be jammed, I won't be crammed on a bicycle built for two.'"

It was good to see her smile, knowing he'd been able to distract her from her worries. He was about to respond in kind, something about how sweet she'd look on the seat, but in the spirit of Anti-Flirting Week, he stopped himself. Any talk about her seat could only lead to trouble. Instead, he absently hummed the tune as he kept his eyes on the window. After a measure or two, she was humming along with him, and the sound of it was sweeter than any conversation he could remember. No words to stumble over, no chance of saying the wrong thing. No possibility of misunderstanding, and no expectation of a perfect note. No harmony, but an imperfect unison. After a repeated chorus, in a moment of unspoken agreement they drifted into silence, and that was somehow sweeter than the song.

The moment the train came to its final stop, Max assumed

the responsibility of leading this expedition of sorts. He handed Monica down the steep steps, hailed a cab, and read the address from the Capitol Bank and Loan stationery. Monica didn't look at him once. She absorbed the unfolding city as though she'd never seen it before, like she was searching for some sort of clue to its place in her life.

Max watched her in the same way.

The cab came to a stop in front of a modest home on a street lined with other modest homes. Two-storied and narrow, it had a closed-in front porch and an exterior badly in need of paint. Upon closer inspection, *modest* may have been too kind a word. It was just shy of dilapidated, suffering from years of indifference and neglect. A curious neighbor pressed her nose up against the front window in the house next door, and on the other side of the street, a woman strolled a tired-looking pram. Scattered dog barks came from behind tall wooden fences.

Monica clutched her coat's collar to her throat as if protecting herself. Max handed the cabbie's fare through the window and stood with her as the car drove away.

"Are you ready?" he asked, placing a tentative touch to the small of her back.

She took a breath deep enough to feel through his fingers. "As I'll ever be."

He let her take the first stride, following right behind until they got to the steps. Fearing they and the porch boards might be weak, he went ahead, grimacing as the wood creaked beneath his weight. As promised, the screened door was open, as was the front door to the house. Here Max took the lead again, grasping the knob and pushing the door. That done, he held back, watching Monica take another series of deep breaths before stepping over the threshold.

With shades drawn against the afternoon sun, the house was dark, and it was a few minutes before their eyes could adjust. Once they did, Max saw nothing more than a small, simple home—a front room with generations of peeling wallpaper, a cold, black fireplace, and empty light fixtures.

"'Be it ever so humble,'" Monica said, strolling the circumference, her finger tracing the wainscoting.

"Do you remember it?"

"I remember it different. It always used to smell like coffee and bacon, except on Tuesdays when Mom would scrub it top to bottom. Then it smelled like lemon oil."

"Those are nice memories to have."

She shrugged. "If you say so."

"I say so."

She turned and looked behind him. "Those must be the *personal effects*."

He looked over his shoulder and saw two slat-back chairs and another, which, even in this light, looked like it had been upholstered sometime before the Civil War. Heaped on and around the chairs was a series of open cardboard boxes, their contents haphazardly piled within.

"That was my father's chair," Monica said. "Mom hated it and wouldn't take it to the new house. I guess whoever was living here had the same taste."

"It's not so bad." Max snapped up a blind, filling the room with dust-dancing gray light. Closer inspection tempted him to recant his statement. It was an odd, mossy green, upholstered in a fabric that called to mind images of ancient Egypt—palm trees and fronds going every which direction. The fabric was nearly worn away on the arms, a testament perhaps to its comfort and use, if not its charm.

"You should take it," Max said, responding to the sentimental-ity in her gaze. "For your apartment."

"I don't have an *apartment*. I have a room. It won't fit, and if I tried to slip it into the parlor, I'd probably be thrown out on the street."

"Then I'll take it."

"You're nuts."

"You've seen my house. I need another chair. If nothing else, for Paolo."

"He might shred it." She touched the place where her father's head must have lolled in sleep.

"I won't let him. What else do we have?"

It turned out not to be much. A teakettle, a few chipped dishes, a water-swollen ledger book, its figures lost in a smear of ink. One smaller box was crammed with sales slips dating back to 1915, and another held magazines of the same antiquity.

"Do you realize," Max said, scooting a box across the floor with his toe, "I was able to fit everything I own in less than this? I'm having my entire life shipped from Los Angeles."

"My mother let me take two suitcases when she threw me out of the Georgetown house. When we left this place? I just came home from school one day and a bunch of strangers were loading everything onto a lorry. Everything in my—"

She stopped and clapped a hand to her mouth, her eyes dart-ing toward the stairs. And then she was gone.

Her feet pounded up the stairs as he imagined they'd done thousands of times. He intended to afford her privacy, until the sounds of pounding and scraping appealed to his protective nature. Three at a time, he followed her upstairs, peeking into one cold, gray room after another before finding her in a small, slope-ceilinged space. A faded carpet covered most of the floor, save for an area where she'd pulled a corner back. She was on her knees, struggling with something on the floor.

"Help me?" she said, looking over her shoulder.

"What are you doing?"

"There's a loose floorboard here, but it's warped or something. I can't—get—it—open."

She spoke with effort, and he went to his knees beside her. Her only tool was a thin finger wedged between the boards.

"Wait here."

He went back downstairs, rummaged through the boxes, and found a dull but not rusty knife, sturdy enough to provide the needed leverage. Up the stairs again, where Monica sat, studying her finger.

"Splinter?" Max asked.

"No. Just sore," she said, shaking it.

Max went to his knees and took over the operations, prying the board up with relative ease. What lay in the shallow space beneath he couldn't tell right away, as Monica leapt into his field of vision, dove in, and whispered, "I can't believe it," as she emerged clutching a book and an unkempt bundle of papers to her heart.

"Treasure?"

"Something like that." She let the papers drop to her lap while she held the book with near reverence. "*Pride and Prejudice*. The first novel I ever read—the first *real* novel. Mom never liked to see me with a big, thick book. Said I would ruin my eyes and get a stoop in my shoulder, not to mention that men didn't like bookish girls."

Max wanted to say that her mother had been wrong—about everything. Instead, he asked, "May I?" and took the book from her, thumbing through the gold-edged pages to study the exquisite, detailed illustrations.

"I devoured it," she said. "I bought a new copy, but it's not the same."

"I've never read it."

She reached over and pressed the book to his chest. "Then you must. Keep this; add it to your collection."

She turned to the scattered papers, ignoring the fact that he wasn't taking his eyes off her. Never had he seen her this unguarded—no coy flapper flirtations, no ruse of respectability. Just the girl in her childhood room. He longed to know what was scribbled on those pages, but respect kept him from asking outright. Besides, it was almost a luxurious thing to take his fill of her this way, watching the tiniest changes in her expression. A parting of her lips, a narrowing of eyes, a nose wrinkled in reaction to a piece of long-forgotten prose.

"It's my writing." The room echoed with her awe.

"I figured as much."

"Stories. I was a regular little Jo March." She clarified, "*Little Women*."

"You hid those, too?"

She shuffled them. "No real reason. It just didn't seem like anybody would care."

He cared.

"And now—" she clutched them to her chest—"I'd rather die than let anyone see them."

He knew better than to grab for them but said, "Are you sure? After all, I am an editor."

"Oh no . . ."

Like a sprite she leapt to her feet, and before he could unfold himself, she'd bolted through the door. He found her downstairs, having emptied the small box of old sales receipts and stuffed her pages within.

"A quick perusal?" he said, making a mock attempt at stealing the box.

"Nope." She held the box above her head, a useless move given the difference in their heights. As he was about to prove it such, she took a quick step and jumped up onto her father's chair, contorting her body to find balance on the uneven cushion.

"Careful," Max said, offering his shoulder to steady her.

Continuing the game, she held the box high, still not out of his reach, and they laughed when he easily plucked it from her grip.

"What now?" she said, breathless. He was breathless too, though neither had run very far or very hard. "You have my favorite book and my only stories. You've got my whole life, the only things I've ever really loved, right there in your hands."

Standing as she was, on her father's chair, her face was perfectly aligned to his. Her lips perfectly aligned to his. Here was a moment when the innocence of the child she'd been wrapped clear around the woman she'd become. He leaned forward, bent slightly, to deposit the book and the box on the cushion of the chair, bringing his face dangerously close to the warm nape of her pale neck as he did so. That done, his hands empty, there was nothing to do but to slide them beneath her coat, around her thin waist, with every intention of lifting her down to safety, but then her hand was cool upon his cheek, and there seemed nowhere else to go but toward her. Nothing else to do but kiss her. And when he did, when his lips first touched, then consumed hers, he felt the fervent stirrings of a man who had finally found his home.

Without losing each other's touch, Monica knocked back his hat brim, took his glasses from his face and put them—somewhere; he didn't know or care. She wrapped her arms around his neck, pulling him closer, their bodies the sole source of heat in the cold room.

Max had kissed women before, but never like this, never as an act of such cumulative longing. Never as a fulfillment of a million imagined embraces, both this and all that could follow. Never with a woman who had so been kissed before. And more. Because he knew—she'd so much as told him—that Monica was far more versed in all things carnal. But here, for a while, for one more minute, he could pretend she was the girl from this house. Innocent. Dreamy. Quiet and bookish and—

"Oh, Max . . ."

She moved, drawing him closer. Making her body shimmy against his, and the heat coming through her dress tossed out all thoughts of the girl tucked up in the attic with her novel. A sound came from her throat the likes of which he'd never heard before, and he wanted nothing more than to hear it again.

Then, "Max . . ." and another sound, more graveled, like a cough, and she pulled away.

"Max." Now she hissed his name, tapped his shoulder, and pointed to an old, stooped gentleman wearing a cable-knit sweater under a pair of loose-fitting overalls.

"You the owners?" He spoke through a bushy moustache. He brought a gnarled hand up to his mouth, indicating that Max may have some substance obscuring his as well.

"N-no," Max stammered, reaching for his handkerchief after helping Monica safely to the floor. "Not currently."

"Formerly?" the man said.

"Somewhat," Monica said. She ran her fingers through her hair before good-naturedly helping Max wipe away the remnants of her lipstick. "From a way back."

"So any of this junk yours?"

"Watch it," Max said, accepting his glasses from Monica. "You know what they say about one man's rubbish."

"It's another man's job to haul away," the hauler said. "Just tell me what you're takin' and what I'm takin'."

Max looked to Monica, who had gathered her book and her box of stories. "Do you think there's anything else?"

She gave the piles a mere passing glance. "No."

"Well, then." Max reached into his vest pocket and pulled out a small white calling card, one left over from his time in Los Angeles. He turned it over, asked the mover if he could borrow the pencil above his ear, and carefully printed Uncle Edward's—his—address on the back. "If you would, have the chair delivered to this address."

The mover looked at the card, then at Max. His jaw went slack. "You've gotta be kiddin' me. That's at least—"

"Worth your while," Max said, handing over three dollars. "And I'll pay you twice that when it's delivered."

The mover remained incredulous. "Nine bucks?"

"Max, that's ridiculous. It's just an old chair."

"Are you kidding? Nothing's too good for Paolo."

Her eyes glistened with gratitude. He would have paid tenfold to have her look at him like that. He loved her. If they'd never kissed or never would again, that fact wouldn't change. He wanted to tell her, right there with the moustachioed mover as a witness, but on the reasonable chance that she did not return his feelings equally, he stopped short of declaration. Instead, he took her childhood belongings, tucked them under one arm, and offered her the other to escort her from the home in grand style. Before they crossed the threshold into the winter's afternoon, she stopped and turned them to look one last time upon the dreary, gray room.

"'And of this place, I might have been mistress.'"

The affectation in her voice surely meant this was a quote, but he couldn't place it. Then she patted the book, saying, "Read it."

And he promised her he would.

CHAPTER 21

Don't wink—a flutter of one eye may cause a tear in the other.
ANTI-FLIRT CLUB RULE #5

SHE'D HALFWAY HOPED TO CONTINUE THE KISS in the taxi ride back to the train station, but since Max had given his last three dollars to the mover for the chair, they'd been at the mercy of that same man for a ride. Once the final portable property of her childhood home had been loaded within the wooden slats of the truck, Monica was handed up into the cab while Max sat in the back, feet dangling over the side. Then it was a mad dash to catch the four o'clock, grabbing the only two seats together—right across from a fat, irascible woman and her sullen, drool-crusted child. Thankfully, Max gave up his attempts to engage either of them in travel banter. Even better, the child whined incessantly about needing to go to the lavatory and the mother finally acquiesced, leaving Max and Monica in peace.

"Alone at last," Max said, touching his forehead to hers.

"Maybe he'll lock himself in there."

"*He?* Are you sure? I thought it was a girl."

299

"Sorry road for her if it is," Monica said.

Then he kissed her. Nothing like before, when her feet pooled in her shoes and her head sizzled like frost on a furnace. But sweet and soft, somehow making everything and everybody else on the train disappear behind a curtain of touch and taste.

He pulled away, looking satisfied but not smug, and said, "I hope I'm not causing you to violate the vows of Anti-Flirt Week."

"That depends. Are you teasing me?"

He shook his head. Slowly. "Are you?"

She held her head steady and answered, truthfully, "I don't think so."

Her answer brought a decidedly less satisfied look to his face, and he blinked precisely five times.

"What does that mean, exactly?"

"Well, I don't know, *exactly*. Who knows anything exactly?"

He just kept looking at her and blinking, making her wish she could disappear during that tiny space of time when his eyes were closed and reappear again, as sure of her feelings as he apparently was of his.

Monica stretched up, hoping for another kiss, but the woman and child had returned, the latter unceremoniously stomping on her foot. Whatever question, answer, and conversation had been left unspoken would have to wait until they could get away from their gloomy audience.

She ran her fingers listlessly over the lid of the box containing her childhood stories, then lifted it and shuffled through the pages themselves. Leaning against Max's shoulder, she offered one up as a little light reading material. Perfect for the train.

"Is there a monkey in it?"

She knew he meant no harm by the question, and she found her own defensiveness surprising.

"No monkey. Just a girl." She scanned a few lines, though simply seeing the paper was enough to bring the words back in full detail. "She makes sashes out of butterfly wings for the women in her town to wear when they march in the suffrage parade. But then all the women fly away. What do you think Freud would make of that?"

"I like monkeys better." This from the child sitting across from her.

Monica lifted one eyebrow, sending the child to melt against its mother's arm.

"How old were you when you wrote that?" Max asked, either intrigued or amused.

"Seven? Eight? Before the war, when getting the vote was my mother's passion of the day."

He held out a hand. "May I?"

All of a sudden, those pages filled with her juvenile, practiced script seemed to be spun from her very soul, and to simply hand them over, a betrayal of the child who wrote them.

"You have enough to read right now," she said, nodding her head toward the book in his lap. "*Pride and Prejudice*, remember?"

"I liked *Emma* better." This from the child's mother, who was not so easily intimidated by Monica's raised brow.

So they rode in silence, with unfinished kisses and conversations and stories between them.

They lit from the train at Union Station amid a throng of travelers. The sound of a thousand voices filled the space between the marble floors and columned walls. The last of the day's sunlight poured through the windows in the vaulted ceiling. With silent complicity they joined their fellow travelers, funneling their way toward the exit gates.

"I think I have enough for us to ride a streetcar," Monica said, digging in her purse as she walked. "Why don't you come back to my place for supper?" She tried to think of anything that would give her more time with him. She'd broken some sort of spell on the train and felt close to begging for a chance to make it right again. "Tuesday night, probably beef stew. Mrs. Kinship makes it with pearl onions."

"I don't think so," he said after seeming to weigh a world's worth of options. "When I left the office this morning, I had no idea I'd be gone all day. Not that it wasn't a wonderful way to spend an afternoon."

"Then come with me." She clutched his sleeve. "If not to my house, anywhere. You must be hungry too. I'm starved. How about Chinese? There's a great place just a couple of blocks—"

"Stop," he said, but gently, with his fingers touched against her face.

"What did I do?" She felt the first sting of tears, and they clogged her throat so, she feared she wouldn't be heard over the din of the crowd. "What did I say? I feel like I ruined something, but I don't know what, or how." She felt herself escalating to hysteria, and were they anywhere else but Union Station, they might have accrued the attention of some passersby.

"Come here," he said, putting his arm around her shoulders in a now-familiar protective way and ushering her to one of the wooden benches near the entrance. He sat her down and moved in close, blocking out everything—the ticket booths, the clock, the hawkers of peanuts and magazines. Only Max, with a blur of activity behind him.

"Something happened back there at that house," he said with exaggerated authority.

"No kidding," she said, confused by his adamant tone. "I was there, remember?" She leaned in, ready for it to happen again.

"Stop." Again, this time more forceful. "It's something I think I've wanted for a long time. With you, and maybe even before you."

"Before me?"

"There's never been a woman that I thought—that . . . I loved. And I'm in love with you, Monica. I think I have been since the day I met you. That first morning, at the funeral, when you called me Griffin."

Her mind followed him back to that moment, unable to recall anything other than nervous amusement at her own cleverness.

"And there were times—moments—when I thought you felt the same. Somewhat the same. So this afternoon, when you kissed me, when you let me kiss you . . ." He paused, bemused by his own declaration, looking to the passing commuters as if they would tell him all he needed to hear. "But here you are, not exactly leaping at the chance to say you're in love with me too."

"Oh, Max." No man had ever declared love for her. Not in a setting like this, anyway. Not with daylight and witnesses, speaking from a clear and sober mind. "How could I be?"

He sat a little straighter, a little farther away. "So how could you—what made you let me kiss you like that?"

She shrugged and clutched her stories. "Playing house?"

It was exactly the wrong thing to say, flirtatious and cruel in the face of his sincerity. He physically recoiled from her, and she wished she could reel her words back in and bring him back with them.

"Max—"

"Of course. What did I expect?"

Now it was her turn to draw back. "That was cruel."

"I'm sorry."

It was an apology delivered with pity, not just for his remark but for the reputation that prompted it. She silently sent it back.

❧

Max opted to go to the *Capitol Chatter* offices rather than to his home, hoping a few matters of business would distract him from the afternoon. He arrived to find only Zelda, with a neatly typed list of the girls who had come for the receptionist position. Barely perceptible tick marks spoke of Zelda's personal opinion, and there were few who passed her muster.

"Everything is fine with Miss Monica?" she asked with her specific blend of maternal austerity.

"All's well," he replied, making no attempt to convince her. He told of their visit to the bank, of Monica's inheritance and the discovery under the floorboard, forging on regardless of the tug at his conscience that he may be betraying her confidence. He hadn't seen anything in this city as dependable as Zelda Ovenoff's ability to keep a secret.

"And I am thinking there is something else," Zelda said, "though it is not my place to know, maybe."

They were sitting at the large conference table, drinking coffee and picking at the last of the Danish from earlier in the day.

"I kissed her," he said, trying hard not to relive the experience in Mrs. Ovenoff's presence.

"Oh, how wonderful." She squeezed his hand, and he felt a little embarrassed, like he'd just been awarded a prize he didn't deserve.

"Maybe," he said. "I mean, yes, wonderful, but then, after, I think I might have chased her away."

"Nonsense. Who would run from a man like you?"

"A woman like Monica, apparently."

Zelda tucked a soft finger under his chin and forced him to look up. "Tell me this. Do you love her?"

"I think so, and that's the problem."

"How, a problem?"

"Because she doesn't love me."

"And what makes you say this?"

"Because she told me."

"Ah." She released him and wrapped her hands around her coffee cup but didn't raise it for a drink. "You think because she cannot say her feelings, she must not have them."

"That's not it." But of course it was.

"Not once, in all of our time together, did Edward Moore tell me he loved me. But I know he did. It is one thing to say and quite another to do."

"I'm just beginning to think she's not the right girl for me."

"And that is just the important word. *Girl.* She may be twenty years old, but she is, in so many ways, still a child."

And in so many ways a woman.

"Maybe I'm the childish one," he said. "I should know better."

"Love knows nothing but moment to moment. Be honest and true in each one, and expect nothing more from her."

"Is that how it was with you and Uncle Edward?"

She closed her eyes for a moment before responding. "Yes. And we had our measure of happiness."

He didn't believe her and said so. "If you loved each other and you were both alone, why didn't you—?"

"Marry? It is sometimes more complicated. Edward had been alone for so long. A bachelor. And I think he was set in his ways. Not willing, I think, to give up those quiet moments of his life."

"But did you ever ask him?"

She looked shocked. "To marry me?"

"Not exactly, but hint. That you wanted more."

"My life, all I have wanted was my own home, with my own

man. Always I lived on the edge of somebody else's family. And here I had this little bit. I was afraid if I asked for more, I would lose what little I had. It had to be enough for me."

"So, regrets?"

"We were patient with each other. Like the Good Book says. Love is patient. And love is kind. That's what we were to each other. We didn't know he had so little time. Maybe we should have. We were old. Not so old, but not young like you two."

The weight of her wisdom wrapped around him, anchored by God's Word. Patience. Kindness. Both thrown away on that train-station bench.

Zelda's hand was covering his again, this time warm from her coffee cup. "You have time. To wait, until each of you can fully be what the other needs. And right now there is time for you to make right whatever it is you think you have done wrong."

"Right now? I don't think she wants to talk to me."

"She wants to. I know this more than anything."

Zelda lifted his hand to her lips and kissed it before standing to gather her purse and coat and hat.

"I will see you in the morning, Mr. Moore. Good luck."

He didn't need luck; he needed grace. From God for his behavior, from Monica for his judgment. Left alone after Zelda's departure, he laid his glasses on the table and buried his face in his hands.

"Father—" He barely had the word out of his mouth before an overwhelming longing for his parents washed away the rest of his prayer. They'd both been gone for years, and he'd made several life decisions without their counsel, but something about this, the deep-down desire to create a new family with this woman, made him feel so utterly alone. He looked up, pressed his knuckles to his lips, and thought about Zelda's final, loving gesture. Here he'd been given the wisdom of a woman, spoken with the breath of a mother, and if he listened close enough, he would no doubt hear the words of his Father, too.

"Father, I love her." Hadn't he spoken these very words aloud just days before? *I love her, and I desire her, and even if she loves me, I don't know that she is what you want for me. And I've tried, always, to do what you would have me do. You've taken my mother and my father and my home and my past. I want her. Give her to me. Let her love me, and I promise she'll love you, too.*

Selfish, he knew, but how wrong could it be to care about a woman?

And yet he'd hurt her with a single careless comment. How vain had he been to think his love alone could save her? That his forgiveness mattered, when it was God's forgiveness she should be seeking?

Combing through their conversations, he tried to remember a single time he'd made it clear to her how the grace of God could bring the peace she must be seeking. They shared the orphan's plight, but Max had the constant presence of a heavenly Father to turn to. Did she? He was fairly certain she did not, and it tore at him with an urgency beyond his own reconciliation with her. God had taken her father, her mother, her home, and her memories too. And he, Max, had fallen so short in showing her how God's love—not his own—could take the place of all she'd lost.

If nothing else, he had to make that right. He had to talk to her tonight.

ᐳ CHAPTER 22 ᐸ

Nothing is a waste of time if you use the experience wisely.

AUGUSTE RODIN

DUSK LURKED by the time she walked into the common parlor, given three line changes taking the streetcar home from the train station. Whether or how Max got home, she didn't know. Forget him if he hadn't learned to always keep a stash of nickels for the car. Big romantic gesture, buying that ratty old chair. Foolish, stupid if it kept him stranded. Even more if he thought it was going to get him permanently hitched to her. She knew her value; she had a lot of things given to her by a lot of great guys. And he was ready to spend nine dollars on a piece of trash.

Then again, there was that moment, there on the bench in the train station after her little joke, when he'd looked at her like *she* was the piece of trash. Since when did a kiss mean you were ready to fall in love? Because if she knew nothing else about Max Moore, she knew he wasn't one to toss that word around lightly. What would he have done if she'd said it back, if she'd thrown her arms around him like Mary Pickford in a final scene? Would they be on a honeymoon before the week's end? The thought was terrifying. Or at least it should be.

The parlor felt blessedly warm and welcoming the minute she walked in. Mr. Davenport had taken up residence in his favorite chair but had not yet begun playing his records. Instead, he sat reading a magazine and looked up with an air of relief when she walked through the door.

"Evening, Mr. D."

"Ah, what a welcome sight you are, young lady."

"Really?" He'd never made her feel welcome a moment in her life.

"Perhaps now, if the telephone rings, you can take the call."

As if on cue, the phone jangled, and at his stern direction, Monica lifted the earpiece from its cradle. "Hello?"

"There's my Mousie."

Charlie, and from the richness of his speech, he'd been drunk for a while.

"What are you calling me for?"

"I can't . . . since seein' you that night. Did you get my flowers?"

Monica glanced in at the dining room table where Mrs. Kinship had added some greenery to the meager bouquet, creating quite a pleasing centerpiece.

"Yeah. Five roses. What a Rockefeller."

"Come have a drink with me."

"No."

"Come dance with me."

"Good-bye, Charlie."

She hung up the phone and took off her hat and coat, hanging both on empty wooden hooks in the entryway. The flat, narrow box of her stories sat deep in one of the pockets, and there it would stay for now. She was exhausted, and the sofa in front of the window loomed far more inviting than a trek to her room. The scent of Mrs. Kinship's beef stew wafted from the kitchen, igniting her hunger. Twenty minutes until six meant so many minutes until supper. Until then she would collapse, her head on one of the embroidered pillows, her eyes closed, with Mr. Davenport reading aloud at her invitation.

Just as she sat, the phone jangled again. She and Mr. Davenport exchanged a commiserative look, and she dragged herself across the room to answer it, again.

"Mousie! Come dance with me."

She could hear the music playing in the background, loud and lively. A familiar place to become lost. She should go. What else would be expected? Max's words nibbled at her resolve, but not enough.

"Find another girl, Charlie."

"C'mon, baby. You know there's no one else even comes close."

"And quit calling."

"Then how 'bout I come over, huh? Like old times, sneakin' up real quiet."

"Not on your life." But the line had gone dead.

Mrs. Kinship came out from the kitchen, brandishing a wooden spoon. "Is that fool calling again?"

"I'm sorry," Monica said. "I'm sure he'll get the message soon."

"Well, I hope to goodness. What he's doing to Mr. Davenport's nerves." She clucked her tongue. "Supper's up in a few minutes, if you care to join us this evening."

"Yes, thank you. I'm starved."

"Well, it's a good, hearty stew. Looks like you can use it."

"Sister, you've no idea."

"Why don't you go on up to your room? I'll bring you a tray."

"Would you?" The offer alone lifted the weight of the day,

and the unprecedented friendliness warmed her as much as the food would.

"Let that phone ring itself silly. Never cared for them things anyway."

As if on cue, the telephone answered the insult, jangling unapologetically.

Mrs. Kinship lunged for it. "Let me at that thing."

"No," Monica intervened. "He's my problem."

Determined to put Charlie off once and for all, she took a deep breath before answering with all the hostility she could muster.

"Monica?" The soft surprise in Max's voice caught her off guard, and she grabbed the edge of the telephone table to keep herself steady.

"Oh, it's you."

"Is everything all right? You sound upset."

"Of course. It's just that we're about to sit down to supper here."

"I'm sorry," he said. "I don't like the way we left things today."

"Exactly what does that mean?"

"It means—" a long, crackling pause—"can I see you again tonight? Maybe you could save me a bowl of stew? Or we could meet each other somewhere?"

Monica twisted the telephone cord around her finger and gazed around the room. There was Mr. Davenport trying to appear absorbed in his magazine, even though his reading glasses hung from his vest pocket, and Mrs. Kinship tapping her spoon against her hip in a rhythm just short of menacing. Every inch of space was stuffed with furniture and carpets and knickknacks and rubber plants. It was soft and home, and she wanted him here, but not tonight. Not with the risk of Charlie making good on his threat to come for a visit. It certainly wouldn't do to have the two of them colliding on the front porch.

"I don't think so," she said finally. "It's nothing to do with you. I'm just beat is all. It was quite a day."

"That it was." Though he spoke over the phone, she could picture him and knew a quick smile had punctuated the sentence. "But I don't want to wait until tomorrow."

"It's already so late."

"It's not quite six o'clock. Even I've been known to stay up past suppertime. I'll see you at eight."

"They don't like me to have—"

"I'll bring dessert."

For the second time in just a few minutes, she heard the phone line go dead in her ear.

She smiled weakly at Mrs. Kinship. "That was the nice one."

Mrs. Kinship expressed a host of opinions in a single sniff before turning on her heel and walking back into the kitchen. Without a doubt, Monica knew she'd lost her chance at a cozy, comfortable supper upstairs. Sighing, she followed with Mr. Davenport on her heels into the kitchen, where they gathered around the small table. Mr. and Mrs. Grayson, the landlords, were apparently dining with friends, but Anna arrived as Mrs. Kinship set the steaming pot of stew in the middle of the table.

"Well," she said, singling out Monica, "look who's joining us this evening."

"Exciting day at the library?" Immediately, Monica regretted the mocking tone in her voice. In many ways, she envied Anna's job.

"Oh, you know," Anna said. "Shelve one, shelved them all." It was a joke Monica had coined not long after joining the household, and not a particularly funny one at that, yet Anna brought it out regularly and still delivered it with a deep-set giggle. It was a great irony that Anna worked in the library without having a particular love of books. It was the quiet she sought, the peace and quiet. Monica often thought it was a waste.

Had the Graysons been home, they'd be eating in the dining room, but given their absence, supper was served in the kitchen, where they each took their familiar seats. Dinner was a silent affair, as most of them were whenever the elderly couple was not there to, if nothing else, speak with each other. Not an uncomfortable silence, though. Rather a familiar one, with compliments to the chef and observations of the weather bobbing to the surface.

What thoughts could possibly be roaming through the minds of these people, Monica could hardly imagine. She kept her demeanor calm, alternating bites of savory beef with those of softened potatoes or flavorful carrots. Each bite ushered in a different thought about a different man. Max was wonderful. Charlie could ruin everything. Kissing Max. Fending off Charlie. Kissing Max again. And again, maybe here in their very parlor, after everyone departed to their solitude. Unless Charlie showed up.

Occasionally the telephone would ring, setting everybody on edge but sending nobody to answer. If it was Max on the other end, perhaps he would become discouraged with his plan to visit. If it was Charlie? Well, at least he wasn't on his way over yet.

"I'm afraid I need to run out for just a minute." Monica patted her lips and chin with her napkin and set it on the table beside her.

"I thought you had company coming over," Mrs. Kinship said as she began to clear the table.

"Company?" Anna was always pleased to participate in any bit of Monica's life.

"I should be back well before then." If she hurried.

She ran upstairs to her room and rummaged through the

tossings of paper until she found the card Charlie had sent with the roses. JJ's. A fun place run by an affable Irishman. Good drinks, sometimes music, and a regular crowd that assembled almost any night of the week.

Monica changed into a warmer dress and lower heels to accommodate the walk. Normally she wouldn't be caught dead in anything this frumpy for a night out, no matter how casual the place. But she didn't want to get Charlie heated up any more than he already was, and it didn't hurt that she'd look kind of homey when Max came over. Downstairs, she glanced at the clock while tugging on her hat. She had a little over an hour, plenty of time to head Max off at the pass. She looked back to see Anna's wide, moonlike face behind hers in the mirror's reflection.

"Maybe I should go with you."

"Not tonight, kid. This place isn't for you."

"*Kid*? I'm older than you."

"But I have experience in spades."

The angle of her hat perfected, she wrapped a scarf around her neck and touched fresh lipstick to her lips. No need to look like an absolute farmer. She met Anna's eyes in the mirror.

"I may have a gentleman coming to call this evening." *A gentleman coming to call.* She loved the propriety of it all.

"So why are you leaving?"

"Because I may have *another* gentleman coming to call, and I don't want their paths to cross. If the first one, Charlie—you've met him; he was here the other night—shows up, tell him I've gone to meet him. He'll know where, and he'll go away. And if the second one, Max—tall, wears glasses—arrives, tell him—"

"You've gone to meet the first one?"

"No! Don't mention anything like that. Just tell him that I'm trying, really trying, to get home."

Anna looked at her with something akin to worship. "Oh, how I envy your life. How exciting everything must be."

"Yeah?" Monica pulled on her coat. "Well, right back atcha half the time." She reached into her pocket and pulled out the box of stories. "Do me a favor? Take this up to my room for me?"

Anna studied it. "What's this? Another token from yet another man?"

"Nothing quite so interesting, I'm afraid. Just a few scribbles from my childhood. Probably the last things I've ever truly enjoyed writing."

Her explanation triggered a new reverence.

"How lovely. But I'll wait. Maybe we can read them together? Make some hot chocolate?"

"Sure," Monica said, adding a breathless "It's a date" while subjecting herself to the girl's enthusiastic embrace.

Then it was out the door.

She walked at a near-scurrying pace, both to feed her nerves and to warm her body. *Please, please, please be there.* Maybe she'd asked for this kind of predicament, leading Charlie on the same way she'd led Max, making him think she was available at his whim. After all, she had been for months, in clandestine meetings in dark, crowded places all over the city. She'd given him her time and her body, and even a little bit of her heart. They'd even gone so far as to declare a love for one another, such as it was, in slurred and stumbling conversations.

But that was before Max. And before Alice Reighly. And before this clear, cold walk that was emptying her head of nostalgic affection with every step.

She wasn't his Mousie anymore.

Halfway to JJ's, she wished she'd taken a car, and she vowed to do so for the journey home. She didn't have a watch, but when she asked a fellow pedestrian the time, she found more than twenty minutes had passed since she left the house.

Wait for me, Max. If he showed up at all. Then again, when had he ever not been a man of his word? *Wait for me.* Not that she had anything new to say. And she dreaded that he had something new for her to hear. Like he didn't love her after all. Or she was fired. Or he'd decided to take her to bed just because he knew he could.

During the grocery's business hours, the entrance to JJ's was through an innocuous-looking door at the back of the shop. After hours, one had to navigate a menacing alley, dodging trash and dogs and unsupervised hooligan children. She thought briefly of Paolo, wondering if he'd spent his time away from her in such a place, feeding off scraps and mice. If so, no more, and she stopped just short of envying him.

The alley entrance to JJ's was unmarked and unlit, as was the bell one rang in order to gain admittance. Regulars knew the button was nestled in a certain brick four rows up from the ground; newcomers didn't know at all and weren't welcome. This being Monica's first time to come alone, she had no one to act as lookout to be sure her moves were undetected, but her own surveillance assured her that she was alone. Under any other circumstances in a dark alley, that fact might have met with trepidation. Now, she reached down, found the submerged button, pushed it, and waited. Seconds later, an opening appeared in what had looked like a solid door, and a soft yellow light shone through. A familiar face appeared. At least, a familiar brow.

"Sorry, lady. We're closed. Come back at seven tomorrow morning."

"I'm looking for Charlie." For a time, that had been the actual code. "Is he still here?"

"Is he? Take him off our hands, would ya? He's a mess."

With that, the door opened just wide enough to allow Monica to slip through before Benny the brow closed it. After that, a heavier door, insulated to keep the sounds of people and music from seeping to the outside. This he opened with equal ease, releasing the sound of raucous laughter underscored by a single brave piano. The room was far too small for the riotous crowd, and Monica sidled her way between the patrons, often seeing nothing but jackets and shirts and suspenders in her line of vision. Instead, she trained her ear for Charlie's distinctive laugh, the one that started with a shout. It wasn't long before she heard it. She bumpered her way toward the source, back toward the bar, recognizing his square form underneath the suit that seemed simultaneously rumpled and stretched. His head turned, offering the familiar profile, his hat pushed to the back of his head, and then his mouth unhinged at the last joke.

"Charlie!" She had to shout his name three times over before he responded, and when he did, she could tell she was initially out of focus.

"There's my little Mousie." He approached her, slow and unsteady, holding out his hand in a pinching gesture as if he could pick her up by some thin, whiplike tail.

She held up a hand. "Stop right there. You gotta leave me alone, Charlie. Understand? It's over."

Unfazed, he draped himself over her, drunker than she'd ever seen him, and she staggered under his weight. "Baby—" his breath launched a second assault, sour and wet—"with girls like you, it's never over."

She strained to look up and over him, her eyes frantically searching for somebody to come to her aid, but his comrades at the bar were more amused than alarmed.

318

Monica heaved. "Get *off* me!" She managed to slip away, a move apparently worthy of applause from the onlookers.

Someone shouted something about putting ten bucks on the mouse, which drew a fresh burst of laughter, including Charlie's. Monica stood in the midst of it, fueled by fresh anger. How could she ever have thought this creep was charming, or witty, or even civilized?

"You leave me alone, Charlie. Do you hear me?" Overwhelming superiority made her feel ten feet tall. Or at least six. "You don't call me, and you don't come by my place. Understand? You do, and I'll put your name and face on the front page of my paper with a story juicy enough to keep your wife entertained all the way through breakfast. Understand?"

By the end of her tirade, she felt like she'd won ten bucks for every patron ready to put money on her, because Charlie was reeling from the sheer force of her words. A beat of actual silence intervened as all waited for Charlie's response. He, for his part, looked deflated, small enough for her to kick around, and for good measure she did just that, landing her foot against his shin hard enough to make him wince but not fall over.

This further moved the crowd to her favor, and they burst forth in cheers. Somebody came up behind her, grabbed her hand, and raised it above her head in victory. Then, next thing she knew, someone else pressed a glass into it, and facing a semicircle of drinks raised in her honor, she acknowledged her fans and drank it down.

It was strong, cheap, like it always was in this place, and by the time she finished, she felt halfway to drunk. There was a ringing in her ears like she'd never experienced before, not with any amount of drink. She closed her eyes and shook her head, but it only intensified, growing more sharp and shrill. When she opened them again, she noticed the look of absolute terror on Charlie's face. She turned to focus on what he was seeing behind her, and that's when Monica realized the sound wasn't coming from inside her head at all, but from the thin whistle between the pursed lips of a granite-faced man she hadn't noticed until now. He, too, held his hand high, and in it was something shiny and gold and shield-shaped. Another man, older and grizzled, held up a similar object and shouted lyrics to the tweets.

"Ladies and gentlemen! We are federal marshals! This is a raid, and you are all hereby arrested for the illegal manufacture and purchase of alcohol."

The crowd roared around his words, only causing his voice to escalate.

Whether out of habit or blind fear, Monica found herself reaching for Charlie, felt his square, tough hand grasping hers. It was a necessary island of comfort in such a storm of confusion. She stepped closer, hoping against hope she could simply disappear behind his bulk and slip away to safety at the first opportunity.

"Ah, geez," Charlie said, struck with new sobriety, "my wife's gonna kill me."

And she decided she was better off alone.

Max realized immediately after hanging up that he had no address and therefore no way to find her. Both of his repeated attempts to call went unanswered, even after the operator verified that there was nothing wrong with the line. Finally, he called young Trevor, who provided not only the address but the quickest route to get there on foot. His steps followed Trevor's words, past the bank where they'd shared a drink, and Sobek's, where they'd shared coffee and pastry. In fact, he managed to slip in just before Mrs. Sobek locked up for the night and purchase the last custard pie.

Trevor had given him a detailed description of the house itself, three-storied with a large front window, and now it appeared just as he'd pictured. He stood at the foot of the steps, holding the white box by its string. Remembering the time on the clock at Sobek's, he judged it to be a little past eight, just as he'd promised. He climbed the wide steps to the front door and rang the bell, impressed with the chimes he heard ringing within.

A plain, plump young woman answered, seeming to size him up on the porch.

He removed his hat. "Is Monica Bisbaine at home?"

"Who should I say is calling?"

"My name's Max. Max Moore."

She rolled her eyes as if calculating, then smiled and said, "Please, come in. She's not home right now, but we're expecting her back shortly."

Confused, Max walked through the open door. "Not home?"

"She had an errand," the girl answered with a studied propriety. "But we're expecting her back any moment. My name's Anna, by the way."

"Nice to meet you, Anna." She took his hat and coat and finally his pie, thanking him for his kindness before handing it off to a thin, middle-aged woman who appeared silently at his side.

"I'll take this to the kitchen until Monica gets back. She's run an errand, but we're expecting her back at any moment."

"All right," he said, bemused at their identical responses.

The women—Anna and, he learned, Mrs. Kinship—invited him to sit in the front parlor, brought him a cup of tea, and introduced him to Mr. Davenport, who also informed him that they were expecting Monica to return at any moment. Max sipped the tea and took in the room. Plush, comfortable, well-worn. He felt immediately welcome, and for the first few minutes the conversation was easy and consistent, about him, about them, and the weather. When the clock chimed eight thirty, however, and the "any moment" of Monica's arrival didn't materialize, the talk suffered, becoming stilted and intermittent with long, fidgety silences.

"Where, exactly, did she say that she was going?" Max asked.

"She didn't, exactly," Anna said, clearly uncomfortable. "But that's our Monica, always running off somewhere. Dancing, mostly—something I don't care for at all."

Mrs. Kinship nudged her with an elbow.

"It's just that she was expecting me at eight," Max said, hoping he didn't sound as petulant as he felt. "It seems odd that she wouldn't mention having an errand."

"She decided rather suddenly," Mrs. Kinship said. "During dinner, and ran right out."

"Most unusual," Mr. Davenport said absently. "Most of her gentlemen call for her at the house, like you are now."

"Mr. Davenport!" Mrs. Kinship chastised.

"It's all right," Max soothed. He recalled her demeanor on the phone and the look on her face when she walked away from him in the station. Of course she had someone waiting to—

Stop.

If there was another man, it was just such an assumption that had driven her to him.

"I'm beginning to get a little worried, truth be told," Mrs. Kinship said. "That lecher was calling all evening." She reached over and patted Max's knee. "Drunk, he was. A most unpleasant fellow. Never liked him."

Max could picture the fellow, if it was the same one. The lout from the diner. He curled and uncurled his fist in memory. "Did she say where she was going?"

"No," Anna said. "You never know with her. She goes to the most glamorous places." She leaned forward, whispering. "I think, even, a few speakeasies. So exciting."

Max looked for the others to comment on Anna's observation, and it dawned on him. They didn't know. None of these three people had a clue about Monica's job, where she went and why.

"Maybe she left some sort of note?" After all, she was a writer, and writers made notes.

"Not for any of us," Mrs. Kinship said.

"Maybe—" he cleared his throat, not wanting to seem improper—"maybe somewhere in her room? On her desk?"

Mrs. Kinship snorted. "Not likely."

"You should go look," Anna said, standing. "Would that be all right with you, Mrs. K.?"

"You know the Graysons don't approve."

"I'll go with him," the younger woman eagerly volunteered.

"Thank you," Max said, "but I think it would be best if I went alone. I wouldn't want anyone to get the wrong idea."

Apparently, he couldn't have said anything to please her more, because she blushed and giggled in something close to joy and eagerly agreed.

In truth, he simply wanted a moment alone with his thoughts.

He wondered whether he would need a key, but he found the room—last on the left—to be unlocked. What he was looking for, he didn't know. Maybe nothing, but the nascent discomfort he'd felt since learning that Monica was out "on an errand" was on its way to a full-grown fear.

He ran his hand along the inside of the doorway, eventually finding the switch that brought the room to light. And there she was. Monica. Not the woman herself, of course, but every inch of it the essence of her. The bed was made with a plush cover of quilted silk, half of it obscured by clothing. Moreover, clothing was draped on the bedpost and the bureau, piled on the floor, hanging from hooks. The room smelled of coffee and . . . something else—soft, like powder. An enormous mirror was draped with scarves and necklaces; the dressing table was a sea of jars and bottles—a myriad of all that enhanced her beauty. And books? She may have stood in awe of his collection, but if someone were to gather all she had, sort and shelve them, hers would rival. They were piled and pyramided on and under every possible surface. Finally, on a small folding table flush against the window, a small, portable typewriter. How anyone could write anything in this nest of a room was beyond him.

But then, nothing about Monica had ever really been in his grasp.

Here, a witness to her systematic messiness, the idea of finding a clue as to her present whereabouts seemed more ridiculous than ever. An archaeological approach would mean sifting through the topmost layer of litter surrounding the coffeepot, but he was reluctant to dive into her privacy. Then he remembered that guy, Charlie, and the primitive, hungry way he'd looked at her, and started reading everything in sight. Shopping lists, abandoned Monkey Business columns, scattered humorous rhymes, and then something not in her own hand.

I miss you, my little Mousie. One more chance? JJ's tonight.

The endearment was the one the creep had used in the diner; he could almost hear the slur.

As he puzzled over how he could possibly find this place without being killed or arrested, the sound of the telephone downstairs offered a ring of hope. This hardly seemed a household of people who would receive phone calls after nine o'clock at night, so it must be Monica. Her, or the creep calling to look for her. Either way, it meant someone he had to talk to.

Stuffing the note into his pocket, he hurried downstairs to find Mrs. Kinship listening intently, a look of grave concern on her face.

"Is it her?" Max asked.

She nodded.

"Let me talk to her."

She shook her head, holding up a single finger to stop him in his tracks. "What should I tell him?" She listened again. "And what do you need us to do?" After this, a series of humming agreements, then a promise to do all that she could, and then, to Max's utter amazement and frustration, she hung up.

"I wanted to talk with her," he said, fighting to keep his voice calm. He could barely explain this urgency to himself, let alone this woman he didn't know. "I think I know where she is."

"I don't think you do," Mrs. Kinship said.

"I found a note."

When he held it out to her, she did that sideways sniff he saw for the third time that evening and said, "Figures."

"Do you know where this is?" She hardly seemed like the type to be able to point him to a place that may well be a nightclub, but it was worth asking.

"She's not there. Come into the kitchen."

He followed, too stunned to do anything else. She went straight to a cabinet in the far corner, opened it, and pointed to a cracker tin on the top shelf.

"Can you reach that down for me?"

"Certainly." It was an easy reach. He held it, drumming his

fingers against the tin, wondering how he could hold it hostage without coming across as some menacing bully. "Where is she?"

Mrs. Kinship glowered, held out her hand, and he silently handed over the tin.

"She told me to tell you she had a meeting with some club. That you would know what she was talking about."

Relief surged through him. Of course. It was Anti-Flirt Week, after all. It figured they would have a meeting.

"But that's not where she is." Mrs. Kinship popped the lid off and reached inside, pulling out a few rumpled dollars and a handful of change before instructing him to put the tin back. "She's been arrested, rounded up in a raid in one of them places. Bound to happen sooner or later."

His stomach sank as she spoke. The fact that she was in jail and the fact that she went to meet *him* battled as to which was most troubling.

Just then, Anna poked her head inside the kitchen. "Mr. Davenport and I were wondering if that was Monica on the phone." She turned to Max. "Did you find anything?"

"Everything is fine," Mrs. Kinship said before he could get a word out. She tucked the money into her apron pocket. "She and this one had a misunderstanding. Seems they were supposed to meet up at some swanky place."

"Oh," Anna said, crestfallen. "Mr. Davenport is ready to retire to his room, but he'll be happy to know all is well, at least."

"Well, if you ask me," Mrs. Kinship said, without a trace of compassion, "we've all spent quite enough time worrying about Miss Monica this evening. I'm already over an hour late for work. Will you go put poor Davenport's mind at ease?"

Anna, clearly dismissed, gave Max one more wistful look, and it crossed his mind that his life might be far less complicated if he could love a sweet, simple girl like her instead of one rounded up in a speakeasy and sitting in jail. The minute she left, Mrs. Kinship took the money from her apron pocket and pressed it into his hand.

"It's five dollars' bail, she says. Go get our girl."

❧ CHAPTER 23 ❧

*Don't let elderly men with an eye to a flirtation pat you on
the shoulder and take a fatherly interest in you. Those are
usually the kind who want to forget they are fathers.*
ANTI-FLIRT CLUB RULE #9

THE COP HELD ON TO HER ELBOW throughout the phone conversation, tightening his grip the second she replaced the earpiece
in the cradle.

"Watch it," Monica said, attempting to tug it back.

"Listen, sister, we got a lotta people waiting to get their phone
call same as you."

"Yeah? Well, if anybody would listen to me, there'd be one less.
I haven't committed any crime, Officer—" she glanced down to
see the name written at the top of the report—"Meeks." He was
a solid block of a man, his beefy fingers easily encircling the arm
encased in her coat sleeve. "You see, I'm a writer—"

"Well, then, you can write up a nice story to tell the judge at
your court date."

"No, I mean I write for a paper. *Capitol Chatter.* I was doing some research." It wasn't the total truth, but then she wasn't in front of that judge yet.

"I don't ever look at that rag. See enough of that stuff every day with my own eyes, you know what I mean? But my girl? She's a different story."

"Then ask her." They were moving along at a good clip, Monica's feet barely touching the floor. The cell, crowded with the dozen or so women who had been at JJ's along with a few unsavory perpetrators of other crimes, loomed closer with each step. She tried in vain to dig in her heels; it was up to her words to get herself out of this mess.

"I write for the paper. That's what I do. I go to places like that and write about them. Monkey Business."

That got his attention, and he stopped.

The two holding cells—one for men, one for women—each had three solid cinder-block walls, the fourth comprised of bars stretching from ceiling to floor with a locked sliding door camouflaged within. He'd brought her from the front desk, where each prisoner had been allowed to make a single phone call, and he'd stopped right in the middle, putting them in view of the occupants of both cells.

"You that Monkey?" he said, with what she imagined to be hopeful affection. "My girlfriend reads you every week."

"Yes!" Relief rushed over her. "See? I'm not just—"

"And after she reads it, I get all the guff about not being exciting enough for her. That I don't buy her nice things or take her to swanky clubs, never mind that it's my job."

"Oh." Hope closed shut. "If it helps any, I tend to exaggerate."

"That don't help." He tightened his grip. "Let's see what everybody else thinks." He puffed up and hollered. "Well, whaddya know about that, everybody? We got us a monkey in the cage!"

If he expected a riotous reception to his joke, he must have felt disappointed, because the crowd of men offered little more than a grumble, and the women simply jeered.

"That did not make them happy," Officer Meeks said. "Seems like they might feel a little resentful, you writin' about all these places, tipping off the Feds and all."

"I didn't tip anybody off to anything," she said, once again being moved along. "Maybe once, but that place needed to be shut down."

"Hey, Mousie." It was Charlie, his face pressed up between the bars. "I think it best you pipe down right about now."

She lunged, and Officer Meeks pulled her back, up against his chest while her feet danced in the air.

"This is all your fault, Charlie—"

"Cut it out!" Officer Meeks turned his body, making a blue wool wall between them. "You'll have time to kiss and make up on the other side."

"Fat chance of that," Monica said over the sound of the opening and slamming of the women's cell door.

There was one empty seat on the long bench lining the wall; Monica sank down on it, burying her face in her hands.

"Monkey girl," the woman next to her said derisively. It felt like a life sentence.

She pressed her cheekbones into the heels of her hands, welcoming the darkness, but conscious enough of her makeup. She'd been strong enough not to cry so far; why take a chance on smearing it all now? It would take all the dignity she could muster to face Mrs. Kinship when she arrived to post bail.

The conversations around her were surprisingly inane. Clothes and lipstick and Rudy Valentino—like they were all lined up at a drugstore counter getting egg creams instead of lumped together in a holding cell.

"I could watch him all day long," one woman said, speaking around a massive wad of chewing gum. "Give me a handful of movie tickets and a couple of baloney sandwiches, and I wouldn't have to move all day."

The girls listening laughed, and one said if she was going to spend the day in a dark room with him, she sure didn't want him up on no screen. And they laughed some more.

Monica pulled in tighter, willing herself to disappear. She'd spend the rest of her life happily in solitary confinement if it meant getting away from here right now.

Someone tugged the collar on her coat. "So, tell me," a voice pierced through the darkness, "this monkey fur, monkey girl?"

Monica looked up to see who had spoken. A tall girl with brown hair nearly the same shade as her hat. She had a smear of lipstick on her teeth that no one had bothered to tell her about, which made her a person even more reviled than Monica. Motivated more by superiority than kindness, Monica told her.

"What's it to you?" she retorted, though careful to keep her lips covering the offending stain. Then she strode off, as far as a girl can stride in a room not much bigger than her apartment.

"Some girls just aren't made out for friends." This from the woman sitting next to her, whose face was familiar from other nights on the town. She was doughy-soft and pale, and she sat with her legs crossed at the ankle, the way ladies were supposed to.

"I'm thinking I might be one of them," Monica said. "I can't seem to keep anybody in my life."

"Looks like you had a fellow at the place back there."

"Him I don't want to keep."

"You ever been arrested before?" She spoke with surprising nonchalance.

"No. Have you?"

She held up three fingers. "Atlantic City, Philadelphia, and here. This is the nicest by far."

"Glad we could accommodate you."

"It's not so bad, you know. Few hours here, pay a fine, and then it's back in the saddle. Me, I figure you'll never get warm if you spend your life afraid of getting burned."

"Well, aren't you the philosopher? What's your name?"

"Samantha." She reached a hand over to shake. "Nice to finally meet you."

"I apologize for the circumstances."

The two leaned back against the wall. Samantha offered up a cigarette, which Monica refused, and another attempt at conversation, which she also refused.

One by one the men and women were led out, escorted to the front desk to make their phone call, then back again. The cells were side by side, and from her recessed seat, she couldn't tell when Charlie was taken. Not that she cared. Tonight should end it all for sure. Perhaps she'd been foolish to think she could stay with a guy as long as she did with Charlie and expect everything to end all cut and clean. Most guys were more than happy to go away, move on.

Max certainly was.

A girl takes five seconds to clear her head and decide if she's in love or not and he's ready to write the whole thing off. Had her pegged for being fast, and maybe she was, but fast girls fell in love too, didn't they? It just maybe wasn't so obvious when it happened. Sometimes a girl needed to think. For a few minutes, maybe longer. What could that hurt?

"Samantha Pedronski?" Officer Meeks studied his clipboard and repeated the name, louder.

Monica nudged. "Is that you?"

"Yeah." She took a final drag on her cigarette and crushed it out on the floor.

"Then why don't you go?" Monica spoke quietly, out of the side of her mouth, not wanting to be the one to turn the spotlight on this girl who seemed determined to hide.

"I got no one to call. At least not that can come get me tonight."

"No friends even?"

Samantha gave a quaking smile. "All my friends are right here. We might have to find a way to bail each other out."

"Samantha Pedronski!" Officer Meeks's voice was hoarse from shouting.

"Hold your garters!" Monica yelled back. "Her lawyer's office doesn't open 'til nine."

"Well, why didn't ya say so in the first place?" he said before moving on to the next name on his list.

"You're a quick wit," Samantha said, watching the one with lipstick on her teeth exit.

"I spend a lot of time making up stories. In fact, most of my life is a lie."

"You're kidding. So a few months ago, when you went to Romo's and pocketed the coffee cup? That didn't happen?"

Monica winced with the memory, having given it very little thought since the incident occurred.

"It was an espresso cup." Tiny little thing, almost doll-sized. "Yeah, I took it."

"And when you went up to Atlantic City and saw the guy getting his face kicked in on the beach? Was that true?"

Monica nodded, recalling in the pit of her stomach the sickening sound of that face-crushing encounter. Two men in expensive suits, blood staining the white foam of the surf.

"Everything I write about is true. I think the lie comes from making everybody think it's a swell way to live. Because lately it doesn't seem so wonderful. Look where it got me."

Samantha shrugged. "There's worse places, I guess."

"Maybe," Monica conceded, "but there's better, too."

Officer Meeks was back with the girl who, after thanking him with exaggerated charm for his escort, revealed that she had taken the time to wipe the lipstick off her teeth at some point. He slid the door shut and locked it before looking off to the side and saying, "Five minutes, buddy. Not a minute more. I don't know if the big boys want any of this in the press at all."

"That's all I need, Officer. Thanks."

The familiar voice brought Monica flying from the bench to grasp the cold iron bars, pressing her face between them. "Tony!"

He turned to look at her, unbelieving at first, then put a finger to his lips and scurried over until he was nose-to-nose with her, speaking quick and quiet like a rat. "What are you doing here?"

"Same as everybody," she whispered. "Family reunion."

"Not so funny, sister. You know whose place this was?"

She shook her head as much as the bars would allow, and he dropped his voice even softer.

"King's."

"As in, Jim King? The guy who—?"

"*Pffft.*" Tony cut her off, but they were both thinking of the man who had come into the office a month ago. Obviously Hoofers had not been his only establishment.

Monica gripped the bars tighter, her hands now equally cold. "He's going to think I tipped somebody off."

"He's not here," Tony said. "You can bet if the Feds ever got ahold of him, they'd have someplace better to take him than a local lockup. Besides, you never wrote about the place, did you?"

"Not with any details."

"And nobody knows you, so—"

"Hey, cop!" The girl with the newly clean smile was now standing right next to Monica, her face pressed through the bars. "How come the monkey girl gets a visitor? Maybe I wanna visitor too!"

"He's not a visitor," Monica hissed, hoping her hint would stave off further shouting. "He's with the press. Same as me."

"Oh, of course," she said in a quieter, if still nasty, tone. "Journalism at its finest."

It was all Monica could do to stop from kicking her and thereby giving Tony a new story to report. But there were more pressing questions.

"Does Max know?"

"That I'm here?"

"That *I'm* here," Monica said, not at all certain of what she wanted the answer to that question to be.

"I don't check with Max for all my stories. I figure I can sell this two ways. For the *Chatter*, it's a cautionary tale of the evils of drink. For some bigger fish, it's the story of the takedown of a gangster. Either way, I get a picture."

He stepped back and began rummaging through the worn leather bag slung over his shoulder. "The light in here is lousy," he said, producing a camera, "but sometimes ya gotta make do."

"There's a third story." The words seemed to tumble through her lips no sooner than entering her head.

"Yeah? What's that?"

"Monkey Business goes to jail?"

"Oh yeah?" He looked up from fiddling with the camera. "I can see that. Kinda cute, you standin' there behind the bars. Then we'll do one of them treatments—cut your face out of the picture and put a monkey's there instead. Protect your anonymity, as it was. Might be a nice feature to add all around, the pictures. You could have Monkey at the park, Monkey at the White House. Even Monkey at the zoo. Feedin' an elephant, maybe."

She could picture it too. Her body, her clothes—finally getting the attention they deserved—posed all over the city. And just above her shoulders, maybe even under her hat, that doodled little monkey face that ran in place of a byline. What a fine joke. What a clever idea that would have been all along, but she hadn't thought of it then, and such a monstrosity wasn't her idea now.

"No, Tony." She interrupted him in the middle of a delightful Monkey in a bathing suit. "My picture, my face. My name."

"You've gotta be kiddin' me, kid."

She looked over her shoulder at Samantha, pale and puffy, sharing a smoke with another woman. What kind of girl had she been three arrests ago? Monica didn't want to find out. Now she pulled her coat close around her, closing the collar up around her nose. The dying taste of her last drink lingered, a constant reminder of what brought her here. Not just that one drink tonight, but all the ones before. All the nights before. Maybe she'd just been lucky, beating the odds, keeping herself at the right places. Never going to the same place too often, never staying too long. *Slippery*—that's what Edward Moore had called her. *"Like the law don't stick to you."*

"Nope," she said, turning back to Tony. "I'm coming clean. Max can run it as a straight story, 'Monkey Out of Business' or something like that. I just think it's time for me to move on to something more . . . I don't know . . . responsible."

Tony gave her an inscrutable look, but before he could say anything more, the police warden hollered again. "Hey, Mr. Reporter. You got one more minute."

"I'm workin' on it," Tony replied, exhibiting the same impatience.

Monica was grateful for the interruption, thinking Tony might not be the best person to handle such a half-baked idea. Max deserved to be the first to know, both as her boss and . . . whatever else he'd become. If she was going to hand Monkey over to anybody, it should be him.

"Hold this, will ya?" Tony handed the camera to Monica while he rummaged in his bag for a new flash. It was heavy, boxy, and bulky. She'd never understand how Tony could handle it with such ease, let alone carry it around all day.

"Now," he said with a glance up, "step back a little, and to the left." He directed with one hand while looking down through the viewer. "Maybe one more step? I wanna get as much of you as I can in the shot. The way the light's makin' these shadows, it's a beautiful thing, kid. Beautiful. You ready to hold nice and still for me?"

Behind her, her fellow prisoners caught on to what was happening, and whether it was to be included or excluded from the photograph, a mad scramble of women erupted.

Monica stood in perfect motionlessness. The flash exploded in a burst of cleansing light, taking with it her secrets. In just a few days, everyone would see her face, know her name. Well, *everyone* might be an exaggeration. Only those who'd been blindly following her all this time. She felt the weight of their adoration heavy on her shoulders for one burning moment, and then it drifted off with the light. For a full minute after, she stood, blinded, but as she blinked, the world came back into focus, and she stepped forward to grab the bars for balance, freer than she'd ever been.

There was a spot, dead center above her tailbone, like a button of pain holding together a body's worth of dull aches. The room was cold with the same unchanging dull light. No windows, no clock, no reliable way to mark the passage of time other than asking, and nobody wanted to talk to her. Even Samantha had abandoned their budding friendship, having enticed all the girls to fill the bench, leaving Monica to sit on the cold slab of floor. Officer Meeks hadn't made an appearance in ages, not since issuing the final "Pipe down!" after Tony left, taking his camera and notepad with him. A few of the men had been willing to talk—as unnamed sources, of course—and a few of the women thought it would be a gas to have their picture taken, but Officer Meeks had pulled him out before anybody got their full say. They'd been left with no recourse other than to voice their renewed frustrations.

Monica had jumped on the tail end of the shouts, hollering a plea for Tony to please not tell the boss, when she heard the sound of a key at the top of the passageway followed by the familiar squeaking step of Officer Meeks. He appeared at the door of the women's cell, looking none the worse for wear for his shift, and read the name off a card in his hand.

"Elsa DiMonaco!"

A doe-eyed, round-hipped girl hopped up like she'd just won a prize and sashayed to the open door, blowing kisses as she left. A few of the men were called out too, chuckling profanities as they left.

"Now, see?" Samantha spoke from her perch in the center of the bench, the agreed-upon queen of the cell. "That's nice. In Atlantic City they make you stay all night, no matter what. No one gets out until 7 a.m., when the shift changes. Keeps 'em from sending all us drunks straight out into the street."

Monica wanted to say that she wasn't a drunk, but the coating on her tongue wouldn't let her speak such a thing. Besides, her throat clamped shut with the thought of staying for an entire night. Did Mrs. Kinship know she could come right away? Tonight? She'd seemed so calm on the telephone. Calm, and something else. Resigned? Unsurprised? She'd never been a fan of Monica and her late nights, her dates, her poorly concealed attempts at covering her boyfriends' tracks. All this time, Monica had been dreading that moment when she would have to face her dour-mouthed neighbor with scraped-together humility and gratitude. Now she welcomed that moment. She practiced her smile into the darkness of her coat.

Again the squeak of Officer Meeks's shoes. *Meeks squeaks.* She crossed her fingers and repeated it three times before realizing she had no reason to remember such a clever phrase. There wouldn't be another column.

He called out three of the men, none of the women. Every muscle in Monica's body protested as she shifted her weight, making her feel old. Everything about today made her feel old. That empty house. The way she'd left the train station wanting nothing more than a plate of stew and a good night's sleep. The fact that she could sit here now and think about Max like he was some long-lost love.

And here she was, not yet one-and-twenty.

She may not have a home of her own, but as of today, she had money to buy one. She could find a new job, a new town, a new guy. Or none of those. She could go to college, or Paris, or South America—someplace warm.

She could write. That little bundle of stories belonged to a girl who wanted to be a writer. Now she was just a girl who made a joke of herself with her words. Maybe she could buy a cabin in Maine or a flat in London. Or California. Max had said she'd like it there. Everything was new, he'd said. Fresh. Fast. Perfect for a flirty girl. He didn't know she had this old soul.

Then again, he didn't know she was ready for a new one, either. And maybe, when he found out, it wouldn't be too late to ask for his forgiveness.

Those Meeks squeaks, again. And this time he called her name. She had to lift her head from the tunnel she'd created with her coat collar and ask to hear it again.

"Monica Bisbaine. Right?"

Her cellmates echoed with "monkey girl" while Monica, muscles aching with cold and bones popping, unfolded herself from the floor. She ignored them. Two more minutes and she'd never see any of them again.

As she and Meeks passed the men's cell, she heard Charlie call out—"Monica, Mousie, sweetheart"—but she looked straight ahead at the back of Meeks's neck.

The cold went with her, seeped into her legs, her back, and places in between. She may have been walking with the gait of a crippled old woman, but it was the heart of a little girl beating within her. She didn't want to face Mrs. Kinship, but she did want to go home. And after that, like any good child grown up, she wanted to go away.

~§ CHAPTER 24 ह~

*Don't annex all the men you can get—by flirting
with many, you may lose out on the one.*

ANTI-FLIRT CLUB RULE #7

MRS. KINSHIP'S KITCHEN MONEY burned in his pocket. It might be the price to be paid for Monica's crime; he just wished he could be the one to pay it. After all, he'd played some role in the crime's commission. Had he tempered his kiss, had he censored his love, had he simply accepted an invitation for a dinner of beef stew, he might be walking away from her house under very different circumstances. Or maybe, given the coziness of the parlor, he might still be there.

It was quite a distance from the house to the station, but the only alternative was to ask Mrs. Kinship for car fare. He prayed with each step, asking God to protect Monica with every breath, both coming quicker and quicker as he closed in. He'd never been to the police station before, of course, and he'd never come close to seeing a jail cell. In his mind, Monica was cold and small, huddled in a dark corner, prodded and mistreated by moose-like prison matrons.

He broke into a run, dodging around strolling couples and parked cars with the passion and ease of his high school football days. Unfortunately, those days were long past, and by the time he arrived at the steps of the precinct office he had to bring himself to a stop, braced against a lamppost. A slow, wet snow had started to fall; when he looked up, he could see individual flakes dancing in the light. He stayed and watched, choosing a flake and then trying to match his breath to its descent.

Give her that kind of peace, Lord.

"That you, boss?"

The clipped, nasal voice of Tony Manarola interrupted his prayer.

"Tony?" He held out a gloved hand. "What in the world are you doing here? Who called you?"

Tony simply touched his nose in answer to the first question and shot the second right back to Max.

"I was at her house," Max said, allowing Tony to intuit what he wished.

"She never mentioned she talked to you."

"She didn't—wait, you've seen her?"

"Yeah," Tony said, and Max didn't need to be a street reporter to know there was something Tony was holding back. He also knew no amount of peppering with questions would ever bring it out. "You here to bust her out?"

"*Bail* her out, yes." Though the former wouldn't be out of the question, if necessary.

"Good." Tony sounded as protective as Max felt. "I'll let her give you the details."

Tony tipped his hat and was about to walk away when Max stopped him with a tap on his arm.

"I've never done this before," he said somewhat sheepishly. "Bail someone out, I mean. I'm not sure I know exactly what to do."

"Look, boss. I'm press; I gotta stay out of it. You ever get a coat out of check before? Then you can do this. Give 'em the name, give 'em the money, and take her home. Big roundups like this? They don't want no fuss."

"All right," Max said, slightly more at ease, though he couldn't help cringing at the looming next question. "One last thing. I—I don't have car fare. For her, not me. I'm fine to walk, but she won't be in any shape for that."

A slow grin unfurled across Tony's grizzled face. "Well, ain't you the attentive boss?"

"I can't help but feel responsible. Because of the paper. If it weren't for that column, she might not even be in those places."

"Maybe so." He delivered a light punch to Max's shoulder. "Don't worry about the ride, boss. I'll take care of it." Within a few steps, he'd disappeared into the street.

Gathering courage, Max ascended the steps to the front door, holding it open for a man and woman exiting the station. She had dark hair and a sharp tongue, if her rapid-fire Italian words were any indication. Her companion—older, stooped, defeated—winced in their wake. It was a puzzle, who was the liberator of whom. Either way, they appeared to be in for a long, hostile night.

Inside, the station was a bustle of activity. A wooden counter stretched from wall to wall, and behind it, a dozen police officers manned their desks. The cacophony of ringing telephones and clattering typewriters underscored shouted demands for lawyers and quiet—all permeated with a fog of cigarette smoke and profanity.

Keeping Tony's analogy of the coat check in mind, Max stepped up to the counter and drummed his fingers on its surface, waiting to be noticed. It didn't take long.

"Who ya here for?" The officer—Meeks, according to the colleague who'd shouted, "Hey, Meeks! Front desk!"—looked like a solid brick of a man, though worn a bit at the edges.

"Miss Bisbaine. Miss Monica Bisbaine."

Officer Meeks muttered the name over and over, shuffling through a sheaf of papers in a folder before finding what he needed. "Ah, yeah." He looked up at Max and smiled, revealing a row of strong, cinder-block-like teeth. "Monkey girl. Ain't you the lucky guy?"

"Excuse me?" How could the officer have possibly known that? Unless they'd somehow worked it out of her. He was ready to jump over the counter and land himself in jail.

"She's a corker, she is."

Rather than risk his freedom for an explanation, Max calmly said, "I'm here to pay her fine."

Officer Meeks studied him again, squinting. "Not sure you're what she's expecting. Talked to a woman on the phone. A Mrs.—"

"I'm here to pay her fine," Max repeated, planting his palms on the counter and looming closer. "Does it matter whom she called?"

"No, sir." There was a mocking element to Meeks's response. "I see you're not bailin' out the fellow she came in with." He tapped his cap. "Smart move, that. Leavin' him locked up."

Patience was about to lose the battle with prudence as Max worked to keep his voice calm. "I was told the fine is five dollars. Is that correct?" He pulled the money from his pocket, making a show of unfolding the bills, smoothing them on the countertop.

"Yeah, that's it," Officer Meeks said, reluctantly giving up his game. He opened a large, leather-bound ledger, made a few notes, then turned it for Max to sign. There was her name, and next to it, his. The purchase price noted in the column between.

"Wait here," Officer Meeks said. "I'll go get your girl."

The wall behind him was lined with rough wooden chairs, most of them occupied with rumpled-looking women who appeared far too comfortable in this environment. He caught the eye of one, tipped his hat, and received a dismissive snort in return.

Long before he saw her, he heard her voice saying, "What do you mean, a gentleman?" Then she emerged from a back hallway, unceremoniously escorted on the arm of Officer Meeks.

The sight of her stole his breath. She looked so little in contrast to the wall of a man beside her. Her face was pale, the meticulous lining of her eyes now smeared, making her look like a woodcut of an orphan from some Dickensian novel. Without their usual crimson hue, her lips looked more like pale-pink petals, and now they were parted in surprise.

There was a visible slowing to her steps, and Meeks hauled her along like she weighed considerably more than she did. Still, he soldiered on, bringing her to a place at the counter where he reached down, slid a latch, and lifted it, allowing Monica safe passage to the other side.

"Here ya go, mister. She's all yours."

His instinct was to take her in his arms, but at the first hint of his intentions, she braced her hands against his chest, and any idea he had of her weakness disappeared in the strength of her barricade.

"What are you doing here?" Her voice little more than a whisper.

"The other lady at your boardinghouse, Mrs. Kinship—"

"She wasn't supposed to tell you."

He searched her eyes, looking for any hint of gratitude or warmth, but saw only steeled dark.

"I guess she's not great at keeping a secret. Would you like me to have the nice officer take you back? I could get a refund and use the money for cab fare home."

Always before, when they'd been short with each other, she'd softened at a joke. But not this night. Grim-faced, she took her purse, handed across the counter by Officer Meeks, and brushed right past Max, heading for the front door.

"Darling, wait." He made a play to touch her arm, but she reeled away from his grip.

"Don't touch me."

He recognized more pain than anger in her directive and therefore pursued her again, this time forcefully drawing her to him.

"Are you sure you want to accost me in a roomful of police officers?" she said. "I don't even have to scream, but I will."

He crouched to better meet her eyes. "Where are you going?"

"Home."

"Then wait. Tony's coming with a ride."

That stopped her. "You saw Tony?"

"Yes."

By now they'd captured the attention of the weary women waiting in the chairs. They sat forward, clutching their purses to their hearts. One of them whispered, "Who's Tony?"

"Listen, lovebirds," Officer Meeks said. "The lady's free to go. So go."

"In a minute," Max said.

"Now," Meeks countered.

"Come on," Monica said, grabbing Max's arm. "I could use some fresh air."

Left with little choice, Max led the way, holding the door open, touching the small of Monica's back as she passed through. The snow was falling harder now, thick white flakes against the cool black sky. She immediately turned her face up, blinking as they landed on her long, thick lashes.

"I love snow," she said, as if she stood alone behind its curtain.

Max watched as the falling flakes worked a sort of magic, cooling her spirit. She closed her eyes and emitted a sigh big enough to see, leaving her mouth open as if to drink in the sky. Never had he seen her this unguarded, this serene—certainly not what he'd expected after the ordeal she must have been through.

The snow was beginning to stick, forming a lacy cover on her shoulders. She heaved them again in a breath that seemed to signal relief. Or perhaps release. Either way, it was clear that she was not the same woman who had run away from Union Station. He heard himself saying, "'Come now, and let us reason together, saith the Lord: though your sins be as scarlet, they shall be as white as snow.'"

She looked at him sidelong. "What is that supposed to mean?"

"Just something I think about," he said, treading carefully, "whenever I see snow."

"Is it, really?" Her suspicion threatened his peace. "So tell me, Max. How shall we reason together, you and me?"

"I think it's more important that we reason with God first." He chose his words carefully, prayerfully, trying to remember the promises he'd made to himself and his Father just hours ago. "I've spent some time doing that tonight."

"And did you have many scarlet sins?" A snowflake landed on her lip and stayed there, a beckoning crystal.

"A few," he confessed.

"I can't imagine."

"They're mostly to do with you."

A pale shadow of her flirtatious self broke through. "Well, then, maybe I can."

He looked beyond her, down the street. Where was Tony with the car? "There's so much I have to tell you. So much I should have told you already."

"About what? You have some sort of secret life or something?"

"In a way."

"Applesauce," she said. "I've never known anybody more straitlaced than you."

"What I mean is that . . . I worry about you, Monica. I know you don't want me to, and I probably don't have a right to, but . . . I can't help it. What happened tonight, well, that's just part of the danger you're in."

Her face lost its flirtatious edge as he spoke, sobering with every word. "I know, Max."

"Do you know what's really at stake here?"

"My eternal soul?" The edge of mockery was back. "If it eases your conscience any, I did a lot of thinking myself tonight. And I think I'm ready to come clean."

He let her words settle for a moment, seeing before him a new creation, fresh as the snowflakes on her shoulder. She had that sense of bewilderment he'd seen on the faces of all those who'd experienced redemption at Sister Aimee's altar, and he could only hope that somehow, despite his bumbling, the grace of God had become real to her within the walls of the jail cell.

He burst forth with an enthusiastic "Darling!" and took her

up into his arms. She felt close to weightless, and he swung a full circle before finally setting her softly down. "You can't imagine what it means to me."

Her laughter came in short breaths. "I knew you'd appreciate my decision. Tony wasn't nearly as enthusiastic."

"Tony?" Why would Tony care?

"But I told him it was settled. He wasn't convinced, but he took my picture anyway, and I want you to run it. I'll leave it to you, or even Tony, to write the story. I don't trust myself to be objective. Headline it whatever you want. 'Monkey Bars'—that's clever—or 'Monkey Unmasked.' Run it right next to my column if you want. You're the boss. But I want a byline on my last column. I think I owe that to the girls."

She was talking at such a rapid pace, one puff of steam after another floating away with each new direction. Max struggled to make sense, feeling like he was experiencing a long stretch of conversation from a movie, waiting for a title card to interrupt with clarification. His heart longed for an answer, longed to know that she fully shared his faith, because he wanted her to share his life. The more she talked, the less he understood, so he started back at the beginning.

"Tony took your picture?"

Startled, she backtracked her thoughts. "Yeah. In the jail itself. So it's a news story, my arrest, but also works on a more symbolic level, don't you think? A way to expose Monkey Business and kill her off."

"I didn't know you wanted to kill her off."

"I didn't, either. But things change."

Just then the door to the police station opened, and a man and woman emerged, walking in stony silence. The man he recognized, and his hand ached remembering the feel of his face slamming against it. The woman was quite pretty, with a sweet face pinched in disappointment. He could see, too, from her posture, that what first appeared as an unattractive girth was, in fact, an advanced pregnancy. Monica tracked their every step with her eyes, though they—Charlie and his wife—looked steadily forward.

"I should say something," Monica said so quietly her words were carried by the steam from her breath.

"Why?"

"She should know. She deserves to know."

Max took her by the shoulders and turned her to look at him. "She knows." In his heart, he knew he spoke the truth. "Maybe not about you specifically, but you saw her face. She knows."

Tears pooled in Monica's eyes. "I want her to know that I'm sorry."

"God knows that you're sorry. He will forgive you. Her? Maybe not."

The couple had turned left upon reaching the sidewalk, and Monica craned her neck to look behind Max, watching. After a bit, she turned her attention back to him.

"One of those scarlet sins, then?"

"White as snow," he said. "Just ask him and believe."

"What about you, Max?"

"Me?"

"Do you think there's anything I can do to make you forgive me? Erase my past?"

"Monica—"

He interrupted his own dispensation with a kiss, her mouth the only spot of warmth in all the world around him. She responded at first, greeting him with the faintest taste of whiskey. When they parted, amicable and sated, he took her face in his gloved hands and touched his lips briefly to her temple.

"To think," he said, seeing only her face before him, "I took you to one of the most beautiful churches in our country, and you had to go to prison to have a true experience with God."

Her eyes clouded. "Max . . ." She brought her hands up to his and pulled them away. "I'm not sure I had a religious experience tonight. I don't want to disappoint you."

"As if you could." He cocked his head to one side, then the other. "Seeing you here, right now. It's like I'm looking at you for the first time."

"That's because I don't have anything to hide from you anymore." She gave her arms a flightless flop at her sides. "This is it. This is me."

"Darling—" he took off his glove and laid his hand against her face, needing to feel the touch of her skin—"understand this. I love you. More, I think, than you can possibly imagine. What I said today, at the train, was thoughtless. Impatient."

"You deserve better."

"I deserve nothing. Even so, God loves me. He's given me everything I need. And that includes you—as you are. Whether you believe it yet or not."

"That's just it, Max. I don't believe, not like you do. I don't understand; I don't *feel*."

"Do you trust me?"

"Yes," she said, as if her fate depended on it.

"Then we'll start there. I won't hurt you, Monica, and I won't go away. My home is here, and I hope someday my home will be with you."

The sound of a car's horn blared between them, and he turned to see an ancient automobile rounding the corner, black smoke billowing behind. No roof, no doors; it seemed to be held together by the rattle of the engine alone. At the wheel, looking just a little sleepy, Trevor brought it to a sputtering stop at the curb. There had to be a better time to have this conversation. In the morning, maybe, over doughnuts and coffee at Sobek's. Or even Thursday, with the new issue of *Capitol Chatter* on the stands. He could call her into his office after a celebration of her first byline.

Together, they studied Trevor's sputtering car. It had only one passenger seat and no backseat at all, thus deciding definitively that Max would not be escorting her home. Just as well. He pictured her room, strewn with everything she owned, her bed covered with a thick, warm quilt. More than anything now, he wanted her home and safe. Trevor could make that happen; he could not.

"Until then," Max said with a grand gesture. "Your chariot awaits."

Monica drew him down to speak close to his ear. "You know, if you're going to stay in this town, you might want to get an automobile."

"You manage just fine without one."

"There's always a man to give me a ride."

"Remember your mission. No flirting with men in cars, remember? You still have the rest of the week to play along."

"That's just for this week. Get a car, and I'll flirt with you forever."

She pulled him to her and kissed him before jaunting off to Trevor's automobile without any bit of a glance back to see that he had followed.

"Mr. Manarola called me and said you might need a ride home." Trevor's voice fell short of being fully given over to that of a man.

"Thanks," Monica said, clambering into the seat.

Trevor leaned forward. "How about you, Mr. Moore?"

There might be room on the bench seat, with Monica nestled in warmth between them, but the falling snow offered a cocooning silence, enough to keep his thoughts safely tucked beneath his hat.

He saw her then as he had that first day, her eyes large and brown, white flakes of snow reflected on their surfaces. She'd called him Griffin. The name of an invisible man. And as he watched her settling into Trevor's idling car, he longed for it to be true. To be invisible. To disappear within this storm. To climb in, unseen beside her, and wrap himself around her, ready to appear when her heart searched for him again.

"No, thanks," he said with a friendly slap on the front panel of the car. "I'll walk."

"Suit yourself," Trevor said, and with a great sputtering display, they lurched away from the curb. The hour was late, leaving the street empty. Trevor steered the car in a wide U-turn but stopped midway as Monica hopped out and ran back to Max, right into him, actually, laying her palms flat against his chest, feeling for his heart.

"I just need to know," she said, the snow nearly thick enough now to make a lace curtain between them. "When you say you love me, do you mean it? Do you really, really mean it?"

"Yes," he said, without hesitation. If she could accept his love without condition, give her heart to him, this bumbling, imperfect man, could they not together give it over to one more worthy? "Can I ask you a question?"

"Anything."

"When you say you don't love me, do you mean that?"

She sparkled with snow and mischief. "I don't think so. That might have been the Monkey talking."

AN EXCITING PREVIEW OF ALLISON PITTMAN'S NEXT BOOK, *ALL FOR A SISTER*

HE'D BEEN SITTING on the other side of the desk. Staring, not speaking, while the clock ticked away another five minutes. Dana sat perfectly still in her wooden chair, knowing the slightest movement would send an echoing creak into the musty, solid silence.

"Do you know who I am?" He spoke without removing the thin cigarette holder from between his lips, and it bobbed with each word.

"Celeste said you make movies."

"That I do." His voice was deep; his words, clipped.

Celeste had called him a kraut—German. Which meant nothing to Dana except that they had been the enemy in the war. He seemed too old to have been a soldier. His hair, short and iron-gray, sprang stick-straw straight above a tan, angular face. Werner Ostermann, according to the name on the brass plate on his desk, and on the door, and on the small scrap of paper folded neatly in her pocket. "And you want to make a movie about me."

"That I do." He gave no verbal elaboration, only bored his gaze deeper.

Instinctively, she reached for her hair to stroke the long tresses, seeking the comfort she'd always found in their weight, but her fingers found only the soft, curling fringe peeking below her hat. Slowly, she returned her hand to her lap, pleased at having done so without eliciting the tiniest noise from the chair. "I suppose I don't know how that is possible."

His mouth spread into a wide grin and he removed the cigarette holder, balancing it across a shallow dish on the corner of the paper-strewn desk. One dropped cinder, and the entire small office would go up in flames.

"Nothing more than a thousand pictures shining on a screen. And each picture tells a story."

"I don't have a story."

"I disagree."

She wanted to argue. After all, she'd been to a movie. Three, in fact, just since her arrival in California. One about a man who met Jesus and raced chariots. Another about a woman who rode white horses in the circus, and the last about a hideous monster lurking in the shadows of a castle. That one she couldn't watch, except through a thin slit between her fingers as she covered her eyes. Celeste had been squealing beside her. *Dana! Dana! You're missing the best part!*

"I've done nothing for anybody to see," she said, fighting hard to keep her voice above a whisper. "What could you possibly put on film?"

He held his hands in front of his face, angling them against each other until he'd created an open square through which he looked at her with one open eye and said, "Take off your hat."

"My hat?" she questioned, but she obeyed.

He stretched his arms out further. "I can see the entire story in your eyes. With a camera and some music, I could make a movie just right here. But—" he dropped his hands—"only I would understand it, and art must be shared."

She turned the hat over and over in her hands. "I'm not art."

"No. But Celeste is. Your story. Her face."

He slammed his hand on top of the desk as if delivering a verdict. Dana flinched at the gesture, nearly dropping her hat. It really was a beautiful thing—a bell-shaped dome, flipped rim, and a wide blue ribbon punctuated by a perfect silk flower. She put it back on her head, not bothering to try for the perfect angle the way Celeste did, and sat up straight.

"Why do you need me, then? You know the story. I hear it was in all the papers."

He picked up a handful of folded newspapers and held them aloft. "These tell me nothing. They have no heart."

"Neither do I." She said it with convincing flatness, or so she thought.

Ostermann burst out with a short, bitter laugh. "So dramatic. Perhaps you are the one to be the actress in the film?"

He was joking with her, of course. Something she was still training her ear to detect.

"What do you want to know? They said I killed a child. They put me in prison. And then they let me out, and I came here. All that time between—sixteen years, Mr. Ostermann; nearly half my life—nothing happened. I went nowhere, saw no one, did nothing. Who would come to the theater to see an empty screen?"

"There is no such thing as *nothing*. You tell me—all of this nothingness. Surely I am not the first to ask?"

Far from the first. There'd been a journalist in Chicago, and even two on the train, pestering her with questions. How did it feel to be free after all this time? What did she want to do? Where did she want to go? What was the connection between her and the lovely Celeste DuFrane? Their queries pelted her like stones, chipping away at the wall she'd built around her—far higher and stronger than those of Bridewell.

But this felt different. Ostermann's office was close and plain and gray, lit only by a small, open window high up on the opposite wall. Under his scrutiny, she felt the space closing in, and the odd comfort of the confinement frightened her.

"Will you leave the door open? So I can leave if I want?"

"Of course." His expression lacked any hint of triumph as he stood, walked out from behind his desk, and spoke curtly through the opened door. Within seconds, the capable, sturdy woman who had greeted Dana in the outer office came in carrying a small notebook and a sharpened pencil.

"This is Miss Lynch. She will be taking notes as you speak. Is that all right with you?"

"Of course," Dana said, purposefully repeating his words, trying to match his tone. She turned to acknowledge Miss Lynch, who sat in a chair to the left and slightly behind her. In the meantime, Werner Ostermann settled himself back behind his messy piles and lit a fresh cigarette.

"Do you mind?" Dana said, emboldened. "I'm not used to the smell, and the smoke burns my eyes."

He said nothing but stubbed out the offensive thing.

"Thank you."

"Proceed." He opened his hands toward her, inviting.

Again the clock ticked silence, the only other sound being the soft clearing of Miss Lynch's throat.

"Where should I begin?" Dana's voice was little more than a whisper, so soft she could feel Miss Lynch craning closer.

"I believe it was Oliver Twist who began with his birth, but I

360

don't think we need to go back that far. Perhaps the night you were arrested?"

She shook her head. "I don't remember much about that." It was a truth that had not served her well.

"Perhaps, then, a memory from before?"

Before she went to prison, he meant, but those memories were equally shrouded. Still, she closed her eyes and took in a deep breath, seeing a small, pale hand pushing aside a curtain.

"My mother and I lived in a small apartment on the third floor above a grocer. . . ."

DISCUSSION QUESTIONS

1. At the beginning of the book, Monica seems to embrace a loose, immoral lifestyle. Do you think that's who she really is? Why or why not?

2. Often we find things in our lives to hide behind the way Monica hides behind Monkey, her newspaper persona. What are some of the things Monica is trying to avoid? What are some things in your life that you are tempted to hide behind, and what are you trying to avoid?

3. Max is all alone in the world, even more so after his uncle dies. How does that affect him? What steps does he take to develop a support network? What kind of support network do you have? How might you strengthen it?

4. Monica, too, is all alone. What kinds of people has she filled her life with? Some of her choices were set in motion when she was an adolescent. Are there things you did as a teenager that have adversely affected your adult life? What kind of counsel do you wish you had received? What might have helped Monica to make wiser choices?

5. How does the Anti-Flirt Club challenge Monica? Do you think her reaction to the club is realistic? Why or why not?

6. The Anti-Flirt Club was a real organization and Alice Reighly a real person. How effective do you suppose the organization was? What do you think motivated Miss Reighly?

7. The issues the Anti-Flirt Club addressed seem quite tame by today's standards. Why is that? Which of its rules is most applicable today? If someone were to start a twenty-first-century version of the club, what additional rules might be included?

8. Max finds himself almost instantly attracted to Monica, even though on the surface she is not the kind of woman he expects to share his life with. Did you find that believable? Do you have any experience with "love at first sight"? Do you think sometimes it can be—or can develop into—the real thing? Why or why not?

9. What is your impression of the relationship between Zelda Ovenoff and Edward Moore? In what ways do you suppose the friendship brought joy to each of them? Why do you think they never married? How are Max and Monica similar to Edward and Zelda? Do you see their relationship playing out in similar or different ways in the future?

10. At the end of the book, Monica realizes she needs to discover who she really is, and Max hopes she will come to find her identity in God's forgiveness and love. We often try to make ourselves look either better or worse than we actually are. Why do you think we do that? What are some ways we can determine the accuracy of our self-image or the image we project to others? Read 2 Corinthians 5:17 and Galatians 2:20. What do these verses say about the true identity of those who are in Christ?

A NOTE FROM THE AUTHOR

I HAVE BEEN OVERWHELMED by the reception of the first book in this series, *All for a Song*. I have an amazing support system of friends and family—and readers. When I am writing, I always look for that moment in the middle of a story, when something will happen or a character will say something, and I'll think, *Ooooh. They're going to love this!* I write with all of you in my heart, and I deliver my stories with all my prayers, and I'm so, so thankful that God has allowed us to take this journey together.

We call the years in which these stories are set the Roaring Twenties, and they were indeed a time of roaring change. Men returned from fighting the Great War on foreign soil with a new taste for sophistication and adventure. Women, having won the right to vote, stormed the walls of feminine convention, shedding their long hair and long skirts in a new zest for freedom. Thrust into a world where wild parties replaced church socials and cars with rumble seats stole the road from Sunday buggy rides, young girls saw the fair-skinned, long-legged flapper heralded as the new feminine ideal.

And then there was Monica.

People often ask me where I get my stories, and sometimes it's a long, difficult answer. But this one was easy. From the start I was eager to delve into some of the more fun (some would say *sinful*) aspects of the 1920s and also to bring back a couple of characters from *All for a Song*—Sister Aimee and Roland—for cameos. But the story itself came from a paragraph in one of the books I was reading as research for the series—*Flapper,* by Joshua Zeitz. (Go read it!) There really was a New York journalist/columnist who went by the pseudonym Lipstick, and she was the real-life Carrie Bradshaw of the Jazz Age. You could even say she was a pre-Internet blogger! Then, in an odd little book I picked up in a treasure trove of a basement/used bookstore, I saw a tiny picture of Alice Reighly, who headed up something called an "Anti-Flirt Club." I knew I had to bring these very real women into my story. I kept Alice, reimagined Lipstick, and put Max together from scratch. So that in itself was fascinating, but then as I coupled it with exploring the ideas of hiding, invisibility, and secrecy, piece by piece the novel fell into place.

I had a lot of fun with Max and Monica—they may be one of my favorite couples. I'd love to hear your thoughts too. Contact me through my website (www.allisonpittman.com), connect with me on the Allison Pittman Author Page on Facebook, or follow me on Twitter @allisonkpittman.

ABOUT THE AUTHOR

Award-winning author **ALLISON PITTMAN** left a seventeen-year teaching career in 2005 to follow the Lord's calling into the world of Christian fiction, and God continues to bless her step of faith. Her novels *For Time and Eternity* and *Forsaking All Others* were both finalists for the Christy Award for excellence in Christian fiction, and her novel *Stealing Home* won the American Christian Fiction Writers' Carol Award. She heads up a successful, thriving writers group in San Antonio, Texas, where she lives with her husband, Mike, their three sons, and the canine star of the family—Stella.

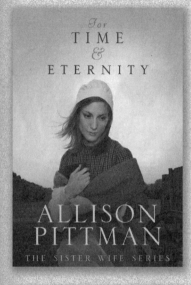
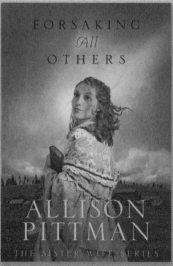